The Betrayers

HAROLD ROBBINS
AND JUNIUS PODRUG

The BETRAYERS

A TOM DOHERTY ASSOCIATES BOOK
NEW YORK

THE BETRAYERS

Copyright © 2004 by Jann Robbins and Junius Podrug

This book is printed on acid-free paper.

A Forge Book
Published by Tom Doherty Associates, LLC
175 Fifth Avenue
New York, NY 10010

www.tor.com

Forge® is a registered trademark of Tom Doherty Associates, LLC.

ISBN 0-765-30810-X (hc)
EAN 978-0765-30810-8 (hc)

ISBN 0-765-31269-7 (first international trade paperback edition)
EAN 978-0765-31269-3 (first international trade paperback edition)

First Edition: September 2004

Printed in the United States of America

0 9 8 7 6 5 4 3 2 1

Harold Robbins

left behind a rich heritage of novel ideas

and works in progress when he passed away in 1997.

Harold Robbins's estate and his editor worked with

a carefully selected writer to organize and complete

Harold Robbins's ideas to create this novel,

inspired by his storytelling brilliance,

in a manner faithful to

the Robbins style.

For

Robert Gleason

Acknowledgments

*With thanks to Dr. Jeffrey Kruger, M.B.E.,
René Kruger, Elizabeth Winick, Hildegarde Krische,
and Jann Robbins*

The Betrayers

1

❖

Havana, Cuba, 1958

She had nightheat, the sensuous quality in a woman that made men ache with desire. A body made for sin, skin the color of light cinnamon, fire-green emerald eyes, wet red lips. Her legs were long and slender, legs that would strap a man and squeeze while he made love to her.

Havana was the most sensuous city in the world, exotic, erotic, filled with beautiful women who had virgin-whore complexes—hot Latin blood that made them intensely passionate while their cultural and religious training had told them sex was *sin*.

Regardless of the sexual conflicts put on them, there were no women as sexually provocative as the women of Havana. They came in all shades, from light brown to the sheen of ebony, though a few had skin as white as a Swedish winter. Whatever their skin color, there was fire between their legs. When men entered them, they became *one* with the male, cocking their legs back so the men could get in tight and hard, grabbing flesh with long nails and pulling the male stalk in harder and harder. That was why the best whores in the world were in Havana, too—they enjoyed their work.

We were on the balcony of my room above the Malecón, the

❖

broad thoroughfare that ran along the waterfront. Flowing in from our right was a narrow, twisted Old Town street filled with centuries-old colonial buildings draped with overhanging balconies. It was early evening. A cool breeze skimmed across the bay and flowed up to my balcony.

She was leaning dangerously over the railing, enjoying the colorful insanity of the La Habanas at carnival time, a sea of colorful costumes, bizarre floats and loud music. Old Town was rocking—drums, rumba music, and a band playing La Cucaracha competed for air time on the streets below. *Muñecones*, satirical figures of famous faces, led the big parade, with a caricature of Sergeant Batista, the rank that the dictator of Cuba held when he led the 1933 Sergeant's Revolt, drawing cheers and jeers as it came down the waterfront street.

The streets were filled with flashy costumes, exciting music, swaying hips and conga lines, and most of all the soul of the Caribbean, all on a sultry summer night—along with enough beer and rum to float the U.S.S. *Maine. Por los santos*, "for the saints," was the salute given for the first drink out of a bottle. And the saints were very thirsty this carnival night.

Fireworks burst over the harbor as I stood behind the woman and stared at her. I had never made love to a woman like her. Most women either made love to me because of lust, or they wanted something—clothes, jewels, the good life or the protection money buys. None had ever gotten under my skin. Until tonight.

This woman was impressed with neither my money nor what I packed in my pants.

It was a man's world from frozen pole to pole, and nowhere was it as much of a man's world as the hot Latin regions of the Caribbean where women were either pampered and kept in golden cages—or abused by being treated as sex objects or work animals.

Once in a while some seer, usually a woman with a man's job, would predict that there would be a time when women would be sexually and economically equal, but I was sure I'd never see it in my lifetime.

❖

But this woman was different from any woman I'd met. It wasn't just that she conveyed an aura of independence, but that she knew she was my equal in every meaning of the word. I sensed it the moment I had seen her across the arena at a cockfight. Not a very auspicious place to find a woman who set my world on fire, but this was Havana.

She was neither saint nor whore—she wasn't someone who could be pigeonholed as a type. Rather, she was pure female, unaffected by what the male of the species wanted her to be.

She leaned against the railing, bent over, her hips vacillating to the music, her buttocks grinding up and down in the skintight dress. She was in her early twenties, a time in life when a woman's body was still fit and firm. My juices boiled as I watched the sensuous movement of her body, imagining her with no clothes on, my own nakedness pressing up against her.

I had once seen a ram in rut run up from behind an ewe and jump on her as if he needed a fuck for dear life.

That's how I felt about this woman—I needed her for dear life.

Her sequined white dress was several inches above the knees, her long legs were covered by black silk net stockings, her white cloth shoes had silver-plated spiked heels.

I came up behind her and put my hands on her hips, pushing myself against her. She felt my hardness and turned to look at me. If eyes were windows to the soul, my eyes revealed the good, the bad and the ugly, some dirty deals, some midnight meets, some things I wouldn't want to brag about in mixed company. Hers were temple doors, hiding secrets.

Our lips met and I kissed her gently at first, just brushing her lips, then pressed harder, my cock jerking up another notch as our tongues found each other.

I pulled her dress up above her hips and lifted her onto my hardness. There were a thousand people below, hell, maybe there were ten thousand, but they were all drunk—and so were the saints.

As I entered her, I knew I was violating my most sacred principle—*never fall in love.* I had spent most of my life avoiding the pain of loss. It was a sickness—to love and lose and never want to love again.

But I knew this was the *one.* I hadn't chosen her, hadn't thought about what life would be like with her—or without her— or even if she thought the same about me. It had just happened. I saw her across the arena and I knew that I couldn't hide behind my fears anymore, that I wouldn't be able to live without lying in bed at night with her at my side, without seeing her body naked beside mine, running my hand down her body to the feminine mystery between her legs.

As I held her, as our bodies flowed with the erotic rhythm of lovemaking, her tight body squeezing my phallus that had entered between her legs, I had a terrible thought, a moment of precognition, that made me both sad and frightened.

I would love her.

Yet I knew I would lose her.

LENINGRAD

THE SIEGE OF LENINGRAD

In scale, the tragedy of Leningrad dwarfs even the Warsaw ghetto or Hiroshima.

The siege was the longest a great city has undergone since Biblical times.

It was endured by more than three million people, of whom just under one-half died . . . most of them in six months—from late October 1941 through mid-April 1942—when the temperature went from 20 to 30 degrees below zero, and there was no heat, no light, no transport, no food or water; the front was still active; bombs and shells rained down; and the cannibals—some say—became king.

HARRISON E. SALISBURY,
THE 900 DAYS

$\mathcal{D}uring$ the terrible winter of the siege:

With his back to the post, a man sits on the snow, tall, wrapped in rags, over his shoulders a knapsack. He is all huddled up against the post. Apparently he was on his way to the Finland Station, got tired, and sat down. For two weeks while I was going back and forth to the hospital, he "sat."

1. Without his knapsack
2. Without his rags
3. In his underwear
4. Naked
5. A skeleton with ripped-out entrails

They took him away in May.

CYNTHIA SIMMONS AND NINA PERLINA,
WRITING THE SIEGE OF LENINGRAD
(DIARY OF VERA SERGEEVNA KOSTROVITSKAIA,
BALLERINA AND DANCE TEACHER)

2

❖

Nicholaus Cutter, February 1942

They took me out of Leningrad on Wednesday in a truck loaded with other children. I planned my escape from the truck so I could start back to the city to find my mother.

We had ridden out of the city in the dump bed of a sand-and-gravel truck. We drove in the darkness, the thump of the truck's old pistons keeping pace with the artillery the invaders were using to rain death all night upon the city. When the sun came up, Nazi bombers would join the murderous assault.

There were twenty-five or thirty of us, boys and girls, all under thirteen years old, bundled in winter coats and packed into the truck bed. Lena, a girl beside me, trembled as artillery shells pounded a district the truck rumbled through. Like all of us she was pale and bone-thin. We spent two days together back at the departure station and I knew that she had lost both her parents. Most of us had lost at least one parent. Some had lost their entire families, mother and father, brothers and sisters, even grandparents. A few whose mothers had died still had fathers fighting at the front.

"Why do they hate us?" she asked.

❖

Her question was barely audible. It wasn't meant to be heard, anyway. We were all weak and tired from months of hunger and sometimes thoughts just dribbled off our lips like drips from a leaky faucet.

"They don't hate us," I said. "They think we're animals. People kill animals."

That was what my mother had told me. The Germans thought of themselves as a master race and Russians as animals that could be bred and trained to serve them. But first they had to kill enough of us so the rest obeyed. "They think they can whip us like dogs, that we will just lie down and whimper," my mother had said. Our people had staggered from blows but had not fallen. Some people said we fought too hard, that if we just gave up they would kill fewer of us. "But then they would be right," my mother had said. "We would not be human."

A light drizzle of ice followed us out of the city. As I sat on the cold metal truck bed, rocking back and forth as the truck went from one rut to another, I thought about what it was like the year before, a time before the war started. I thought about how I greeted the first snow of winter with laughter and glee, of snowball fights and a trip to the country where we rode on a horse-drawn sled.

That was before the invaders came, before hunger and cold death stalked us, a time when we went to a warm bed with our bellies full, a time before the world turned rabid.

The Hun had come in September, destroying everything that stood in their way. The Germans called their sudden, overwhelming attacks using tanks, war planes and fast moving troops "blitzkrieg," lightning war. Neither our soldiers nor our generals had experienced anything like the mechanized fighting units that came at them like a storm of murderous steel demons from hell. The brutal war machine sent our troops reeling back. Our armies were crushed by the blitzkrieg, trampled beneath the onslaught of steel and bullets. The German advance was not stopped until they were in the suburbs of Moscow and Leningrad.

We heard rumors that the Poles, Baltic peoples and even Russians had greeted the invaders as liberators, assuming that they

❖

would be an improvement over the regime we lived under, but soon those whispers of glee were replaced by ones of horror as word spread of atrocities committed by the conquerors.

That invasion began five months ago, and the war had raged on, with Leningrad violated and abused by the struggle between ruthless armies. The Horsemen of the Apocalypse rode with the invaders, malevolent storms of death, disease and famine gripping Leningrad as a violent winter lashed the city while enemy artillery and bombs rained murder from the skies.

The worse fate was not to die quickly from the explosion of a bomb or murderous shrapnel from artillery—it was to die slowly of starvation and lost hope, as you watched family, friends and neighbors wither and drop like leaves on a dying tree.

Have you ever seen anyone starve to death? Have you seen someone you love get thinner and weaker everyday, fading like sand slipping between your fingers, too weak to keep the flame of life glowing? That was how my mother was when they pulled me away from her, pale and weak, sand slipping between my fingers.

I had to get off this truck that was carrying me out of the city, further away from my mother, and make my way back to help her.

PETER THE GREAT HAD built our city atop rivers and swamps two and a half centuries earlier with the Baltic Sea on the west and Lake Lagoda, the largest lake in Europe, to the east. The Germans had not been able to completely surround the city because of the two bodies of water. But the Baltic was no help to us because the German navy would be waiting for our ships if they tried to leave the harbor. Besides, the sea froze in the winter, trapping our fleet anyway, making the ships sitting ducks for the Nazi fighter planes and bombers that swarmed overhead.

But the lake was different. When winter howled, the lake froze in places solid enough for trucks to cross under the cover of darkness. Daredevil runs by truckers carried a little food into the city and children out, the drivers praying for moonless nights as they raced across the frozen lake to the Soviet forces on the other side.

❖

I didn't know how far we were from the city when the truck stopped. We had left late at night and drove slowly with the truck lights off, but we never made it across the lake. We had to stop because enemy fire had hit a convoy earlier and the burning hulks were blocking the road. Once the debris was removed, we would have to wait for night to fall again because we wouldn't have time to get across the lake before the sun rose, making the truck an easy target for the *Messerschmitts* that would scream overhead.

"We wait for darkness," the driver told us, after he pulled the truck to the side of the road and got out. "Otherwise we have no chance of making it."

No one said a word. We huddled under a stiff white canvas used as camouflage and waited for our ration.

The driver brought a cotton duffle bag out of the cab and set it on the snow. He opened one end of the bag to expose long loaves of bread. It was black bread, coarse and usually with a little sawdust added at the plants to increase the number of loaves. No one cared about the taste. We would have eaten dirt if we were told it was nourishing.

Drawing out a loaf at a time, he tore off pieces and handed them up to us. Each of us watched the driver intently, waiting for our piece. A few months ago, it would have been a piece of bread, not very inviting, perhaps not even eaten because it didn't come with a slab of butter or spread with sweetened fruit. Now a little bread was life itself.

"Roast chicken and borscht," he said, as he carefully tore off a portion.

It was his idea of humor. I could not remember what a piece of chicken or a bowl of borscht tasted like. The words didn't even make my mouth water. Starvation had left my body numb. No one around me smiled at the words, either.

Over two million people were in the city when the war started. Five months ago the streets were filled with cars and trucks and trolleys, the sidewalks crowded with people rushing and bustling, talking and arguing, leaving trails of cigarette smoke behind them

❖

and sometimes vodka fumes. Half of the people in the city, a million souls, had already died, mostly from hunger. It was now a quiet city—when the bombs and shells weren't raining—cold and quiet with snow covering everything, with few nonmilitary vehicles moving, no trams or trains rattling down tracks, no chatter of conversation on the streets, no loud voices, not even the smell of cigarette smoke in the crisp clean winter air as you walked past people on the sidewalks. A city of people with white, haggard faces, people without smiles and hope, without light in their eyes—people who would surrender without a fight when death came knocking.

"Walking, breathing ghosts," my mother called the children and people of Leningrad. "The flesh is gone from our bodies and all that is left is a little bit of our soul. When we give up the spirit, we don't even get to go to heaven because we're Communists."

She hadn't always talked like that, critical of the regime. In the old days, before war clouds gathered over Europe, the three of us—my mother, father and me—would sit together in our warm little apartment. For a Leningrader, I had an unusual pedigree—a Russian Jewish mother and a father who was Anglican and British.

We lived on the third floor of a walkup and had two rooms—a kitchen-living room combination and a bedroom. There would be hot food on the stove and bread in the oven. We'd laugh and talk about books and movies and my day at school, but the two of them were careful not to discuss their feelings about work or the government in front of me. From a child's point of view, such parental secrecy was the reason someone invented the keyhole.

Sometimes I shut my eyes and tried to remember every detail of those days before the war, hearing in my mind once again the sound of their laughter, the smell of my mother's cooking, the warmth and comfort and security we shared before the minds of men were afflicted by the madness of death and conquest—before the insane dreams of Hitler and Stalin turned day into night and human lives became the color of blood.

We were entitled to three ounces of bread as our ration. It looked like less than three ounces was being torn off for each of us, but I said nothing and neither did anyone else. To speak up might result in no ration. None of us had any extra fat on our bodies to keep us going if we were not given at least a little food.

Even with many night convoys getting through, only a fraction of the food necessary to support the city was brought in. And no fuel for heat came in at all. Hundreds of thousands of people who were not killed by the bombardments froze and starved.

After he handed out the ration of bread, the driver passed out letters that had been sent to the station in the city where we children had been assembled to await our turn to be evacuated. He shouted, "Nicholaus Pedrovich Cutter."

I went forward and got a small sheet of paper bearing the letterhead of Gorky Hospital. A smudged scribble read, "*Happy birthday, my son, mother loves you.*"

I was eleven years old today.

It was not my mother's handwriting, nor was the simple signature, *Mother,* in her hand.

Lena stared at the note in my hand.

"It's not my mother's handwriting," I said. "She's too weak to write it, or even sign it. An attendant in the hospital must have wrote it."

"My mother is dead," she said in a fragile voice. "I don't know where my father is. He was sent to fight the Hun."

Her eyes were blank. She wasn't talking to me. I think she was remembering, perhaps the warm arms of her mother, her father's strong hug, a big pot of hot soup on the stove.

I stared at the note. The simple message created dread in me. If my mother was too weak to even sign the note, she would die soon. The dead and the dying were things I knew about, things all the children in the city had firsthand knowledge of.

"She's going to die," I told Lena.

She stared at me with blank eyes. She was going to die, too, I thought. She had given up hope.

I climbed off the back and went to the truck cab. I grabbed the door handle and used the running board to step up and knock on the window.

The driver was chewing on a piece of meat. A loaf of bread lay across his lap. It was a week's ration. And he got it by chiseling a little off from each of us. If he was caught, he would be summarily shot. If he was caught plunging a knife into someone's heart, he would get a trial and imprisonment. But to take bread from another's mouth earned the death penalty without a trial.

He saw me looking at the big chunk of bread. He rolled down the window, his expression ugly.

"I have to return to the city," I told him.

He stared at me as if I'd just told him that I needed to go to Mars.

"Fuck your mother, what are you talking about?"

The expression he used was not a slight to my mother, but the standard street expletive for anger and exasperation. Before the war, I had heard it once at school. Now it was almost a common salutation.

"Get back on the track," he said, "before I take you to the Haymarket, you little bastard."

I jumped down from the cab and went back and crawled under the canvas next to Lena. No one had moved or even shifted position.

The driver didn't have to explain his threat. The Haymarket was the place in the city where a black market in food and other things was conducted. People brought family heirlooms to the market—jewels and art and fine furs left from before the revolution twenty-five years ago—to sell them for a little meat or a few ounces of grain stolen by gangs of food thieves. Physical possessions, heirlooms, fine watches, gems, wads of rubles—none of it had the value of food. On good days, the meat was horsemeat. Dogs, cats and rats had been devoured early. Work horses weren't slaughtered until they fell.

Like the Stone Age, where fire, shelter and the day's kill meant survival, the siege of Leningrad had taken the city back to the most basic fundamentals of human survival.

A common joke was that a Fabergé egg worth a king's ransom wouldn't buy a dozen hen eggs. People said that there was trade in a stranger foodstuff than eggs, and that the tender meat of children was preferred over other cuts.

❖

THE DRIVER LEFT THE cab and joined a group of other truckers who had gathered at a fire started in a metal barrel. They talked as they heated snow for hot water to drink. A few had tea.

I listened to their conversations from the back of the truck.

"Half the city is dead already," our driver said. He spit, and the spittle turned to ice before it hit the frozen ground. "It's good people are dying, it leaves more food for the living. Besides, those not strong enough to live need to make way for the rest of us."

I didn't think it would be good if my mother died. In some small way I understood that she had been so battered and abused by cold and hunger that death would take her beyond sorrow. But that did not help the ache of loneliness and despair in my heart as I realized that I was the only family she had. I didn't want her to die alone. I needed to get to her, be at her side, tell her that I didn't want her to die.

After he finished drinking hot water with the other truckers, our driver climbed back into the cab, no doubt covering himself with a fur blanket.

The children huddled together in the back of the truck, shivering under the oiled canvas tarp as light snow fell. There was no laughter, no jokes, no talking. We were all too cold, too numb from months of shock and hunger to do little more than sit quietly. My mother said that the children of Leningrad no longer laughed or even smiled. But I saw hopelessness in the eyes and on the faces of everyone on the streets, not just the young. Hopelessness, helplessness, even surrender. So many horrors confronted us each day that our minds balked at accepting any more. There was a time early in the siege when people cried and complained, but no one had the energy anymore for anger or grief. There were neither tears nor smiles. The deprivations had created not just a grim gravity in everyone, but in some people, like our driver and the black marketeers who specialized in exotic meats, it had brought out a cruel streak.

Or maybe the driver's attitude was just a human survival instinct. Perhaps if I had been the biggest and strongest, I would

❖

have cut the rations of the others to make sure my belly was full. Hunger was a strange new sensation for all of us. At first it was an urgent growling in my stomach, then a feeling of light-headedness and even increased energy. But the shot of energy lasted only a short time. In its stead came the sickness of starvation, a lack of strength that made getting out of bed and walking across a room a chore. The final stage was weakness and a dull ache that engulfed my whole body, a vague pain gripping my entire body that never went away, that made even thinking difficult.

I saw the starvation disease all around me, at first in the very old and very young, and then slowly infecting everyone—they became confused, dull-witted, lethargic. People collapsed in the streets, some convulsing in seizures, others just sitting down to quietly die. An old woman who lived in our apartment building just sat down on the front steps and never got up again, passing into a coma and then to the sanctuary of death.

My mother said that God was on the side of the Germans because He sent icy storms to make our hunger more miserable.

It was strange to hear her talk of God. Officially, God did not exist in the Soviet Union.

At the evacuation station where we were held before being placed in the back of the truck for the lake crossing, we were given an ounce of bread and a cup of hot water with salt for breakfast. At lunchtime, we received two ounces of bread, a spoon of butter, a bowl of soup made from frozen beets and a little linseed-oil cake. Many of us who still had parents or siblings poured half of the soup into a jam jar and threw in other scraps and took the food back to them because they were starving. I took my jar each day to the hospital where my mother lay on the floor on a mattress. There was no more food in the hospital than other places in the city, each patient getting only the starvation ration of three ounces of bread a day. I helped her into a sitting position and made her drink the liquid.

Now I felt the jar beneath my coat. I had put half of my soup and bread in the jar, intending to take it to my mother at the hospital, but hadn't gotten the chance because we were suddenly

❖

locked up. The supervisor at the evaluation station realized that some of us would run away to return to our parents rather than be shipped out. He was right about me. Had I known I would be transported from the city, I would have run away to be with my mother. As soon as lunch was over, he locked us in a room, held prisoner until night fell and we were loaded into the truck.

I shut my eyes and tried to sleep. The stronger children pushed their way back in the truck to get more heat from the surrounding bodies, but I deliberately stayed on the outer edge and curled into a fetal position to keep as much body heat as I could.

When the first crack of light arrived, I slipped off the back of the truck.

I was driven not only by my own need for my mother, but to save her after what she had done for me. I overheard a nurse at the hospital say my mother was weak because she had slipped me a little of her own bread ration each day. To help me survive, she had sacrificed herself.

As I walked down the frozen road I realized that if my mother died, I would be all alone in the world.

❖

3

❖

Peter Cutter, Munich, 1930

"He spiels all that morality stuff, but he's fucking his young niece."

Peter and the man who spoke to him, Josef Krausner, were on the outer edge of the crowd with their backs to the wall of a building. Peter took his eyes off the man who was powerfully haranguing the crowd from the flatbed of a truck. Prudently, neither he nor Krausner wore a red star on their lapel that would identify them as the Communists they were. A large crowd packed the square to hear the man on the truck speak, and neither the speaker nor the crowd were friendly to the followers of Karl Marx and the Bolsheviks. *Nazis* is what the orator and his followers called their organization.

"How do you know?" Peter asked.

"A man named Otto Strasser has broken off from him and started his own political party. He and his brother have been close friends with this man. He says incest is only one of his sex crimes, the least of them. He's not married, is said to be shy around women in public, but in private does very outlandish things with them."

"Like what?"

Krausner grinned. "We're all perverts, aren't we? There's nothing like some sexual scandal to pique our interest. He likes to have

❖

women beat on him, even whip him, while he's naked. Then he lies down and he eats their cunts and lets them piss on him. He doesn't like to use his cock. Maybe he doesn't have one. I heard he lost one of his nuts in the war, but maybe he got the whole set of tools whacked off."

"And he wants to be leader of a master race," Peter said.

Peter Cutter was British, but he spoke German to Krausner with hardly a hint of accent. Twenty-six years old, Peter had graduated from Cambridge with advanced degrees in Central and Eastern European language and cultural studies. Besides his native tongue, he was fluent in high and low German, Polish, Russian, Czech and Hungarian. A middle-class "intellectual Marxist" whose political views were born and nurtured from collegian discussions and philosophical treatises, he had come to Germany to live with a coal-mining family to experience the poverty and suffering of the masses under the capitalistic system he believed enslaved workers.

It was a particularly appalling time economically all over the world. After the First World War ended eleven years before, most of war-ravaged Europe had fallen into a terrible economic collapse. The war had brought the demise of the Russian Empire and the rise of the Bolsheviks, the German and Austro-Hungarian empires disintegrated and the countries of Poland, Czechoslovakia, Hungary, Austria and Yugoslavia erupted out of the turmoil. In the wake of the governmental paralysis came unemployment and spiraling inflation that spawned political chaos. Much of Europe was a boiling cauldron of conflicting "isms" as Fascism, Nazism, Socialism and Communism battled in the streets for control of governments and the minds of people.

It was a world of political violence and political confusion—the speaker on the truck called his political party National Socialism, Nazism for short, despite the fact the party was antisocialistic, while his Fascist pal in Italy, Mussolini, got his start in politics by founding a "socialist" newspaper. Now both men had private armies and engaged in terrorist campaigns against liberals, "left-wingers," socialists and communists, burning down their oppo-

❖

nents' headquarters and terrorizing their supporters with humiliation, beatings and even murder.

Peter had not come to Munich to see the man on the truck speak, but to participate in a march by German Communists. He felt both excitement and fear—with anticommunists convening in large numbers for the Nazi rally, there was danger of violent confrontation. Although he thought of himself as a soldier for Communism, just as some missionaries think of themselves as soldiers for Christ, he was not a man of action, but a thin, medium-build young man with a friendly face, unruly short blond hair, kindly gray eyes and scholarly gold-rimmed eyeglasses.

The last—and only—fight he had been in had resulted in a black eye in the fourth grade. His opponent had nary a scratch.

The man on the truck, an Austrian named Adolf Hitler, was not well known to the general public outside of Germany, but had gathered an impressive 18 percent of the national vote in a recent election. It was not enough to place him at the head of the government, but it was shocking considering that any rational person would question the man's insane views.

Hitler thundered to the crowd, "There are two great evils in this world that keep the German people oppressed and the German nation from taking its rightful place as the leader of all nations. Jews and Marxism are the destroyers of our Aryan culture, are the filthy, diseased parasites that infect our culture and keep us from our greatness!"

As he listened to the man haranguing the crowd and studied the faces of those around him, Peter was stunned by the impression that the man was making on the people. The audience was buying into the ridiculous tirade.

"Look at their faces," he whispered to Krausner. "They love him and they accept his lies with the awe and reverence of Moses receiving the Ten Commandments. Besides his powerful voice and dramatic gestures, he's telling these people that they are the greatest on earth, that they should rule the world. He gives them Jews as scapegoats to blame for their own failures and the terrible economy, and Communist conspiracies to make them fearful."

❖

"Brilliant. Devilish. Insane," Krausner said. "We offer them a society in which there will always be full employment, bread on the table, and an equal share of all the fruits of labor, and they listen to this maniac who calls people 'parasites' and instills in them that Jews and communists are infecting them with a disease that is keeping them from ruling the world."

"Look at the joy and veneration on their faces," Peter said. "His voice is reaching inside them and touching something, the type of preternatural emotion that you see on people enraptured by religious ceremonies. He makes Jews the incarnation of evil, responsible for all their troubles, like a witch doctor telling the tribe one of its members has to be killed because he's responsible for the tribe's failure in the hunt. And these people believe every word, every lie. Look at the bliss and nervous energy of these sheep suckling on these lies. What fools!"

Peter shook his head. "I'm dumbfounded that the common man can be so completely stupid and naïve. And I don't think the rest of the world has any inkling about what this man is talking about, what danger he can be. I heard he wrote a book filled with these crazy ideas. I'm going to read it."

"There is a social disease," Krausner said, disgusted. "It's National Socialism. It's a killer disease with pogroms against the Jews and the murder of our comrades in communism. That's the true illness spreading throughout Germany as a pandemic. And it's not just a contagion among people out of work, not just among bakers and clerks who fear for their jobs and for bread on the table. The big bankers and industrialists running this country see this madman as a wedge against the Communist Revolution that would tear down the pillars of privilege they reside upon."

"Maybe the incest with the niece and his sexual perversions should be well publicized."

Krausner shook his head. "Coming from us, it would sound like smear tactics. And it's the type of story no newspaper would carry. Papers that get too critical of these animals are liable to find themselves bombed and their editors murdered."

❖

A young woman was pushing her way through the crowd toward them.

"Comrade Menchik," Krausner whispered. "A secretary at the Russian Embassy in Berlin. She was sent here to help assist in the preparations for the parade. A very good organizer."

Peter guessed the woman's age at four or five years younger than his twenty-six. She had light brown hair pulled back tightly in a bun and large brown eyes. His first impression was that she was modestly attractive, but her physical appearance conveyed more than the sexual nuances members of the opposite sex convey to each other. There was a serious cast to her features, a studiousness that he himself was often accused of having. Like the proverbial absentminded scientist, Peter and Comrade Menchik both saw the world as a place that needed constant study and analysis.

"Comrade Menchik, Comrade Cutter," Krausner said.

She offered a handshake. Peter was caught by surprise at the strength of her grip.

"We are assembling six blocks from here," she said, quietly. "We will keep a block away from this square as we march."

"Just a block? That will still provoke the Nazis," Peter said.

She stared at him and frowned. "Of course, that is our purpose. We will be attacked by these fascists, the police will intervene on their side, and many of us will receive the blows of martyrs. But the world will have another example of how these brutal animals treat anyone who does not agree with their sick theories." She gave Peter a look, sizing him up. "Are you up to this, Comrade Britisher? Perhaps you are more used to defending our movement in the drawing room over a cup of tea rather than on the streets with blood."

He flushed. "I'm up to anything you are."

"Isn't she a tiger?" Krausner said, grinning. "That's why the Embassy sends her around to organize demonstrations. She's wonderful at making a man stand up for himself . . . when he is shitting his pants from fright."

What annoyed Peter the most was that the woman had seen through him instantly. He was a drawing-room revolutionary.

4

❖

Peter mulled over the young woman's accusation that he was a drawing-room revolutionary as he walked toward the rendezvous point where the Communists were forming for their march through the streets. Although he was little more than middle-class in terms of British society, by comparison with the poor of Eastern Europe, he was privileged.

His own father, Charles Cutter, was a minor British government career official, a supervising engineer in the electrical works of West Dorset. Asked to describe his father at a meeting of a Communist cell, he told the group of Reds that his father was a sturdy, pipe-smoking English yeoman, a stouthearted man of the kind who made Britain the empire that the sun never set upon.

That description of his father brought criticism from his fellow radicals because they tended to see people in economic terms, as the exploited and the exploiters, and the British Empire was high on the list of exploiters. Although Peter, too, saw the world through eyes tinted by the economics of oppression, he didn't think of his own family as part of those dynamics. His father was just a rather reserved and stern older man, who took little interest in politics—

though he didn't temper his own feelings about his son being a radical. Like most young intellectuals of Peter's time, being a "Red" was not in his family's ancestral makeup, and by all the odds of heredity and environment, he should never have been drawn to Marxism.

He grew up next to the sea, in the picturesque fishing village of Lyme Regis at the foot of the cold, dark and windy waters of the English Channel. Like his father, he was bright, a good student, but while his father excelled at technical studies—math and physical science—Peter was drawn to the humanities—philosophy, politics, languages and other human concerns.

Intensely intellectual, a hardworking student, Peter won a Queen's scholarship to Cambridge, where he excelled at Central and Eastern European languages, speaking fluent German, Russian and Hungarian, hoping for a career in the foreign service because he loved traveling and experiencing different cultures.

He entered Cambridge in 1922 and stayed there during most of that decade. In America, it was the decade of the Roaring Twenties, a vibrant, noisy time when Prohibition was in and morality went on vacation. In Europe, it was a more somber era. Germany was shackled by its crushing defeat in war and peace terms that kept it from recovering—people were out of work, and inflation was so hyper it was no joke that it took a wheelbarrow full of German marks to buy a loaf of bread. The rest of Central and Eastern Europe were no better off. The Russian Empire had fallen to the Communists, the Tsar and his family murdered, and the country transposed into the Union of Soviet Socialist Republics. Following Lenin's death in 1924, Stalin and Trotsky spent the rest of the decade battling for power before Trotsky went into exile in 1929, later to be murdered by assassins sent by Stalin.

While a dynamic economy, booming stock market, jazz and the Charleston—knees-bent, toes-in, heels-out—were the rage in America, in Europe there was economic depression that got even sicker as the American stock market and economy went into a tailspin after the 1929 crash and the Great Depression was ushered in. The frightful economic conditions stirred social upheaval.

❖

Fighting in the streets between socialists and fascists when Peter entered college in 1922 had, by the 1930s, become murder in the streets as the "isms" violently collided.

Peter evolved into young manhood on the British Isles as the British labor movement fought the factory owners for employment rights and continental Europeans tore at each other's entrails. While his father, who had never left Britain except for a stint in the navy, saw a world where the well-defined social orders of the past should be maintained, Peter saw a world of have-and-have-nots, of greedy factory owners and workers without food to feed their families.

Traveling in Eastern and Central Europe—Germany, Austria, Hungary and Czechoslovakia—to advance his knowledge of the languages, he saw an even wider gulf between rich and poor. Already a socialist and Marxist, when he returned to Britain he joined a Communist cell.

The leader of the cell gave him an assignment to live with a working-class family to broaden his awareness of the suffering of the people. Living for a month with a coal-mining family in the Ruhr, he saw firsthand how the poor suffered under terrible living conditions and dangerous working ones. He had even shown up "for work" one day in the mine, falling into line with workers to see what it was like to work in a hot black hole hundreds of feet below the surface. Exposed by a supervisor, he was taken back atop and would have been prosecuted but he managed to talk his way out of it, putting across a story that he was a British university student doing research. Had the mine management found out he was a Communist, he would have been given a good beating before being turned over to the police.

A week ago he had been instructed by his cell leader to leave the countryside and go to Munich to help build membership and organize resistance. The Communist march set for the same day and area as the Nazi rally made him nervous. It was planned to interfere with the Nazi meeting, sure to provoke a confrontation. He was bothered by the idea of violence on two levels—his own per-

❖

sonal safety and his philosophy that a communist society could be achieved by peaceful means.

He didn't think of himself as a coward, but he also wasn't practiced in the way of violence. Nor was he eager to be martyred—he wanted to live to see Communism victorious, not die for it. The idea of getting clubbed by a policeman or having to fight a Nazi brute knotted his stomach.

Even though he was frightened, he kept one foot in front of the other, kept himself moving in the direction where the Communists were gathering. He would not let down his comrades, nor would he humiliate himself in front of the firebrand from Berlin. Comrade Menchik had not only jabbed him through the chink in his armor, she had aroused a more fundamental aspect of mankind than bread and bullets. *Lust.* He didn't particularly find himself attractive or desirable, although women, especially ones older than him, let him know otherwise. But the young Russian firebrand had stirred his blood.

His sole sexual experience, beyond breast-petting and finger-fucking with a university girlfriend, and a brief and unsatisfactory "experiment" with the boy he roomed with when he attended a private prep school, had been losing his cherry to an older member of the Cambridge Communist cell he belonged to.

She was the wife of a university don who was also a member of the cell. Peter had been invited to their country home for a weekend visit. After he retired, the don's wife came in, took off her robe—totally naked—and crawled into bed with him. She explained that they had an "open" marriage and that if he liked, he could also have sex with the don. He had been too mortified to get it up even for her, much less climbing into bed with an older man. However, she had helped him along by stroking his penis until it finally came erect, and then pulled him into her.

He had come quickly—and prematurely—as much out of fright as pleasure, and had left for town early the next morning to avoid any sort of tit-for-tat that the professor might expect after letting his wife fuck him.

❖

His reserve and shyness around women had cost him many opportunities for intimacies, but he had regretted few of them. He was very much more interested in cerebral matters than those of the flesh. In his own mind, he was reserving his passions for the cause of revolution. But Comrade Menchik had challenged him both intellectually and emotionally, arousing in him an instant sexual attraction.

As he hurried down the street, he tried to imagine her naked body in his mind.

❖

5

❖

"You are late."

Comrade Menchik glared at him.

"I shall have to mention your tardiness when I do a report on the demonstration."

Peter gaped at her. "Why? Look around you, people are still arriving."

"These are workers who had to leave jobs and family to come here at great personal sacrifice. All you had to do was get your bourgeois little ass in line—*on time!*"

He gaped as she gave him her back and walked away, leaving him angry and frustrated.

What a bitch!

Someone slapped him on the shoulder.

"Are you ready to fight the Nazis thugs?"

It was Krausner.

"I'm ready to kick your Berlin friend in the ass. The girl just berated me like she was a colonel of artillery."

Krausner laughed. "You're not the first one to want to do something with her ass, but not every man wants to kick it. Most of us

❖

41

want to stick our sausage in it. Some women who come into the cause believe in a bit of communal love to go with a communal economy. Personally, I'd like to give Comrade Menchik a taste of my sausage, but she isn't the communal-love type. But I have never seen her so completely antagonistic toward anyone in the Party as she is with you, my friend. She seems to have taken an instant dislike for you."

Krausner moved away to greet an arriving Party member.

Peter struggled with anger, resentment, frustration and inexorable attraction before he sought out Comrade Menchik in the crowd. At first he told himself he wanted to get close enough to tell her off, but deep down he realized that he merely wanted to get *close enough*—period.

A dog, he told himself, *a whipped dog that lies at its master's feet and whimpers, that's what I am.*

The verbal dressing-down she gave him had gotten him sexually aroused. Watching her work the crowd, going from one member to another to give instructions and encouragement, watching her eyes sparkle when she laughed, her breasts strut out, made him horny.

He got close enough to her so he could listen to her instructions, even though Krausner had told him the drill earlier. They were to march down the middle of the street, sticking together, singing a communist song. They were to start no trouble with the police or Nazis. But everyone knew trouble would come, anyway. Even policemen who had not been attracted to Nazism were anticommunist. The marchers could expect no quarter from the Nazis and no help from the police.

As he mingled, he listened to "veterans" of previous marches talk of police brutality, of comrades run down by police horses and clubbed by Nazis brutes. He wiped his wet palms on the sides of his pants. He became more excited and nervous as the time to march arrived.

There were three hundred of them, a motley bunch: factory workers and miners, women store clerks and men employed in low-level government jobs; an old man and woman with white hair and a young woman with a baby in her arms, but most of the marchers were middle-aged and younger, at least half of them university students. Most wore black mourning bands on their arms to commemorate the death of two young Communists who were brutally murdered by fascist thugs called the Sturmabteilung, the SA, a paramilitary group loyal to Adolf Hitler.

These so-called Storm Troopers attacked the two students in a beer hall when the two dared to sing *"L'Internationale,"* the anthem of socialism and communism written by a nineteenth-century Parisian transport worker. The Communist students had burst out with the song right after the Nazis finished singing *"Horst Wessel Lied,"* a song dedicated to a low-life Nazi student killed in a brawl with Communists in Berlin. The man in charge of Nazi propaganda, Joseph Goebbels, had cleverly turned Horst Wessel, a bohemian slum dweller, into a martyr for the Nazi cause by having a song composed about his "martyrdom."

Storm Troopers were waiting when the two young students left the beer hall. They dragged the youths into an alley and beat them to death.

As the march started, the word went out to pin red stars on lapels. Peter pinned his on and began marching under a banner of the hammer and sickle. As he marched, he joined the others singing *"L'Internationale."*

"Arise, the wretched of the world!"

"We were nothing—thus let us be everything!"

As they walked, he pushed his way through the crowd until he was positioned next to Comrade Menchik. As he came up alongside, he asked, "What is your first name?"

"'Comrade,' the same as yours, *Comrade.*"

"Have we met before?" he asked.

"Met?" She glanced at him. "No, I don't think so."

"Then why are you angry at me?"

She stiffened and shot him a look. "I'm not angry at you."

"Yes, you are, from the very first moment we were introduced. You were friendly to Krausner and caustic to me."

They marched together for a moment before she answered.

❖

"I am not angry at you *personally*, I am angry at what you represent. You British and Americans play at being Communists. You believe it is an intellectual pursuit, something to debate with school chums. You forget that it is warfare between the classes, that at some point you must pick up a gun or a shovel, or use your bare hands if there is no other weapon, and go into the streets and fight. Without blood spilled, bourgeois society, with its class distinctions of workers and capitalists, will never be destroyed and the proletariat will not become the masters of their own fate. When I see you British take to the streets and spill blood for the cause, I will have respect."

"I don't need your respect. In case you haven't noticed, I'm in the streets right now."

He moved away from her, angry. But after a moment his anger faded and he was a little amused at her attacks on him. In truth, he had met many other continental European Communists with the same attitude about British and American Communists. And he admired their courage and determination. He had come to the continent not only to experience firsthand the plight of the German worker, but to test his own mettle.

He watched her as they marched and sang, her chin lifted high, her face glowing with determination. She wore the hat and pants of a Bolshevik worker, but had a red rose in the front of her blouse. He tried to keep beside her but lost his position as enthusiastic marchers surged by him. As he marched and sang with his comrades, his fear and nervousness was replaced by a swelling of pride and camaraderie.

She looked back, caught him looking at her, and linked her arm with a man next to her and lifted her chin higher. He laughed, delighted at her antics, thrilled to be finally on a street, demonstrating for the cause he had adopted as his life's work.

The anthem faded as the marchers turned a corner. Down the block stood a line of mounted German police, their spiked helmets and spit-polished leather shining, blocking their passage. Behind the marchers, several trucks pulled up and began unloading uni-

❖

formed men carrying clubs and shields. The marchers slowly came to a halt.

"Rohm's storm troopers!" Comrade Menchik said.

"They're blocking us, they won't let us through," someone else yelled.

It took a moment for Peter to understand. It was the police who were blocking them, preventing them from leaving the street so that the Storm Troopers would have their way with them.

He felt the wave of fear and anticipation that went through the crowd, sucking it in, raising his own fear level. His elation was suddenly gone. These were the dreaded brown-shirt paramilitary thugs that carried out the bloody street battles and violent harassment of Jews that the Nazis had become identified with.

He gawked as Comrade Menchik stepped forward and threw a rock at the line of Storm Troopers. *My God, she's insane,* he thought.

It broke the dam.

The brown-shirt Nazis waded into the demonstrators, swinging clubs. The demonstrators had been warned not to carry any weapons out of fear of confrontation with the police. Now they were easy victims for the thugs.

Peter was carried along as the panicked radicals tried to escape the brown shirts by rushing the police lines. The line of mounted officers drew their sabers and surged forward on their horses, ramming the demonstrators and bringing their sabers down on them.

Peter was unexpectedly knocked off his feet by a horse. Rolling to avoid being crushed, he got to his hands and knees just as an officer's saber came down on his head and he went down again.

He lay stunned, unable to move. His vision blurred for a moment and his head buzzed as the screams, shouts and commotion swirled around him, the pounding of hooves pelting the cobblestones. He sat up and felt the blood on his face.

Almost immediately, a pair of hands helped him to his feet.

"We have to hurry."

❖

It was Comrade Menchik.

She pulled him along by the arm roughly and he staggered beside her, almost losing his footing, but she kept him from going down.

"Hurry, hurry."

❖

6

❖

They darted into an empty alley two blocks down the street, a rush of adrenaline carrying them away from the fray.

Peter closed his eyes and leaned back against the wall, his heart still racing. He was nervous, hyper, but strangely elated. This is why he had come, to march in a demonstration, albeit getting attacked hadn't been part of his plan. He almost couldn't remember getting hit on his head, it had happened all so quickly. But now he was beginning to feel a dull ache on his forehead.

He winced when Comrade Menchik touched his face.

"You're bleeding, a cut on your forehead."

"I don't care." He touched the blood with his fingers and held it up to her. "British blood, you see, we can bleed for the cause."

"It's just a scratch. Better Communists than you have given their lives for the cause."

"Is that what it's going to take to impress you? My life?"

"It would take a miracle, and those are no longer sanctioned by the Party." She looked both ways down the alley. "When we go back out onto the street, we have to pretend we're just out for a stroll.

❖

Pull your hat down over your wound." She removed the hammer-and-sickle emblem and red star from her clothes.

"Where are we going?"

"To a safe place. It's only about five blocks from here. Are you okay, can you walk?"

"Sure, like you said, it's just a scratch. Let's go."

Moving back into the street, she held his arm and they proceeded to walk at a leisurely pace, ignoring the drama around them, as policemen on foot, horses and horse wagons rushed by them.

"Just smile and nod as they go by," she told him.

He waited until they had passed before he said, "The police were helping those fascists."

"Of course. They're part of the system of keeping the people oppressed. Why should that surprise you?"

She was slamming him again, he thought.

"It didn't. Like everyone else, I knew the police were on the side of the fascists. I was just making a comment. Why do you have to kick my feet out from under me every time I say anything?"

She was silent for a moment. "You stood up fine during the altercation."

"Thanks. Maybe next time I'll lose an arm or a leg and please you even more. Why did you bother saving me back there? You could have left me to be martyred."

"Comrades don't abandon each other."

She stopped in front of a brown building, weather-worn and neglected, with iron railings over the lower windows. By the door stood a planter box devoid of any plants.

"Here we are."

Once inside, they went up a spiral wood staircase to the third floor and paused by a door. The whole building, Peter thought, needed a coat of paint, but he had a good feeling about it. It was old but it had character. She opened the door and locked it behind them once they were inside.

"Come in the bathroom, I want to get a closer look at your head."

❖

"Is this your apartment?"

"No. It belongs to a friend. I live in Berlin."

It was one large room with a bathroom. A pot-bellied stove stood in one corner of the room, along with a small table and two chairs. On the other side separated by a room divider was a small divan and double-size bed. The whole room felt warm and cozy, simple yet homey. Judging from the flowers he saw in several places, he assumed her friend was a woman. "Is your friend a woman?"

She didn't answer him as he followed her into the bathroom.

"I was right, it's just a scratch," she said, washing the wound with rubbing alcohol. "You're a bleeder, aren't you?"

He examined the wound in the mirror. "It's a bloody damn bludgeoning, not a scratch."

"You men. You're all babies. You'll live."

"You sound disappointed."

"No, just not overly interested. I've seen worse—on better men."

He swayed dizzily and she grabbed him and steadied him. "I feel like I'm going to faint."

"Come sit down on the bed."

She helped him to the bed and he fell onto it, taking her with him. At first she struggled to get out from under him but he held her down and kissed her on the mouth. She didn't resist the kiss, but pushed him back after their lips parted.

"You're not hurt."

"Yes, I am. My heart hurts."

"You're lying."

"True, but that's irrelevant. I wanted to kiss you from the moment I saw you."

He looked at her thoughtfully. He had never met anyone like her. None of the other women he had been with, which hadn't been many, had ever attracted him sexually. There was something different about Comrade Menchik. It wasn't that she was any prettier than the other women he had dated. Probably not any smarter. But there was an essence, a feminine mystique about her that drew him inexorably to her—even when she was stepping on his ego.

❖

"What is it about you that makes me want to make love to you?"

"It's your irresponsibility toward the suffering of your fellow man. You're not a revolutionary, you're a lackey for capitalist—"

He put his finger on her lips. "Ssshh. You're a woman. I'm a man. Let's not talk about politics."

He kissed her again, fondling her breast with his hand.

"What do you think you're doing?"

"About to make love to you."

"Then stop acting like you're still in an English drawing room. We're adults. Sex was popular when humans were living in trees, so let's go at it like the animals we are."

She sat up and unbuttoned her shirt and threw it over the bed. With one swift move, she unclasped her flesh-colored bra and tossed it. Her porcelain breasts were full and round, the rosy nipples already were hard. They were the most beautiful breasts he had ever seen. Not even the pictures of the women's breasts at the British Museum, which is where he saw most of the breasts in his life, compared. He had an urge to suck them right away and was about to do so when she quickly bent down and removed her boots. Then she stood up and dropped her pants. She wasn't wearing any underwear. She turned around and faced him.

"What are you waiting for?"

He hadn't made any move to get undressed yet. He was too mesmerized by her body, her nakedness. Standing totally naked in front of him, his eyes passed over her pubic hair, slightly darker than her light brown hair, and focused on a mole on her abdomen just below her belly button. It caught his eye. It was perfectly round, almost black. There was something even sensuous about it.

"What are you staring at?"

He didn't realize he had been staring. "You have a beautiful body." She was neither thin nor fleshy, the muscles well-toned and defined.

"You're not lying again, are you?"

"No," his dry mouth croaked.

❖

"Good, because I know what you need. The doctor will fix you up."

She undid the buttons on his shirt and flung it over the bed. "Just close your eyes and leave everything to me." She pushed him back down on the bed. Her fingertips moved playfully down his chest, around his belly button and over the bulge already getting hard beneath his trousers.

He could feel the heat rising in him. As a male he was culturally molded to be the aggressor; it was titillating for him to experience her taking the lead. For a woman who gave the impression that her main interest in life was revolution, her femininity surprised him.

She got on top of him, spreading her knees slowly apart, her wiry pubic hair brushing against his waist before she slid down over his legs. "You British schoolboys are not used to being with a real woman, are you?"

She undid his belt and the top button of his pants and pulled the zipper down. "You bugger other boys and they bugger you. But I'm not a schoolboy," she whispered in his ear, letting her hard nipples brush against his chest.

He opened his eyes. The ache in his groin was growing.

"I didn't tell you to open your eyes. Keep them closed," she ordered.

She took out his rigid cock through the opening of his underwear and started massaging, slowly at first, then more fervently, finally putting her wet mouth on his organ.

The urgency in his body mounted. "I can't stand it anymore. I'm going to explode." He rolled her over on her back and thrust himself inside her. She was already wet. The rhythm of their bodies carried together and they both climaxed quickly. He kissed each of her nipples before he fell back on the bed, spent from his orgasm.

When he rolled on his side and looked at her, her eyes were closed. Her body glistened. He watched the motion of her breasts move up and down as she breathed. He guided his hand over her smooth stomach, down between her thighs, and began massaging her clitoris. Watching her body respond to his touch got him aroused again.

"Oh, God," she moaned, spreading her legs apart. "I'm going to come again."

He felt the surge of excitement in his body. He pushed himself inside her as her whole body shuddered against him, his own climax following immediately.

"Vera," she cried out.

He looked at her puzzled. "What?"

"My first name is Vera," she said, smiling at him. "If we're going to be lovers, we might as well call each other by our first names, don't you think . . . Peter?"

❖

7

❖

Vera Menchik Cutter, Leningrad, 1939

Vera sat on a wood chair with her back to the wall outside the Radio Leningrad meeting room where Peter was being interviewed. Married nearly nine years, Peter and she both were employed at Radio Leningrad and had a seven-year-old son, Nicholaus.

Her thoughts were on both Peter and Nicky as she sat stiffly, her hands tightly clasped in her lap, her knees together, holding in her tension. What was being said, being determined in the room, could affect them the rest of their lives.

She could hear the murmurs of voices in the meeting room behind her. Peter's voice became loud for a second and she involuntarily started. She didn't know what was said, but she had doubts that he had the tact to keep from putting his foot in his mouth. To be questioned about one's loyalty to Stalin was dangerous for anyone. For Peter, who wore his heart on his sleeve and exposed his emotions to everyone, it was particularly dangerous. The fact that he was a foreigner, permitted to emigrate to the Soviet Union to be part of the socialist revolution, did not help his cause. When she returned to Leningrad married to an Englishman, she was envied. But now that they lived in a society in which people were trying to

❖

get *out* of the country, anyone who had come *in* voluntarily was looked upon with a mean sort of jealousy.

She kept her facial features completely neutral. There were two women in the room, the clerical staff for the committee. It would not do well to show *any* emotion at the proceedings her husband was going through. The slightest sign of emotion—for or against her husband—would be grounds to question *her* loyalty to Stalin, regardless of how the investigation into Peter's actions went.

She knew there were three people in the room besides Peter: a commissar sent from Leningrad's Communist Party headquarters to preside over the hearing, and two members of the Patriotic Workers Committee of the radio station. The function of the committee was to investigate allegations of disloyalty to Stalin or the Party. It was a frightening experience to be targeted by the committee. While on paper the committee only made brief, vague "recommendations," in fact it was a court of last resort and, more often than not, judge and jury.

Peter was called before the investigating committee to defend an anonymous accusation that could be interpreted as criticism of Stalin. *Khozyain*, "the Boss," is what many Party insiders called Stalin—it was the old Russian name for master or landlord, a word once used by serfs to refer to the landowners who owned them. And he had a stranglehold on the Soviet Union tighter than any Tsar, even Ivan the Terrible who had clutched the Russian Empire in an iron fist.

A few days earlier, Soviet troops had launched an attack on Poland. The strike followed a surprise assault on Poland by Nazi Germany seventeen days before. The coordinated invasions brought out an even bigger surprise. Hitler and Stalin, the Nazi and the Communist—sworn blood enemies—had signed a secret pact dividing Poland between them. *A pact between devils.*

That the two sworn enemies of world politics, Hitler and Stalin, could violate every political principle that they respectively espoused to attack a small, neutral country sent a shock wave through the world. These two dictators had publicly proclaimed animosity and hostility toward each other's regime not unlike the zeal with which Christian crusaders and Muslims did battle.

Yet they had signed a secret pact of nonaggression toward each other, and between them swallowed a small, neutral country.

While the rest of the world could proclaim its displeasure at the hypocrisy, it was a death sentence in the Soviet Union to criticize the actions of the leader.

Poor Peter, hopelessly idealistic, intellectually naïve, impulsively—*and dangerously*—honest, had expressed his dismay over the pact before his coworkers. Unfortunately, the Soviet Union he came to eight years earlier was not the paradise of the proletariat that he thought it was. And things only got worse. Since that time, Stalin had consolidated his powers until he was the sole master of the nation, a brutal master who killed millions from crazed paranoia and kept the entire country in a constant state of fear and paranoia.

The sexual passion that instantly flared between Peter and Vera in Munich grew into love as the two teamed up to lead more demonstrations and communist recruitment in Germany. After Vera became pregnant, they married in Berlin.

Idealistic young Marxists, they saw themselves as pioneers who could help build the perfect socialist state in the ashes of the decadent, corrupt old Russian empire. Vera's elderly mother shared an apartment with her in Leningrad and they decided they would live there with her. Peter took Vera to England to meet his father before they set sail for Leningrad. A baby boy, Nicholaus Pedrovich Cutter, arrived prematurely and unexpectedly during the visit.

Peter's mother had passed away when he was still a child. His father argued with them to stay, but they spoke of the oppression of the proletariat by a capitalist society, of a monopoly of the "tools" of production by a privileged few, of social injustices and evils they saw Communism curing, of joining the common workers to build the perfect society. His father just sat there and stared at them openmouthed.

The utopian view they had of the Soviet Union in 1930 slowly

❖

withered, twisted and soured as Stalin set out to create a society in which everyone was equal—but some were more equal than others, a government that was totalitarian and subservient to him— compelling tens of millions of rustic households into collective farms, and instituting crash industrialization that enslaved the common worker to the factory wheel.

Anyone who resisted or criticized the plans was arrested, shot or imprisoned in an expanding network of gulag concentration camps. Many people, perhaps numbering into the millions, simply disappeared.

By the late 1930s, prominent people who dared to be critical of the leader and weren't outright murdered or shipped off to the camps were touted as traitors in show trials, quickly found guilty with fabricated confessions and shot in the traditional Soviet manner—a single shot to the head. Why waste bullets on garbage, the apparatchiks reasoned.

Instead of the utopian society Peter and Vera were to be pioneer builders of, they found themselves trapped in a totalitarian dictatorship that oppressed everyone beneath "the Boss," a system in which ideas and suggestions to improve society were strangled with bureaucratic apparatchik red tape, or kept secret because of fear of the countless spies-upon-spies. People looked over their shoulders, not out of paranoia, but heightened awareness that they, their spouse, children—*anyone*—could be next.

No one could be trusted.

No one trusted anyone else.

People at work spied on each other.

Neighbors reported negative attitudes about the Party to block committees.

Children were taught in school to inform on their parents.

"How is your Nicky? My son sees him at school."

The question startled Vera out of her brown study. It came from the younger of the two women who served the committee as clericals.

Vera forced a smile. "He's doing well. He performs exceptionally at school, but only if he enjoys the subject, of course." *And I teach him not to inform on his mother and father*, she thought.

She didn't know if the younger woman or the older one was an informer. Probably both. The spies and toadies of the security police, the NKVD, were everywhere. There was rumor that there would be a letup of the ruthless elimination of alleged enemies of the state when Yezhov, the short, lame NKVD chief known as "the Dwarf," suddenly disappeared. He was presumed murdered by the Boss for any number of reasons—or for no reason at all. But his successor, Beria, was already making a name for himself as cruel and unmerciful. It was said that Beria had his chauffeur drive him down Moscow streets at night, looking for young women and girls to prey upon. When he saw one he liked, he had her picked up and delivered back after he raped and abused her. Husbands or parents who objected "disappeared."

The older clerical worker left the room with papers in her hand. The other woman looked around confidentially, then whispered to Vera. "You know what they say, if the commissar berates the person being investigated, it's okay. If he smiles, watch out. The next thing you know, there will be a knock on your door in the middle of the night."

Vera just smiled her thanks to hide her dread but said nothing. The woman might be testing her, trying to solicit a negative comment about the committee that could be reported. But Vera had heard the same thing about the committee's procedures. It was rumored that it was better to get publicly reproved for your political sins than merely dismissed after the hearing. The latter could mean that your punishment was to be decided by a higher official, whose authority was more far-reaching than a low-ranking commissar.

She didn't want to think about any of the possibilities. She wanted to go home, be with Peter and Nicky, cook a pot of borscht and a leg of lamb she had stood in line for two hours the previous day to buy.

Why didn't Peter learn to keep his mouth shut?

It had been that way during their entire marriage. They both

❖

turned their back on an ordinary life in Britain to make Leningrad their home, accepting the challenge to create a utopian society. When things started going bad in the country, when the chilling realization came home that they were trapped in a brutal, totalitarian regime, Vera had the good sense to keep her mouth shut outside the home to protect her family. But Peter was impulsive and instinctively honest.

The door to the meeting-room door suddenly opened and Vera started. She forced herself to remain seated and kept her features blank to keep from exposing emotions that could be interpreted as an admission of guilt.

The commissar stepped out first, followed by Peter.

"Comrade Cutter, we appreciate your attendance. You may return to your duties."

Peter joined Vera and they boarded an elevator. He started to say something and she shook her head. As far as she knew, the elevators were bugged. In fact, she was certain they were. They were walking on the street toward the trolley that would take them home before she asked him the question that was eating at her.

"What did the committee, the commissar, say about the charges?"

"They asked me questions about what I said. I told them that I was caught by surprise by news of the Polish invasion, that I meant no disrespect."

"What did the commissar say about that?"

"Very little. You heard him when I was leaving. He said very little during the meeting. The other two committee members asked questions, mostly the commissar just listened."

"Did he tell you that you were wrong, that you made an error of judgment?"

Peter grinned. "No, he was actually quite pleasant. A very reasonable man."

The hair rose on the back of her neck.

❖

8

❖

Vera went through the motions of cooking dinner, with both her and Peter trying to keep the mood light for Nicky's sake. But Nicky was perceptive for an eight-year-old. While he looked like his father, an attractive young male with light blond hair, he thought like his mother. He was quick for his age, analytical far beyond his years.

She never had any fear that he would report any anti-Soviet conversations at school, no matter who questioned him. She had told him that if asked by his teachers or anyone else what his mother and father talked about, he was to tell them honestly about every conversation they had about home and school—about dinner, clothes, cleaning the apartment, his school work. But he was never to reveal any conversation about their work or thoughts. Did they love Stalin? Yes! Was life good? Yes!

There were not many eight-year-olds who would fully understand that his loose lips could bring harm to his parents, but Nicky was not just mature for his age, he had inherited Vera's street smarts.

The downside of Nicky's ability to read people and situations was that it was impossible to keep a secret around him.

"What's the matter?" he asked his mother and father. "You both look worried."

"Eat your borscht," Vera told him. "Tonight you're sleeping in our bed, we're sleeping on the couch."

The couch folded down to accommodate both of them. She needed to talk and didn't want to be cooped up in the tiny bedroom.

The apartment was just two rooms—a combination kitchen-living room and a small bedroom. They shared a toilet and shower down the hall with the three other apartments on the floor. But they were lucky to have a two-room apartment to themselves. After Vera's mother passed away, they feared that they would be assigned another person, or even another couple, to share the two rooms with.

There was a severe housing shortage in the country, just as there was a severe shortage of anything people really needed. The production-oriented communist system managed to manufacture an endless number of things that no one had use for—or didn't work—while skimping on housing and consumer products. The system didn't work but no one criticized it. People were afraid to complain or even comment upon it.

When Nicky was sent off to bed and the bedroom door shut, the two of them unfolded the couch but sat up to talk, Vera on the couch, Peter on a chair facing her.

"Don't be worried," he said. "I think everything will be all right. I'm sure the commissar would have been tougher if there were going to be any real repercussions."

She didn't want to repeat what the clerical worker at the committee had said for fear it could come true. Nor remind him of another rumor they both knew—that there was literally a quota system for offices and factories to discover and turn in dissenters, whether they existed or not. To meet the quota, some committees in factories and offices simply drew a name out of a hat, with the unlucky person whose name was picked turned in as a counterrevolutionary. Other facilities based it on merit—or on who complained the loudest.

Vera couldn't help but be recriminatory toward Peter. He had been in the country long enough to know when to keep his mouth shut. It wasn't the first time his criticism of the system had caused a problem.

"You weren't thinking about me and Nicky when you opened your mouth," she said.

He rubbed his face with his hands. "It just came as such a surprise. One day we are the enemy of fascism and the next we are brothers with that maniac Hitler in Germany. I was a fool to believe that a barbaric, backward country like Russia could be the home of a utopian society. The people in this country have no history, no experience in self-government. From the Mongols to the tsars and the Communists, they've always been ruled but never ruled themselves. Hell, look at the way they treat Jews, hardly better than Hitler and his pals."

"You have a way out," she said. "Nicky is a British citizen, too, he was born there. We can apply for exit permits for both of you."

"You know they won't let you come."

"I will stay and join you later."

"No, they will never let you go. And I don't think they'll let me go, either, not now, it's too late. They know I'm critical of the system, they don't want a disillusioned Communist to return to the West and tell people what it's really like in a society in which the apparatchiks have the mentality of steel filing cabinets—they store everything, forget nothing, but are so fearful of having an original thought that they can't process the information they have. And if it doesn't have the Party stamp, it stays in the back of the filing cabinet."

"There! That's the sort of comment that got you in trouble."

He climbed onto the couch and lay his head on her shoulder.

"I'm sorry, sweetheart, I'm sorry I put you and Nicky into danger. But I can't leave without you." He sat up. "Do you think they'd let Nicky go to Britain to live with my father?"

❖

"I don't know, what excuse would we have? That we don't want him brainwashed in a Soviet school system where children are taught to spy on their parents?"

"We could ask to send him for a visit."

She shook her head. "I don't know, I don't want to think about it tonight." She held his face in her hands. "You can never say anything again that in any way challenges the Party line."

"I know, I know."

"Another mistake and Nicky will be an orphan and I will have to find a new husband, one with his lips sewn shut."

"That will never happen."

What she didn't say was that in her heart, she thought it was too late. It was a cruel system that never forgave or forgot.

She put her arms around him and hugged him. She couldn't shake the sense of dread that she had been experiencing since the summons came for Peter to appear before the committee. Everyone knew that they came at night, taking people out of their homes, putting them in black cars without markings. Often, the person was never seen or heard from again.

If they came for him, would they take her, too? And her son? Surely they didn't hurt children. But she wasn't so sure.

"I'm sure I covered myself with the commissar," he said.

She hugged him with all her strength.

She didn't share his sense of confidence.

❖

9

❖

It was three in the morning when the pounding on the door was heard.

They woke up and turned on the lamp next to the couch. Neither of them spoke, but just stared at each other.

Peter was terrified. "They've come for me."

She got up and went to the door. "Who is it?"

"Officers of the People's Commissariat of Internal Affairs."

NKVD. Secret police.

"What do you want?"

Her voice shook. She knew what they wanted. She knew the time had come.

"Open the door. This is official business."

Nicky came out of the bedroom with sleep in his eyes. "What is it? What's happening?"

Peter was suddenly beside Vera.

"Take Nicky into the bedroom. I'll deal with this."

His voice was calm but his face was pale and drawn.

She grabbed him. "Peter!"

He pushed her back. "Take care of Nicky."

❖

The pounding came again. She grabbed Nicky and forced him into the bedroom, telling him to be quiet as questions poured from him.

She closed the bedroom door as Peter was opening the apartment door, exposing two burly men in black suits.

It wasn't until later that she realized Peter had worn his pants, shirt and socks to bed.

He had known they were coming for him.

❖

10

❖

Charles Cutter opened the envelope from Russia as soon as he found it in his mailbox. Inside was a plain piece of paper, with a typed message.

> *My Dear Father-In-Law Charles Lawwood Cutter:*
>
> *I regret to inform you that my husband, your son, Peter Charles Cutter, was killed instantly in an automobile accident.*
>
> *He will be mourned by me and your grandson, Nicholaus Pedrovich Cutter.*
>
> *There will be no viewing of the body. It was Peter's wishes that in case of death, his body be cremated. His ashes were scattered in the Neva.*
>
> *Your Daughter-in-Law,*
> *Vera Menchik Cutter*

Charles Cutter's hands shook as he read the letter.

"Murderers," he muttered. "Murdering commie bastards."

❖

11

❖

Nicholaus Cutter, Leningrad, 1942

The other children gave me only dull stares as they watched me slip off the truck and walk away, down the road toward Leningrad.

The driver would not have stopped me even if he saw me leave—a missing child meant another bread ration for him. When—*if*—there was a head count at the other end, it would be assumed I became delusional from deprivations and wandered away, freezing to death or becoming a meal for a wild animal . . . some of which walked on two feet.

I trudged on snow and ice. The only thing making the "road" different from the rest of the frozen terrain were the tire marks on it. I followed the tracks in the direction the truck had come. There were other trucks parked along the road, like the one I had been in, covered with white camouflage canvas. The only person I saw outside the vehicles was a driver relieving himself on the side of the road. The trucks would stay put for the entire day, waiting until darkness fell before they attempted the run across the frozen lake to the Soviet forces on the other side.

I had no idea of how far I was from the hospital in the city or even if I was going in the right direction. I only knew the direction

❖

the truck had brought us. I wore a heavy down coat that went from a hood covering my head to the tops of my shoes. I wrapped my scarf around my face and pulled the coat hood tight to keep out the blistering cold. The glove on my left hand had worn away, leaving my little finger exposed. I kept that hand in my pocket as much as possible. I was numb all over, but that finger felt on fire.

The authorities had actually started the process of evacuating children from the city soon after the Germans attacked and began driving back our forces on the Polish front. But too little, too late, was done before the enemy was at our gates and had the city nearly surrounded.

While my mother was functioning, she never wanted me shipped out of the city, knowing she would never see me again. People believed that those left in the city would all die and that the children being taken out were to be adopted by others. Many parents in the city felt the same way, refusing to let their children go. But that was in the beginning. As the siege wore on, as the last fuel was used for heat and apartments and homes became subzero and starvation set in, the weakness started and then death became more common than life, which only made my mother regret keeping me in the city. But I didn't want to leave her. We needed each other. After my father died, she became more and more fearful and withdrawn, worrying that men would come in the night and take her and I would be left an orphan.

Her fears increased that I would be left alone in the world as war and a pandemic of starvation and deprivations descended upon us like all the plagues of Egypt. Each day my mother and I, and everyone I saw around us, became weaker from hunger and cold. It became an effort just to stay *alive*.

At first, as family members died, they were taken to a cemetery and buried. I saw them on the streets every day, people pulling a child's snow sled behind them—a man or woman pulling the body of a spouse or child, a child pulling a parent's body—taking the bodies to the cemetery. But soon the ground froze hard and the number of bodies became overwhelming for the gravediggers who couldn't do the hard physical work on the small ration of food they were given.

❖

At the same time, it became more and more difficult for family members to get their dead loved ones out of their house or apartment as their strength faded. If they had a two-room apartment, they would put the bodies in the bedroom. With temperatures in unheated rooms as subzero frigid as it was outside, the bodies stayed frozen. People in one-room apartments would wrap the body in a sheet and drag it down to the street where bodies were stacked like cords of wood.

My mother at first was the strongest one in our neighborhood, taking care of me but helping other people, organizing people still on their feet to help the sick and dying. But when she fell down some icy steps as she helped an elderly woman move the body of her husband onto the sidewalk, there was a change in her. She claimed she wasn't hurt, but I didn't know if she had broken something internally because she was never quite the same after that. She grew weaker and weaker each day, her skin turning the bloodless pale of the dead bodies I'd seen.

When my mother was too ill to even take the small ration of food we got each day, and I saw death and defeat in her eyes, I got her into my sled in front of our apartment building with the help of a man who lived beneath us. I pulled the sled down the frozen streets to the hospital and asked them to save her.

They laid her on a thin mattress on the floor of a room that had almost wall-to-wall mattresses. An attendant told me I had to go to a place where children were kept as they waited for a chance to be evacuated from the city. But I held onto my mother, crying for her, as I was pulled away. Like her, I knew that if we were ever separated we would never see each other again. And I had no one to ask for help to save my mother and keep us together.

I knew my father had some family left in the village in England where he had been born, but I knew nothing of them, though my mother believed my father's own father was still alive. My Russian relatives were even more sparse. There had been mention when my Russian grandmother died when I was six that she had a sister somewhere near Novgorod, but my mother had been unable to contact her after Grandmother died.

❖

As a Russian, I had three names—Nicholaus Pedrovich Cutter. Nicholaus after my mother's father, and Pedrovich, which meant "son of Peter."

I had been told that Peter, my father, had died in an automobile accident. But I still remembered that night when men came into our apartment and my mother took me back into the bedroom. I never saw my father again. And I found my mother's grief was strange—rather than just grieving for my father, she seemed to be constantly worried about me, as if she might go to work in the morning and never see me again.

I missed my father. I guess it was natural that I felt a little closer to my mother than my father, but I loved both of them and felt the loss when he was gone.

A month ago, when my mother was weak and suffering from the starvation disease, almost delirious, she told me that "they" had killed him. But then she had panicked and told me never to say such a thing to anyone.

I promised her I wouldn't, but when I pressed her further to find out who "they" were, I got no answer. She just kept warning me never to say anything.

I knew I had to get to my mother before "they" took her, too.

There was little movement on the road besides the pad of my feet. It was early morning and very cold. I saw an occasional guard hut with a sentry hiding inside from the cold, muffled in winter uniform, the barrels of rifles sticking out.

No refugees were trudging toward the road over the frozen lake because the escape route was reserved for "official business." The food brought in was so little anyway it merely prolonged death. The route back out was also reserved for official business, used mostly for the movement of troops and the evacuation of children when a truck was available. Anyone who tried to leave the city without permission was considered a traitor and shot on sight. I'd heard stories of people who had gone out to sentry shacks and asked to be shot, saying they were too weak to kill themselves.

As I trudged slowly down the road, occasionally vehicles would

❖

pass me, mostly small trucks, a size it was hoped that Nazi fighter planes and dive bombers wouldn't bother with.

There was no longer any public transportation in the city except feet. What the bombs and artillery barrages didn't destroy were covered by snow and ice: cars, trucks, buses, trams, frozen in place by the winter storms when the trains and vehicles ran out of fuel or electricity. The frozen forms were ghosts reminding us of the world that existed before the Great Patriotic War erupted and the world became a living hell.

After walking for an hour, the lack of food caught up with me. My legs felt weak and I slowed my pace until I walked staring down at my feet, willing one foot forward after another. I could barely lift them. It seemed like I was wearing concrete shoes. I just kept pulling them off the ground and putting them back down, over and over. Finally, weak, I staggered to a post and leaned against it.

I felt the jar with watery soup inside my coat, keeping warm against my skin. I hadn't had any food since the partial ration the driver gave us last night. I needed the food but I couldn't take it. A little nourishment might be all that stood between my mother and her slipping beyond life.

I had to keep moving or I would freeze to death. I pushed away from the pole and again forced one foot in front of the other, more of a shuffle than a walk, half-dragging my feet.

A small truck, a little bit larger than a pickup, pulled up next to me. It had the markings of a soap factory on the side door. With the changes in production, the factory probably now produced explosives.

The driver leaned over from behind the wheel and rolled down the passenger window.

"Where you going, boy?"

"Gorky Hospital, to see my mother."

"Where's your father?"

"Gone."

"Get in, I'll give you a ride into the city."

I stared at him, locking eyes. During the past three years, the world kept shifting and changing configuration under my feet, as if I was standing in a dark kaleidoscope that someone was turning. Before my father left us and the Germans came, I would not have given a second thought to jumping into the truck. Now I stared at the man, sizing him up.

He was big, bear-big, with long hair falling from under his fur hat, a heavy beard and large frame covered by a long animal-hair coat. His eyes were dark and hard and he reminded me of the pictures I'd seen of Rasputin, the mad monk who had whispered dark words into the ears of the imperial family before the revolution.

But there was one other thing I noticed. His face was pale and I could tell from the way the hat and coat fit him that he had lost weight. That made me trust him. Like most good people, he lacked sufficient food. It was the fat cats who bought and sold God-knows-what on the black market that I feared.

I climbed into the truck.

❖

12

❖

"What are you doing out on the road?" the man asked.

"I was in a transport."

"You left it to return to your mother?"

I nodded.

"Good boy. Stay with your mother. No one knows what's happening to the children trucked out. Besides, the war will be over soon."

He patted my leg.

"The Boss himself is coming to Leningrad to fight the Germans. Those bastards will put their tails between their legs and go home when our Josef comes after them."

He went on and on about how the tide of the war was going to turn, going down the list of Soviet heroes who would do the fighting. Some were names I'd heard my mother speak of as being dead or have fallen out of favor and shipped off to Siberia. The old bear of a man was quite mad. But as we came onto city streets and I saw the familiar stacks of bodies piled on corners and the frozen ghost of a street car with a passenger, frozen in death, still sitting in it, I realized that he was the lucky one. When horrors became unimag-

❖

inable, to retreat inside your mind to a place where life was good was not insanity but salvation.

The streets were almost empty. Before the war, the sidewalks and roadways were crowded with people from early morning until late at night. Now, no one left their living space except to get their ration or report for their work, if they still had a job and were able to physically do it. I'd heard that people who held down jobs got an extra ounce or two of bread each day.

The people on the streets looked as gray as the day. No one moved with a spirited step. I suppose if they did, they would be accused of black marketeering, hoarding or cannibalism.

There was no snow removal except where necessary to keep military traffic moving.

He pulled over on Voinoya Street, letting a battle tank rumble by.

"The hospital is down that street, to your right. Here, this is for being a good boy."

Out of his pocket he handed me a small, round piece of hard candy. I examined it as I went down the street, pinching off a piece of black hair, and smelled the candy—who knew what the old bear could be passing out for candy? It had a distinctive smell, but I couldn't remember what it was called.

I licked the piece of candy. It tasted a little soapy but I realized what the smell was—mint, it was a piece of hard candy with a mint taste. I hadn't had a piece of candy for months. I broke it in half with my teeth and put one piece away for my mother. I sucked on the other piece as I walked down the street. My mouth puckered a little at the strange sweetness, but I couldn't remember anything that tasted so good. I sucked it, careful not to get greedy and break it down with my teeth because it wouldn't last as long if I crushed it. The sweetness made my heart beat faster and my step lighter.

As I came up to the long set of granite steps leading into the hospital, an old woman came down the street. She stared at me with horror in her eyes as I went by her.

"They stole it," she kept repeating, "they stole it and now I'll die."

❖

Feeling the bottle of food for my mother inside my clothes, I continued on. I knew what she meant. Someone had taken or tricked her out of her ration card. It was a death sentence in the starving city. She would not be able to get the card replaced. There was a process for replacing a lost or stolen card, but it took weeks. And it only took a day or two to starve to death when you were malnourished to begin with.

I stopped halfway up the stairs and thought for a moment, trying to remember what the world was like before it became hell. Maybe it was because of the bitter cold, but I couldn't remember the good times. I continued going up the steps but at a slow pace, worried about what was waiting for me, that my mother might already be gone. I went up the steps with dread.

The interior was dark, lit only by the gray light coming through windows. Interior corridors leading off the main reception area were dimly lit, small wattage bulbs taking the edge off darkness. People were lined up six deep at the long reception counter, many of them sitting on the floor as they waited their turn to be admitted or check on relatives. Despite the number of people, there was little noise and no aggressive behavior. No one had the energy.

I headed for the dark stairwell to the second-floor ward where my mother had been the last time I saw her.

There were only a few beds in the long, high-ceiling ward for all the patients. It was a woman's ward and most of the women were on mattresses on the floor. I felt the coolness in the ward, not bitter cold but not entirely comfortable, either. The nurse in the room wore a heavy sweater. She was busy with a woman and paid no attention to me.

I went directly down the line of women in the direction of where I had last seen my mother. I avoided meeting the eye of the patients who looked up at me as I walked by. There was no hope in any of them. No matter what illness they suffered, for a certainty the condition that would kill them was the same disease that was pandemic in the city under siege: starvation.

It was a matter of supply and demand, my mother had told me the first night we went to bed hungry. There simply wasn't enough

❖

food to feed the people in the city. But unlike the truck driver's notion that great numbers of people dying created a bigger supply for the living, the ration given to each person remained the same. If it created any spare food, it went to the troops fighting the war—and as everyone knew, to high-ranking apparatchiks.

I almost passed my mother. I stared down at her, my heart squeezed by icy fingers. She was pale and gray, her hair gone almost white even though she was still a young woman in terms of her age. Her pallid, brittle, and undernourished skin was pulled tight across her bones, creating the look of a skeleton with dried skin.

She was still breathing, but her eyes were closed. She lay without a blanket covering her. The woman next to her had two blankets and I pulled one off of her. As I did, I realized the woman was dead, so I took both blankets and covered my mother with them.

I knelt down beside her. "Mama, Mama, it's me."

Her eyes opened and I could see that she was having a hard time focusing.

"Mama, I've brought food."

She said something, a mumbled whisper, but I couldn't make out the words.

I struggled out the bottle from under my bulky clothes and unscrewed the cap. I tried to lift her into a sitting position but couldn't and managed to spill some of the precious contents of the soup jar.

She spoke my name in a hoarse whisper.

"I'm going to take care of you," I told her. "I'm not leaving you again."

"Nicky . . ." She stared up at me and clutched at my coat.

"It's okay, Mama, I'll take care of you."

"Watch out," she said with that hoarse whisper, "don't let them . . . don't let them hurt you."

She released air through her mouth and went limp in my arms. I dropped the jar and hugged her. "Mama, Mama."

I don't know how long I held her. The nurse pulled me away and covered her with the blankets.

❖

"Look at your finger," she said.

I shook my head, my mind too soaked with emotion to comprehend what she was talking about.

"Your little finger, it's frostbitten. You're going to lose it."

❖

13

❖

Red October Home for Boys,

Leningrad, 1945

"Here comes Four-Fingers!" Pavel Ivanovich yelled as I came out of the building.

I stopped two steps from the bottom, making me taller than I would be if I was on ground level with Pavel.

Lev, my bunkmate, was surrounded by Pavel and his pals. We called them the Gang of Nine because there were nine of the bastards, all a year older than my fourteen, getting around that age when they would be sent to work camps to get them out of the orphanage and mold them into model Soviet workers.

Pavel wasn't the biggest of the bunch but he was the meanest and the toughest. He had that kind of build that was hard to fight—short, stocky, solid. He'd put down his big shaved head and ram your face while he slammed both fists like pistons into your stomach. I kept to myself and didn't belong to a gang, but I had had a lot of fights because that was just the way of life when you spent twenty-four hours a day with twelve hundred other boys. I hadn't fought Pavel yet, but because I had a reputation as the toughest

❖

kid in my barracks, I would be a target. Especially when he had his pals around to back him up.

We were all survivors of the siege of Leningrad, all had lost our families, our homes. Some, like Pavel, had lost their humanity. I didn't have a list of what I lost, though the most obvious was my little finger. It had been amputated because of frostbite. It saved my life, because I was kept in the hospital for weeks and given an extra ration each day because I had had an operation.

The German siege of the city was over, but it had lasted over two years, nearly nine hundred days. Our troops had finally pushed back the invaders and kept up the pressure. Now it was said our troops were in Berlin itself.

"I'm going to stomp this little anti-Communist toad," Pavel told me. "He believes in God. You want some of it?" He shook his fist at me. It was a small, solid, mean fist, all bone, and scarred from use on people he didn't like or just wanted to stomp.

Lev was my age, but like many of the children of the siege, his growth had been stunted by the earlier starvation. His family had been Jewish. I guess that somehow equated to Pavel as a belief in a higher authority than the Party. Pavel was one of those whose main objective in life was to become a member of the Party so he could be above other people and bully them. That didn't exactly fit into the Communist theory we got a dose of every day in the classroom, but no one would accuse Pavel of thinking too much—or of the theoretical system working well in actual practice.

Pavel reminded me of someone, I could never remember who, but his round shaven head, bull neck and flat broad features had struck a cord in me from the first time I met him. He had only been here at the Home for a year after being transferred from another orphanage. There were stories he'd been shipped out because he'd beaten another boy so bad the kid was permanently brain damaged. Since Pavel's own boasts were the source of the stories, and he had stomped more than one kid since he'd arrived, I didn't doubt that he had a history of violence.

"I hear you're a God-lover, too," Pavel said. "Your mother was

Jewish, your father was British. Think you're better than the rest of us?"

I shook my head. "I really don't think anything about you, or God, or anything else except what's for supper."

My knees weren't shaking but I was worried. Pavel was an animal and he was out to get me. Because I didn't belong to a gang and was a loner pretty much, he knew I wouldn't have anyone backing me up. My usual good sense told me to turn around and go back into the building. I had an idea that picking on Lev was just an opportunity to pick a fight with me. There was something about me that ticked Pavel off. Maybe it was the fact that I had a reputation for not permitting myself to be bullied, even by older boys. Or maybe I just breathed the same air Pavel did and he wanted more of it.

There had been trouble brewing between me and the bastard, rumors that he was going to stomp me. Now he was here, in front of my barracks, picking on a kid identified as my friend. Not that Lev was actually a friend. I had no friends, I was a loner. But we shared the same bunk and he liked to hang around with me. I kind of ran interference for him because he was scrawny, and he helped me with my school work because I hated paperwork.

"I can take care of myself," Lev said. His voice trembled and his knees were shaking, but he had his fists clenched and he was going to go down fighting. Not that it would take much for Pavel to stomp him. Pavel was twice as thick as Lev and the extra was all muscle.

I didn't need a fortune-teller's ball to tell me that Pavel was picking a fight with Lev to pick one with me. He was a smart bastard. He didn't pick the fight directly with me because he knew I'd have to fight if painted into a corner by him coming at me. He thought he could take me—so did I—but why risk it when he could get more mileage out of arranging a situation in which I could show a yellow back and walk away while he beat up Lev?

No one would ever accuse Pavel of having too many brains, but he was cunning like a feral animal, and in a stone-age environment where brawn was king, brainy guys like Lev had no chance.

❖

Pavel head-butted Lev, hitting him in the nose, sending the smaller boy flying backwards, blood squirting.

Like a bull that had just gored one picador and quickly swung around to gut another, Pavel turned to smash me. I went into motion the moment his head spattered poor Lev's nose. As his head came back around, I kicked, the tip of my shoe catching him in the jaw. We wore steel-capped shoes because they lasted longer and could be handed down time after time. You could run a truck over the caps and it wouldn't dent them.

It was a beautiful kick, not one I would have managed had I been standing on the ground, but being two steps up, and a little taller than Pavel, the kick had the force of a shoed horse.

Pavel's lower jaw drove his teeth up against his upper. Shattered teeth and blood sprayed.

It was a beautiful moment, but it was over in a flash. Known for my speed, I spun on my heel and went back up the steps toward the barracks door with eight of the Gang of Nine hot on my heels.

I didn't quite get the door opened when fists started pounding my head and bodies slammed into me.

"Stop it!"

A voice of authority roared and the world stood still.

T-34 stood in the half-open door and gave us a look that would have turned lesser boys into stone. One of the boys attacking me stumbled against her because he didn't quite have his footing. She hit him back-handed, smacking him across the face. He flew backwards, down the steps.

She was all muscle, built a little like Pavel, but taller and broader. Before the war, in her younger days, she had been selected for the All-Soviet shot-putting team. She had a real name, Comrade Renko, but we all knew her as T-34, the name of the Soviet battle tanks that drove over the backs of Germans all the way to Berlin.

"Get outta here!"

Eight of the Gang of Nine scrambled to get clear of T-34's fury, with me on their heels. I would have taken a stomping by the gang over facing the fury of T-34. A school with twelve hundred orphans

❖

who had survived hell and damnation and were almost all completely unmanageable was not a job for the timid. And Comrade Renko was about as timid as a wolfhound.

I never made it off the landing. She caught me by the ear and jerked me back, nearly ripping off my ear.

"Akkkkk!"

She pulled me inside the building and down the corridor. I went, staggering off balance alongside her to keep my ear attached to the side of my head. At her office door, she let go of my ear and gave me a shove into the office.

T-34 was the barracks monitor, the live-in headmistress over the two hundred boys in the building. I heard she had been assigned as a medical orderly during the battle for the city, but had picked up a rifle and joined the troops on the front lines.

Because of her big boned, muscular frame, some of the boys claimed that T-34 was really a man with long hair and big breasts, but no one questioned her gender to her face—or her sexual preference, which seemed to be the barracks mistress next door, a woman who was only a slightly smaller version of T-34. No one had actually seen the two do anything, but suspicions got raised and rumor and innuendo flew each time the woman visited T-34 in her quarters and T-34's door got locked and the curtains drawn.

The bottom of the building contained her offices and quarters, the kitchen, mess hall and rec room. We boys were crowded in bunks on the floor above. The building was wood, poorly insulated, cold most of the year but an oven during the couple of months of the year the region experienced sweltering heat.

"Take down your pants and bend over."

"Comrade Mistress Renko—"

"Shut up. Do as I say. Pull down your pants."

I undid my belt and let my pants drop to my ankles.

She removed an ugly, coarse piece of knotted rope from its place of honor on the wall. The yellowish rope material was stained with blood. Some of it was my own.

"You are incorrigible."

"I was attacked."

❖

"You struck the first blow."

"Only after Pavel hit Lev."

"I saw only your kick."

"Comrade—"

"Bend over, grab your ankles."

I groaned as she came at me, slapping the coarse rope in the palm of her hand. She was a big woman, with big hands and muscular arms. A big woman who liked pain. *Other people's pain.*

"I've been trying to be good—"

"You are the smartest boy in the barracks and your grades are the worst. Unless you start studying and participating in school activities and Young Communist meetings, you will not be sent to the university but to a labor camp in Siberia. Do you know what the temperature is in Siberia?"

"I'll change, I promise."

"Too late. Drop your underwear, grab your ankles. You know the rules."

The "rules" were that for each whelp I made, or if I let go of my ankles, she would add another swat.

She hit me and I choked back a cry. Then again and a third time.

"Stay put," she told me.

Out of the corner of my eye I saw her set down the rope and pick up a jar and unscrew the cap. I had no idea of what was in the jar. Knowing T-34, it could have been salve—or battery acid.

She poured an oily substance into her hand and stood beside me.

"I don't know what to do about you, Nicholaus Pedrovich."

She rubbed the oil on my bare buttocks. I flinched, expecting it to burn, but it was cool and soothing.

T-34 was not noted for her tender ministries after a lashing. Nor did she use the Russian "familiar" of a boy's first and middle name.

I wondered what she was up to.

As she pushed against me, caressing my rear, I felt the powerful muscles in her hip. *Great Lenin's Tomb!* I hoped T-34 was not

❖

getting sexually aroused. There was common kidding among the boys about what it would be like to have sex with the barracks matron, but it was universally agreed that a mere boy might not survive the experience.

Her hand was cool and moist against my damaged rear.

Then it slipped between my legs. I almost cried out as her fingers caressed my testicles. My penis jerked alive as her fingers gently rubbed my balls.

I must have looked stupid, like I was ready to launch like a rocket, holding onto my ankles with legs spread, cock erect and my mouth gaped wide open. I didn't know what to say. She was scaring the hell out of me and making me feel really good at the same time. The only sex I'd ever had was in my bed at night stroking my own cock. I passed on doing it with other boys or letting them pull my cock like some of them did. One of the boys would even do it to others with his mouth for a ruble. But this was the first time anyone had touched my genitals.

"Nicholaus Pedrovich."

Her voice was soft and gentle, almost purring, a voice from T-34 that I'd never heard before.

"Yes, Comrade." My voice quavered.

"I want something from you."

"Something?" My legs trembled. My cock throbbed. *Fuck your mother!* T-34 was going to rape me!

She grabbed my balls and squeezed so hard I yelped.

"Vodka! Bring me vodka!"

❖

14

❖

Vodka. The milk and honey of all the Russians and their Soviet brothers. The name itself literally meant "water" and referred to the "waters of life."

The British and Americans had their whiskeys and beers, the Europeans their wines and beers, the Japanese their sake and beers, but no libation so nourished the soul or dominated a culture as vodka did in Russia.

The Russian solution to the fact that vodka had made drunks out of millions of people was simple: "Vodka is our enemy, so we will utterly consume it!"

But there is also another old expression about the national drink—*vodka spoils everything but the glass!*

Whatever it was—and if it's any good, it's tasteless, colorless and odorless—and whatever it does—create ruin in the lives of tens of millions or make daily survival more palatable—it was always in high demand.

They say that garlic was Russian penicillin. But vodka was nourishment for the Russian soul. When there was a shortage, tempers rose, the murder rate went up, production fell. Yet, occa-

❖

sionally the apparatchiks cut back on the supply of the stuff on the grounds that too many citizens were drunk too much of the time, though the real reason was that they just hated people having something to fall back onto that gave them comfort in this bleak society we lived in.

The Bolsheviks, certain that vodka was the scourge of the common man, outlawed it soon after the revolution, but eventually had to back down, no doubt because the men and women of the those days also needed to have their souls nourished with something besides ideology.

Now, with the war literally won, the rationing of vodka was back, the government ordering the distilleries to cut back on the production of this nectar of Russian gods.

That was the reason T-34 told me she wanted vodka—there was a shortage of it. Unless you were in the upper echelon, you had to spend many hours in line to buy a bottle and what was a mere bottle to any self-respecting man or woman?

How did I fit into this great national scheme in which an orphanage barracks matron finds herself unable to quench her thirst because the government was trying to dry out Russia and the rest of the Soviet republics? How did a mere school boy fit into the historical epoch of rationing vodka, thus making it liquid gold to the deprived?

It was those criminal tendencies that T-34 complained I had, though I never really thought of myself as a criminal. Of course, what a crime was depended on what side you were on. The Huns killed millions and called it war, not crime. I wasn't quite in that category, but even at fourteen I preferred not to think of myself as a criminal. Opportunist, yes.

All boys fourteen or over at the orphanage were apprenticed to factories or offices to learn a trade that would become their livelihood once they finished school. I was officially apprenticed to a tire factory. Under the Soviet system, my future was laid out in a clear and precise manner—I would spend the rest of my days standing at an assembly line, helping turn hot rubber into tires. I would be a productive citizen, a good Communist.

❖

However, T-34 was right about me. There was a flaw in my character. Rather than being a good Communist, or at least a good Communist Youth, I found myself attracted to free enterprise. That attraction created an inherent problem of logistics and perception because there was no legitimate free enterprise in the Great Socialist State.

Actually, though, while there was not supposed to be any free enterprise in the Soviet Union, there was one form of capitalism that existed everywhere in the country, with a big city like Leningrad being particularly susceptible to it: crime.

The government's clamp-down on vodka production opened a door for black marketeers, some of whom were no doubt the same people who traded in stolen food—and human flesh—during the 900-Day Seige.

The interesting thing about black marketeering was that although few crimes of violence, even most homicides, were punishable by death, the Boss, Josef Stalin, hated private enterprise enough to make buying and selling for profit a death sentence. But human nature being what it is, it wasn't a deterrent. The system was puritanical and corrupt at the same time, money had a loud voice even in a Communist society, only an occasional black marketeer was actually sentenced to death—usually when an execution quota needed to be met—and no one planned on getting caught, anyway.

Through another boy in the barracks, I had made contact last year with an underground entrepreneur, a one-armed former war hero named Sergi, who bought and sold whatever he could get his hands on. At that time, Kremlin-quality cigarettes, made from tobaccos grown in the Georgia and Abkhazia regions, were in high demand on the black market. My job was to deliver packs to Sergi's timid customers, the ones who were too afraid of a prison sentence to come to the Haymarket and make an overt purchase.

Sergi was the boss of the organization, what Russians call the *vor v zakone*. The name implied a relationship of honor and loyalty among thieves, but Sergi never struck me as someone who would sacrifice himself for his underlings. I never did quite understand

❖

what his war "heroics" were. He didn't strike me as the type who would risk his life for anyone else. I asked once, but got snapped at for asking. I guess just surviving, even with only one arm, was tantamount to heroics.

I couldn't figure out what he did with the stacks of rubles he collected, either. He certainly didn't share with anyone else—as far as I could see, everyone was paid in cigarettes or other barter items. Nor did he spend any of the rubles on shaving gear, haircuts or fancy clothes. He had a scruffy beard, unkempt hair and clothes and tattoos on both arms.

The tattoos were a symptom of how unsophisticated the Russian justice system was. Criminals proudly wore tattoos as a badge of honor and police officers somehow didn't notice that most of the criminal underworld had branded themselves. Or maybe they didn't care. Once when he'd had too much of his own bootlegged brew, Sergi explained the cops-and-criminals system to me. "They don't understand economic crimes because they don't understand economics," he said. Being an entrepreneur, buying low and selling high, jacking up prices when the supply went down and the demand went up, bartering, things that came "naturally" to people in the West, were alien to people raised and educated under the Soviet system. "I even have a hard time finding police to bribe," he complained. "Not only are they scared, but most of them don't understand the concept of having more rubles in your pocket than you need for today's expenses."

I was paid in cigarettes, which I used in exchange to buy little luxuries like candy and better food than the cabbage soup and potatoes we got at least twice a day at the orphanage.

The enterprising Sergi had moved from cigarettes to vodka when the law of supply and demand shifted. His vodka supply came from a collective farm near Lake Lagoda that grew potatoes. Vodka, like everything else, was a state monopoly, and the farm was not authorized to produce it. That worked out well for them and Sergi, because he wasn't authorized to distribute it, either.

With vodka, I had the same delivery job that I had with cigarettes, using my school bag to hide the bottles in and hand-

❖

delivering them to shy customers, but Sergi still paid me off in cigarettes because they were easier for me to exchange for other
goods and vodka was too valuable to waste on a delivery boy.

It wasn't hard to figure out how T-34 discovered I was delivering the brew—there weren't many secrets when you lived in one
big room with a couple hundred other boys.

Early the next morning, I rode on the passenger side of Sergi's
old truck as I drove with him to the collective farm to pick up a
supply of the bootlegged brew. It was my first trip to the farm and
I volunteered to come along and help Sergi load because I needed
to talk to him about T-34's thirst.

"Why do they make vodka at the farm?" I asked.

"Potatoes, that's all they grow and the government demands
their crop for the army. Worse, with the Huns cleared from the
land, other farms are growing food and now there are too many potatoes. So they turn the potatoes into something they can use to
barter with other collectives and factories for their goods." Sergi
grinned. "And I give them a supply of rubles so they can buy things
that they can't barter for with their home brew."

No one seemed to find the Soviet system of economics in which
collective farms and factories survived on a system of fraud and
deception as irrational. I did only because of listening at the keyhole to late-night discussions between my mother and father when
they used to talk about the system. But I was taught to keep my
mouth shut about criticizing the system. I couldn't even intimate
to Sergi that the system was wrong. It was a far worse offense to
criticize the system than it was to violate it.

"Won't they get arrested if anyone finds out?" I asked.

Sergi shrugged. "They don't announce their vodka production
in *Pravda,* but everyone knows half the collective farms in the
country make moonshine. The farmers wash the inspectors' hands
and the inspectors wash theirs, the inspectors and their bosses get
paid off in vodka and everyone is happy unless some naïve apparatchik from Moscow shows up and turns things sour. When that
happens, the government shuts down the still and shoots the col-

❖

lective's director. Six months later, they have a new director and the stills start boiling again."

I broached the subject of getting vodka for T-34, emphasizing the urgency without mentioning that she was going to rip off my balls if I didn't get it. Instead, I concocted a story that my very life was in peril.

"Fuck your mother! The bitch pays for it like everyone else."

No one would accuse Sergi of being a sentimentalist. He rather reminded me of a scruffy river rat and he frequently acted the way a rat would when other rats want a piece of the cheese. That's how I came to think of him—Sergi the Rat.

"Tell the bitch she can pay or drink sewer water," he said.

"I'll pay for it."

"It would take you a month of deliveries to pay for a bottle of vodka."

I shut up because he was right. But where there is a will, there is a way. I would just have to steal an occasional bottle from him. That way I could satisfy T-34 and keep the cigarettes I got for making deliveries. I didn't consider it underhanded because I knew when it came down to it, Sergi was not a true Russian gang boss. Since he was only going to look after his own needs, I would have to look after my own.

"I heard some of the moonshine is made so badly it kills people," I said.

I changed the subject so he wouldn't read my guilty mind. Being a thief, I was certain he knew exactly what other thieves were thinking. That information came from T-34, who warned me she'd rip off my balls and stuff them in my mouth if I brought her vodka that made her sick.

Sergi gave me another who-gives-a-shit shrug. "Hundreds of people, maybe thousands, die every year from alcohol poisoning, but who cares? They have to die of something, better to die from bad Russian vodka than a Hun's bullet or strangled by an apparatchik's red tape."

As he spoke, I thought of the five-liter petrol cans in the back of the truck. We would fill the cans with vodka at the plant and bring them back to the garage where they would be used to fill bottles. Back at the garage, Sergi had poured the last petrol from one of the cans into the truck and then tossed the empty can into the back to be filled with vodka.

When I asked about the residue of petrol left in the can, he did one of his who-gives-a-shit shrugs and said, "No problem, it'll just give the vodka a little flavor. People who buy bootlegged brew aren't particular about anything except how many swigs it takes for them to forget what their life is like."

The farm was huge, thousands of acres that were once in the hands of some boyar or hundreds of peasants. Now the land, literally at gunpoint, like most of the farmland in the country, had been turned into a state or collective farm where hundreds of people worked. My mother told me many people had died, perhaps millions, resisting the forced move from their own plots of land into state and collective farms. Everyone knew people were dying or being shipped off to hard labor camps for resisting, but no one said anything about the atrocities. And certainly the slaughter was not discussed in *Pravda*—the national news organ whose name meant "truth" in Russian.

At the farm, one of the men took the passenger seat and I climbed into the truck bed with the petrol cans. The farmer directed Sergi down dirt roads to a place where the still was hidden behind tall walls of baled hay.

In the clearing between the walls of hay were a series of metal tanks I took to be boilers. As Sergi talked business with the foreman of the bootlegging operation, I got another employee to explain the process for making vodka.

"It starts with digging the potatoes and cleaning them. They get chopped and crushed and wetted and we heat them into a slush in those big vats. We call the process a 'wash.'"

The vats were metal pots with wood fires underneath.

"We let the potatoes ferment for a few days and add some yeast. That produces a small percentage of alcohol in the concoction. What comes out is drunken potatoes!"

❖

He laughed and I laughed with him.

"Then comes the difficult part," he said, "getting rid of the potato residue so the liquid is clear and distilling the liquid so that it rises from seven or eight percent alcohol to fifty percent or more. We put the liquid in a pot still"—he pointed at taller vats, also with fires beneath—"and heat it again. When it heats up, the liquid turns into steam, vapor, and rises into these pipes coming out of the top of the still. These are condensation pipes. We pour cold water on them to keep them cool. Inside the pipes, the vapors cool and turn back into liquid, basically water with an alcohol content."

He shook his forefinger at me. "Now here's the trick. We have to increase the percentage of alcohol in the water four or five times from what it originally was. How do you imagine we do that by boiling it?"

"I don't know."

"Of course you don't know, that's why you're buying it instead of making it. But it's really very simple, and clever. Alcohol has a lower boiling point than water. What we do is heat the liquid enough so more alcohol is turned into steam than water, so when the steam is condensed back to a liquid, there is a higher alcohol percentage than there was before." He slapped the side of his leg. "Is that not clever and simple?"

He was right. Before visiting the bootlegging still, I assumed that making vodka was a complicated process involving huge machinery. To see it being made in a farm field with wood fires and crudely made vats was an eye opener.

"We'll be here for a couple hours," Sergi told me. "We have to wait for the farm boss to come. In the meantime, I will decide which cans I will take."

"How do you do it? Taste it?"

"Taste this swill? Do you think I'm crazy? I smell it. The bad stuff usually smells like cooked cabbage, sometimes like meat. I've seen it smell like warm piss, which it probably was. I'll call you when I need you to load."

He had already told me the routine—we'd pour vodka from five-liter milk cans into the petrol cans. Back at the garage, he'd

❖

add some essence of lemon, lime, cherry, or whatever he could get his hands on, before we bottled much of it. The flavoring would hide some of the smell and rough flavor that came with the boot-legged "potato water."

I wandered around, watching the farmers making their brew. I spotted bow and arrows sitting in a corner and I went over and picked up the bow and tested the string.

"Ever use a bow and arrow?" my vodka guide asked.

"We made them at the orphanage, but not this good."

"Go ahead, take it and bring back some rabbit for supper. I'm damn tired of eating potatoes three times a day."

I grabbed the bow and arrow and headed out to slay a dragon. One with bunny ears.

Born and raised surrounded by asphalt and concrete in a big city, I hadn't been into the countryside since I hopped off the back of a truck one frozen day and headed back into the city to find my mother.

I thought about the good times as I trudged across the fields, about my mother and my father, about being on a rowboat on Lake Lagoda and laughing and shouting as my dad rocked the boat until it tipped over.

I stopped at a creek and knelt down and took a drink of water, then continued walking, following the creek. As a city boy, I'd hardly recognize a rabbit if I saw it, much less know how to hunt one. I let loose an arrow at a big black bird, but the arrow went far wide and the bird squawked curses at me as it flew off.

Further down the creek I heard the sounds of laughing and water splashing. They were female voices and I crept up slowly, low to the ground. Tall reeds were between me and the pond and I carefully sneaked through them, making no more noise than a stampeding elephant.

When I got to the edge of the water, I hung back in the reeds. A woman was in the water across the small pond. Her bare back was to me. She turned a little toward me, not directly at me but enough so I could see her naked breast. My heartbeat took off on a wild rhythm. It was the first time I'd actually seen a woman's bare breast.

She didn't seem to notice me but continued to splash water on her breasts as if she was cooling them off.

I heard a noise behind me. As I swung around, a pair of strong hands gave me a shove that sent me flying into the pond. I went in and down and got back onto my feet, coughing and gasping from the water I took in. The person who shoved me dove in and glided by me. It was a woman. She came up next to the other woman and they both laughed at me.

Looking closer, I realized they were really girls, probably in their late teens, four or five years older than me. Both were husky farm girls, used to the hard labor of a farm. They looked like sisters—long blond hair in ponytails, freckles across their noses, light blue eyes, facial skin already showing tiny wrinkles from long hours in hot sun and icy winds.

"Why'd you do that?" I asked.

They stayed in the water up to their necks.

"Because you're a pervert. Aren't you ashamed of yourself, sneaking up on women?"

"I was rabbit hunting."

"I think he was beaver hunting," one girl said to the other. I took her to be the older of the two, maybe no more than a year or two.

They both laughed and I blushed at the accusation.

"What are you doing on the farm? We don't know you."

"I'm with the gang that sells your vodka in Leningrad," I boasted.

"You don't look old enough to be in a gang. You're barely out of diapers."

"I am too old enough. I'm seventeen."

"You think he's old enough to have gone through puberty?" the older one asked.

Her sister shook her head. "I don't know. Why don't you show us, boy."

"Show you what?"

❖

"The hair around your cock. So we can tell if you're old enough."

They howled with laughter. I tried to look unruffled but I could feel my face blushing.

"Oh, let's not pick on him. The poor boy's obviously a virgin."

"I am not!" I lied.

"What do you think, sister?" the older one asked. "Do you think we should give him lessons?"

"Well, let's see." She straightened up, rising enough so both her breasts were out of the water.

I stared at them. It was my first good frontal view of naked breasts.

Her sister lifted one of the breasts up a little. "Do you know what you're supposed to do with a woman's breast?"

They took my silence as ignorance.

"You can caress them with your fingers," she said, massaging the girl's breast and nipple. "And you can lick them with your tongue."

She leaned over and put her mouth on the girl's breast and sucked.

I was completely frozen in place, not sure what to say or do. I was mortified and excited at the same time. My cock was pumping frantically, coming erect.

The younger girl stopped sucking and stood straight again. Her sister got behind her and cupped both her breasts in her hands.

"You can use your hands"—she squeezed the breasts—"or you can use your lips." She ran her lips off the side of the girl's neck. Then they kissed each other on the lips.

"And finally," the younger girl said, cradled back in the other's arms, "you can kiss her cunt."

With her sister holding her from behind, the younger girl raised her legs out of the water and spread them. I gaped at the sight of the pink between her legs when she kicked and sent a wave into my face. I stumbled back and before I knew it, the two

❖

girls had grabbed me and held me under. I fought back, breaking their hold, and came up gasping for air.

They had already climbed out of the pond and disappeared into the reeds when I came out of the water and retrieved my bow and arrow.

I couldn't get the two girls out of my mind as I made my way back to the still. Finally, I went into bushes and relieved myself.

❖

15

❖

Two days later, I went to the garage to make a delivery for Sergi. And to figure out a way to steal a bottle. T-34 had given me a look that told me I better not come back empty-handed.

Sergi was seated at a grease smudged work stand counting dirty ruble notes when I walked in.

I started to say something and he said, "Stop your whining. Something has come up." He indicated four bottles sitting on the table. "Put these in your school bag. Deliver them and you'll get the bottle for the woman."

Two things set off alarm bells in my head. His tone of voice was too kind—Sergi liked to crack orders—and his offer was too generous. The last time I spoke to him, he'd told me I'd have to make deliveries for a month to earn a bottle.

"How do I earn a bottle by making one delivery?"

"Fuck your mother! I give this little piece of shit an opportunity and he asks questions. Get out of here, go to the tire factory. In ten years you'll have black lungs from the smoke in the place and look like you are eighty years old."

I started loading the bottles into my school bag.

❖

THE ADDRESS FOR THE delivery was in the heart of the city near the theatre district, on a street that crossed the canal. I rode the trolley and got off three blocks away from the location. It was after seven and dark by the time I stepped off the trolley. I knew the area. I'd made deliveries in the area for Sergi before, to the apartments of performers and backstage people at the ballet and other theatres.

As I walked, I noticed a black car come slowly down the street behind me and pull to the curb, parking under the dim glow of the street lamp. The sight of the car made my knees weak. I paused by a store window and looked at the car's reflection. No one got out of it. The car just stayed at the curb, probably with its motor running.

It reminded me of the night my father had been taken away as I stood by the bed and stared out the window. I had seen two men push him into the backseat of a black car.

Everyone in the city knew that the NKVD drove that kind of car.

It could have been on the street for any reason, but it scared the hell out of me. I tried to shake it off and kept walking.

Another black car was coming up the street, this one a couple blocks away but coming toward me. It pulled to the curb when it was a block from me and parked under the street lamp.

I paused near another store window, my heart beating in my throat. I didn't know what was coming down, but there was one thing I did understand—Soviet police, the ones on the streets and the secret ones that ride around in black cars, are not subtle. They call the Soviet Union a police state because the police are everywhere, and if not actually present, their presence is felt by a system of spies and informers that permeated every level of society. They had no problem making their presence known wherever they went.

The four bottles in my kit suddenly felt like heavy bricks.

What would they do to me if they caught me? I was only a teenager. Would they send me to a hard labor, convict camp? Shoot me?

❖

I realized that Sergi had set me up. He had been much too generous, offering me a bottle of vodka for making one delivery.

But that didn't make any sense. I wasn't a big enough catch to warrant the secret police. The local police, the militia, were the ones who dealt with low-level crooks like Sergi. The secret police deal with crimes important to the Party, especially political ones.

Sergi was a rat and I had no doubt he would throw me to the police to save his own skin. It may even have been that he had to satisfy a quota system with the police, give them an economic criminal once in a while so they could meet the quota for convictions set in their plan year. That would be very Soviet. But there were others involved; most of his delivery people were adults. It seemed to make more sense to give the police one of them, an adult who they could make more of a show of convicting and sentencing.

No, it just didn't seem right. And I kept seeing my father's face, gripped by fear and courage, as he turned and told my mother to take me into the bedroom. I couldn't remember if it really happened, but in my own mind I saw him turn and look up at the window where I stood before they took him.

I broke into a cold sweat and started shaking at the memory. And I kept walking. The address was on the canal side of the street and I crossed over. The two cars flanking me stayed a block away, still parked at the curb.

I thought about the fact that the men in the two cars seemed to know exactly what my destination was. That was the only way they would have known where to park in order to flank me.

It struck me as I reached the canal sidewalk.

They weren't there just to arrest me. They could already have done that by now. There was someone else they wanted and Sergi was giving them the evidence they needed. *They were going to arrest the person I made the delivery to.*

I can't say that I cared about the person to be arrested. But I did care about the person's family, about how they would take the person out of the house in front of spouse and children. And I did care that I was going to be the tool used and that I would be castigated along with that person. Sergi was a bastard. Life was not fair. I was fucked. I had to go through with the delivery. I was too scared not to.

All those thoughts ran through my head as I paused on a canal bridge. The address I was going to was just across the short span.

I kept seeing the look on my father's face.

Fuck it!

I slipped my school pack off my shoulder and tossed it into the canal.

I went in after it.

I quickly learned that heavy, steel capped boots were wonderful for kicking people's faces but were hell to swim with.

I went down and hit bottom and kicked my way back up.

I heard cursing from men and saw the shine of a flashlight as the current swept me along.

They might be waiting for me when I got back to the barracks, but it was more likely they would go get Sergi and beat the crap out of him.

Maybe even throw his ass in jail.

As I trudged toward the orphanage, wet and cold and miserable, my only thoughts centered on what T-34 was going to do with my balls when she found out I couldn't get her a bottle of vodka.

❖

16

❖

Leningrad Detention Center, 1949

I was eighteen years old when I was finally arrested and looked forward to a long sentence.

"Five years in a labor colony in Siberia," Ivan Denisovich said, with great authority. "But they will hold you for eight more for lack of good behavior, no matter what your behavior. And you will age twenty more years from bad food, freezing weather and hard work. Hard work, did I say? Work that will make your back and feet ache. Laboring work, picking at the frozen tundra with picks and shovels to build a road that will not last the winter. Neither will your toes. They call you Four-Fingers? They will call you No-Toes after a few years stomping on the permafrost."

We sat on the cold, damp concrete floor of the holding cell connected to the City Court building, smoking cigarettes hand-rolled in toilet paper and waiting our turn. There were twelve of us, all waiting to enter the courtroom to be bound over for trial or be pulled out for interrogation prior to trial.

Ivan Denisovich was able to speak with authority on the sentences received by criminals because he had served so many of them.

❖

"It's so damn cold there," Ivan said, "if you rest your butt on the ground for a moment during a work break, your ass and balls freeze. A couple horny dolts snuck off into the woods to corn-hole each other. One got his cock stuck in the other's hole, frozen tight, cock-to-ass as soon as he whipped it out and stuck it in. They had to whack off his cock on the spot."

Ivan could speak on authority about prison sentences, but that didn't make him a Soviet rocket scientist.

"Give me a cigarette," a prisoner said. He had a Gypsy look to him, dark hair, eyes and skin, with greasy long hair and clothes that looked like they were soiled long before he was arrested.

"Fuck your mother," I said. I got off my rear and squatted on my heels, ready to spring at him if he made a move on me. The street insult I gave him was a profane exclamation between friends—but fighting words between strangers. When he told me to give him a cigarette, it wasn't just a request, it was a challenge. If I gave it to him, next he'd want my bed and my ass. I wasn't the biggest guy in the cell, but I wasn't a pushover, either.

He squatted down facing us and grinned. "Can you spare a cigarette, comrade?"

I handed him one of the toilet-paper cigarettes.

"What are you in for?" he asked.

"I'm falsely accused of participating in a gang involved in criminal theft and speculation. Naturally, the accusations are completely false, a miscarriage of Soviet justice. I'm innocent."

Everyone within hearing scoffed at my proclamation of innocence, but it was better to lie than say anything that could come back and bite you. In a society where you may be married to a police spy, or have birthed one, there are as many spies and informers in jails as anywhere else. Probably more.

"First offense?" he asked.

"Yes."

I had been arrested before, but had always squeezed out of it. This time I hadn't been able to sell my innocent-teenager act to the investigator. Someone had told him I was the head of the gang. As usual, my weak link had been a woman—a jealous woman. I had

had a nice racket going. I had a woman who worked at the factory that made Red Star perfume sneak out essence. Flowers were boiled at the plant. The essential oils containing the fragrance evaporated with the steam that rose from the boiling. When the steam condensed back into water, the oil floated on top.

It wasn't unlike the way I saw vodka made four years earlier. Irina worked in the processing area where the concentrated oil was collected. She sneaked out essence in her lunchpail tea bottle. We diluted and bottled the fragrances and sold them at the Haymarket in Red Star bottles that another confederate obtained. At half the price and no standing for hours in line to buy a bottle, the counterfeit was very popular with women.

I bounced around from one scheme to another, avoiding honest work the past few years and had learned well from Sergi before he was sent off to the Gulag shortly after I leaped into a canal.

The counterfeit perfume operation worked fine until Irina caught me in bed with her sister. I tried to explain that it was a case of mistaken identity, they were twins, but she tried to slice me up with a knife before the two sisters began screaming and fighting. The police were called, accusations made, and I found myself in jail. The worse thing was that we hadn't passed the petting stage before we were caught.

"It's a case of mistaken identity and false accusations of criminal conspirators," I said. "The efficient Soviet justice system will ferret out the truth and I will be released and returned to my former role as a valuable asset to our socialist society."

"Good, good, that's a nice speech for the investigator," the Gypsy said. "And your friend is right." He nodded at Ivan, who had turned to give another inmate the benefit of his long years in the justice system. "Five years. It is probably worth ten, but because of your tender age and lack of a prior record, you'll get off with a lesser sentence, unless you annoy the investigator."

"And you, comrade? What is the false accusation against you?"

"Oh, it's not false at all. I killed my lover, my mistress. There are, however, extenuating circumstances. I was drunk, so drunk that I had passed out. When I awoke later, I started drinking

❖

again. While in that state, I discovered that my lover had stolen my *papakha* and sold it. Comrade, can you imagine being in Leningrad in the winter without a fur hat? I beat her to death while under the influence of the vodka and the sudden rage that erupted when I discovered the theft."

"Ah," I nodded knowingly. I was already becoming an expert on the justice system. "So the crime lacks the need for an 'exceptional measure of punishment' that often is prescribed when there is a killing." The exceptional measure referred to was the death penalty. In the Soviet system that constituted a single shot to the head, often given by a "volunteer."

"Exactly so," he said. "Because there is a lack of exceptional measure, I am criminally ill. I can be cured, re-educated and re-turned to society as a useful member."

A guard appeared at the bars of the cell and called out, "Nicholaus Pedrovich Cutter."

"Yes, comrade."

"Your turn to see the investigator."

I gave my lit cigarette to Ivan and followed the guard, ideas buzzing in my head. This was the critical interview. Unlike the system in my father's homeland in Britain, where common law devel-oped and was exported to America, neither the Soviet Union nor the rest of continental Europe used a jury system, nor were crimi-nal proceedings battles between gladiatorial lawyers.

Instead, before a defense attorney entered the picture, a crimi-nal case was thoroughly investigated, including questioning of the defendant by an investigator or even by the "procurator," what the prosecutor was called in the Soviet system. A defendant did not have a right to refuse to answer questions.

When the matter was brought to trial, the defendant was given a defense attorney, who usually received a copy of the investigation file just before the trial was to start. The trial was held before a judge and two lay "assessors." These assessors were common citi-zens who were nominated by the factory or other entity they worked for to serve two weeks a year. While in theory the two as-sessors had a right to vote against the sitting judge's decision, in

❖

practice it was the judge who found guilt or innocence and the assessors merely rubber-stamped the judge's decision.

However, even though the judge had the final say, in actuality the matter was usually decided through the investigation process. Everybody even remotely concerned with the case was questioned and allowed not only to state what they said or heard, but what they thought or believed. A defendant was not expected to deny guilt but to admit it and be given the opportunity to explain why he committed the offense. The chief investigator's final report and conclusions were generally accepted as the case would be decided.

The objective was that no innocent person would be brought to trial and no guilty person would escape punishment. Bottom line, rather than a trial being a search for truth, as it was under the common-law system, only guilty people were put on trial in the Soviet Union.

One could be convicted of a crime even if there were no witnesses or physical evidence that a crime had been committed. "Conviction by analogy" and being a "social danger" were classes of crime that were extremely vague and gave the authorities great leeway in punishing persons who they could not actually prove committed a precise, physical act. There were also secret crimes, ones not published in statutes but known only to a specific set of investigators, procurators and judges.

While I could come up with many objections to the reliability of the Soviet justice system, in this particular case I was guilty and my main concern was how to use the system to avoid being *justly* punished. The theft, counterfeiting and marketing of perfume were just a few of the crimes I had committed since leaving the orphanage at the age of fifteen and hanging out on the streets as a nonproductive member of society.

Cured, re-educated and returned to society as a useful member. The phrase used by the Gypsy ran around my head like a dog chasing its tail. It was the key I needed.

Unlike the British-American system, the Soviet system did not focus on the crime but on the defendant. Everything about the defendant, from the day he was born to the day of the crime, was con-

❖

sidered important. Criminal acts, they believed, were caused by mental illness, and if the defendant could be "cured" of the illness and "re-educated" through medical treatment, he could be returned to society as a useful member.

It was a no-brainer. I could either go off to Siberia for five years, aging two or three years for every year I spent on the frozen tundra, or I could get "treatment" while confined in a mental facility.

There were rumors that the "mental illness" theory about crime had been grossly misused by the authorities, that intellectuals and dissenters who objected to the Soviet political system were thrown into mental hospitals and declared mentally ill, but I was more worried about my tender skin than the theory and practice of Communism.

I had it—I needed to be taught a trade that would benefit Soviet society. I was a poor orphan who never had a chance. I could not earn an honest living because I had no training. If I was sent, say, to a tractor factory, and learned how to make tractors, I would benefit the heroic farmers of our nation.

"It's the task of the justice system to 'remake' me into a good citizen," I said.

"You will get what you deserve," the guard said.

That was the last thing I wanted.

I was running the spiel through my mind when I was led into an interrogation room. A cold fist grabbed my heart when I saw the investigator. I had hoped for one of the women investigators, one I could bring to tears with my poor orphan story as I laid my head against her breasts.

But Comrade Chief Investigator Nevski was a bastard. He was snake-eyes, the black marble, a bad draw at cards. It wasn't just bad luck to have him assigned as the investigator on your case, it was the *worst* luck. He was not the clever detective Porfiry Pedrovich, who used psychology to get Dostoyevsky's Raskolnikov to confess, nor the relentless Javert who pursued Jean Valjean even into the sewers of Paris in Hugo's *Les Misérables*.

Nevski had none of the finesse of these fictional detectives. Rather, he had the mentality of an ox. The government put a yoke on him and sent him down a straight line to plow—and that is what he did, plowing through crime and criminals without ever looking right or left.

Rumor among the criminal milieu of Leningrad was that Nevski totally and completely lacked imagination, that his head was incapable of handling more than one thought at a time, and that he even slept sitting up with his eyes open because he had no need for rest. The word also was that he began his services with the police by cleaning toilets. It goes without saying, no one cleaned toilets as well as Nevski did.

I didn't know which, if any, of the observations were true, but I did know that the bastard had a thick dossier on me and had been waiting patiently for me to trip up so he could hang me by my heels on the spokes of Soviet justice.

He had his head down, light reflecting on his close-shaven skull, when I walked in. He was reading something, my dossier no doubt.

I waited a minute, shifting my weight from one foot to another and cleared my throat. "Comrade—"

"Shut up," he spoke without looking up.

My mind reeled. The poor orphan story was my only defense. I had used it repeatedly over the years. It wouldn't work on Nevski, but at the trial, the defendant is given the last word so he could explain his acts and throw himself on the mercy of the court. I still had an opportunity. If I were lucky enough to get a female judge . . .

Nevski finally looked up at me. His eyes were totally blank.

"You have a disease."

My jaw dropped. "I do?"

"A social disease, one that affects everyone you come into contact with. Do you know what Lenin said about crime?"

I shifted uncomfortably on my feet. "He said many things."

"He said that the smallest illegality, the tiniest violation of the legal order, is a crack in our armor that is used by enemies of the Soviet workers to destroy all they have toiled for. Do you recall learning that in school?"

❖

"Yes, Comrade Investigator."

"You're a liar. You never went to school. You lived on the streets where you became infected by the disease of criminality."

"I'm a poor orphan—"

"Hundreds of thousands of children were left orphaned by the Great Patriotic War. Only a few became career criminals. And only a few of those organized gangs. Only one of those few organized a gang to rob, steal and exploit the Soviet economy. That one person is you."

Nevski had more imagination that I realized. I was nowhere near the gang king he imagined me to be. He was also a great judge of character.

He pointed his finger at me, a fat finger that looked like the barrel of a pistol aimed between my eyes. "It's in your blood. Your father was a bourgeois traitor to the Soviet state."

"My father was a hero who fought for socialism on the streets when you were cleaning shit off of toilet seats."

A red flush began at his bull neck and worked its way up his face. I was a tough kid, I could handle the Gypsy, but Nevski was built much more like a T-34 tank than the barracks matron. He could rip off my arms and legs and beat me with the bloody stumps.

My knees began to shake. I was not only in imminent danger of getting beaten, but I had probably talked myself into ten years instead of the five that the knowledgeable Ivan predicted.

The door opened behind me. A secretary popped her head in.

"The official is here from the British Consulate."

17

❖

John Byrd, the consulate representative, had a long, arched nose, unhealthy blotches on his skin, and as far as I was concerned, the wings of an angel.

"You are a British citizen, young man."

I sat quietly and listened without opening my mouth, a not-very-common experience for me.

"Your grandfather, Charles Lawwood Cutter, died three years ago. In his will, he left funds to conduct an investigation to find you. His son died nearly ten years ago, and the last word he had from your mother was news of your father's death. Following the war, he made inquiries that revealed that your mother had died during the war and that you ended up at an orphanage. However, it was discovered that you left the orphanage—"

"Escaped," Nevski said, "to take to the streets as a criminal."

"Yes, well, as I was saying, it took considerable time to track you down. It was the very fact that you had incurred a police record that resulted in our being able to locate you."

"Does that mean I get an inheritance?" I asked.

"I'm afraid not. Your grandfather was a man of some means,

❖

but far from wealthy. His first wife, your grandmother, the mother of your own father, passed away and he remarried. That marriage produced a daughter, Sarah, who is your aunt, half-blood aunt technically. I suppose because there was thought to be little likelihood that you survived the war or would ever be found, funds were set aside to try and locate you but there is no legacy."

I sighed and looked over at Nevski. I couldn't read anything in his eyes. I grinned at him. "I guess we are right back where we were a few minutes ago when you were questioning me."

"Not exactly," Mr. Byrd said. "As I said, you are a British citizen. While technically the Soviet state could also claim you as its own, or detain you in regard to certain acts"—he coughed politely into his hand—"because of your youth and the tragic circumstances of having lost both parents, arrangements have been made to have you rejoin your last living relative, your aunt."

My jaw dropped for the second time that day.

"*I'm going to Britain?*"

"No, at least not permanently. Your aunt lives in a colony. Have you ever heard of British Honduras?"

I shook my head.

I heard a strange noise beside me. It was Nevski. He was shaking. His face had gone beet-red. I stared at him. He looked like the top was going to blow off his head, a volcano about to erupt. I realized that he was convulsed with laughter and trying to control it.

He leaned toward me and shot spittle at me as he laughed and choked.

"Fuck your mother! You're going to Devil's Island!"

❖

18

❖

Aboard the Queen Elizabeth, North Atlantic, 1949

The smell of money. That was the difference between the communists and the capitalists. The stacks of rubles Sergi the Rat counted back in Leningrad smelled of piss, sweat and bureaucracy. The smell of money in the West was the sensuous scent of Chanel No. 5, the masculine power of a Montecristo cigar from Cuba, a bubbling Chateâu-Thierry champagne and an aged Charente brandy. Born and raised under the dreary austerity of communism, I was hopelessly seduced by the smell of money and the sexual opulence of the West as I experienced the swish of shapely legs in silk stockings and the dynamic clout radiating from men in black tuxedos.

Walking down the ship's deck, stunned by the opulence, I realized that I was stuck on this earth and that there were two types of people on it—the ones with and the ones without. My father had talked about the "haves" and "have nots" as if being poor was a privilege. He was wrong. He had lost his life because he lacked two necessities—*power and influence.*

❖

And having or being without had nothing to do with the difference between communism and capitalism. The Soviet Union was supposed to be a land of equals, but I knew that a privileged few lived lives of luxury while the general masses stood in long lines and worked long hours for basics.

I saw my mother die of starvation while fat-cat apparatchiks with power and influence ate well.

I was never going to be without again.

I was going to get everything those rich people had.

And more.

SIX DAYS BEFORE BOARDING the great ship *Queen Elizabeth,* I sailed out of Leningrad on a freighter flying the Union Jack, sharing a cabin with the ship's oiler. The ship delivered fine machine parts to the Soviets and took on a load of fifty kilo gunny sacks of potatoes. Other than a few conversations with Mr. Byrd, aboard the ship was the first time I'd heard English spoken in any meaningful way since my father died. I started rolling English through my mind and thinking in English from the moment Nevski sent me back to the cell to await processing out. Mr. Byrd was pleased that I spoke English with a British accent. Since I learned it by mimicking my father's accent, it wasn't a surprise to me.

Besides getting what amounted to a refresher course in English aboard the freighter, there were books, a world globe and a complete set of encyclopedias. I used my finger to trace the route that was taking me almost halfway around the world—Leningrad to Liverpool by freighter, Liverpool to New York on the *Queen*, then on another ship down America's Atlantic seaboard, past the tip of Florida and Cuba, across the Caribbean to Belize Town, the capital of the British colony called British Honduras. The colony was tucked right under the southernmost part of Mexico, the region called the Yucatán.

From the encyclopedias, I learned that British Honduras was nowhere near Devil's Island, but like the infamous French island prison, it had considerable jungle and beaches. No one aboard the

❖

freighter had been to the colony or knew much about it. But I was assured that there were real paradises in that part of the world.

Not even Mr. Byrd of the British consulate seemed to know anything about the colony, although he was certain it wasn't as bad as Devil's Island.

After the cold, mean streets of Leningrad, not to mention the dungeonlike stink and dampness of a city jail, I was ready for a lush, warm paradise.

I laid over in Liverpool only for a day before I boarded the floating palace for the trip across the Atlantic to New York. Not that I was treated royally aboard—I traveled steerage class, sharing a room deep in the bowels of the ship with three other, dark-haired, olive-skinned men speaking a tongue unfamiliar to me, Turkish or Greek, I thought.

I was awed by the great transatlantic liner. It was both a floating city and a Leviathan, a monster of the sea, over a thousand feet long. It introduced me to that strange and wondrous new phenomenon—the smell of money.

I got my first sniff of money when I sneaked up to the deck where first-class passengers promenaded. Walking down the deck, I gaped like a country bumpkin on his first trip to the city as women in spike heels, diamond necklaces and sleek dresses came by on the arms of men wearing tuxedos and gold watches. Everything was new and strange to me, but I now realized the difference between communism and capitalism. It had nothing to do with class differences—hell, there were class distinctions in the Soviet Union, the higher up the Party you got, the better your food and housing and car became.

No, there were obvious class differences under communism. The real difference between the Soviets and the West was in consumer products, especially the luxury kind. We Soviets led the world in making battle tanks and refrigerators that didn't work, but try to find a diamond bracelet or sheer silk stockings. Chanel No. 5 dominated the opulent West; in Russia, the government put out a perfume that was jokingly—and only on the sly—referred to as Stalin's Breath.

❖

There was something else I gave a lot of thought to—the family I lost and the one I was on my way to meet. There was no one to see me off at Leningrad—I had no real friends, no close relatives that I knew of. I left nothing behind in the city that I cared about and took nothing with me except the memory of my mother and father. In a strange way, I felt they were coming with me, their spirits beside me.

I knew little about the family I was going to meet. My father's half-sister in British Honduras, Sarah, apparently was my only close relative. "I suppose you'll have cousins in Britain, that sort of thing, it'll all be sorted out when you get to the colony," Mr. Byrd told me. I wondered what she would be like, what her husband was all about. All I knew was that they had no children.

Most of all I wondered about my own qualms about meeting family.

Since the death of my mother, I had been essentially a loner, careful not to have close friendships that would bring pain. I had lost my father when I was eight and my mother when I was eleven. Much of my life had been spent in a time of war and loss. Most of my life had been spent in a struggle for survival. I knew how to survive—to cheat and steal and fight. What I didn't know was how to be normal.

I had been dealing with gang members for so long, fighting over scraps, being devious to avoid the snare of bureaucrats and policemen, I had forgotten what passed for normal. I was eighteen years old now and had been an adult almost half of my life.

I thought about not showing up at the colony, about jumping ship in New York and getting a job. But I couldn't do that—my aunt had paid my fare and at the very least I had to honor her kindness.

My qualms about the future took a back place in my mind as I walked down the ship's first-class deck and experienced the sight, sound and smell of money. I gawked at everything. I hadn't decided yet whether the women in the West were more beautiful than Russian ones, but the way they dressed, with plunging necklines and body-tight dresses, stirred my preternatural juices. A number

❖

of women gave me looks or smiles that to my mind were inviting, but I would quickly look away. Part of my reluctance was the fear of the uninitiated—I would not have admitted it under secret police torture, but I was still a virgin. I was eighteen years old. I had had a couple opportunities to break my cherry, but I had passed, not because I wasn't horny but because the girls who offered me their bodies expected a commitment beyond sex.

There was also the question of being exposed as a fraud. I paid a small bribe to borrow a steward's white coat in order to gain access to the first-class deck and see wonders I had only heard about. But my dark brown pants and scuffed, steel-nosed shoes didn't complete the outfit.

My fears of exposure were realized when a ship's officer stopped in front of me. I was preoccupied looking at the beautiful people and didn't see him until I was almost chest-to-chest with him.

"What are you doing out of uniform?" he demanded.

"I—I ripped my pants, took them to the tailor."

"Report back to your supervisor immediately. You don't belong up here in first class."

"Yes sir!"

I could feel him drilling holes in my back as I marched away. It was probably my steel-toed boots. Even if I'd ripped my pants, the boots were obviously not anything like the polished black shoes the stewards wore. He apparently decided to investigate me further, and I heard him call "Steward" behind me but I pretended I didn't hear him. I went around a corner and into a corridor lined with cabin doors. I took the first stairway down and went around more corridors until I had not only lost him, but had lost myself—the ship was a floating city and I wasn't familiar with the streets.

Avoiding another ship's officer, I went around a corridor and faced a dead end. Only one cabin door was in the hallway. I tried the door and the handle turned. I stuck my head in. It was a one-room suite with an open door to the bathroom. The light was on but no one was home. I slipped in and closed the door almost shut, leaving it open only a fraction of an inch. I used the slim crack to check the corridor to see if the ship's officer was there.

❖

"Are you a thief?"

I almost jumped out of my steel-tocd boots.

A woman had stepped out of the bathroom.

"Naa-no," I stammered.

"Rapist?"

"No!"

"Pity."

"I—I'm sailing steerage, I wanted to see what the upper decks looked like."

"Including the cabins?"

"I thought it was empty. A ship's officer was after me."

"Well, make yourself useful. Come over here and help me with this."

"This" was a bra. I didn't know what to say. She turned to face a full-length mirror and took off her robe, tossing it onto the bed.

She was naked. Suddenly my feet felt like they were in buckets of cement.

"Come over here," she said. "Or do you want me to ring for a ship's officer?"

Dry-mouthed, knees trembling, I shuffled toward her.

She was not a large woman but wasn't small either. Everything was more full about her, nose, mouth, large brown eyes. Her breasts were not as perked as the ones of the young girls I'd petted, but were rounder and fuller and much more buxom than a girl's. She had long black hair that hung in wet straggles. Her bare skin was still moist from stepping out of the shower.

She stood with her back to me as I came up behind her. She slipped her bra over her breasts and held the two straps back for me to link.

I fumbled with the hooks. I didn't know how they went together and I was too nervous to see how simple it was.

Her hands came around her back but instead of hooking the straps, she took my hands.

"You're awfully clumsy. How old are you?"

"Twenty-two," I lied. I could pass for it. All except for my knowledge of women's bras.

❖

"Then you should have more experience."

She pulled my hands forward, in front of her, letting her bra drop. I cupped her breasts with my hands. Her breasts were full and hot. I gently squeezed them, feeling their lushness. I stared at the breasts I was enjoying and the mound of pubic hair.

"Do you want to fuck me?" she asked.

I nodded affirmatively.

"Have you ever been with a woman before?"

"Lots of times," I croaked.

She twisted in my arms, turning to face me. Her lips met mine and she swallowed me, covering my lips with her mouth, fucking my mouth with her tongue.

My knees had stopped shaking and I felt the bulge in my pants growing.

She undid my belt and the top button to my pants, then released the last three buttons and slid her hand down my pants, grabbing my throbbing penis. I went off in her hand, my penis jerking out of control.

"Oh God, I'm sorry. I didn't mean to—"

"It's okay, it's okay, sweetie."

She backed me onto the bed and pulled off my pants and helped me get off my underwear.

"A boy your age can do it more than once."

She spread my legs and knelt on the floor on both knees. She took my penis in both hands and massaged it with her hands, stroking my testicles with her fingers.

"I like it when it's soft," she said. "Let it get hard in my mouth."

She cupped my testicles, rolling her tongue up my stalk until she swallowed my cock. Her mouth was wet and warm. I felt my cock rising as she sucked, growing bigger in her mouth, pumping it as she sucked.

She stood up grinning and climbed on top of me, straddling me. My cock was high and firm.

"This is what's good about getting a young one. Letting it get hard in your mouth and then getting it jabbed up your cunt."

❖

She was wet and ready for me. She took my cock and shoved it inside of her opening.

Oh God, I moaned.

It was a good, uncommunistic expression I learned aboard the British freighter and now it seemed just right. I felt like I was in heaven. I kneaded her large breasts as they hung over me and leaned up to suck them, taking one nipple in my mouth and then the other, as I pumped from beneath her.

For the first time I really felt the power in my male loins. My penis had grown huge. She slid her wet vulva back and forth over it, letting out a little whimper of joy each time she hit her erogenous zone.

I twisted around, lifting her into the air and down onto the bed, keeping her inside me as I came down on top of her. I pumped, lifting myself with my arms and legs as I drove into her. She gasped and grabbed my buttocks, spreading herself wider.

"More, more," she cried, "harder."

As I went in deeper, she let out a cry and arched her back, riding up with me.

I heard the door open and looked over my shoulder, a wave of fear in my gut.

An elderly man had stepped into the cabin. He saw the two of us fucking and stopped dead in his tracks.

"Oh—sorry."

He backed out the door, nearly stumbling over backwards. He disappeared, shutting the door behind him.

I tried to get off but her sharp fingernails dug into my buttocks.

"Don't worry, it was just my husband."

❖

The
CARIBBEAN

If the world had any ends, British Honduras would certainly be one of them.
It is not on the way from anywhere to anywhere else.
It has no strategic value.
It is all but uninhabited.

ALDOUS HUXLEY
BEYOND THE MEXIQUE BAY

British Honduras is the armpit of the British Empire.

JACK WALSH

19

❖

Belize Town, British Honduras, 1949

Novoki, the paradigm of Soviet justice, had been wrong. British Honduras was not Devil's Island.

It was hell itself.

Hot, wet, steamy, oppressive. Like breathing from under the covers of a wet wool blanket. An atmosphere you swam through rather than walked. And were parboiled as you did.

It was early in the morning when the ship dropped anchor in deep water several miles outside Belize Town harbor. "What kind of port city can't handle banana-boat tubs?" I asked the second officer. A week aboard the small American ship had supplied me with another foreign language—American English.

The second officer spit chewing tobacco over the side. "The port's so shallow, most cargo is hauled out in barges and loaded aboard anchored ships. Worst goddamn port in the Caribbean. Half the crew has to stay aboard to man the ship because we can't dock. Whole damn colony is less than two hundred miles long and maybe sixty, seventy miles wide. Almost all of it's jungles and swamps."

❖

I had worked up a sweat just rolling off my bunk and getting dressed. Along with the sweat, I had built up a dread of arriving in the colony from the moment I boarded the banana boat in New York. I knew nothing about the aunt and uncle I was supposed to live with, whether I would be an intruder or welcomed, whether I would like them or hate them or what they would think of me.

As the ship was within range of the city late last night, I realized that the nagging dread was caused by *fear*. The same fear that had shadowed me across the Baltic to Liverpool and across the Atlantic to New York. Now I had to face the fear.

I didn't know if I wanted to deal with that thing called "family." There was a part of me that really wanted to have a warm, familial connection that I saw all around, mom and dad and the kids. But I was afraid to want anything or need anyone. I had learned early in life that if the gods knew you wanted it or needed it, they took it away.

I CAME ASHORE IN a motor launch with the customs official. I hopped onto the dock carrying a duffel bag and wearing a pair of blue-wash jeans, black tennis shoes, and a white T-shirt, all won from sailors on the banana boat in card games. I was also wearing an attitude that I didn't give a damn about anyone or anything.

At the other end of the dock two people were waiting, a man and a woman. The woman smiled and frantically waved a handkerchief as I came off the launch.

I slowed my pace, a little embarrassed, not knowing how to handle her enthusiasm. She hurried down the dock, almost in a run, and gave me a big hug. I accepted it stiffly.

"You look just like your father," Sarah Walsh said. "Nicholaus, it's so good to finally see you."

I liked my aunt immediately.

"Nick."

Uncle Jack Walsh offered a handshake and tried to crush my hand as soon as he had a grip on it. It was a kind of "man thing" to show who's got the biggest balls.

❖

I disliked him on the spot. And I've always been good at first impressions.

We chatted as we walked toward their vehicle, my duffel bag over my shoulder. Or I should say that Sarah chatted. Mostly I listened and Jack looked preoccupied.

My bare arms felt itchy. "What—what?" They were black with flying creatures. I brushed them off in a panic, leaving streaks of blood on my arms.

"You have to wear long sleeves early in the morning and late in the afternoon," Sarah said. "That's when the mosquitoes feed."

I slapped the back of my neck.

"A hat and kerchief will help, too, the battlass and doctor flies feed about the same time," Sarah said. "We rub juice of a plant on our hands and face, it keeps most of the mosquitoes and other pests away, but I'm afraid I didn't think to bring any."

My ankles itched and I rubbed them.

"Sand fleas," she said. She looked distressed.

Mary, mother of God. It was one of the less provocative expressions I had learned on the banana boat. It was one I was going to have plenty of use for. A city where you could poach eggs in a hot wind, a port where ships couldn't dock and people were eaten alive by insects. This truly was hell.

We got into a vintage Land Rover, the unconquerable jeeplike vehicles that transported a generation of the British soldiers and administrators who wielded the power of the Union Jack in the white man's world that was coming under attack around the world by indigenous peoples.

Sarah turned around in the front passenger seat and smiled at me. It was a nice smile. My memory of my father was only hazy, and I couldn't see any resemblance in her. Her hair was darker than I remembered my father's hair. His was very blond, like mine, while hers was what I heard a man on the transatlantic ship refer to as "dishwater blond."

Her complexion was fair, though a little ruddier than my Leningrad paleness. Her cheeks were full and rosy red. The smile she gave me seemed to be always on her lips. Pretty in a plain and

❖

simple way, she was either a compulsively happy person or worked to keep a pleasant outlook in what looked to me to be a dismal place.

"We're so happy you've finally gotten here. We've been waiting anxiously for months, ever since we got word that you had survived the war. We're just thrilled that you're finally with us, aren't we, Jack?"

Jack grunted. He was about my size, five-ten, a little stockier than me, bullnecked with a broad forehead and brown, short-cropped military-style hair. He had a red rash on the side of his neck that he kept scratching, the kind of rash people said came from worry and nerves.

I had picked up other expressions on shipboard and a couple of them fit him—he had a "hard-on" toward life, a "chip on his shoulder."

I wasn't sure if he was angry because I was suddenly plopped onto their laps or if he just was pissed at the world in general.

"I'm afraid Belize Town's not much to look at," Sarah said.

"It's plenty to smell," Jack uttered.

The capital of the colony called British Honduras was an eyesore. It was poor, shabby, dirty and ugly. Most of the houses were unpainted wood, sometimes trimmed in green with the zinc-galvanized metal roofs painted red. Many of the buildings had a splash of color from red and pink bougainvillea and poinciana. The household water supply came from rainwater that washed off roofs and into cisterns and barrels. I learned from Sarah that the houses were propped up several feet off the ground for ventilation and to keep from being flooded as storms and hurricanes blew in. The town was only a little over a foot above sea level, making it vulnerable to high waves.

"We get hurricanes frequently," she said, "but fortunately the killer storms are years apart."

"The hurricane of '31 swept in suddenly and killed over two thousand people and nearly wiped the town clean, no loss there, though. The one of '42 hit us hardest up north and killed—"

❖

"Jack, stop it, I'm sure Nick has seen plenty of bad weather in Leningrad."

"Nothing that wipes out cities," I admitted.

And Jack was right about the smell. Compared to Leningrad, one of the great cities of the world, with monuments cast for the ages, the town was a stinking armpit. "Sewer" was another word that came to mind—it was a shanty town with open ditches that served as sewers. Stink was everywhere—the air stunk, the bay stunk, people I had walked by on my way to the Land Rover stunk.

Onboard the great *Queen*, I'd learned the smell of money. Now I knew the stench of Third World poverty.

I felt alien. The city, the people, the steamy weather, carnivorous bugs, it was nothing like I imagined or had experienced. Even the Soviet officer's comparison to Devil's Island had left me with the impression of a tropical paradise. But not even Satan himself would have lived in this place. Leningrad was cold much of the year, but cold at least was antiseptic.

Jack twisted in the driver's seat and laughed at the look on my face.

"Bloody shitty, isn't it."

"Jack!"

"Woman, you want the boy to deny what his eyes see? What his nose tells him? Look out there, what do you see? Poor blacks wearing rags, with rubber-soled sandals made from used tires. The town's built on a foundation of rum bottles atop a swamp, the houses are rotted shanties propped up on stilts, the waste in the drainage canals along the streets sits and boils and stinks until a rainstorm washes the scum out to sea—and it's back the next day when people flush their toilets. The only saving grace for the place is the occasional hurricane that levels it, blowing it away as if God had spit on it and wiped it clean."

"Rum bottles?" I asked.

"They say pirates put up the first buildings here on swampy ground by propping them up on empty rum bottles."

❖

A waste of good bottles, I thought. After one look at the town, I could think of a better use of the empty bottles—fill them with petrol and add wicks to create the fiery "Molotov cocktails" Russian and Yugoslav guerrilla fighters used against Nazi tanks. Then use the cocktail bombs to burn the place.

"Don't let appearances fool you," Sarah said, "the people might be poor in terms of material things, but they're rich in their appreciation for life and family. And courteous. The word 'no' is hardly part of the Creole psyche. They are so polite and want to please so much, that even if it is impossible, they're more likely to vaguely agree to a request than right-out refuse."

"Can't rely on them," Jack said. "The natives go by a different time clock than the rest of the world. They don't want to work that day, they don't do it. If I had a hundred stout Englishmen—"

Listening to them talk, it struck me that the town was like the "port" that couldn't accommodate ships—nothing made sense.

"There is a mixture of people in the colony," Sarah said. "The majority are called Creoles, they're either of African descent or a mixture of African and European, mostly British. They speak Creole, which is sort of a pidgin English. It will be hard for you to understand at first, but soon you'll pick up the rhythm and it will be just like regular English. In the north, we have mostly Mayan Indians whose descendants fled the Yucatán area during the caste wars in Mexico a hundred years ago. They speak their own Indian dialect and some Spanish. The ones who are in business usually speak English. And of course, there are us British colonials. Some are actually white Creoles, born here, and others like Jack and I came here for the opportunities. We even have some East Indians—"

"Descendants of the murderous sepoy mutineers who massacred our people in India back when."

"The East Indians are very nice people," Sarah said, "you'll meet some up north, good farmers, and I don't know that they're all descendants from the rebels who—"

"There's us and them," Jack said, "whites and blacks, with the browns sticking to themselves mostly. Some of the blacks are getting uppity, troublemakers, think they should be running things. Got themselves political parties, unions, newspapers, stick their nose into everything, try to tell the king's governor how to run the colony. You wait and see, won't be long till they're—"

"Maybe we can talk politics later," Sarah said. "Nick has a lot to digest just being in a new place. Things will make more sense after he gets a feel of the colony."

A man stepped out from an alley and threw a rock at the Land Rover as we came down the street. The rock hit the hood and bounced, hitting the window and ricocheting off.

"*Sonofabitch!*"

Jack slammed on the brakes and flew out of the car. I went out the back door and followed him as he ran to the alley. The man was gone. I had only gotten a brief glance at him. He was a young Creole.

"Bastard," Jack said. The rock had left a small star imprint in the windshield. "That crack will spread until it's across the whole damn window. I'll have to send back home for a replacement."

"Why'd he throw the rock? Do you know him?"

"I don't know who he is, but I know what's he's up to. He's one of the black troublemakers, the ones that are trying to drive us from the colony."

Sarah had joined us on the street. Her smile was replaced by a worry-frown. "There's trouble with one of the groups of Creoles who want the colony to be independent. They want self-government, rather than a British governor taking orders from the colonial office in London. There was an execution today. A Creole was hanged for killing another Creole during a political argument. The killer supported driving us British out, the other man did not. The man who threw the rock was probably sympathetic toward the independence movement."

"If I had gotten him in my sights, he'd be a dead sympathizer," Jack said.

I noticed for the first time that Jack had a revolver in his hand.

A crowd of curious onlookers had gathered, mostly children. I returned their stares as I walked back toward the Land Rover.

❖

They were a ragged lot, barefoot, skinny. Other than the color of their skin, the looks on their faces weren't much different than the street urchins of Leningrad during the war—I saw hunger, poverty and innocence on their faces. But there was one difference. These children were still smiling and laughing, even in their misery. They had a light spirit that had died in the children I was raised with. These children were poor, but they hadn't gotten to the point of starving to death—or being a meal for someone higher on the food chain.

Sarah waved and exchanged greetings with the children. She took a bag of hard candy from the vehicle and passed out pieces to eager hands.

"Let's go," Jack said. His expression didn't leave much doubt as to his opinion of the children.

"We don't live in the town, thank God," Sara said, after we got underway again. "The plantation is nearly a hundred miles north, up near the Mexican border. You'll like it, it's a true paradise."

"A paradise in which you have to worry about stepping on snakes that'll kill you faster than a cobra, crocs that will have you for dinner, spiders—"

"Jack, stop it, you'll frighten the boy."

I could have told her that "the boy" had survived a frozen hell with cannibals that not even crocodiles would want to mess with.

Sarah looked back at me, concern on her face. "I'm sorry this happened, Nick. Belize Town is not a very nice place, but you'll find things much better up north at the plantation."

"What kind of plantation is it? Do you grow bananas?"

"Sugarcane," Jack said.

Sarah gave me that bright, perpetual smile of hers. "We grow the cane and process it into raw sugars and molasses in our own plant. It's really quite interesting. Don't let Jack scare you, there are jungle fevers and things like snakes and crocs—"

"Scorpions as long as your foot—"

"But as you can see, we are still around to talk about them."

"Sounds interesting," I said.

❖

The permafrost of the Soviet Gulag was beginning to sound attractive in comparison to this hot, bugsy hell.

"We have to stop so I can pick up a few things in the general store. You and Jack can have something cold while I do. It's an all-day drive home. I'm afraid the road north isn't much of a road, what there is of it."

JACK AND I SAT at a window table at a small tavern while Sarah disappeared into a store across the street. There were more live flies on the window than dead ones, and there were plenty of those. He ordered beer for both of us and something else. I was sure I had misunderstood the word he used for what he ordered and kept my mouth shut because I thought I heard him order "shit."

"Can't drink the water unless it's been boiled," he said. "Beer is the only salvation for a thirsty man."

The waiter served the beer and then returned a moment later with a big platter holding a roasted fish. It was the ugliest fish I'd ever seen.

"Saltwater catfish," Jack said. "Damn good."

We each forked into it and he was right, it was good fish, thick white meat, moist and tasty.

We made short work of it and he signaled the waiter. "Give us another shittifish."

"What'd you call it?" I asked.

"You heard right. Most of the sewage in the city washes from the streets to the river and down to the bay, where there's a million of these shit-eating catfish waiting for it. That's why they're called shittifish in the local jargon." He grinned. *"Bon appétit."*

I had my fill of fish. I took a swig of cold beer, but couldn't help but wonder where they got the water for the brew.

I had been given fifty British pounds by the Embassy official before I left Leningrad, money from my deceased grandfather's estate, and had doubled it playing dice and cards on two ships. I tried to pay for the meal with a pound note and Jack shoved it back at me. "I can afford some beer and shittifish. We're not on sterling here, anyway, colony's got its own money, pegged to the value of the U.S. dollar. We'll get your pounds exchanged before we leave town."

I thought picking up the tab was courteous—he took it as a slight, as if I thought he was too poor to pick it up. I didn't need a road map to tell me that I would have to walk on eggshells around him.

"Running a sugarcane plantation is hard work," Jack said. "It's a full-time, all-time, everyday job. I work harder than the black-amoors that do the field work. I'm telling you this so you'll understand that we're not rich people, you'll be expected to pull your own weight."

"I'm not afraid of work," I said.

"I'd like to believe that, but I'm afraid I have information to the contrary. A policeman in Leningrad sent the British police commissioner here in the colony a letter stating that you have been involved in criminal activities most of your life. Since you're barely eighteen, that's quite an accomplishment—in the wrong direction."

That bastard Nevski. May he rot in hell. I had been completely wrong about him. The guy did have an imagination—a twisted one. He had gotten his revenge for me slipping out from under the punishment he knew I so well deserved.

"I just want you to know, boy, you're going to be watched. Don't let Sarah's friendly attitude fool you. I'm the boss, not her, and I'm going to make sure you walk a straight line. As far as you're concerned, I'm going to be your judge and jury. You step out of line, go back to your criminal ways, and I'll have you before the police commissioner quick as a wink.

"That goes for work, too. *We* work hard, that means *you* will work hard. I run a tight ship, it's the only way the plantation survives. If that isn't satisfactory for you, as they say, you can take a hike, family or not. My wife thinks a lot of her dead brother, but she forgets that he was the shoddier kind of Red—the egghead intellectual type. He never had a real job, he was one of those university daydreamers who walked around wide-eyed and muttering about social injustices but never got his hands dirty."

❖

"Did you know my father?"

Either my face or my voice signaled that he had gone too far because he looked away, avoiding my eye.

"Never met the man." Jack slapped a roach as big as my thumb as the creature made a sudden dash across the table. "You're going to find out real fast that you'll be shitting out both ends before your stomach gets used to bacteria in the food. You can't drink the water, the beer tastes like piss, you have to take quinine and hope it keeps the chills and raging fevers out of your blood. You work day and night to build something and it gets swept away by floods or hurricanes or the stupidity of an arrogant colonial administrator who knows nothing about what it takes to run a business in the colony or shit on by the blackamoors who care nothing about their culture. The colony has free education and most of the blacks can't even write their name except on a credit chit."

He took a long swig of his beer.

"Sarah and me, we don't agree about how to deal with the natives. The only thing they understand is a strong hand. We Brits didn't build an empire the sun never set on by passing out candy. We did it with guns and guts and that's the only way we're going to keep this colony under control."

I listened and said nothing. In Leningrad, the colonial wars in which people in places like India, Africa and Indochina battled the Western colonial powers had been cast by my Communist teachers and in the news as white European exploiters enslaving indigenous cultures. Personally, I had no opinion as to who was right or wrong and didn't care who won. I had seen enough of war and death.

I also kept my mouth shut because I was seething about his remarks about my father.

Jack chugged his beer and ordered another mug.

"Bloody fucking country. When I make my pile, I'm going back to Manchester and buying myself a nice farm outside the city and a pub inside. And I'm never going to use a piece of sugar again."

❖

20

❖

The road north had ruts big enough to swallow the Land Rover. During the long, slow, treacherous drive, I saw a snake slithering in the foliage on the side of the road and spiders as big as a man's hand scurried across our path. Monkeys screamed and flew from branch to branch, birds with dazzling colors and piercing cries screeched at us.

"Have to watch out for the Tommy Goff's," Jack said.

I looked at him with a questioning face.

"A jumping viper doesn't slither but jumps right at you, likes to spring from trees. Get bit by one, just kiss your ass good-bye."

"Jack, your language. There are jaguars out there, too," Sarah said, "big cats, almost the size of African lions. They're mankillers. Someone told me that the name 'jaguar' is an Indian word that means something like 'kills in one leap.' But you don't have to worry, they don't like people and stay in the jungle."

Mars would not have been stranger to me.

"The road is bad on vehicles and tires," Sarah said, "but archeologists hate it more. The colony's so poor, instead of proper asphalt paving when they put in the road back in the thirties, they used

❖

stones taken from Mayan Indian mounds that are scattered all over. Destroyed a bit of history. I'm told you can still find pottery shards in the rubble."

The wet heat became smothering as we left the coastline and were swallowed by dense jungle.

"It's much hotter away from the coast," Sarah said, "but in the Corozal area where the plantation's located, we get a cool ocean breeze in the afternoons. Really quite pleasant. Corozal Town itself is pretty small; Belize Town has over twenty thousand people, Corozal maybe one tenth that. But it has electric lights and telephone and wireless contact with the capital. Corozal even has a moving picture theatre. Doesn't play anything that hasn't been out for a year or two, but there aren't many towns with their own picture show.

"The northern country where the plantation's located consists of lowlands. The southern half of the colony has mountains. The biggest, Victoria Peak, is almost four thousand feet high. The Caribbean coastline is really quite beautiful. We'll go down it by boat sometime and show it to you. There are barrier reefs and numerous cays, little islands and swamps everywhere, especially along the coast. And then there's the jungle, it's everywhere, too. Lots of hardwood in it, that's really what the colony is famous for, logging of tropical woods."

As we drove, Sarah talked incessantly, first giving me an oral tour of the colony and then telling me stories about my father's family in Britain and her and Jack's life in the colony. I already knew the basics about my British grandfather, whom my mother described as a hardnosed, bourgeois engineer. My father had been his only child until he had remarried after my grandmother passed away. Sarah was the only child of that second marriage. She was about ten years older than me, late twenties, maybe thirty, much younger than my father, who had been her half-brother.

My grandfather left most of his estate to Sarah's mother, putting aside a bit to hunt for me, Jack told me, to extinguish any hope I might have for an inheritance, which I already knew.

"I was just a little girl when I met your mother," Sarah said.

❖

"Peter brought her home from Germany, where they had met and married. He brought her to Lyme Regis to introduce her to the family. It was a triple shock for my father—your grandfather. His new daughter-in-law was Russian, a dyed-in-the-wool communist, and Peter and she were going to live in Leningrad. I guess it was really a quadruple shock because she was also Jewish." Sarah laughed. "I was in the room when Peter announced they were going to live in Leningrad. I thought my father was going to have a coronary on the spot. His face turned beet-red and his jaw hung open."

She turned back in her seat and gave me another one of her nice smiles. "There was a big age difference between your father and I, about fifteen years. He really wasn't a big brother to me, he was gone too much, off to school, then off to Europe and finally off to Russia. Rather, my image of him was that he was idealistic and brave. He made my father angry because they disagreed on politics, but to me he was heroic. I often used to boast to the other children at school that my brother was in Europe fighting the Jerries."

Sarah's eyes misted.

"I remember your mother, too. She was pretty, very pale, one of those real northern Slavic complexions, but very grave, very serious about life. She didn't smile a terrible lot, but she was very nice to me and treated me like a young adult rather than a child. It's too bad you lost both of them."

I looked out the window and didn't say anything. There were no more tears left in me.

She continued on with her chatter. "Jack and I were married when he was a sergeant in the army and I was a nurse. There's lots of class distinctions in the home country, more than you might imagine. We settled here in the colony to get away from all that class snobbery. Back home Jack would be lucky if he could rise to being foreman in a factory but—"

"Will you shut your mouth, woman? You talk—talk—talk. Do you think I want my dirty laundry aired?"

"Well—darling, Nick is family."

Jack eyed me in the rearview mirror. "I seem to recall that his father abandoned his family and his country and went over to the enemy."

"Jack!"

I sat quietly in the backseat with my fist clenched and trembled from rage. It took everything I had to keep myself from smacking Jack across the side of the head. I had come to some conclusions about my new "family."

Sarah was a good person who had a need to help others. She was genuinely happy to see me. Maybe she needed family. She had Jack and no children, not exactly the combination for a homey atmosphere when one of the housemates is a bully.

Jack was caught up in his own needs and had little care about the rest of the world except to strike out when the chip on his shoulder was rattled or it suited his purposes. They were a mismatched pair. Where Sarah was warm and outgoing, Jack was sullen and introspective, and quick to temper. He spoke roughly to his wife, not at all the tone I would expect a good man to use with his wife.

For Sarah's sake, I would have to watch my step and toe the line when it came to Jack. I was family to her, she was truly happy to see me, and I wanted to make sure that I wasn't a disappointment to her, or subject her to lectures for the rest of her life from Jack as to how wrong she had been about "her family." If I walked out now, she would be hurt.

As to Jack . . . well, Jack and I were headed for trouble, but I had to keep my mouth shut for Sarah's sake. But I just didn't know how many more potshots about my father I could take. Or how unhinged I'd become if he said something about my mother.

21

❖

We were bouncing along in bright sunlight one moment and then the sky suddenly turned black and opened up, hitting us with a downpour so thick I could have cut it with a knife. We couldn't see fifty feet in front of the Land Rover.

"The rainy season runs from May to February," Sarah said.

"That only leaves March and April to dry out," I said.

"Yes, and sometimes May, but you get used to it. As you can see, it's quite warm rain. You just go on doing whatever you're doing."

"Unless there's a hurricane," Jack said, grinning. "They come the second half of the year, from July to October, and have winds of over a hundred miles an hour. Sometimes they're so fierce, they destroy everything. The last big one blew away Belize Town and about everything else standing in the country."

Wonderful.

"It's all right," Sarah said, "the last killer hurricane was nearly twenty years ago."

"They're cyclical," Jack said. "We get the small ones frequently, but the big ones come about once every decade. We're just waiting for the next big one. If we survive the hurricanes, you still have to

❖

deal with the plagues of locust, froghoppers. They come in cycles, too, and attack the sugarcane."

"They look like tiny frogs," Sarah said.

"The froghoppers hit in '41, the last killer hurricane in '42. We didn't come to the colony until '46 and we've been waiting for the other shoe to drop ever since."

Wonderful.

The rain let up and we passed a cart pulled by a donkey and loaded high with sugarcane. A black man wearing a straw hat guided the donkey. He smiled and waved as we passed. Sarah waved back.

"You'll find the blackamoors are generally lazy bastards," Jack said.

"Sweetheart, I wish you wouldn't use that word. They're called Creoles, not that ugly old-fashioned word you use."

"I use it because they're lazy and stupid. I'll use a better word when they deserve my respect. I'd hire wetbacks from Mexico, they're better workers, but the colonial government is against it."

Sarah looked anxiously back at me. "The locals are neither of those things, Nick. The fact is, it's difficult for anyone to work hard in the heat and humidity of the tropics. And they certainly aren't stupid people, they just don't have the same desire to make money that we British colonists do. They prefer a simpler life. I find the culture charming."

I didn't ask Jack what the "locals" thought of him, but I suspected that I could make a good guess.

We passed two pretty young Creole teenage girls who exchanged waves and shouted greetings with Sarah as we rumbled by.

Jack glanced back at them in his rearview mirror and then sniggered to me. "One thing a young buck like you is going to enjoy, these native women are free and easy about spreading their legs."

"Jack!"

"*Jack!*" he mocked. "Okay, woman, tell the boy whether I'm lying or exaggerating."

Sarah hesitated before looking back at me, her cheeks redder

❖

than usual. "I'm afraid that he's not exaggerating. The, uh, moral customs are not exactly what they are in British society. To say the least."

"Anytime you feel like it, you just grab one of them and take her into the bushes and give her a poke."

"Jack!"

I had had no interaction with people of color in Leningrad. And while I hated the Soviet system, every school child was taught that all people were entitled to be economically and socially equal—not that it was that way in practice, of course.

My impression of Jack was that besides being uncouth and ignorant, he was the worst kind of economic exploiter, a wannabe British upper-class who had come from the lower classes economically and looked down at others because he was self-conscious about his own circumstances.

"You're going to hear some things about me," Jack said.

"Maybe we should go into that later," Sarah said.

"No, let's get it out in the open. I stand behind the Union Jack, just as I did when I served under it in the army. This place is the slum of the British Empire, but my ancestors fought to get it and I'm willing to fight anyone who wants to take it back. If they can beat me, they can have it. Me and some of the other Brits who feel the same way have formed a *posse comitatus* to help keep order."

"Our own colonial administrators are against it. They say it's taking the law into our own hands," Sarah said. "We shouldn't interfere with the way the colony is administered."

"We're not interfering, woman, we're helping."

"What's a posse comitatus?" I asked.

"It's an old Latin expression. I think it means 'common-law posse,'" Sarah said. "It dates back to medieval times when the shire of the county had the right to call all able-bodied men to arms if it became necessary to maintain order. Jack and some of his friends want to help keep order even if the commissioner says he doesn't need the help."

"When the law can't keep order," Jack said, "we do it for them.

If it means going out at night to pound on doors and drag out bad people and punish them, that's what we do."

Pounding on the door at night. That was how my mother had described the incident in which my father had been taken away.

Jack took on new dimensions in my mind.

❖

22

❖

Sarah was right. The north was paradise compared to Belize Town. But I suspected even Siberia was farther up the rungs of hell than the colony's capital.

We arrived at the Northern District late in the afternoon, passing through Orange Walk Town and following a waterway Sarah called "New River" toward Corozal, about thirty miles downstream. The river was muddy and sluggish. A small coastal motor freighter carried freight and a few passengers along the river. I also saw dug-out canoes Sarah called "doreys," flat-bottomed boats with high flaring sides. The big canoes were loaded with goods—fruits, vegetables, even packaged and canned items—and had several rowers manning oars.

"There's lots of citrus grown around Orange Walk," Sarah said, "that's how it got its name. A 'walk' is a citrus or coconut grove."

We passed sugar plantations, row after row of green stalks an inch or two thick, some not more than a couple feet high to full grown ones fifteen to twenty feet tall.

"It's grass, you know," Sarah said.

❖

"Grass?"

"Sugarcane. It's a form of grass, even though it looks like bamboo. Bamboo is grass, too, isn't it?" she asked Jack.

He grunted affirmatively.

"New River is only about ten miles from Rio Honda, the river that's our border with Mexico," Sarah said. "Further down, our plantation runs along both sides of a branch of the river. I call it ours, but you understand, we just manage the plantation and the sugarcane processing plant for a group of investors back home, a group of Scotsmen from Glasgow. That's what many of the complaints are about, the locals say that all the money from the land ends up in Britain."

That comment caused another spiel from Jack about the lazy, stupid natives.

"That's our Achilles' heel," Sarah said, pointing at a bend in the distance after we left the main river and drove along the smaller stream that led to the plantation. "We built the sugarcane processing plant next to the stream so plantations upriver can float their cane to us in barges to be processed. Much cheaper than horse wagons or trucks. An earthquake two years ago lifted the bed of our stream so much, barges can't make it all the way down to the plant. Instead, the growers haul their cane overland to a processing plant in Orange Walk. We still process for growers who we're the closest for, but that's only a fraction of the cane we have the capacity to handle."

We passed a small village with a mishmash of shacks, some with mud walls and thatched roofs, others with clapboard and tin roofs. Some of the houses looked like they'd been walled with anything handy, from packing crates to a big tin sign advertising tonic water. None of the houses were painted.

The ground was littered with rusting empty cans, bottles, coconut husks, sugarcane debris and other trash. The entire settlement was surrounded by cane fields.

"Many of our full-time workers live here," Sarah said. "They're really lovely people, but I'm afraid their culture has a different view on how to deal with rubbish than we do. The mud-walled houses are called abodes; the ones with thatch you'll hear called 'trash' because that's how the Creoles pronounce thatch."

A tall, middle-aged Creole came out onto the road and Jack pulled over to speak to him. Jack said Samuel was his foreman.

"This is Sarah's nephew," Jack told him. "He'll be working with us."

I stepped out of the vehicle and shook hands with Samuel. He grinned at my pale white complexion.

"Better have a hat," he said. "Or you'll fry."

A mile further down, the plantation house sat a hundred feet from the road within sight of the off-shoot river, cane fields at its back and sides, and larger than most of the houses I had seen on the trip, but not as palatial as I imagined it. It was a rectangular white box, two-storied, with screened verandas in front and on the sides of the house on both the ground and second floor. The building was white, with a greenish zinc roof. Several feet off the ground, three steps led up to the entry porch. The kitchen was in back, separated by a breezeway, to keep the hot cooking fires from heating up the house.

"This is home," Sarah smiled. "It's not Tara but it's where we lay our heads at night."

"Tara?"

"Oh, you probably wouldn't know about a movie called *Gone With the Wind*. Tara was the name of the heroine's plantation house."

"I think I've heard of the movie. A tale of capitalistic exploitation of slaves." I grinned to take the edge off the remark. Actually, the only thing I knew about the movie was a conversation I overheard during a meal onboard the *Queen*.

"Well, let's have something to eat," Sarah said.

We sat in the kitchen at a table with a red-checkered tablecloth and ate cold beef sandwiches. Jack washed his down with more beer—he'd packed down five or six more during the ride home. His face was flushed and his eyes watery.

"Hope this is all right," Sarah said, showing me to a room on

❖

the first floor. "We're just above you. We don't use carpeting because the fleas love the stuff, so you're sure to hear us walking around."

"It's a palace," I told her truthfully. It was the first "room" I'd had to myself.

"We get to bed early here because we start work at the crack of dawn to beat the midday heat." She squeezed my hand. "I really am excited you're with us, Nick. You look so much like Peter, for a moment I thought I was seeing a ghost when you came down the gangplank." She paused at the door. "Don't mind Jack," she said in a low voice. "He's had a hard life. Under it all, he's a good man. He's just had a rough time of it."

Rough time? Because no one gave him money and status as a birthright? Because he had to work to be somebody? I had no sympathy for him.

Later that night I turned off my light and sat on a rocking chair out on the screened porch. I heard Jack and Sarah's footsteps above me. Their bedroom door was open to their screened porch and I could heard the murmuring of their voices as I sat in my underwear and took advantage of the cool breeze.

I must have dozed off for a while because Jack's loud voice awakened me.

"He's a charity case as far as I'm concerned, he has to earn his keep." His tone was beer-soaked.

Sarah asked him to lower his voice.

"Bitch!"

I heard the sound of a slap and froze in my chair. I didn't know what to do. I'd seen plenty of husbands and wives fight, hell, I'd seen a woman go after her husband with a vodka bottle. But they were strangers to me. *Sarah was my family.*

My first instinct was to run upstairs and beat the hell out of the bastard. My heart started to pound. I got up and went quietly back inside and lay on the bed, ignoring a net that made me claustrophobic. I was sure Sarah would be embarrassed if she knew what I had heard.

It was hard to imagine a man hitting someone like Sarah.

❖

These weren't street people, they were a respectable, middle-class—whatever they called it—couple.

And being called *a charity case,* I hadn't heard the expression before, but it wasn't hard to imagine what it meant. It was an insult. And I came from a street culture where insults were answered with blood. But I had to keep my mouth shut and my fists in my pocket. I didn't want to hurt Sarah.

I lay in bed and stared up at the dark ceiling. I was a very mature eighteen year old, not only in appearance but as a result of my struggles in life. Hell, I'd survived the 900 Days, the worst single atrocity ever inflicted upon a city and its people. I had experienced more horrors than the most tried combat veterans.

But even if I was mature in terms of some experiences, there was so much about life I still had to learn. I knew almost nothing about women other than the wonders of their anatomy. I knew they could be courageous. To Sarah, my father had been a heroic figure, but to me, my mother was the braver heart although I loved them both. What I lacked was not only how women viewed life but their relationships with men.

How could a woman permit a man to physically abuse her and not fight back—or at least walk out on the bastard?

I didn't wonder about what made some men strike women. A bully will strike anyone who they can dominate.

One thing had come clear to me: Sarah thought the colony, at least the part where she lived, was paradise. Maybe she was right. But there was a snake in every paradise.

I had found "family" in Sarah, but not a home. I had always looked out for myself and I would have to continue to do so. As much as I liked Sarah and felt her warmth, I could not stay in the house without coming into violent conflict with Jack.

There was another reason why I had to get out.

I felt an immediate affection for Sarah. I had lost everyone I loved. But I wasn't going to let my feelings for her get so strong that I wouldn't be able to handle it when I had to move on.

I would have to fend for myself, not rely on anyone.

❖

The people and places of the colony were alien to me, but in most ways, British Honduras was much less a "jungle" than Leningrad. Mosquitoes and jaguars couldn't compare to the human beasts that had preyed on people during the siege of the city, and were trivial compared to the all-controlling, suffocating and occasionally murderous bureaucracy that kept a tight stranglehold on Soviet life.

Jack's problems with colonial administrators were, as the banana boat captain would say, "a piece of cake" compared to dealing with the brutal apparatchik system in the Soviet Union. Not to pat my own back, but frankly, it was a lot tougher to be a criminal in a police state than in a free society. Besides the spy-on-spy system that permeated every level of society, the Soviet system had more "police" type personnel and no constitutional rights to get in the way of super-efficient "justice." In a country where confession was considered good for the soul, it was not inappropriate to help the tongue loosen with good old-fashioned torture.

I survived on the streets of Leningrad.

I would survive in the jungle of British Honduras.

❖

23

❖

I woke up in a sweat. I had dreamt that I was chased by a huge snake that wrapped itself around my leg and was squeezing the life out of it.

As dawn was breaking, I left the house and walked to the village where we had met Samuel. I was greeted by barking dogs and the smell of food. Smoke curled up from the houses and the smell of food stirred my stomach juices. But I wasn't going to eat until I had earned my keep.

I hung around until Samuel came out of his house. He did a double take when he saw me.

"I'm ready for work."

He stared at me in disbelief. "Work?"

"I want to work."

"What kind of work?"

"The kind you and your men do."

He shook his head. "We do field work. Englishmen don't do that sort of job."

I grinned at him. "I'm not English. I want to learn everything there is to know about sugarcane. And I want to work."

❖

His expression told me that he considered me slightly touched, but he merely grinned and shrugged and said, "Okay, okay, you want to do Creole work, you'll do Creole work."

"Can you teach me about growing sugarcane? Everything about it?"

"There are two people who know everything. God and me. And I am the only one willing to tell you." He suddenly reverted to Creole. "Too much hur-a get dey tomarra, tek time, get dey tiday. You understand?"

"If you take your time, you'll get things done faster."

"Good. Speaking Creole dey firse layson," he said, grinning.

He talked and I listened as we walked along the rows of cane. He spoke perfect English and only slipped into Creole jargon to give me practice listening.

"There are three main things we do in the fields. We call it ditching, seeding and cutting.

"The ditchers dig the trenches that bring water to the cane during the dry season. The original ditches were made by plows pulled by horses, but now your uncle, Mr. Walsh, has a small tractor that makes the ditch. But men with shovels still have to work the trenches, keeping them open.

"The seeders plant the cane. It's a funny name because we don't plant seed, it's just what we call the process. Rather than seed, we plant cuttings about so tall." He indicated about knee high. "The seeders use a measured stick, about five feet long. They lay the stick on the ground to space where they put each plant. You'll see in the fields how fast they work when they make the hole and get the stalk deep enough into it.

"We have some growing all the time, new growth coming up, mature plants being harvested. Because we have sun and rain most of the year, it grows almost all year. It takes about a year, sometimes more, for the plants to get tall enough to be harvested.

"The third job is the cutting. You see how tall the stalks grow?"

We walked up to stalks that soared two and three times my height.

"But before we can cut, the men have to burn off the leaf and

❖

branches. We don't burn the stalk which has the sugar, just the heavy growth of leaves surrounding the stalk."

"Why is that burned away?"

He counted on his fingers. "One, it makes it easier to cut the cane because we can get closer. Two, it drives out the rats. And three, it drives out the snakes."

"Snakes?"

"Cousin to the cobra. If it bites you, we just bury you where you lie."

"Leaping viper?"

"That's his cousin."

I didn't ask anymore about snakes. Some things aren't worth knowing or thinking about. Or worrying about.

"After burning away the leaves, we do the cutting."

Workers were already in fields. We stopped and watched them cutting. Workers literally attacked the cane, wading in and chopping at it, cutting the tall stalks with a machete-looking tool, a large steel blade about eighteen inches long and four or five inches wide, with a wooden handle and small hook in back. The stalks were cut close to the ground.

"There are still leaves left that we don't burn off because they're close to the stalk. They use the hook on the end of the knife to strip it of leaves. They cut the cane at the top joint and then chop it into four- or five-foot lengths. Then they bundle it so it can be hauled to the cane-processing plant."

The cutter piled the cut stalks on the ground and another worker came along, tied them in bundles and loaded them onto donkey carts for transport to the processing plant.

"Where do I start?" I asked.

"Where do you want to start?"

I was burning with nervous energy. I wanted to hit someone with Jack Walsh's face, and attacking the cane seemed like a good way to burn off my aggressions.

"Can I cut?"

"That's not a white man's job—"

"I don't care."

I wanted to learn everything there was about the work and the only way to do it was to get my hands dirty.

Samuel gave me a machete.

As I started for a line of tall stalks, he said, "Remember, my friend, the cane is important, it's more important than you or me. The money produced in the fields of Corozal and Orange Walk feeds thousands of families. Never disrespect the cane. It's what the Mexicans call the Flor de Corozal, the Flower of Corozal. You may not love it, you may grow to fear it or hate it, but never show it disrespect."

I saluted him with my machete and went for the cane.

He called after me. "And watch out for the snakes."

I waded in, like I'd seen the other workers, bending down, cutting the stalks close to the ground.

It was easy work—for a half-hour. Thirty minutes after I started I was drenched in sweat. The early-morning sun beat down on me. I took off my shirt and tied it around my head and let it drape down the back of my neck. And kept chopping.

The other men chattered in that mix-and-match Creole English they spoke as they chopped the cane. I chopped and sweated. I would have given up by now if I hadn't pushed my way in. I would have been humiliated if I quit.

The sun got hotter and I felt as if my blood was boiling.

One moment I was swaying dizzily and the next thing I knew I crashed into a pile of cut cane.

A few minutes later I sat in the shade along the river with Sarah. She had arrived just in time to see me take a nosedive.

"You have to learn to live with the heat," she said. "You wouldn't go outside in Leningrad during the winter without a coat. By the same token, you don't walk around the tropics without a hat."

She had brought me a straw hat, like the other men wore, lemonade, a jug of water, and a piece of stuffed flat bread. She wet her handkerchief with cool water and put it on the back of my neck. She smelled of sweet rose bath oil when she leaned next to me.

"What did Samuel say to you a moment ago?" I asked.

❖

"He blames himself. He said you were so energetic and determined, he forgot you were a backras."

"A what?"

"I think it's Creole for 'raw back.' It's what they call a newcomer, a white person who burns in the sun until the skin peels off." She was silent for a moment. "You left the house without joining us for breakfast."

"I wanted to get to work." I changed the subject. "This stuffed flat bread is good."

"It's called a burrito. It's a cornmeal flat bread, a tortilla, stuffed with black beans and peppers, a Mexican specialty. The Corozal area had a big influx of Indians from Mexico during the caste wars about a hundred years ago, so there's lots of corn and roasted peppers in our diet. From the Creoles, you'll get food from a West Indies culture, plenty of jerk chicken and rice and peas, but the peas are really kidney beans. And don't forget we're British when you're eating roast beef and Yorkshire pudding."

She laughed. It was a nice sound, like a small, harmonious bell.

"You'll have British, Caribbean and Mexican food all on the same day. Things are rather mixed up here. The colony is in Central America, wedged between Mexico and Guatemala, but it's more Caribbean than Latin American. They have a Creole dish here called a pepperpot, it's a mix of whatever, and that's how the colony is. Like that burrito you're eating, you'll find much of the Mexican and Creole food is spicy hot from peppers. I guess the theory seems to be that spicy food helps people in hot climates."

She paused for a moment. "Jack didn't intend for you to work in the fields. He can use an assistant, and he'd feel more comfortable with you than a Creole. He doesn't always get along well with the locals, if you know what I mean. But until you get used to the climate, you don't have to work at all. You caught both of us rather by surprise when Samuel came to the house and told us you insisted upon working in the fields."

"I like learning new things."

I avoided looking at her as I spoke. I noticed the bruise mark on her cheek which she had covered with rouge. It made my blood boil almost as bad as the sun had.

She squeezed my arm. "We really are both very happy to have you here. We haven't had children and have only ourselves for company. You're not a child, of course, but you are family and Jack is already thinking of you like a younger brother."

I kept a straight face at that one.

"When you get to know Jack better, you'll understand why he's like he is. He had a very hard childhood. His father was a laborer who earned too little and drank too much. Jack worked hard in the army for his sergeant's stripes and but it still wasn't enough for him because no matter how good he was, some wet-nosed new officer who got his commission through family connections was above him. Jack never got the chance of good schools or being an officer. It's all rather set at birth, you know.

"Running this plantation has been a godsend, giving him an opportunity to push up the ladder that he never would have gotten back home. But bad luck has plagued us. He convinced the investors to build the sugarcane processing plant, promising them they'd make more money processing cane than growing it. Things were bloody spectacular the first year and then that earthquake shifted the river."

I smiled and tried to appease her.

"I like Jack. I can see he's tough, but I'm sure he's fair. And I'm grateful that you two have let me into your house. But I have a favor to ask."

"Anything."

"I notice there are a lot of small houses, huts, that are empty."

"Those are thatch houses for the seasonal workers we need occasionally when we do major harvesting."

"I'd like to live in one."

"You don't want to be with us?"

"No, it's not that, it's just that I'd like to experience living alone for once. In the orphanage—"

"Oh, of course, you must have lived dormitory style." Her eyes searched my face for the lies. "Well, if that's what you prefer, but

❖

you still must take your meals with us. One thing about the tropics, you don't need much shelter. You just have to make sure you
kill all the scorpions and spiders. And sleep under a net. They can
drop off the ceiling and onto your face while you're sleeping. And
check for snakes. The floors are dirt, you know."

Wonderful.

Sarah and I stared at each other for a moment. Her cheeks
flushed and she gathered up her utensils and left.

AFTER SHE LEFT, I took my baked aching body back to attack the
cane. As I went to war against it, I thought about what had occurred.

For sure, it was no longer possible for me to ever live under the
same roof as my aunt.

I had found myself sexually aroused as she sat close to me.

24

❖

Early in the afternoon, Samuel tapped me on the shoulder as I hacked at cane.

"No more." He jerked his thumb up at the sky. "It's getting so hot, we'll melt down. What I tell you?"

"Tek time get dey tiday," I said.

He led me to a row of empty seasonal worker shacks. One had a roof partly covered with corrugated, galvanized metal. Samuel said it would leak less than a trash house.

"Take this one or take any one you want."

I figured there would be less poisonous insects in the metal-roofed one.

That evening after dinner, while it was still light, I took my duffle bag and a mosquito net and moved into the shack. On the wall were wilted pictures torn out of a magazine of the wedding nearly two years ago of Princess Elizabeth, the heir to the British throne, to Lieutenant Philip Mountbatten. A Bull Dog Beer sign was nailed to the front door to cover a big hole.

I lay down but couldn't sleep, my skin was on fire. Sarah gave me lotion to help with the sunburn. I rubbed more on and tried to

❖

lie down again, but it was too hot to sleep. Instead I got up and followed the sounds of music outside, into the thick vegetation beyond the rows of sugarcane. It was cooler in the brush.

I found Samuel and a group of a dozen men and women gathered around a camp fire, with another fire under a rusty oil drum in a clearing. I recognized the drum with the pipes coming out it. It was cruder, but served the same purpose as the vodka still I'd seen at the collective farm in Russia years ago.

Samuel came over grinning with a tin can in his hand. "Bush rum."

I took a sip of the moonshine. It was molten lava going down my throat. My red face turned fiery.

There was a general laugh among the group. Samuel slapped me on the back.

"You're okay, boy, you no longer a backras, we make you an honorary Creole."

We sat around the fire where meat was being roasted. The men and women tapped bottles, cans and sticks, playing an enthusiastic percussion rhythm Sarah had described as "brukdown" earlier at dinner.

More tin cans of rum and pieces of the roasted meat were passed around.

"Meat's tasty," I told Samuel.

"Gibnut," he said.

"Some kind of rabbit?"

"Rat."

Wonderful.

"Makes me feel like I'm back in Leningrad during the war," I said.

After a couple cups of the raw rum, I leaned back against the tree and let the booze relax me. I didn't feel like my skin was on fire anymore. I didn't feel *anything*.

Through dimmed lids, I watched a young woman, probably a couple years younger than me, dancing to the percussive sounds. She swayed rhythmically in front of me, giving me a seductive grin. She started slowly at first and moved into a frenzy as the mu-

❖

sic got faster. Everything shook under the short, tight-fitting cotton dress.

The music suddenly stopped and she collapsed onto her knees in front of me. Her breasts heaved as she caught her breath and her ebony skin glistened from sweat.

She got to her feet and left the clearing.

I started to get up to follow her. Samuel was suddenly in front of me.

"Drink this, Duende."

He handed me a tin cup of rum. Small dark things were floating in it but I was too far gone to care. I gulped it down and got slowly to my feet, letting the dog running around my head chasing its tail slowly subside. Samuel gave me a grin and nodded in the direction that the girl had gone.

I went into the bush, pushing through the dense vegetation. I was too drunk to question whether I would step on a snake or run into a jaguar—or have a Tommy Goff viper come flying out of a tree. I had something stronger on my mind than danger. Testosterone focused the mind on one thing, an urge that needed to be satisfied.

Following the sounds, I eventually came into a small clearing in front of a green pond. I heard her before I saw her. She came out from behind a tree and was behind me. She gave me a push that sent me flying into the water.

The water was no more than waist high. It was cool and mind-clearing and the first thing that occurred to me was that this was the second time in my life a woman had pushed me into water.

She laughed as she stood on the bank.

"You Englishmen are so easy to trick."

I smiled at her and said, "Why don't you come in and see what other tricks we have up our sleeves?"

"I don't think it's up your sleeve but in your pants that you're talking about."

She pulled her dress off over her head. Her body was young and firm, almost muscular—like Russian farm girls, she worked her whole life in the fields. The back-breaking work under the hot

❖

sun would ultimately ruin her skin and break her bones, but right now she was in her physical prime, her black skin taut and smooth.

Her breasts were round and firm, more than enough, with large, brown, oversized areolae and nipples. The mound of pubic hair had the soft sheen of Russian sable. Some females in their teens were immature but this girl was a young woman already, full-bodied, full of love and passion and wonderful promises.

She came into the water slowly, teasing me with the sight of her supple young body. She suddenly went under, coming up next to me, her hand on my firm stalk.

"It wants something," she said.

I cupped both of her firm breasts gently, savoring each one with my mouth.

She grabbed my head and pulled me hard against her breasts. "Suck harder, they won't break."

I sucked harder, then lifted her up with my hands on her buttocks, as she spread her legs apart and wrapped them tightly around my waist. I entered her quickly and easily and brought her against me, rocking her up and down, letting her clit slide back and forth on my cock. She went wild, slamming herself against me as I held her up, squeezing and giggling.

When we were spent and lay on the grass by the bank, she leaned over and nuzzled my ear. "That was amazing. You Englishmen are usually too uptight for good lovemaking."

I didn't tell her I wasn't really an Englishman. "I saw you this morning coming out of Samuel's. You resemble his wife."

"I'm her sister. I'm also Samuel's wife. Me and my babies live nearby. He has three wives."

Jesus. I had a lot to learn about the Creoles.

"You put a spell on me, Duende."

"What does that mean? Samuel called me that, too."

She laughed. "A duende is a forest creature, a magic beast that lives in the forest and tricks young girls into making love."

"I don't get it, why would he call me that?"

❖

She grabbed my left hand and held it up. "Duendes have only four fingers."

"I see, that's logical."

"I told Samuel you wouldn't need the wee-wee ants because you were a duende."

"What wee-wee ants?"

"The ones in the rum he gave you."

I sat up. "Are you telling me that Samuel put ants in my rum?"

She nodded and grabbed my stalk. "The ants are good, makes your little thing grow big and hard. But I'll tell Samuel not to do it next time. You don't need it."

Ants in my rum.

Wonderful.

❖

25

❖

Garcia's Widow, Corozal District, 1952

Sarita Garcia stood in front of the full-length mirror and examined her naked body. She was critical of what she saw, but shouldn't have been. At forty-four, her breasts, thighs and stomach were firmer than most women half her age, the silken sheen of her black ebony skin almost wrinkle free. As she stared at her body, she tried to image what she would look like if her skin was white or yellow or brown.

She slipped on a simple white cotton shift and went downstairs to the kitchen to prepare dinner, going barefooted and wearing no underclothes to take full advantage of a stingy cool breeze.

As she stirred the pepperpot—a concoction of meat and vegetables that varied in its ingredients in every household—Sarita hummed a tune she had learned as a little girl. She was preparing the dinner for Neil Lawrence, a retired English engineer known throughout the Corozal District as "Suez" because he once worked on the canal and talked incessantly about the marvel of engineering to anyone who was trapped into listening.

Suez came to dinner at least once a week and everyone assumed that they were lovers. Why else would a Englishman visit a

❖

black woman? But they were not lovers. She wasn't sure why he had never married, but she suspected that he really didn't feel any significant sexual attraction to women. Or to men, either. Sarita was wise enough in the ways of the world to realize that not all men or women were sexually motivated—why else would one become a priest or a nun?

Their lack of sexual attraction worked out well because while Sarita enjoyed their conversation and the companionship, she wasn't sexually attracted to him, either. In her culture sex was treated as a natural state of affairs, rather than something to hide in the bedroom under covers.

Early on in their relationship, more out of concern for him than any arousal on her part, after he was feeling relaxed from the Scotch he brought over with him, she had unzipped his pants and taken his penis into her hand, gently pumping it. He calmly sat and talked about the old days at the Suez Canal and drank his liquor without once looking down at what she was doing.

His penis got a bit stiff but never really erupted into a full-blown erection. After a while, she had given up and pushed it back inside his trousers and buttoned him back up again.

Neither of them ever said anything about the incident.

Suez was tall, six feet two, with a knucklebone frame, unruly brown hair and unhealthy skin blotches that looked like he was rusting. He was an intelligent person, well-traveled though rather boring—truly a British gentleman, reserved, well-mannered, but not one to show his emotions.

Even though Sarita had no true friends, and really needed none, he provided a little relief from the everyday monotony of speaking only to the workers at her sugarcane farm and tradespeople.

A widow for ten years now, her husband, Jose Garcia, had been the son of black Creoles, but she was a Garifuna. Her people, who were often called "Black Caribs" and mostly concentrated along the southern coast of the colony, spoke a different language and had a different culture than the Creoles who comprised the majority of the colony's population.

Most Garifuna stayed with their own people along the south-

❖

ern coast, and she had no near neighbors of her kind in the northern area. That made her both unique and different from her Creole, Mexican and British colonial neighbors in many ways.

The Garifuna were a proud, independent and sometimes obstinate people and she shared the traits. What made them different from other New World peoples of African heritage was their ethnicity. The Garifuna prided themselves on not being the descendants of slaves. Their descendants were Africans captured and shipped to the Americas for the slave trade who revolted and fled into the jungle on St. Vincent island in the Caribbean. They intermarried with Carib Indians who also had refused to submit to Europeans.

That ethnic heritage, rebellious African and Amerindian, created a unique race of people whose skin was black but who did not identify with the black culture of other Caribbeans with African blood.

There was another quality that separated the Garifuna from the others—their connection to the world of ancestral spirits. Voodoo Lady, Witch Woman, were names applied to her by Creole neighbors who neither understood the Garifuna *dugu* ceremonies nor had any knowledge that she was in fact a *buyai*, a spirit medium able to make contact with the other world.

People who accused her of being in contact with the spirit world knew only half the truth. The dugu ceremony was performed to contact ancestors. Sarita was a buyai and could perform the traditional ceremony, but for a different reason. She contacted the spirit of her husband and enjoyed sex with it.

She would often lay in bed at night, naked on top of the sheet, close her eyes and begin to utter words that her aunt, a renowned buyai, taught her. The words would come faster and faster, until they were a hum. At some point the words were no longer spoken aloud, but swirled round-and-round dizzily in her head.

Once the words took on a life of their own and no longer needed her to utter them, she would rise from her body, up to the dark ceiling, and look back down at her naked form on the bed and watch her own hands touch her naked breasts and move down between her legs.

❖

Then Jose, her dead husband, would appear by the bed, naked, his powerful manhood erect. To her eye, it was twice the length and thickness of the Englishman's.

As she watched from above, Jose would slowly run his lips down her body, starting from her neck, caressing her breasts, sucking each nipple in his mouth, teasing her belly button. She would spread her legs and arch them back as he worked his way down to her pubic hair and kiss the swollen lips between her legs. And as he used to do when they made love, his lips would travel back up her body, leaving her laughing and shuddering from delight, until he found her mouth, when he would tell her that he was sharing the taste of her sweet cunt . . .

She slammed the dough she was kneading for flat bread on the counter. What did she need a new husband for anyway when she had a ghost lover that raped her in her sleep?

Jose Garcia had been well known in the Corozal District as a good businessman, good by the colony's definition that he made money and usually wasn't particular about how he did it. He inherited a very small sugarcane farm from his parents that he tripled in size, though it still wasn't large enough to be called a plantation. But his most profitable business venture had been in trade goods, especially one item: rum.

Like many Creoles in the sugarcane growing region, Garcia, and his father before him, made bush rum for themselves and their friends. Sugarcane and rum went hand-in-hand.

During the processing of the cane, molasses of several different qualities was produced, the higher qualities of which were good for making rum. After obtaining molasses from the cane processing plant—by hook or by crook—it was a fairly simple process to make rum with a small distiller hidden in the bushes, away from the prying eyes of the police, tax and health authorities.

When Prohibition hit the United States and bootleg booze became a high-ticket item in the early 1920s, the enterprising Garcia turned a barn on his property into a real distillery and began producing it in enough quantity to profitably ship it north on a banana boat to Biloxi, Mississippi.

❖

In 1925, he met and married a seventeen-year-old Garifuna girl who was considered the best-looking woman of her ethnicity in the colony. It was a happy event both sexually and economically, because Sarita was not only warm and sensuous, she had a knack for making rum. After she became the official rum blender of her husband's distillery, Garcia's rum became a favorite among the imbibers of illegal spirits in the States.

The end of Prohibition in 1933 brought that gravy train to a halt. The Garcias had not become rich from the rum business, there was too much overhead due to U.S. Coast Guard seizures and too many bribes to pay, but it had made enough money to increase the size of their sugarcane farm until it was no longer a family affair but a business one.

Unfortunately for Sarita, who didn't plan on becoming a widow anytime soon, and even more unfortunately for Garcia, who didn't plan to die young, instead of retiring on his laurels and sugarcane fields, Garcia was attracted to the darker side of business.

Knowing that there was a small, but profitable market for marijuana in the States, he went into the farming of that plant. It was bad enough that he risked a jail sentence at the hands of the British commissioner, but he made the mistake of luring a Florida "importer" away from a Mexican gentleman who grew a great deal of the plant across the Rio Honda and shipped it north from Chetumal, the Mexican town across the bay from Corozal. That caused the Mexican to one day come across the border and drive the ten miles to Corozal Town where Garcia was drinking in a dingy Creole bar that called itself the Mayfair Pub. He put a bullet between Garcia's eyes and was back across the border before dinnertime.

Sarita buried Jose, let the marijuana field turn back into jungle, kept the still closed, and remained living on the sugarcane farm. She had no interest in business and the farm was enough for her to handle. She also had no interest in getting married again, having had a husband that she loved, lusted and respected. Besides, there weren't any candidates around that could replace him.

She was not that lonely and managed to fulfill much of her sexual needs with her buyai talents.

❖

She heard the front screen door open and Suez's greeting as he came in.

"In the kitchen," she yelled.

"Brought you a little gift," he said, giving her the usual peck on the cheek. He handed her a can of salted herring. "Had a whole case of my favorite brand shipped over from Liverpool."

"Thank you." Just what she needed—salty canned fish when she could buy mouthwatering fresh fish every day of the week in Corozal.

She fixed him a whiskey and soda from the ingredients he brought.

"I want you to meet someone. That young man, Cutter. He might be of help to you."

"Cutter?"

"Nick Cutter, Jack and Sarah Walsh's nephew."

"Oh, yes, I've seen him in town. He came to Corozal two or three years ago, didn't he?"

"Right, rescued from the Reds, Russian born, British father, speaks the King's English like he was raised proper."

"Why do you want me to meet him?"

"He's an enterprising lad, that one, smart. They say he knows more about sugarcane farming and processing than Jack Walsh."

That didn't surprise her. She didn't like Jack Walsh, found his brand of white superiority and quarrelsome personality offensive. Her opinion was one commonly held. He was a big man in the area because he managed the biggest sugarcane plantation and a processing plant, but that gave him power, not respect. She knew what Nick looked like, a pale-skinned, blond young man who appeared to be physically fit.

"Why do you think he can help me?"

"Well, you're always complaining about how you hate to run your farming operation, letting it deteriorate because you're not motivated to keep an eye on the workers so they don't take advantage of you. The Cutter lad might be just the answer. I have it from the horse's mouth that he and Jack Walsh grate on each other—"

"Is there anyone Walsh doesn't rub wrong?"

❖

"Personally, I find the man objectionable on many levels. Arrogant ass, if you know what I mean. One of those men who give colonials a bad name, not good at all in a world in which the Union Jack's been attacked by the locals everywhere. To tell you the truth, I think he's one of those lower-class chaps who resents the upper classes. He probably comes from a Labour Party background but votes the Conservative Party ticket to identify himself with his betters."

"I don't like Jack Walsh, haven't since the day I met him. His wife appears to be nice, too quiet and forgiving, from what I hear. I haven't met the boy. Do you think he's trustworthy?"

"Yes, within reason. I understand he picked up some bad habits under the Reds, but nothing for a friend to worry about, rather reminds me a little of your late husband, a sharp trader, always ready to make a deal, not always concerned about the source of the goods, if you know what I mean. But I'm told by everyone who does business with him that you can count on his word. I got to know the young man making repairs to machinery at Walsh's processing plant. Nick watched every move I made and I'm sure now he can fix that machine himself if it acts up again."

"Have you spoken to him about my place?"

"Actually, he's the one who brought up the subject. Heard from talk among the cane workers that you've been having problems getting the most out of your land. Told me he could run your operation in his spare time and make it worthwhile for both of you."

"Well, then perhaps I should speak to him."

❖

26

❖

Three years in the tropics had left my blond hair almost bleached white and my skin the color of a dull penny. I moved from the seasonal-worker shack after a few months and bought a bungalow from a Brit who went home, claiming he preferred the cold damp of the Isles over the wet-warmth of the tropics. I drove a war surplus American army jeep that I bought on a foray to Mexico City. I still did work for Jack, second to him running the farm and the sugar-cane processing plant, but I had some of my own things going.

My present interest was pre-Columbian artifacts.

It was a natural for the area. The incredible Mayan civilization had occupied southern Mexico and most of Central America, with British Honduras in the center of it, for two or three thousand years. I wasn't much on book learning, but Sarah took an interest in history.

It was hard to imagine that much of the region had been heavily populated by a race of people in many ways more advanced than we were a thousand years ago. Sarah told me that the Mayans built great cities, constructed roads, had sky observatories, and had a calendar more accurate than the one used today.

❖

Sounded like the Romans, except with a lot of jungle.

Then they up and disappeared one day, leaving behind stone cities that got swallowed by jungle, and creating one of those mysteries of the ages that university types loved to debate.

Personally, I didn't think there was much mystery about *why* they left—the damn heat and mosquitoes, snakes and crocodiles were good enough reason.

While I wasn't particularly versed in Mayan history, I had become something of an authority on Mayan antiquities—at least enough to tell the real ones from the fakes.

There were Mayan sites all over Central America and the Yucatán, most of them still covered in jungle. In the Corozal and Orange Walk districts of the colony, every now and then some farmer who was digging a hole to plant yams would come across a piece of stone artwork. Most of it was pretty rough, but once in a while someone came up with a real quality piece.

Naturally, all antiquities had to be turned over to the government. And it was just as natural that few pieces ever were. There was a healthy trade in pre-Columbian artwork, and I had become one of the chief traders in the contraband. Until I got into the trade, it was pretty hand-to-mouth. Most of the stuff got sold for peanuts by the finder, usually to a shop owner. Every couple of months, a dealer from the States would wander through and buy several pieces.

I took the trade door-to-door, putting out the word that I would come to anyone—anywhere, anytime—who had a piece to sell. My contact for resale was an art dealer in Boston I'd met when he was making one of his annual trips in search of antiquities. I packaged the items in parcel boxes and gave them to a deck officer on the sugar boat that hauled most of our production to a plant at Galveston. There, the deck officer mailed the parcel to the Boston art dealer.

The local police called the business smuggling rather than private enterprise, and I had to watch my back.

I was in front of the bungalow negotiating for the head of a Mayan god with an Yucatán Indian when a Morris Minor came into the yard, kicking up dust. It was Sarah, who took as much offense to rumors of my smuggling activities as the local police did.

"Deal," I told the Indian, quickly giving him the money and escorting him to his donkey.

Sarah followed me into the house where I set the head on a table and covered it with a shirt I had taken off earlier and tossed nearby.

"Lemonade?" I asked, already grabbing the pitcher to pour.

"You told me you weren't involved in smuggling."

"True, but—"

"I boasted to Jack about your work preserving artifacts and he told me you were a bloody smuggler. You lied to me."

"No-no-no, listen to me." I gave her my best boyish grin. "I don't consider it smuggling. I'm working to preserve the great Mayan heritage by getting artifacts out of the jungle where they're deteriorating and into the hands of museums where they'll be safe. I'm like those countrymen of yours who stole—uh, I mean, *preserved*— all those antiquities of Greece and Egypt that ended up in the British museum."

"You're a liar and a scoundrel." She said it without malice.

I laughed.

"I really don't know where you learned such things. Your father was such an honest, idealistic, intellectual—"

"I'm sorry to say that my father didn't live long enough to pass on any of his fine qualities."

"I'm sorry, Nicky, I didn't mean to be hard on you."

Okay, I deliberately played the sympathy card, I knew my father was a soft spot with her. She was the only one I let call me Nicky. It sounded like a little kid's name, but it also came with the warmth of family. Jack and I were barely on civil terms. I kept away from him as much as possible even when working at the farm and plant, but I had grown even fonder of Sarah. I was careful to never show anything but familial respect for her. The closest thing to intimacy was a friendly peck on the cheek. I still went to dinner at their house a couple of times a month, but I did that for Sarah's sake.

❖

"You're not hard on me. I deserve it. I try to walk the straight and narrow, but I just keep slipping off." That was a lie, of course. I didn't slip off, I jumped off with both feet every chance I got.

"Nicky, I—I—"

"What is it?" I asked, letting my eyes linger on her longer than I should have.

"I don't know. You and Jack seem to constantly be on the outs."

I shrugged. "We get along okay."

"Like a cat and dog. I think he's jealous of you."

"What?"

"I really do. You seem to succeed at everything you do and manage to do it without antagonizing everyone around you. Poor Jack just can't help offending people."

I wanted to say that "poor Jack" would be less abrasive to people if he didn't try to bully them, but I never badmouthed him to her. I wished she'd kick him in the butt, but she loved him and seemed to have endless patience and tolerance for his transgressions.

"There's something else you should know."

"Yeah . . . ?"

"I think the police commissioner is extremely interested in your, uh, 'artifact preservation' activities."

"Uh huh. Where'd you hear that?"

"A little birdie told me."

She avoided my eyes.

It was Jack. The bastard had hollered me off to the cops.

"I've got to get back. I'll take this and make sure it gets to the local preservation society."

She grabbed the head and I grabbed her. She held onto the head and twisted in my arms. The button flew off the top of her light dress. Her face came around to me and for a stunning moment we were only a kiss apart.

I found myself kissing her, pressing her breasts again my bare chest. At first she was stiff, then suddenly her lips met mine hungrily.

She broke away and staggered back, locking eyes with me.

"I—I—" She dropped the head and ran out the door.

❖

I stood still, not moving a muscle. I didn't know what to think. Then I cursed myself.

The last thing I wanted to do was complicate Sarah's life. It was a stupid move on my part. I didn't want to hurt her.

Damn, damn, damn.

I was all stirred up. I took some deep breaths to get my breathing going and my testosterone cooled off.

I picked up the head. It wasn't damaged. The Mayans knew how to make them so they lasted.

A more pressing matter than my sexual transgressions was at hand. Jack had ratted me out to the police, so I could expect an official visit at any time. Things went slow in the colony, but it was inevitable that the local police inspector would get it ultimately into gear and pay me a visit.

One option would be to simply get rid of the incriminating evidence, but I had too much into it—and was too innately greedy—to get rid of my stock in trade. I grabbed a fisherman's net that Suez and I used to drop into the bay and drag behind his boat as we drank beer and talked about "old times." I filled the net with the four artifacts I had and took them out to a pond a hundred meters behind my bungalow. I tied one of the lines from the net to a limb that hung out into the water and tossed the bundle into the pond. It sank out of sight in the dark green water. The local inspector wasn't a rocket scientist and it would take at least someone capable of reaching the moon to figure out that my hoard was stashed in the murky waters.

I went back into the house, completely satisfied with my deception, wondering only if the crocodiles out at the pond would eat stone.

❖

27

❖

A few days later I was in Corozal making a deal on another artifact that I was helping preserve for prosperity when I got a message from Jack that there was mechanical trouble at the sugarcane processing plant.

I hadn't given up the artifact business, but the police interest in my activities—despite the fact the inspector found nothing when he made a search—had cooled the trade, which left me flapping around, looking for another way to make money. I still worked for Jack, helping him run the plantation and processing plant, but it was a part-time job for me for two reasons—he didn't pay me much, and I avoided too much direct contact with him simply because I didn't like him. Now that I knew he'd hollered me out to the authorities, I liked him even less.

One of the first lessons I learned in gangs on the streets of Leningrad was to always stand back-to-back when me and my mates were in a fight with outsiders. Jack had never learned the lesson. It never bothered him that getting me into the police commissioner's clink might embarrass his wife because I was "family."

❖

The only reason I wasn't in the clink was because Sarah had warned me.

Hanging around Jack really had diminishing returns. The more I had gotten to know him, the less I liked him. He treated Sarah badly and made no bones about the fact he had girlfriends. I didn't care what he did in private, but when I'd see him at a Corozal bar with a couple whores hanging onto him, I wanted to kick his ass for not having any class.

Suez's pickup was already there when I pulled into the plant. The retired engineer was good at what he called bailing-wire-and-chewing-gum repairs on the plant equipment. I hopped out of the jeep and waved to the outside workers, returning their greetings as I hurried toward the plant entrance.

The plant was a mile downriver from the heart of the plantation, where Jack and Sarah's living quarters were located, and had been positioned to take advantage of plantations with river access. It was operating at half-capacity since the earthquake lifted the river bottom. I'd come to think of the earthquake as an attitude adjustment God gave Jack. But it didn't improve the bastard's disposition.

The plant was a large, rambling, awkward set of tin buildings that looked like a barn and a couple sheds shoved together, set at a wide point in the river where there was room for river barges to tie up.

The cane came in by cart, truck and barge, where it was processed into raw sugar and grades of molasses for export.

Already trimmed in the field, the pieces of cane were put into a cutter that had revolving blades that chopped and shredded it. The cutter was the problem at the moment. Suez had told Jack repeatedly that the engine that ran it needed to be replaced, but Jack kept having him patch it up rather than lower the plant's poor cash flow by spending the money for a new machine.

I liked Suez. He was very British, proper, stuffy, but had a good dry—and wry—sense of humor. Most of all, I liked his range of technical knowledge. I was always fascinated about the way things work, and he knew, as I suppose the English grandfather I never met knew, how one piece of something fitted into another and did this or that. I spent many hours at his place, learning about machines and equipment. He could be a big bore, though, talking about his work on maintenance of the Suez Canal during the 1930s and the war years. His backyard was laid out as a miniature Suez Canal with ponds for the Mediterranean and Red Sea. Circling it was a model train he called the Orient Express.

He retired after the war and came to the colony to live with his cousin, a widow. She died before his feet touched land and he moved into her house and soon became a colonial character.

After I bought the army surplus jeep, he guided me as I literally field-stripped the jeep's engine and put it back together so that it worked *almost* as well as it did before. Jack didn't know it, but I could have repaired any machinery in the plant. I didn't let him know my mechanical talents because I would have gotten my hands dirty for nothing, he wouldn't have even given me his gratitude.

Even though most people called him Suez, which was how I thought of him, I was always polite and called him Mr. Lawrence. He never asked me to call him by his first name and, in fact, I didn't know what it was.

I found him up to his knees in grease and curses by the cutter.

"That bad?" I asked.

"Worse."

"Terminal?"

"Worse. It will work for another couple months and your uncle will call me again to fix it."

The sugarcane stalks were brought through big double-doors and into the plant where they were fed into the cutter. After they were cut and shredded, they were fed into a crusher, where they were squeezed to get the juice out.

Once the sugar juice was extracted, the vegetable residue left from the crushed cane, bagasse, was allowed to further dry. It would become important in the process.

The sugarcane juice had to be boiled at several stages and that took heat. It would have been too expensive to import petroleum to

❖

fire the boilers. Fortunately, the dry bagasse burned well, thus the sugarcane not only provided the essence to be extracted, it even provided the energy source for the extraction. Without the bagasse, wood, coal or petrol would have to be used, and that would make processing the cane much more expensive.

From the crusher, the juice flowed to a tank with another fire heating it, then to a second heated tank, this one an evaporator that had an opening at the top that allowed steam to escape and the juice to condense into a thicker syrup. At that point we added already processed sugar granules to the mixture. The granules acted as seed crystals, which helped the syrup crystallize.

When as much sugar as possible had crystallized in the syrup, the mixture was spun in a centrifuge, which separated the remaining syrup from the raw sugar crystals, separating out the crystals and allowing them to dry.

Bags were filled with the crystals, which were pale brown to yellow colored. This was the raw sugar, which was stacked on barges that were towed to Boliso Town where the bags were loaded onto freighters. At the receiving end, usually Britain and the States, the raw sugar was remelted and processed at a refinery into retail and wholesale baking products.

Sugar is sweet, but there was a byproduct of it that interested me even more.

Molasses.

For some people, it's the syrup you put on pancakes, use in cookies and candy or even put in feed for cattle. For me, molasses had more exotic—and profitable—aspects. I got the idea from the local bush-rum stills and the vodka still I saw in Russia.

Why not make vodka from sugarcane juice?

When sugar was boiled at the plantation's processing plant, some of the juice extracted didn't turn into sugar crystals, but stayed in syrup form. The juice was called molasses. It got separated in several stages, creating different grades of molasses that were put to different uses.

The first separation of molasses from the sugar crystal process created molasses that was the sweetest and lightest in color. This was considered a premium product. One use of it was to make fine rums.

The second extraction created a darker molasses—also used in rum, candy making and cooking, but wasn't as sweet and light as the first extraction, and not considered as high quality.

The final separation of sugar crystals from liquid created a dark, heavy, thick and sticky syrup with little sugar content. This was called blackstrap molasses. Blackstrap and the rest of the residue was mostly turned into animal feed and sold to farmers. There wasn't a big market for it among the poor farmers of the colony, and it was too cheap to export, so a lot of it was just poured into our fields under Jack's theory that it would make a good fertilizer.

Bush rums were made by Creoles out of anything they could find to create the product. Much of it wasn't true rum but *tafia*, made from impure molasses.

Now that smuggling pre-Columbian antiquities had been reduced to a crawl, I had to figure out a way to make money. And that wasn't easy in the colony. Life was hard. This wasn't Hong Kong or Bermuda. No tourists came here to spend money. We didn't have oil wells or fine resorts or anything else that made money. Sugarcane, bananas and logging were not the games of kings, but of absentee British owners who tried to get as much work for as little money out of the locals. I couldn't make a fortune working at the plantation—any real money to be made was kept by Jack and he wasn't getting rich. He spent half his time pleading with the Scottish investors not to sell out, promising them things were going to get better.

The idea of turning sugarcane into vodka had been the reason I had Suez talk to Garcia's widow.

Suez stood up, wiping his greasy hands on cloth. "Throw the switch," he told Allen, the Creole shift foreman.

Allen threw the switch and the cutter choked, coughed and spit into action.

I walked Suez to his car.

❖

"By the way, Nick, I talked to Garcia's widow about you," he said.

"Does she have a first name? Everyone calls her Garcia's widow."

He thought for a moment. "Sarita. She'd like to meet you. She's tired of hassling with the workers. She has a few good year-round people, but the ones she brings in for the harvest cheat her. Just drop by and say hello so she can get your measure."

"Good. Thanks, I appreciate it." I could have approached the woman myself, but figured it was better if Suez talked to her first. Jack had alienated so many people in the colony, I didn't know what my reception would be if someone like Suez wasn't vouching for me. Especially when she found out I had little actual interest in running her farm.

"What's your uncle going to say when he finds out you're running the widow's operation?"

"I don't care what he says. He's gotten enough of my sweat."

"I heard he hit another worker. He's getting a mean reputation, drinking and—"

"Fucking." I said what Suez was too polite to say.

"That too. Well, I have to get back to my own digs and get some work done. Drop over in a day or two and I'll take you for a ride in my Bulldog. I can fly us almost anywhere in the Caribbean."

"I'll wait until you have parachutes."

His Bulldog was the remains of a two-seater plane he bought that had been used in government mapping operations before it did a nosedive on takeoff. He had put it back together, but I wasn't anxious to find out if all the screws and bolts were tight.

Jack pulled up in his Land Rover before I'd made it back into the plant.

"Suez been here?"

"He just left. It's been patched again."

"Fucking climate, people rust in it, no wonder equipment never lasts. Did you take care of the problem with the southwest fields? I want those lazy bastards fired."

"I took care of it." Without firing anyone. The workers weren't lazy—they were offended by Jack calling them "blackamoors." He was the only one who used the demeaning phrase for black Creoles. No one ever told him that you can get more work out of people with sugar than vinegar.

"Don't let it happen again. Next time it does, I'm going to take it out of your hide."

I could smell the booze on him. And the cunt. He'd been out fucking around behind Sarah's back again, this time in broad daylight on a work day.

I blew. "What did you say? You're gonna what?" I squared off to him with my fists clenched. "I'm tired of taking your shit. I'm outta here. You keep it up and no one will work with you."

"I don't need you. Up yours. Go on, get out."

He stomped off and I went to my jeep. I drove like a maniac to the plantation. I no longer had any personal items there, but I knew family dinners were going to be a thing of the past and I had to say something to Sarah. I hadn't been able to face her since I kissed her in my bungalow.

She was on her knees working in the garden when I pulled in and hopped out of the jeep. She looked up and smiled as I came over.

"Nicky, I was just thinking about you. I got the nicest beef roast—" She stopped when she saw my face. "What's wrong?"

"I just quit."

She got to her feet and brushed off her knees.

"I was wondering when it was going to happen. Jack is a bit difficult—"

"No, he's impossible." I almost said he was a "prick" but Sarah wasn't the kind of woman that deserved such language. "I'm sorry, Sarah. You've been really terrific to me, but I couldn't take it anymore."

"I understand. What are you going to do?"

"I don't know, I have a few things in the fire."

She shook her head. "You're not going to—"

I grinned and shook my head. "I'm all through with the Mayan stuff. It's the straight and narrow for me now." It was better to lie to a nice person like Sarah than worry her.

"I spoke to the police inspector about you," she said. "I told him you were a good boy, just a little wild."

We both laughed at the description.

She sighed. "Well, you can still come to dinners—"

"You know I can't."

Her cheeks blushed because my comment cut both ways.

"Oh God, I'll miss your pretty face at dinner."

She gave me a hug and I held her tight. She suddenly broke loose.

"Jack!"

The fucker had pulled up and was staring at us through the windshield of the Rover.

I squeezed Sarah's hand and gave her a peck on the cheek. "I'll see you later."

Jack got out of the Rover and slammed the door as I walked toward him and the jeep. His face was red and his eyes ugly with rage.

"There's nothing between Sarah and me, and you know that," I said. "You lay one hand on her and I'm going to beat the shit out of you."

"You're gonna what?"

I got into his face. "You heard me, you prick. I'm not a ninety-pound woman. You hit Sarah and you'll be shipped back home in a pine box."

I got into the jeep and left before I did anything I would regret. I hadn't lied to Jack, though, when I said I'd kill the sonofabitch if he hit Sarah. I was that sick of him and his bullshit.

Instead of heading home, I turned toward the farm of Garcia's widow.

❖

28

❖

"You know I'm Garifuna," she said.

We were walking the farm. It was considered a big farm, but only a fraction the size of the plantation that Jack ran. Another difference was that the plantation was owned by half a dozen investors while Sarita Garcia's farm belonged to her alone. It wasn't a big enough place to get rich on, but it could provide a good living if it was managed correctly.

"Yes, I know, it's a mixture of Carib Indians and African slaves."

"No, not slaves. Our ancestors escaped from the slave ships and fought the slave owners until they were granted their freedom. That is the difference between us and the Creoles; they are descendants of slaves, we never submitted."

Suez had told me about the Garifuna, and I had also heard stories about her from others—people called her "Voodoo Lady" because her people claim to be able to connect to the spirit world. But the only spirits I was interested in were the ones that came out of a bottle when you drank from it.

Personally, I didn't care what they called her. All I knew was

❖

that she was the most sensuous women I had seen in the region. There were many good-looking Creole girls around, a few Mexican ones also, but none of them stirred my furnace like this woman. I'd seen her before at the marketplace in Corozal, but hadn't gotten a real close look at her. Suez thought she was in her forties, but to me she looked much younger than that. I couldn't help but notice her lush body, full and succulent, as I was walking up to her porch when she came out of the house, barefooted and wearing the standard loose, cotton shift that permitted some ventilation in the humid climate.

As we walked, I pointed to a section of sugarcane that was scrawnier and paler than the tall, green stalks they should have been.

"You've got too much water. The water table's too high. You need ditches to draw off some of it."

"Yes, my husband used to do that with some of the fields, I remember him talking about too much water in some places, not enough in other places. You understand, I have little interest in the farm. My family says I should sell it and move back with them on the south coast, but I have been here for over half of my life. Besides, the weather is hotter there." She smiled. "The mosquitoes are bigger there, too."

"It's going to take a bit of work, getting the place operating again as it should. I'd be willing to manage it for you for a percentage of the harvest."

"Yes, that would be fine, but why?"

"Why what?"

"Why do you want to do it?"

I stopped and faced her. "That's a strange question. I'm an experienced sugarcane field manager, I'm out of a job." I shrugged. "Why not?"

She stared at me, her eyes examining me. "You are a very young man, but you have old eyes."

"I'm getting wrinkles?"

"No wrinkles. Your face is young, and perhaps to some women you would be called handsome."

❖

"Thanks."

"But your eyes are old. My husband's eyes were that way, even when his face was young. He had seen much in life, did much, and it aged his soul while his face remained young."

"You know I'm not British, not really."

"Yes, Russian, they say, but I don't know anything about your people. Suez says they are cruel, violent and dangerous, but that you're more English than Russian. I don't know about your people, but I do know that even though you are still young, you have been involved in many things. So I ask you again. Why do you come to me and offer to help run my small, poor farm? You can make more money smuggling Indian curios, can you not?"

"Christ, you are a witch. Did your husband ever get away with lying to you?"

"My husband lied to me only once. And I told him that if he did it again, I would cut off something that was lower than his nose."

This was not a woman I wanted to screw—financially, at least. There was a mystic quality about her, a spiritualism that supported the allegations that she was a witch, but there was also a toughness. Mr. Garcia had no doubt walked the line when it came to her.

I steered her toward an old tin barn.

"That was your husband's distillery, wasn't it?"

"Yes."

"Mind if I take a look?"

We pulled open the tall double doors at both ends to let in light and air. Holes in the ceiling let in sunlight and no doubt plenty of rain. I walked around the vats and condenser pipes. Everything seemed to still be in place. Some pipes were rusty, but the vats themselves were not. They appeared to be made of a high quality metal, certainly better than the battered old pots cane workers used in their bush-rum stills.

"It looks like it's all still together. Probably usable?" I asked.

"With some work, yes."

I was certain I could get Suez to help me get the equipment running. It was far less complicated than the sugarcane machinery. There were few moving parts, mostly just copper tanks, piping and burners.

"You know a little about distilling rum," she said.

"Not really."

She gave me a curious look. "I've heard that you invested in a bush-rum distillery with Samuel, Walsh's foreman. Been selling the moonshine to bars in Corozal and Orange Walk."

"Then why did you ask me?"

"To see how big a lie you would tell."

I cleared my throat. *Bloody damn witch.* "All right, I know a *little* about distilling. But this is a professional operation. And I promise not to lie to you—if you promise not to read my mind anymore."

She smiled as she waved at the equipment. "Garcia tried to produce rum with a forty-five percent alcohol content, but often it was higher. There are three processes to distilling. Fermented molasses and water is heated in the still." She pointed at a boiler tank. "We use bagasse to boil the liquid, just as you do at the sugarcane plant. The boiling turns the liquid into vapor, it goes through the condenser . . ."

"The boiling is done at precise temperatures to increase the alcohol content, I know."

I also knew that molasses was allowed to ferment to increase its alcohol content before it was distilled to increase the alcohol percentage. Rum with a forty-five percent alcohol level, called "ninety proof" in some countries, was pretty average.

"I've heard that your late husband's rums were extremely good."

"He called his original rums kill-devil after a rum made by slaves in the early days of sugarcane production in the West Indies. It was not high quality, but I worked with him on giving it good taste. Good rums are like good whiskeys or any other fine liquor— they are aged and blended. Garcia was an impatient man—his rums came out of the distillery and into the bottle, sometimes with a high enough alcohol content that you could burn swamps with them."

"That was back during American Prohibition, wasn't it, the 1920s."

"Up to 1933, that's when the Americans legalized alcohol again."

"It wasn't profitable to operate the distillery after that?"

"The colony is a very poor place, poor even in comparison to its neighbors and the Caribbean islands we are most culturally connected with." She shrugged. "Half the rum consumed is made by bush distilleries. And in those days, when my husband was alive, the colonial administrator was a teetotaler who discouraged rum production; he thought demon rum was bad for the 'natives.'"

I laughed with her. I had a simple solution for uptight guys like the late administrator—getting laid. There was nothing like a good fuck to relax a man and soften his worldview about liquor and lust.

"Yes," she smiled, "I saw his wife once. Both of them looked like they wore pajamas to bed. In the tropics."

Christ. The woman was a mind reader.

"It's too bad, though, that Garcia didn't try to stay in the legitimate end of the business. Our brew had obtained a good reputation as a moonshine. I always thought we should have sold it as a premium rum rather than just bootleg, but Garcia was as much of a criminal as a businessman." She smiled. "You remind me of him, his business methods."

I took that to be a compliment—of sorts. I thought it was odd that she referred to her husband by his last name.

"So that is why you want to work my sugarcane," she said, "you want to distill rum."

"I understand that the colonial administration is now more worried about unemployment than drunkenness and it's easier to get a distillery license."

"True, true, but why does the colony need another distillery? The ones that are already here make little money."

"I was more interested in export," I said.

"Export? You think colony rum could compete against the fine rums made in Barbados, Puerto Rico, Jamaica? Those rums are aged for years, sometimes up to ten years, often in expensive oak barrels. Even after that, they're blended with other rums to make a fine product. This little distillery turns out poor quality rum,

❖

that's all. It would cost a great deal of money to turn it into a distillery that could compete with them. Most of the rum distribution is controlled by the West Indies cartel, so you're not even competing against individual brands, but by a cartel as powerful as some small countries."

"I don't plan on competing with anyone. Your husband successfully turned out a product—"

"During the American Prohibition, a time when people would have drunk toilet water if you told them it was ninety proof. And it was perfectly illegal. Garcia was a better business person than me. I thought our rum was good and should be sold legitimately, but he knew how difficult it would have been to break into the market, that's why he stayed with bootlegging and went into another business after the moonshine business dried up."

"Well, I plan to be perfectly illegal, too." I grinned at her. "Besides, I plan to make vodka."

I finally got a surprised look from her. I might as well have told her I planned to distill petrol.

"Vodka? What is that?"

"A liquor you don't find in places like British Honduras, or even Mexico or the Caribbean. It's big in some parts of Europe, Russia and the rest of the Soviet Union, Poland, Sweden—it's even getting popular in the States."

"What does it taste like?"

"The best vodka has no taste. It's clear, tasteless and odorless."

She wrinkled her nose. "Who would want to pay for a drink that has no taste or smell?"

"Millions of people, actually. Vodka is popular straight, what the British call 'neat.' But like Mexican tequila and some rums, it can also be used as a base liquor, meaning that it's used as the alcoholic base for mixed drinks."

She shook her head. "This is a poor colony—"

"No, actually I'm not talking about selling it in the colony, not in any significant quantity. I have a contact in the States, in a city called Boston, north of New York. The man's an antique dealer, but his family's in the liquor business. If I can make vodka, bottle it

❖

and give it labels that claim it's made in Moscow, he can distribute it in the States."

"I see, it's another form of bootlegging."

I grinned. "You can call it that."

"What do you make vodka from?"

"Molasses from sugarcane. It's not exactly the preferred ingredient, in Russia they prefer rye, wheat, potatoes, but even molasses can be used. It's all done in the distilling. Once we get a clear liquid, with about forty percent alcohol and as little taste as possible, we've done our job."

"But people who drink vodka will be able to tell it's not as good as other brands, or the real brand that you're labeling it with."

"No, they won't, because it's not being sold retail. My friend's company sells liquor to bars and restaurants, and will sell it as a mix only. No one will be able to tell the difference. They'll get the vodka at half of what they pay for it shipped over from Europe, the bars will be happy because they're buying it cheap and charging for the good stuff, and it's not bootlegging under American law."

"Just what Garcia did," she said. "You know how my husband died, don't you? One of his under-the-table business deals went sour. But I don't suppose there is anything I can say to stop you?"

"You can run me off the place."

She shook her head. "And miss all of the excitement? And the nice music and good food at your wake?"

"I have a question," I said. "Rum is a lot like vodka. You can drink it straight or use it as a mix. In fact, most people like it as a mix or with different ingredients. You completely change the taste by adding banana, orange, coconut, spices, and so forth."

"Yes . . ."

"But from what I understand in talking with Samuel, you blend a terrific rum, one that not only tastes good, but has an, uh, exotic effect."

"Some men believe that my rum made them much more potent in bed."

"What do you think?"

❖

"I believe it's what a man has in his mind that makes his manhood potent. If men believe that rum will make them better lovers . . ." She shrugged.

My mind was churning. I was getting an idea, an expansion of my bootleg liquor.

"Now you are scheming more."

"Will you stop reading my mind?"

She looked around clandestinely and then leaned toward me to whisper.

"Let me tell you a secret. I'm not a mind reader. I'm a *face* reader!"

WE SAT ON HER porch and drank lemonade that had a kick to it while we negotiated the terms. We made a simple deal on the distillery— I did all the work, paid all the expenses and gave her 25 percent of the net profit. On managing the farm, I took the quarter percentage.

I told her what was spinning around in my head about rum.

"When I was down in Belize Town a while back, I had an interesting conversation in a bar with a liquor salesman for the West Indies cartel. I was mulling over the vodka idea and was getting a notion of how the liquor business worked. He knew nothing about vodka except that he saw it in some of the better bars and clubs in Caribbean hotspots, but he gave me an eye-opener as to how the cartel operates.

"As you know, they sell to thousands of bars and restaurants in the Caribbean, controlling the distribution of almost all the rum sold by the glass. And they're complete bastards. They keep tight control on the market and treat their employees as if slavery were still legal. The salesman is being fired because he has some medical problems and the company wants to get rid of him. That makes him real unhappy because he started working for them before I was born. He told me that the cartel forces bars and restaurants to pay a premium price for the basic rums that are used in mixed

❖

drinks. These rums are the cheapest to produce, but the distillers want the prices kept up because if the basics get too cheap, it will cut into the sales of the premium aged and blended rums."

I paused. "Are you following me?"

"I have ears, don't I?"

I grinned. "Nice ears, too, perfect for nibbling."

"Before you spin too much wool, please understand that I am a widow, not a fool. You won't make any financial deals with me by offering me your little manhood. You would be surprised how many offers I get from full-*grown* men who think they can get into my money jar by getting into my honey pot."

"Sarita, let me assure you that nothing about sex in the colony surprises me. And let me further assure you that I am *full*-grown."

I took a closer look at my lemonade. I was getting horny just sitting across from this mature sensuous woman. Did she spike my lemonade with some of that aphrodisiac that she was famous for putting into rum?

"You think that you will sell your basic rum to the cartel's customers at a lower price. There are two things wrong with your plan. The first is that the cartel *controls* the distribution of rum everywhere in the Caribbean. They could underprice you—"

"Not without cutting their own throats."

"Or they can swat you away like a fly. There was a rum distillery here in the district that was driven out of business by the cartel, did you know that?"

"I heard it burned."

"You heard right. It burned to the ground after it tried to sell its products directly to bars and restaurants outside the colony. One night there was a fire, and no more distillery."

"Well, I don't plan on being that much of an annoyance. The cartel sales rep told me that that distillery had openly challenged the cartel, a challenge they couldn't afford to ignore. My business plan is different." I was making the business plan up as I went, but it was pouring out in gushes. Basically, it was similar to how I saw the vodka scam.

❖

"This salesman has worked the Caribbean for over twenty years. He knows the territory. He's in the process of retiring. I'm sure I can get him to work for me under the table, give him a piece of the action on whatever he brings in, a commission. He'll get orders for basic rum and we'll provide the product in unlabeled bottles. The bar, restaurant, or whoever is buying the product will put their own label on it. We can provide them with a variety of labels, have a print shop in Belize Town do them."

"You think the cartel won't know where the rum is coming from just because it's unlabeled?"

"Not at all. I just don't intend on making rum a big business, that's all. I see vodka as where the money is, and it's the safe bet. There aren't any vodka cartels that will break our kneecaps if they find out their product is being imitated. America's a wide-open market for vodka, that's where the big money will be. We'll just pick up a little money with rum in the Caribbean."

She looked at my pants. "Do you have someone in your pocket?"

"Excuse me?"

"You keep saying 'we' as if you had someone who was insane enough to get involved in this crazy scheme with you."

"Trust me, Sarita, you'll have no problems except figuring out how to spend all the money that pours in."

"Understand this, my fine Russian, Britisher, whatever you are. If you get my distillery burnt because you've antagonized the cartel, I'm going to put a curse on you that will burn your grown-man ass."

"You said you weren't a witch."

"I never said I wasn't a bitch."

❖

29

❖

Sarah came into the kitchen from the garden to check on the progress of Ann, a Creole girl helping Sarah while the girl's aunt, who was employed as their cook, took a trip to Belize Town to attend a wedding.

"Ann?"

Yams waiting to be peeled were sitting on the counter along with the knife Sarah had given the girl to use. Sarah shook her head. Her regular cook was a dream, but this girl acted like she had been taken away from something important—like hanging around street corners in Corozal Town flirting with boys. She was a pretty thing, but one look at her attitude and Sarah had correctly decided the girl would not be much help around the kitchen.

Noise came from the breezeway that lay between the kitchen and the main house. It sounded like giggling. Sarah's immediate impression was that Ann was outside talking to friends when she should be in the kitchen working.

The door to the breezeway was ajar. Sarah opened it and stopped, stunned. Ann was bent forward against the breezeway wall with her skirt hiked up, her buttocks exposed. Behind her was

❖

Jack, his pants and shorts down, pumping his penis frantically in and out. He looked over at Sarah but didn't stop what he was doing.

The scene disgusted her. She slammed the door shut and spun around, heading back to the sink where she picked up the sharp knife lying on the counter and started peeling the yams, her face flushed, her mind swirling, her hands moving in a blur, slicing the skin off the vegetables. She worked in such a frenzy, the knife slipped and she cried out as the sharp blade caught her finger. She immediately dropped the knife in the sink. She decided to go out the back door of the kitchen and around the house to enter by the front instead of passing Jack and the girl again.

The blood was trickling down her finger as she went to her bathroom and grabbed a cloth to stop the bleeding. With her hands shaking, she managed to get down a headache powder, only to throw it up, gagging. She went and sat on the edge of the bed. She couldn't cry. She had cried too much over Jack, so much that there were no tears left. She knew he was unfaithful to her, but this was the first time she had personally witnessed it. He hadn't even cared that she would catch him.

What went wrong between them? she asked herself. She instinctively knew the question should have been, What was ever right? It hadn't been right since the beginning. She blamed herself, her failures, her inadequacies, for Jack's wandering.

They had met in Brighton in 1945 during a celebration of the news that Berlin had fallen. Jack was a sergeant in the army's quartermaster corps and she was a nurse at an army hospital. She had been immediately taken by his brash, assertive personality, even by the undercurrent of aggression that she sensed lay just beneath the surface. She had been born and raised on the small farm her father maintained when he went into semiretirement. She considered herself more countrified than city-wise, as neither pretty nor ugly, as neither intelligent nor base stupid. At school she had not been brilliant, as her older half-brother, Nick's father, had been, nor had she gathered many friends. Average was how she thought of herself, with little to offer a nice-looking, ambitious young man who intended to make something of himself after he got out of the army.

❖

Like most girls her age, she thought sex was something that was supposed to come only after marriage. She had no knowledge of birth-control methods, although she heard the other nurses openly talk about the "rubbers" men used.

During the celebration dance, Jack had nearly gotten into a fight with another soldier after he and the man rudely bumped into each other on the dance floor, both a bit tipsy. Jack was quick to anger and the other man had backed down, but the military police officer asked Jack to leave. She left with him. He took her out back where a friend's car was parked. They got into the backseat and Jack pulled out a whiskey flask. He took long swigs and gave it to her. She hated the taste, the burning sensation, but she had fallen for Jack and would have drunk plumber's drain cleaner if he'd asked her.

They had started with kissing and then his hand went inside her blouse and pulled off her bra. Her breasts were full and firm and they were her one secret vanity. He told her they were "better than most I've seen" and that made her happy. His hand went up her dress and inside her drawers. It was the first time she had done any heavy petting, the first time a man had touched her between the legs. She was intoxicated with Jack and she surrendered herself to him as he found her love button. His touch put her on fire. She had no idea that a man's fingers could create such desire in her.

Her good sense told her she should not permit it, but she didn't resist as he pulled up her skirt and slipped off her panties. He pulled off his own pants and shorts and she stared at the sight of his erect penis. "Biggest cock in the unit," he told her, grabbing it and wagging it. "Take it." He forced her hand over it and she gripped it, feeling its masculine power. "Taste it," he told her. He pushed her head down to it and she resisted, not knowing what she was supposed to do. His cock was red and swollen, almost purple in the dim light coming from a nearby street lamp. "Put it in your mouth," he said, but she couldn't bring herself to do it, she was too frightened. She kissed the tip of it and pulled herself away.

He grabbed her by her bare legs and pulled her across the seat,

❖

forcing her down, clumsily getting on top of her. There wasn't enough room across the backseat for them to stretch out and his knees were bent, his legs up, as he straddled atop her. She was wet, dripping from excitement, as he slid into her with surprising ease. His penis encountered her maidenhead and she cried out as he broke through.

The ecstasy was short. His cock exploded in her, pumping wildly. She spread her legs wider, enraptured by the sensation, but then he was spent. He pulled away from her and sat up, taking a swig from his whiskey flask, no concern for her own pleasure.

Two months later, when he returned from an assignment on the French coast, she broke the news to him that she was pregnant.

The fact that she was expecting had been worrisome and exciting to her. It turned into a horror when she saw his face as he got the news. "Fucking bitch," he said. He raised his hand in a fist and she had staggered backwards, almost falling.

Fucking bitch. She heard the words over and over during the four years they had been married. He had done "the right thing," as he put it, by marrying her. Her father had not been pleased by the news but had given her an advance on her modest inheritance as a wedding present. That advance was enough for them to come to the colony where Jack had a cousin who was running the plantation. He taught Jack how to grow and process sugarcane and then quickly returned to England.

Fucking bitch. How many times had he used that phrase when he was down or angry and blamed her for the failures in his life? She remembered the first time he hit her. They were newly married and she was five months pregnant when he found out that he'd lost part of the money her father gave them. He had foolishly trusted an army buddy who had a sure thing, selling used army tires to civilians desperate for anything with rubber still on that a car could ride on, but the friend ended up getting arrested because he was stealing the tires.

Jack had gotten drunk at the news. Liquor did something to him. Her father said he couldn't hold his liquor. She didn't know exactly what that meant, but it was obvious that alcohol seemed to

❖

have the effect of releasing his aggressions, of making him louder and angrier.

She came up from behind him as he sat on a stuffed chair and drank beer, putting her arms around his neck to soothe his hurt.

"Get away from me, you fucking bitch!" Without turning, he hit her with his fist, smacking her in the face. She was knocked backwards, hitting a table and falling over. Her nose bled and swelled.

It wasn't until an hour later that she noticed the bleeding from between her legs. At the hospital, she told them she had tripped and fallen.

She lost the baby that night and spent four days in the hospital fighting an infection. When she got out of the hospital, carrying the news that she would never have a child, Jack was contrite, almost painfully remorseful.

She never said a word about the incident, about the loss of the child she carried or the ones she never would have. Neither of them ever spoke about it.

His repentance lasted three months before he got drunk and hit her again.

It soon became a cycle in their lives, a way of living. Anger would slowly build up in him, over a period of weeks, sometimes months; then he would hit her, lashing out at her, calling her names, blaming her for his failures, taunting her that he could have been somebody if she hadn't tricked him into marrying her.

Afterwards he would hold her, sometimes even cry as he hugged her and told her how much he loved her and how sorry he was.

Her logical mind told her that she wasn't at blame for the beatings, but she carried guilt for the pregnancy that forced him into marrying her, a voice inside her saying that she was a failure, that had she been a better wife, a better person, Jack would have treated her better, that she was only getting what she deserved.

Her head pounded. She went into the bathroom and took more of the headache powder, then took off her clothes and lay atop the bed with a cool wet cloth across her forehead, her eyes closed. In her mind she could still visualize Jack and the girl, his penis inside her, Jack pumping back and forth. She hated the scene, hated Jack

❖

for the humiliation, but in a strange way, she found herself getting aroused. Sex between her and Jack had never been as exciting as it was the first time in the backseat of a car. He always seemed to get aroused quickly and ejaculate fast. She had heard that some women had orgasms during sex, but she had never experienced one, although when Jack's penis penetrated against her clitoris just right, she had at times become extremely aroused.

But she never got that release, that electrifying sensation she had heard another woman describe to her. She had been terribly embarrassed by the woman's bluntness over tea and biscuits, but the conversation seemed to come back to her at certain times of the month when she felt eager for a man's touch.

She felt that same feeling of need for sexual release last night when she went to bed and Jack snored next to her, and again that morning when she awoke and he was already gone. She tried to get rid of the image of Jack fucking a girl who was probably no more than sixteen or seventeen, but it kept coming back to her, replaying in her mind. Ann was an attractive young woman, just the type to attract a philanderer like Jack, though she suspected Jack was easily attracted to almost anything feminine.

Jack must have seen her in the kitchen and chased her into the breezeway, Sarah thought, the girl giving just enough resistance to make it interesting. Caught in the breezeway, probably kissed her—no, that wasn't like Jack, he probably first went for her breasts, he liked breasts, "I'm a breast man," he said, the first time he petted hers. Sarah noticed the girl's breasts when she peered at them from the kitchen; they were full and firm, just the kind Jack liked. The girl probably didn't wear underwear, not all women did in the hot climate, and Jack liked that, too. He would often point out the ones that weren't wearing anything under their dresses when they drove along the road or through town.

Replaying the scene in her mind again, she found that Jack was no longer in the picture—*suddenly it was Nick*. She saw him naked, glowing white against the satin ebony of the girl's dark body, pulling his hips back and forth, his cock slipping back and forth in the girl's vagina.

❖

She had seen Nick naked one day when she carried a lunch for him out to the fields. A worker told her he'd gone down to the river to cool off. She arrived at the riverbank just as he came out of the water, unaware of her presence.

He was tall and slender, his skin almost hairless, his pubic hair golden. She noticed his penis had not been erect, but was full, unlike Jack's unless he was aroused. She had seen the male genitals when she was a nurse but had had a clinical detachment for them. They looked like limp little white snails when they were down and an angry rhino horn when excited. Seeing Nick's penis had aroused her more than she'd been aroused since the first time she and Jack had made love.

She realized that it wasn't just seeing his male organ that day that got her excited. There was something about Nick that had stirred her womanhood. In a way, she supposed, it was the fact that she had admired his father so much. She had to admit to herself that when she was a young girl going through puberty, she even had fantasies about having sex with his father. She was aware that children raised in the same household generally were not sexually attracted to each other, but by the time she was a young girl, Peter was gone from the house, off to college and Europe.

From the moment she met Nick, she had felt sexual tension between them. Once she had even seen him get an erection when they were sitting close together, talking. It had excited her and she had gone to bed that night thinking about Nick and his naked body. Was it incest if he was only her half-nephew? She had gotten immediate guilt as the word *incest* ran through her head.

The image was in her mind now, about the full penis she'd seen getting erect, about him entering the girl her husband had been fucking.

As she lay on the bed, her hand went inside her panties and between her legs. She was already wet. The flow of sexual juices increased as she rubbed the lips of her vulva. Her fingers found her sensitive clitoris and she gently massaged it as she imagined herself lying on the bed as Nick stood by the bed, the girl bent over in front of him, his penis in her, stroking her, as Jack called it, "doggy style."

As the girl bent over the bed, she leaned farther down, until her head hovered above Sarah's. Sarah pushed her breast at the girl. Smiling, the girl took the breast between her full lips and wrapped her tongue around the nipple and sucked.

Sarah's hands found the girl's ripe breasts and fondled them, then pulled her down so Sarah could take the breasts in her mouth. Slowly the girl's tongue moved down Sarah's waist and thighs to the bushy mound of hair between her legs.

Nick withdrew from the girl and mounted Sarah, his stiff white cock thrusting between her legs, caressing her love button as he slid back and forth. . . .

❖

30

❖

Corozal, 1955

"It keeps your pecker stiff."

That was my explanation to Suez for why Sarita Garcia's rum was such a hit. We had just returned from a trip to Havana, Cuba, landing at a small "airfield"—basically a level pasture near his house—and had gotten out of his plane when I answered his question.

He had flown us to Havana and back in his two-seater Bulldog. I had been driven to letting him fly me to Havana by the Mother of All Necessities—*money*. My venture into the booze-distilling business had taken a queer sort of turn—no one gave a damn about my counterfeit-label vodka, no one gave a damn about my counterfeit-label rum, but the one product that I manufactured under my own brand name was a big hit.

We had a bumpy trip home, hitting updrafts and down-drafts and headwinds and tailwinds until I was ready to get out at ten thousand feet and walk.

"Chin up, lad," Suez said, after we dropped five hundred feet in seconds and my stomach ended up between my teeth. "We'll tough it up all right."

❖

"Fuck you and your good spirits. Just get me back to earth."

"Hurricane weather," Suez said. "I feel it in my bones."

You didn't need Sarita's Garifuna magic or Suez's weather-sensitive bones to know a blow was coming—it was September, the middle of the hurricane season. I was just glad to get my feet on the ground before the heavy winds and downpour started. I'd been through good blows every year during the six years I'd been in the colony, but for people who'd lived through one or two really devastating hurricanes, the same thought was always on their minds—was this year's going to be another Big One?

"I don't feel a thing when I drink the stuff," I said, still answering his question about Sarita's rum concoction, "but everyone I talk to claims it makes them horny. Men swear on the stuff and women have been buying it for their men."

Garcia's Widow was the name I had jokingly given the brand when Sarita insisted on brewing her own rum concoction. She was a lush, sensuous widow, and again, jokingly, I had used a picture of her in a black widow's dress and red rose on the label. It wasn't long until that label was becoming a name brand everywhere in the West Indies. I had gone to Havana to make peace with the cartel that controlled the region's rum business, agreeing to stop counterfeiting labels and pushing my own brand with their help.

"It just goes to show you," Suez said, "the honest path is always the best path."

"Right." Right, hell. "Honest" success had come to me purely by accident. And I didn't know how really honest it was to sell booze as an aphrodisiac, anyway.

"I think we made it back just in time," Suez said. "Can you feel it? It's going to be a big one."

We drove in silence for a moment before I spoke aloud a thought that had been nagging me since I left Havana. "I'm going to Havana."

"You just got back from there."

"I mean, I'm going to go there to live." I had been really struck by the city, by its energy, beautiful women, exciting cafes and casi-

❖

nos. "I don't see spending the rest of my life in the colony; there's an exciting world out there."

"You can't keep them down on the farm once they've seen Par-ee," Suez sang. "I've been expecting it. But what about the distill-ing business?"

"I'll take it with me. Cuba produces more sugarcane than the colony does. Sarita won't mind, I'll buy her out. She's been talking about going back down south, anyway. With the money she's made, she'll be Queen of the Garifuna."

There was nothing holding me in the colony. Suez and Sarita were friends, and I'd made other friends, but I had not permitted myself to become emotionally attached to anyone. The one exception was Sarah. I felt a strong connection with her. And pain for her. The years had not improved Jack's temperament—or his phi-landering. My social relationship with him was limited to a brief nod and a muttered, "How you doing?"

"So the colony isn't good enough for you, eh?" Suez said. "Would think New York or London would be more up your alley."

"Too much gray concrete, car exhaust and people too stressed out by everyday life to be polite. They remind me of Leningrad."

I was tired of jungle, dirt roads, sleepy villages and watching out for snakes in the sugarcane fields. Add to that outdoor loos with spiders and scorpions sleeping under the toilet lid—or even just stepping into vegetation to relieve one's self and wondering what was going to take a bite out of your rear end when you squatted.

I wanted lights and action and women who sparkled with dia-monds and slinky dresses and smelled of exotic perfumes.

"They're all hiding," Suez said.

"Who's hiding?"

"The birds and bees and beasts of the forest. Notice how quiet it is? They've gone under cover. They can feel it in their bones, too, there's a big blow coming. You know what happened in '31 in Belize Town, don't you?"

"Bunch of people got killed."

"It was the way they got it that was insane. They were hav-ing some sort of festival, just like the Flower Celebration they're having in Corozal today. People were literally caught out in the open when the storm suddenly struck, hundred-and-fifty-mile-an-hour winds, ten-foot waves swept across the town, thousands drowned."

I left Suez muttering about tropical storms and went to my place and got changed to go into town. The Flower Celebration was about the same as all the festivals that the town threw—an excuse for people to get together and dance and drink. It wasn't for me, there was no one I really wanted to socialize with, but I was antsy and didn't want to stick around the house.

I drove into town and walked around, a cold beer in hand. The town square was alive with people having fun, music, dancing, laughing and talking. Carnival time was better than the daily drudge, but the town just wasn't for me, period. Corozal was a nice, sleepy little place, sitting pretty on the bay, just ten miles from the Mexican border. Refugees fleeing from the caste war between mestizos and Indios in the Yucatán started the town a hundred years ago, naming it after the cohune palm, a symbol of fertility because *cohune* in the vernacular referred to a man's testicles. The connotations of its name was the only risqué thing about the town. Even murders were few and far between.

The town was probably a good place to come to die after living a good life, but not somewhere I wanted to hang around and wait to die. I was sure there was more action on one block of Havana than in the whole colony. In the colony, the women looked tame and the men looked like farmers. I heard that carnival time in places like Havana and Rio was so wild, it could burn the hair off your chest. Carnival in Corozal was definitely for family and friends.

Suez's melodious refrain *"After you've seen Par-ee!"* ran around my head as I walked along the outer edge of the square.

Coming to a side street, I saw Sarah's Morris Minor parked halfway down the block in front of the general store. And Jack coming up the street with a floozy. I recognized the woman, she was a *puta*, a whore, from Chetumal, the town on the Mexican side of the bay. I'd seen her in a bar last week with Jack. The swine couldn't keep his hands off of her. It pissed me off, royally. Screwing around

❖

was one thing, but doing it publicly, rubbing Sarah's face in his dirt, was a dirty trick to play on her.

Shit!

Sarah came out of the general store and almost walked into them. I froze. I couldn't hear what was being said, there was too much noise from the band playing in the middle of the square, but Jack's face turned ugly. I saw Sarah turn to go to her car but he grabbed her arm and swung her around to face him. He hit her across the face, causing her to stumble back against the car, dropping her packages.

My heart started pumping. I went for Jack and ran full-pedal as Sarah got into her car and drove away. He stood in the street calling her a fucking bitch. He must have the heard the pound of my feet because he whipped around. I hit him with my right shoulder, trying to slam it into his solar plexus, but he turned sideways and I gave him only a glancing blow. I stumbled by him and he staggered back.

I swung around ready to come back at him. He crouched down, his hand to his boot, and pulled out what he called his "pig-sticker," a bone-handled hunting knife he kept in a boot sheath. I knew I had the advantage, so I kicked him in the face while he was still crouched, catching him under the chin. I was only sorry I hadn't wore my old steel-toed boots because he would have been laid out for the duration. But I was wearing deerskin sandals with soles made from rubber tires. Instead of going out, he just fell back down on his rump.

Before I knew it, a screaming, clawing tiger jumped on my back and clawed at my eyes with long fingernails. I spun around in a circle, trying to get Jack's bitch off my back, but I went off balance and started to stagger. I threw myself backwards at Jack as he was getting up, literally falling against him with the puta still on my back. We went down, all three of us, with the woman finally letting go when she screamed that Jack had cut her.

She scrambled out of the way with a cut on her arm as Jack started up again. I was on my feet first and I hit him with a right that caught him at the temple. He needed the hand holding the knife to brace himself from going back down, and as soon as he lowered his hand I hit him again with a right and then kept pounding his face until he was on the ground on his back.

I stared down at him for a moment. He tried to get up and I kicked him hard in the stomach.

The puta gave me a detailed verbal description of my inadequate manhood, my perverted sex life, my dubious sexuality. I thought my Spanish was pretty good, half the population in the district spoke it, but she knew insults that I had never heard.

I went back to the square and to the side street where I had parked the jeep. The fight had not attracted much attention with the festival goers—they had more important things to worry about.

The bumpy weather that Suez and I had at our tail flying in from Havana had finally reached Corozal. One minute people were drinking and dancing and the next everyone was scrambling to their cars or otherwise hurrying home with high winds blowing. I'd heard stories about how fast a hurricane could suddenly hit land. I never comprehended that it could really happen in such a short time. The horrors of storms that suddenly blew ashore and killed and injured thousands was on my mind and I'm sure everyone else's as the wind velocity picked up.

I headed out on the river road that led to the plantation and my place beyond. The wind kicked up a notch every mile I put under me. Then the sky opened up. The jeep's rag top had been patched so often it looked like a crazy quilt. And was about as porous as mosquito netting.

Sarah's little Minor wasn't at the plantation when I drove in. "Damn."

I backed the jeep up and turned around, heading for my place. I was worried about her. She needed to get shelter during the storm. The plantation house was not bad shelter. Neither were abode buildings—as long as the roofs stayed on.

Wind howled at me. By the time I made it to the dirt road leading into my yard, palm fronds and sugarcanes were being danger-ously whipped around. A ten-foot sugarcane stalk came at my windshield like a hurtled spear. I instinctively ducked but it went over the car.

The Minor was parked in front of my bungalow.

31

❖

Sarah was facing the glass door that led out to the backyard, her back to me, when I came in. The French patio doors were rattling from the storm. So was the roof. It felt as though it would lift off at any moment.

I didn't know what to say. This was the one person in the world who I cared for. Looking at her, I saw my father and my mother, I saw the warmth of a winter fire, the smell of hot soup coming from a pot on the stove, my mother and father playfully dueling with words in their contrasting views of the world. What I saw was family, all that I had left. There was something between us that I had with no other person on earth—*blood love.* She was all that I had and I would protect her with my life.

"It's over," she said.

She turned around to face me. Her cheek was raw. The bruise was turning black.

"I've been a stupid fool. I should have left him years ago."

I shrugged. "We all make mistakes."

"Jack wasn't a mistake, he was God's punishment for whatever

❖

HAROLD ROBBINS and JUNIUS PODRUG

sins I've committed." She laughed. "Maybe the devil was testing me, to see how I survived living in hell."

She suddenly broke into tears. I took her in my arms and held her tight. She shook as she sobbed.

"I loved him, God, I don't know why, I still love him."

"You wouldn't—"

She pushed back and looked at me. "Oh, God, no. He doesn't want me, I should have left him long ago for his sake. He didn't respect me."

"He's an ass, don't blame yourself."

"It's not his fault, I wasn't good enough—"

"Don't talk like that!" I grabbed her by the arms and shook her. "Stop it, don't ever say that again. Listen to me, dammit. *You're the only one who can make you feel inferior.* The Jacks of this world can't do it, only you can. If you don't respect yourself, how do you expect anyone else to?"

She started sobbing again. I helped her to the couch and just held her. Christ, that's all she needed was an idiot giving her a lecture when she was down. I was right, though. Jack didn't cut her any slack, whipped her like a dog, because he didn't respect her. Bullies only pick on people they don't respect. And they have a shark's instinct for finding victims. Jack bullied and abused Sarah because he unconsciously sensed Sarah would be an easy victim.

But this wasn't something she could learn from a lecture while she was suffering. Sarah was smart. When she got away from Jack, got some fresh air, in a new environment where she didn't have to be on the defensive all the time, she would realize that she was a person of value who didn't have to be anyone's punching bag.

I stroked her hair as she emptied her emotions on my shoulder.

"I'm sorry, I'm sorry," she sobbed.

"It's okay."

The storm outside got angrier. The wind howled, the house shook, it felt like the house would go airborne. It was getting scary, but running outside to the flying debris would have been worse.

She slowly lost her tears and raised her head to look into my eyes. Her eyes were misted.

I fought my urge, but it was no good. It seemed natural to me. My lips met hers. They brushed, barely touching. Her lips were warm and lush and tasted like honey.

"Isn't that a pretty picture?"

I nearly jumped out of my pants. It was the voice of doom.

The wind battered the house, threatening to take it off its hinges and send it flying, taking it out of the colony and off to the Land of Oz.

Only it wasn't funny.

Jack had a gun in his hand.

"You've been fucking my wife."

Not yet.

Wind raged against the bungalow, shaking the walls, pressing against the windows. Sugarcane debris, palm fronds and rain were hitting the bungalow like an artillery barrage. Rain slammed against the windows, threatening to burst in. I had a feeling the whole damn colony was about to be washed away, swept out to sea.

Sarah pulled away from me to walk toward Jack. I grabbed her arm to stop her but she twisted away.

"No, Nicky, I've been afraid too long."

"I'm going to kill both of you, no one will blame me, it's the law of the land. I caught you two together."

"Stop it, Jack," she said.

"What makes it so disgusting is not only that you've been unfaithful to your loving husband, but you dirty slut, you fucked your own nephew."

"You are the one who is disgusting, Jack," she said. "You've taken out all your failures, all your pain, on me. Go ahead and shoot me. It will put me out of my misery. I'd rather die than put up with you another day. Go ahead, you bastard, shoot me."

I jerked her back and stepped in front of her. He aimed the gun at my chest.

❖

"I hated you from the moment I saw you, you little prick," he said.

The front window suddenly exploded with glass and water. Sarah and I were both blown back by the burst.

Jack dropped to his knees. He stared at us, his mouth gaped open, and then he fell forward on the floor, a stalk of sugarcane imbedded between his shoulder blades.

32

❖

A week after the storm blew out, I drove Sarah to the airfield out
side of Belize Town. She was scheduled on a Pan Am flight to New
York and from there she was taking another flight to London.

We had spoken little since the death of Jack. He had been only
one of many who died at the hands of the barbaric storm. It had
been hell in the colony since the hurricane, as the survivors dug
out and the dead were buried. Corozal was almost blown entirely
off the map. There were only a few buildings left standing.

Sarah had insisted that Jack's body be returned to Britain. "He
was never comfortable in the colony," she said, "he'd rest better on
home ground. There are too many bad memories here for him."

I found her attitude about Jack incomprehensible. The man
abused her, cheated on her, blamed her for his failures, treated her
like a doormat, said he was going to kill her—yet she loved him.
Regardless of what she said to his face in those last minutes, she
was devastated by his death. It taught me something about love—
it didn't have to make sense. People didn't choose who they loved.
It was something that just happened and when it did, you were
helpless.

❖

"You have no interest in coming to Britain?" she asked.

I shook my head. "I've spent most of my life in a cold climate. The Caribbean sun has gotten into my blood."

I got her onto the plane and went back to Corozal to wrap up my life in the colony. There was Sarita to settle with and Suez to say goodbye to. I needed to take care of shipping Sarah's things and to make sure she had a good financial start back home.

After that, Havana was my next stop.

❖

Rum, Cigars
and Women

IN THE MOUNTAINS WITH FIDEL CASTRO

One night, only a short time before we discovered he was a traitor, Eutimio complained that he had no blanket and asked Fidel to lend him one. It was a cold February night, up in the hills. Fidel replied that if he gave Eutimio his blanket, they would both be cold; that it was better to share the blanket, topped by two of Fidel's coats. That night, Eutimio Guerra, armed with a 45-caliber pistol that Casillas had given him to use against Fidel, and two hand grenades that were to be used to cover his getaway once the crime was committed, slept side by side with our leader. . . . Throughout the night, a great part of the Revolution depended on the thoughts of courage, fear, scruples, ambition, power, and money running through the mind of a traitor.

CHE GUEVARA,
REMINISCENCES

THE ROOT OF ALL EVIL

It was all dominated by the sweet, sickening odor of sugar. Columbus had brought sugarcane to the neighboring island of Hispaniola (now the Dominican Republic and Haiti) on his second voyage in 1493. From there it was taken to Cuba by the Spanish conquerors.

The evil that sugar brought with it was slavery . . .

The sugar plantations brought enormous profits. . . .

HERBERT MATTHEWS,
REVOLUTION IN CUBA

33

❖

Havana, Cuba, 1958

The last time I was in this boxing arena I saw a bout between Carmen Basilo and Sugar Ray Robinson, two of the greatest middleweights that ever put on gloves. Now I was back to see another match, actually a series of fights between what you might call bantamweights. And, unlike our "civilized" boxing matches where men only die by accident, if getting pounded for up to fifteen rounds can be called an accident, the fights I was about to see were real blood sports—the loser usually died. It wasn't unlike the bloodthirsty gladiatorial games that Roman emperors used to entertain their subjects with—a battle to the death by two well-armed, superbly trained, ruthless opponents.

But you could say there was some chickenshit to the games.

I was in the arena to see cockfights.

Until I hit Havana, I had no idea that cockfighting was an organized, world-class sport that could fill the same arena where world champion boxers stood toe-to-toe. In a little while, bad-tempered roosters with razors strapped to their legs were going to fly at each other and go at it until the ring was thick with blood and feathers. I heard that cockfights were conducted out in the

❖

215

bush of British Honduras, but there were more people in this arena than in the whole northern part of the colony.

All to see chickens get bloodied.

But several years in Cuba's golden city had taught me a lot of things about people and places, not the least of which was to keep one eye on my back and another one on my wallet.

"Isn't this great?" Jose asked. "Look at them, they're bloodthirsty animals, savage beasts. They can't wait, they want to see the blood flowing, they want to smell the fear."

Jose was a high ranking official in Cuba's ministry of economics. He was the bagman I paid off to do business in Cuba. That business included my rum distillery, a cigar factory, sugarcane fields and occasional flyers into whatever popped up. Right now I was interested in the casino business. There were casinos on what they were calling "the Strip" in Las Vegas, but that was in the Western desert, thousands of miles from the East Coast. Havana was something like eighty miles off Florida, just a short hop over by plane or boat. That made it gambling heaven for Easterners.

The "bloodthirsty animals" Jose was referring to weren't the fighting cocks, but the audience. There had to be several thousand people in the stadium, and about ninety percent were men. They were excited, loud and anxious. Money flashed everywhere, fingers were held up, hats waved, all in some code that was indecipherable to me but seemed to be understood by everyone else. From a peso to a thousand pesos, sweating, excited men were placing bets.

The only time I got sweaty and excited is when I'm lying with a naked woman and my hands and lips are feeling all of the mysteries of the feminine body. But these men were getting themselves worked up into an orgiastic state about a couple fuckin' chickens slicing each other to ribbons.

It made no sense to me. But you could learn more about human nature watching the audience in a cockfight than a season reading Freud. I'm sure if Freud and Jung had spent more time watching people get off over chicken blood, they would have had less confidence about the rationality of the human race.

"Rabid dogs," I said.

❖

"Señor?"

"Rabid dogs, these people are nuts, they're all worked up over killer chickens."

"*Sí! Sí!* Isn't it wonderful. See the red—I tell you, Señor Cutter, put your money on the red, only on the red, look at him, his trainer can hardly keep him back, he wants to fight, he wants to kill, he smells the blood of the other chicken and now he wants to taste it."

I swear, Jose was almost drooling. Mother of God, could people really get this excited about chickens killing each other? I've seen men getting rabid over cockroaches, too, racing them for money, treating the bugs better than they do their wives and kids.

"I like the red, too," Vincent said. He was wide-eyed as he watched the two trainers bring the cocks into the middle of the ring and poke them at each other, getting them pissed and in a murderous rage.

Vincent was an executive with Havana's Tropical Paradise Casino. I didn't know exactly what his title was, or even exactly what his function was. Someone told me it was his job to kill people who cost the casino money, whatever that meant. But in Havana, when you were told that someone was a killer, you just nodded your head, same as if you'd been told they go to church on Sunday. Especially when it was so logical and reasonable. Havana's casinos were mob owned, mostly the New York Italian crowd with a Jew named Meyer Lansky pulling the strings. Murder just went with the territory.

Basically, I had come to the cockfight because Jose asked me to and Vincent came along because he wanted to talk to me. Jose wanted his payoff, and "winning" it at a cockfight was as good a ploy as any, and Vincent wanted to sell me a piece of a mob-owned casino.

Havana was quite a town. Where else could you bribe a public official and do business with a mobster, all at the same blood sport?

"There's not much in life as exciting and satisfying as owning a casino," Vincent told me as we rode over in my chauffeur-driven Cadillac. Detroit cranked out their new models months before the calendar year, and I had a 1959 Eldorado Biarritz shipped over, hot

❖

off the assembly line. A big car was mucho status in Cuba, and there was nothing bigger than this new Cad that had enough chrome to plate a battleship and fins you could rollerskate on. The car had white leather seats that electrically adjusted six ways, a white convertible top, double headlights with double utility lights underneath. Only ninety-nine of these babies came with bucket seats, and mine was one of them. It packed a V8 with 390 horses and sat on big fat whitewalls. The paint was metallic Persian Sand.

I grew up believing that men loved power and women loved soft things, but Havana proved me dead wrong. Women were the power lovers. It was the female of the species who drove men to flex their muscles and rev their engines. If there ever was a pussy mobile, the kind of heap that attracted women in and their clothes off, it was this beautiful chunk of metal from Detroit.

I LIT A CIGAR for Vincent—not one of my own, which more often than not were counterfeits of fine, hand-rolled brand name smokes, but a Montecristo that was made specially for me and carried my company name, Cutter, Ltd., and logo, the head of a leaping viper. I spent so much of my time worrying about the vipers in the colony, I decided to keep one around. Maybe it would make people afraid of screwing with me.

Vincent nodded at the *Totalmente a mano,* "handmade", statement on the label and the well-veined, even textured wrapper.

There were three parts to a cigar—the filler in a superior cigar was the long leaf stuff in the center, the binder was the first layer holding the filler together, and the wrapper was the crème de la crème—the outer wrap that you saw with your eyes and accounted for over half the taste.

Vincent gave me his seal of approval. "Good earthy aroma, has a hint of coffee and honeyed tones, good brand," he said.

"Actually, these are made especially for me. They're not really *hand* rolled, but rolled between the thighs of virgins."

"No shit." He looked at the cigar with renewed respect. "Get me some boxes of these. The boys back in New York will get a kick out of sucking on 'em."

He went on philosophizing about gambling. "There's only one thing I can think of that equals the thrill of handling huge amounts of pure cash, tens, twenties, even ones and quarters. You ever seen how much quarters add up to? You know, they don't even bother counting change, no shit, they just weigh it. But, like I was saying, there's only one thing that comes close to that kind of excitement and satisfaction, and that's being a pimp with a first-class stable of babes."

"A pimp?"

"Can you imagine what it must be like to come up to babes and just rip open their blouses and feel their boobs anytime you liked, or pull down their panties and rub their cunts until they're juicy and bend them over a table and hump them doggy style? Then send them out to fuck and rob some dumb-ass john and pocket every dollar their sorry asses earn?"

Yeah, Vincent and Jose were a couple of real intellectual types. The kind you find in the south Bronx at construction sites and along the Brooklyn docks. I had to wonder sometimes why I got along so well with them.

The arena had that steamy, stinky jockstrap smell of a dressing room after a sports match. Along with the damp-sour sports smell was the acrid odor of cheap cigar and cigarette smoke, enough to give a nonsmoker in the place black lung disease—the whole damn place was clouded by smoke. You didn't have to light up, just take a deep breath in and you could blow out smoke rings.

It was my night out with "the boys," a couple guys I would never have associated with except for business purposes. Back at my hotel, cooling their spiked heels and net stockings in the lounge, were four Havana *putas*, a set of twins apiece for Jose and Vincent, part of the payoff to the government official for turning his head when I violated the rules and to the gangster for offering to let me in on a piece of a casino. The twins were a nice touch, I

❖

thought. My reputation in the city was of a can-do guy who pays his debts. They were even more interesting because Jose was a switch-hitter—naturally his set were boy-girl fraternal twins.

Let me tell you, there were no whores like Havana whores. In my opinion, the street girls of Havana were unmatched in spicy sex appeal. There was something about the women of Havana that made them great sluts. In most places, it was the losers who turned to prostitution—drug addicts, women with no self-respect, abused women. But in Havana, the babes were first cabin, all of them, maybe because they knew they were hot stuff. Even the male prostitutes had great asses, which I found out third-hand—occasionally I had to pay off a guy who, like Jose, preferred to get his action through the back door.

It was no skin off my nose, as my American friends would say. Live and let live, just make sure you get your share of the take.

"There are two ways they prepare the spurs on the cocks," Jose said, almost overwhelmed by the anticipation of seeing blood.

"Spurs?"

"Bony growths at the back of their legs. Some birds get their spurs cut off and the owner attaches a razor to it, other types fight Caribbean-style, with the bony spur sharpened until it can cut like a razor."

As he spoke, the trainers in the ring were agitating the birds, getting ready for the match, poking them at each other, teasing until the birds were wild-eyed and literally foaming at the beak to start drawing blood.

"They're not ordinary chickens, you know," Vincent, the pimp expert, said. "Fighting cocks are bred, cross-bred and bred again, until they're large birds with the speed and aggression necessary to win. It's a real science to breed the little fuckers. But you gotta have some street smarts to choose the right birds." The casino man tapped his temple. "Just like boxers, it's all up here. You either think you're a winner or you lose. You can't win unless you're all psyched out with how great you are. It's the same with the cocks; some of them think they're winners. It's the cock that believes it's the meanest and the toughest that's gonna win."

❖

Jose spoke to a man standing in the aisle below us. He muttered some particularly foul Spanish after they finished.

"There's a rumor that one of the birds has poison on its spikes. That's what the bastardos do, they cheat so any scratch will kill their opponent's bird."

"Did you find out which bird has the poison?" I asked, not really caring. It sounded like a rumor, the same sort of thing you hear about boxers having eye irritation on their gloves.

"No one knows. I wish I did, I'd bet on it."

"Uh, are there rules like the Marquis of Queensbury stuff they have in boxing?" I asked.

"*Naturalamente*," Jose said. "If they go down for the count, or if they run away or die, they lose."

"You have to understand that these birds are serious warriors," the casino man said. "They're like them gladiators that used to fight to the death. These birds even have to fast for two days before their big fight, kept all that time in darkness and isolation. And you know the most important thing they must avoid?"

"Sex?" I asked facetiously, taking a wild guess.

"*Correcto!*" Jose said. "*Si, amigo,* you know the routine. No sex, not even a peck before a match. Reduces their strength. And just before the match, they bring in a case of hens and tempt the cock with it. When he gets it up, they pull the hens away to really piss the cock off."

"Watch their moves closely," Vincent said, "you'll see that the winners are true artists, martial artists of the jujitsu kind. If you held your hand in front of one of these killers, they would slice it to ribbons in seconds. I knew a guy once, when I was a kid in the Bronx, who could handle a shiv that way. He used to slice the neck of pigeons, not all the way through, just so they'd run around spraying blood until they fell."

Listening to the two foaming at the mouth at the idea of a couple chickens shredding each other with sharp claws and razor blades made me feel like I had fallen into the same hole Alice had—but Havana was a long way from Wonderland.

It had been three years since I left British Honduras on the

❖

heels of a hurricane and an even greater tempest in my personal life. The years swept by like the one hundred and fifty-mile-per-hour winds of the hurricane. I came to Havana, the heart of the world of rum, sugarcane and cigars—and beautiful women—to establish the Garcia's Widow brand as a premium rum, taking its place among the best in the world. Other than an occasional buy or sale of a plantation, I stayed away from growing and process-ing sugarcane—hell, half of Cuba was involved in growing the cane. Instead, I let others grow it and bought the molasses to make rum.

I had to move my operation from Corozal to Havana to keep it growing. It wasn't just that Cuba was the center of the Caribbean rum world, but Corozal was out of the way, with no port, and too many restrictions. And when it became necessary to skirt a few rules and regulations, it was easier to bribe a Cuban official than a British one. *Mordida,* "the bite," a payment to a public official, was the rule of law in Mexico and the Caribbean. Unlike Anglo coun-tries like Britain and America, the passage of money to a public of-ficial was not considered a bribe, or something immoral to give or receive. Rather, it was considered a reward for an official to do their job. And it wasn't possible to do business in the Caribbean and stay strictly on the up-and-up without it. Everybody was on the take or making the payments.

Bottom line, I had needed to get out of the colony and into the world. Corozal was no place for a young man. And no place for any-one who wanted more of a piece of the world than jungle and swamps.

Tonight I was working both ends against the middle. I had brought the two men to the cock fight not only to stroke them—yeah, I was picking up the bill even if they lost money betting—but more to grind my own axe.

My real objective in attending the cock fight was in the VIP box a third of the way across the arena. There were two men in the box I wanted to meet. One of them, Ramfis Trujillo, the son of General Trujillo, dictator of the Dominican Republic, was my main objec-tive.

❖

There were two vicious, rotten, corrupt murderous bastards of dictators in the Caribbean: Batista, who treated Cuba like the personal fief of a robber baron, was the bad man in Havana. The other dictator, General Trujillo, was just as much of a murderous, ruthless bastard. He had been running the Dominican Republic, a country a couple hundred miles east of Cuba, for three decades. And spilled more blood every year than the world series of cockfighting.

The other man in the VIP box I wanted to meet was Porfirio Rubirosa. He was technically Trujillo's ambassador to Cuba, but in reality was the dictator's goodwill ambassador to anywhere Trujillo wanted to send him. Rubi, as he was called, was an international celebrity. He was world famous as a lover, jet-setter and polo player. In a sense, he put the Dominican Republic name more on the map than cartographers.

The much-married playboy had wed two beautiful French actresses, and two of the richest women in the world—Doris Duke, a tobacco heiress, and Barbara Hutton, the Woolworth heiress. Both heiresses were immensely wealthy. They showered him with millions, not to mention his first marriage was to Trujillo's own daughter, Flor de Oro, "Flower of Gold."

The marriage to Flor de Oro created something of a play on names since Rubirosa meant "red rose." After she married Rubi, Flor's name became Flower of Gold Red Rose.

A woman high in Havana society confided in me that Rubi had a cock a foot long and that it operated like a jackhammer. She admitted that she got the description through double-or triple-hearsay.

My suspicion was that his dick size was wishful thinking by sex-starved women. Besides, the guy's charm would be more important to a woman than the size of his cock, especially to women who had all the money in the world to buy male meat. I don't think his secret was in his pants, but in the fact that he knew how to wine and dine a woman, how to touch a woman's heart—he came across as one part innocent schoolboy and one part Latin lover.

I didn't care about his male parts or his charms, but I did want to connect with him for my own reasons. Like I said, I had my own axe to grind.

❖

The casino man nudged me when he saw me looking at the Dominican Republic group.

"Trujillo sent his son to show support for his pal Batista because we Americans have abandoned Havana. Batista says the Americanos are hypocrites and bastardos for refusing to ship him more guns to kill his people with. He's right. When he was killing peasants and *winning* the war, it was carte blanche for military aid from us folk. Hell, he was an American hero, John Wayne and apple pie, as long as he was bringing home the bacon. It's only now when he's killing peasants and *losing* the war that Eisenhower and his State Department people have gotten a dose of morality."

The man spoke quietly so Jose wouldn't hear him. Jose was a government official and talking defeat in Cuba was a no-no, even though the current political situation was about as promising for Batista as it was for the Roman emperor when the barbarians were at the gates of Rome with battering rams. Every day the political—and military—situation in Cuba deteriorated. There was violence on the streets, attacks against public officials and businessmen, ambushes on the roads getting closer and closer to the metropolitan areas.

Half of Havana looked wound up and ready to explode; the other half was partying and fucking like there was no tomorrow— and it was getting to look like they had the right idea.

All the commotion was caused by a young, small-time lawyer named Fidel Castro. He had a ragtag army of a few hundred hungry guerrillas who were playing hell with Batista's well-equipped professional army. Who the hell would have thought that some guy without real military training could take on a professional army— and beat it? Castro was the illegitimate son of a sugarcane farmer, one of five kids by the farmer's cook. Not a real auspicious beginning for someone who wants to run the country.

Five years ago, on July 26, 1953, Castro, a twenty-seven-year-old Cuban attorney no one had ever heard of, led an almost-suicidal attack against a Batista army unit, probably planning on

❖

getting martyred for his commie cause, was arrested, jailed, sentenced to fifteen years and later released in a political amnesty.

When he got out of jail, he formed a revolutionary group called the Twenty-sixth of July movement. In 1956, Castro and about eighty men of the movement crammed into a small fishing vessel, the *Granma,* and "invaded" Cuba. Everything went wrong. They were ambushed by Batista's army and only about nine or ten of them escaped, including Castro and a wounded comrade named Che Guevara.

Fleeing the coast, they got into the mountains and hid—but they didn't quit. From the mountains, they continued to fight, slowly building up an army. And others joined in the fight against Batista. In March 1957, a group calling themselves the Revolutionary Directorate shot their way into the presidential palace and almost managed to kill Batista before they were gunned down.

The writing on the wall about the regime had been getting clearer and bloodier. Just a few months earlier, a general strike occurred. Since then, Batista's forces failed to suppress two major rebel offensives. Recently Batista began an assault on Castro's stronghold in the Sierra Maestra. More than ten thousand government soldiers failed to dislodge Castro's ragtag army during the Battle of Jigue. Now we'd heard that this rebel army had moved out of its mountain sanctuary and onto the plains, pushing the government troops back.

But no one talked defeat openly—Batista's men would shoot you on the spot. Anyone with a loaded gun was judge-jury-executioner.

It was the disintegration of the regime that got me interested in the people in the VIP box. I'd experienced one commie regime and I wasn't planning on dealing with another one. There was talk of American businessmen in town bragging that they were buying up companies at fire-sale prices, confident they would be able to deal with the new regime if—when—Batista fell.

When I heard people opining that they could deal with revolutionary hotheads like this guy Castro, I'm reminded of the fact that

❖

on at least a couple of occasions, Castro threw down his life for the cause, ready to be martyred. He wasn't the kind of guy I could talk business with. Especially in the hot, idealistic stage when revolutionary hotheads would be shooting fat cats like me.

It was time to abandon ship, and I needed a lifeboat.

❖

34

❖

I took another look at the people in the VIP box, sizing them up.

The women in the box weren't Havana whores. Attractive, but not sluts, they struck me as Ramfis's and Rubi's hometown party girls rather than strange stuff picked up in Havana. One of them caught my eye and kept me tuning in. She wasn't the best looking or the best stacked—in fact I took her to be the younger sister of a woman hanging onto Ramfis—but there was something about her that captured my attention.

She wasn't a party girl, I was sure of that; she lacked that wide-eyed, silly-grinned, dazed look of having hot Latin music constantly beating in her head. Instead, she looked like a woman who knew how to use her mind—and that was no small accomplishment.

It was a man's world all over and particularly in the Latin part of it. For men at the top, women were little more than sexual toys. Some sage at a nightclub last week had claimed that someday women would have the same rights and opportunities as men, but that got a big laugh, even from the women present at the table.

Maybe because my mother had been a strong-willed, intelli-

❖

gent woman, I didn't find myself attracted to women who thought their greatest worth was in bed.

The woman who looked like she knew her own mind caught me staring at her. She frowned and looked away, her nose up a couple inches to let me know I was beneath her.

I chuckled to myself. She was no doubt right about my social status—I ranked somewhere above common criminals and far below old money—but I'd make her pay for that snub.

The cockfight was about to begin when I looked over and saw the young woman who had turned her nose up at me leave the group and go down the steps to an exit tunnel.

In the ring below, the two trainers sent their birds at each other. The entire audience went to their feet with a roar. My two companions were busy foaming at the mouth as blood and feathers splattered the referee in the ring.

I was already down to the bottom of the steps by the time the first blood flowed. I went out the exit passageway to the dirt parking lot. The place was loaded with gun-toting soldiers. It wasn't uncommon to see them. There was no place you could go today in Havana without running into them. With the son of a neighboring dictator in attendance, the arena was crawling with even more of them.

My blond hair got me by as a non-Cuban, which took me out of the revolutionary category, so the guards just gave me cursory glances as I strolled by them.

The woman with the intellectual face and cold nose was smoking a cigarette, leaning against a car. She looked even better up close.

"May I join you?" I asked.

She looked me up and down, head to toe, with steel eyes. "No."

I guess she didn't like what she saw. She turned her nose up again.

"You keep lifting your nose up that high, and you'll have to cut it off because it's frostbitten. Happened to me once." I showed her my hand with the missing little finger.

❖

She could have cared less as she took a drag on her cigarette and slowly let it out.

An argument broke out in the parking lot, a couple of putas yelling at each other. The yelling quickly turned into screaming and it looked like any moment a cat fight would erupt. As the guards moved toward the two combatants, I turned away from the woman with her nose in the air and started back to the passageway. I was at the entrance tunnel when a man carrying a paper bag hurried quickly toward the entrance. He wore a straw hat pulled down low on his head and a red bandanna almost pulled across his face.

"Hey, wait a minute," I said, "what do you have in the bag?"

He started to brush by me and I grabbed at the bag. It fell at my feet and he turned and ran. The smell of gas filled the air.

I followed after the man as he disappeared into the darkness. I heard the girl with the cold nose yelling for the soldiers. They turned and hurried back, forgetting about the two putas who by now had also taken a powder.

"Over there," I said, in Spanish, "he went in that direction."

They ran in the direction I pointed as I came trotting back to where the girl was standing. Already the place was starting to swarm with plainclothes cops, uniformed police and militia. A policeman had torn open the bag to expose a broken wine bottle that had been filled with gas.

"What is it?" I asked.

"A Molotov cocktail," the girl with the cold nose said.

"A what?"

"A bomb, a bottle filled with gas. Light the wick, throw it, boom."

Ramfis, Rubi and the rest of the Dominican Republic clan came out of the exit tunnel surrounded by guards.

"Luz, we're leaving," Rubi said to the young woman I was talking to.

"This man made the bomber drop his bag," she said.

Rubi spoke to the man next to him. "Get his information."

❖

A great roar erupted in the arena. Some chicken must have gotten it.

The woman named Luz glanced back at me as she got into the limousine. It wasn't an unfriendly look, but there was a hint of puzzlement in it.

As I watched the San Dominicans pour into limousines, the man who Rubi Rubirosa had spoken to approached me. He was a toady character, very dark, short, with black unfriendly eyes and thin, cruel lips. He introduced himself as Johnny Mena.

"I am a security officer with the Dominican Republic," he said. "If I may have your name and address, por favor, I am certain my superiors will want to show their appreciation for your quick action."

I gave him the particulars he wanted.

"How is it that you spotted the man as a potential assassin?" he asked.

"I smelled gasoline as he brushed by me. And it looked like the bag he was carrying was half-soaked with it."

"If I may be permitted to ask a question . . ."

"Of course."

"Why did you leave the cock fight just when it was beginning?"

I grinned. "I had been giving a pretty girl the eye earlier. When I saw her leave, I thought she was signaling me to join her."

"Ah, I see. And was she?"

"Of course. She just wants to play hard to get."

"Well, señor, I wish you luck on your chase. This woman is noted in my country as one who uses her mouth to tell off a man as quickly as some women use theirs to give pleasure to a man."

"Gracias."

He saluted me. "De nada. You will hear from my superiors, I am certain."

I stood and watched as he and the last of the Dominican Republic limos left. As I turned to go back inside to rejoin my bloodthirsty friends, a man came up beside me.

"Such excitement. And you are a hero," he said, grinning.

"And you stink of gas," I said. "Get out of here. I'll send the rest of your money over by messenger."

❖

I went back inside, thinking about the look Luz had given me. Her name meant light. I liked it. It fit her. But I was bothered by the look she had given me. Had she seen that I sent the police in the wrong direction to find the "assassin"? Or had I slipped up another way with my charade and made her suspicious?

Whatever it was, I hoped she didn't blow my game. I had spent a lot of money and took a hell of a risk to pull off my "heroic" save of Ramfis Trujillo's life. Besides the actor carrying the Molotov cocktail, the two putas arguing in the parking lot had also been part of the crew.

I had big plans for the Dominican Republic.

But the look the woman gave me was disturbing.

It was as if she had looked into my soul and seen every dirty trick I'd ever pulled.

❖

35

❖

I got rid of Vincent the casino man and Jose the corrupt government official by joining them with the twins—almost literally—
and put myself into a tux. It was time to follow up on my heroics at
the cockfight by showing up at a casino—not the Tropical Paradise
that Vincent was trying to get me to buy into but the Grand Presi-
dente, the classiest hotel-casino in Havana. The fact it was owned
by mob money and Batista got a cut of every dollar that went
across the tables was just par for what passed for culture and
morality in Cuba. I fit nicely in the mold.

As I came up the steps of the casino, I recognized a couple of
the plainclothes security men that had been protecting Trujillo, Jr.,
and his crew back at the cockfight. I nodded to them, hoping one of
them would report my arrival.

The floor manager greeted me and shook my hand. "Do you
wish company tonight, Señor Cutter?"

He wasn't talking about a tour guide. The lounge had putas
lined up at the bar like horses at the starting gate.

Not having whores hanging around loose was the mark of a
classy joint.

❖

"No, I'm just going to drop a few pesos and have a drink."

Careful not to be caught staring, or even acknowledging their presence, I spotted the Dominican Republic group in a roped off baccarat area. The men were playing cards, smoking cigars and drinking, while the women were hovering around, looking beautiful, picking at the banquet that had been set out for them. Luz was with them, but her frozen features signaled that she was bored by the whole thing.

I headed for a roulette table on the other side of the casino. I wanted to be spotted, but I didn't want them to know it.

I loved the excitement of casinos—all that lush money and naked desire for it—but I didn't like to gamble. A universal law of mathematics turned me off from tossing my own money on the green felt tables—the odds always favored the house. For everyone who had a run of luck and won a few bucks, a hundred others lost.

I sat down at a roulette table, tossed a wad of bills across for chips, and ordered vodka. In Russia, vodka was soul food. In the Caribbean, they had hardly heard of it, and as Sarita pointed out, weren't ready to turn in their rum for it. But I had a case of Moskovskaya stashed at every casino in town, making sure they kept a couple bottles in the freezer at all times to be ready when I walked in. Despite my aversion to gambling, casinos were a great place to do business—and make payoffs. I deliberately drank vodka not only out of personal taste, but for its mystique—vodka was suddenly popular in the West because a British writer named Ian Fleming was writing books about a spy named James Bond who liked his vodka martinis shaken, not stirred. On more than one occasion, business people I'd been introduced to at a nightclub or casino remembered me because of the frozen vodka. I still sold the stuff in the states, but it was a cheap knockoff, rotgut I wouldn't drink myself.

My buy-in at the roulette table had dwindled in half when she came up and sat down next to me.

I grinned at Luz. "We meet again."

"Life's full of coincidences."

"Maybe it's fate that our trails keep crossing. Aren't there people in India who think everything's predestined? That a person's

❖

kismet determines what their destiny will be?" I leaned closer to her, drinking in the arousing scent of jasmine. "Do you suppose that you and I are meant to be lovers?"

She leaned closer to me, until her lips were only a kiss away.

"If that's true," she whispered, "I'll cut my wrists." She got up. "Ramfis wishes to thank you personally for your assistance."

"Ramfis?"

"Rafael Trujillo, the son of General Trujillo of the Dominican Republic. You remember, don't you? The cockfight, the Molotov cocktail, you being proclaimed as a hero?"

I followed her across the casino floor to the dictator's son and his entourage. I wondered what it was about her that let her read me so well for the lying, conniving bastard that I was.

Along the way, I asked, "Is there something about me that caused you to hate me on sight? Or are you a bitch to everyone?"

"Rubi had you checked out with the Cuban police," she said, without missing a step. "You claim to be a businessman, but you're also a bootlegger, smuggler and opportunist. You might be British or Russian, no one knows for sure exactly who you are or where you're from, the certainty is that you know how to make money and it's not always done honestly."

"And those are my good traits. I also cheat old women, kick dogs and take candy from babies."

She stopped and faced me before we reached the inner sanctum and spoke in a low voice. "I don't know what your game is, Señor Cutter, and I don't care. Deal however you like with the others, but don't think you fool me. I smelled trouble from the moment I saw you at the arena, and it wasn't coming from that bottle of petrol. What do you call them in your native country—Molotov cocktails?"

"Jesus, do you have my number."

She did a double-take and for once didn't know what to say. The others couldn't have heard our conversation but they were laughing as I came into the inner area.

Fuck your mother! Now that she knew I was Russian, she was able to confirm that her initial assessment of me was right. She

❖

had me down pat because she knew I had lied about something back at the arena. The fact I'd blown it had slid right by me because I didn't realize I would be dealing with a woman who had brains and street smarts. She had called the bottle of gas a Molotov cocktail back at the arena and I had played dumb and acted like I didn't know what the phrase meant. Jesus H. Christ. She now knew I was born and raised in Russia. I had to know what the hell it was, it was named after the Soviet foreign minister, probably the most famous man in the country after Stalin. Every Russian schoolboy knew what a Molotov cocktail was.

She had good suspicion that I lied. But what else had she surmised? Did she know I had set the whole thing up to meet Ramfis? That sounded like to much of a leap even for a smart girl like her to make.

Ramfis offered me a limp-fish handshake, about what I expected. My research revealed that he had been made an army colonel at the age of five and a general by the time he was ten. Some people would call that "soft-landings." Regardless of what you called it, having a dictator father who robbed and raped a country was not the best character model for a child.

He was tall, much taller than Rubi, and very Latin looking with a thin black mustache and pleasant mannerisms.

"You have my apologies, Señor Cutter," he said, grinning. "We could see that Luz was chewing on your ear as she brought you over. You must forgive us for sending our ice princess with the invitation to join us. We had hoped that because you were acquainted earlier, she might warm up to you. But, alas, you are another of the many men whom she has cut the *cohunes* off of."

That got a good laugh from everyone but Luz. I couldn't help but wonder if she had ratted on me about her suspicions. I didn't think she had because Ramfis didn't seem on guard while talking to me.

"Is her father rich?" I asked.

"Rich?" The question stumbled Ramfis. It got another double-take from Luz.

"I was just wondering. I imagine he would have to be a very

rich man to afford the dowry that would be necessary to get her married."

Another good laugh from the crowd—even Luz's lips trembled. I hope it was caused by trying to hold back a smile and not rage.

Rubi stepped up and gave me a warm, firm handshake. "Now, amigos, you shouldn't say such things, you are embarrassing poor Luz. It is not her fault that she has both brains and beauty. She is the loveliest flower of our country—and the most intelligent. What more could any man ask for?"

Luz gave Rubi a kiss on the cheek. "There is one true gentleman left in the world and it is you, Rubi."

Why couldn't I come up with things like Rubi said to women?

Rubi said, "Señor Cutter—Nick, if I may?"

"Certainly."

"Nick, we are truly in your debt for your quick action tonight. I am especially grateful to you. Had I reported to the general that his beloved son had been harmed while in my custody, he would have had my skin peeled off, piece by piece."

I was given a drink, a cigar and a chair, and we settled in for a blow-by-blow account of how I had thwarted the fire bomber. Unfortunately, Luz was in earshot range so I couldn't color my actions too much. I basically gave them an honest description—leaving out the fact that I had hired the man. I was a little nervous at first, but lightened up when it became clear Luz hadn't shared her suspicions about me with them.

In terms of my deeds, I didn't have to color the story—Rubi basically repeated it, but when it came from his mouth, it sounded like I had single-handedly taken on Fidel Castro and his rebel army.

The guy oozed charm, both to men and women. When Ramfis made an off-color joke about the bust size of one of the women hanging onto him, Rubi smoothed it out with a compliment. As Luz said, he was a perfect gentlemen. But I knew that coming in. I had thoroughly checked him out. Ramfis was my ticket into the Dominican Republic, but Rubi was the man to open the door so my ticket would get stamped.

❖

It was definitely a man's world, and Rubirosa managed to be both a man's man—and a ladies' man. He was as famous for his daring stunts on the polo field as he was in bed. Polo might be a rich man's game, but galloping around with a thousand pounds of horse between your legs while swinging a big mallet wasn't for the faint of heart. It wasn't for me—I'd just as soon ride a torpedo than a horse.

Rubi's family's owned a coffee plantation in the Dominican Republic. His father was appointed counselor to the embassy in Paris, and Rubi grew up in Paris, getting a worldly education that wouldn't have been possible in his own country. Good looking, multilingual with impeccable manners, he moved smoothly in social circles.

His first marriage was one that would help him for the rest of his life—Flor de Oro, Trujillo's Flower of Gold. The marriage was a stormy one and soon ended in divorce, but Trujillo must have understood that his daughter was not easy to live with because he forgave his now former son-in-law and provided him with diplomatic posts and personal wealth. Trujillo was smart—his country was noted for little more than him being a brutal dictator before Rubi became an international celebrity.

From my contact I found out that Rubi had other qualities that made him irresistible to women besides the reputed size of his cock—he shot blanks, so a woman didn't have to worry about getting pregnant, and he managed to give a woman an exceptional amount of sexual pleasure before he shot off.

"I've heard he jerks off in the afternoon before sleeping with a woman at night," my feminine informant told me. "That way he comes across in bed as if he can last forever."

My evaluation of the two men was interrupted by the sinister-looking dwarf who had introduced himself as a Dominican Republic security officer back at the cockfight. He wasn't really a dwarf, though he was a bit short and heavy set. Rather than his height, it was his dark persona, accentuated by slightly slanted eyes and slightly receding double chin, that left the impression that he was in some way darkly different than the rest of us.

I'd asked Jose if Mena was Ramfis's bodyguard, and was surprised when he told me Mena was not merely a security officer. Jose knew all about Mena because the man had a reputation. Mena was half Latino, half German. Technically he was in charge of Trujillo's Military Intelligence Service—called the SIM in the Dominican Republic. "Secret police, assassins, thugs, torture, censorship," Jose had said. "We could use someone as efficient as Johnny Mena and his SIM here in Havana."

"So we see you again, Señor Cutter," Mena said. "Surprisingly, the police did not catch the man with the bomb. They were not able to even find the putas that had distracted the guards. What do you think of such police work?"

I wasn't sure if I was being baited, so I lapsed into the truth, facts they knew themselves. "Have you tried driving across the island? You can cross most of this country east-to-west in an hour by car, but you wouldn't live to tell about it. People die every day, some of them are rebels, but it's even getting difficult to tell which side anyone is on."

"Johnny," Ramfis said, "we are guests in Cuba, it would not be polite for us to talk local politics. Besides, it is not Señor Cutter's duty to find those who try to kill me, it's yours."

"You must join us tomorrow morning when we take on the Havana polo club," Rubi said to me, quickly changing the subject.

From body language and tone of voice, I got the impression that the dictator's son and the dictator's henchmen were not on the friendliest of terms.

"These Cubans have boasted loudly that they are going to stomp us," Rubi said. "Ramfis and I plan to teach them a lesson."

"I'd love to attend but I have an appointment tomorrow afternoon, one I can't change."

"Ah, that means the woman has a husband and she must meet you at a precise time," Rubi said.

"No such luck. My contact is a man." I leaned closer to Rubi and Ramfis. "I would appreciate it if you keep this strictly confidential, but I am meeting a man who has a treasure map."

Both of them cracked up. Even the dour Mena joined in the laughter.

❖

"Ah, another map to sunken treasure. How many treasure maps have you been offered this week?" Rubi asked Ramfis.

"Counting the one to Captain Lopez's million pieces of eight waiting at ten fathoms, five maps," Ramfis said. "But the week is young."

Rubi gave me a friendly tap on the shoulder. "I apologize for taking the liberty of laughing, amigo, please don't take offense, but when you spend your whole life in the Caribbean, it is inevitable that you will come across many stories of treasure—and many offers to sell them."

"You're right, that's why I would never get involved. I'm just going to talk to this archives guy and tell him to take a hike, as the Americans say."

"The archives guy?" Rubi asked.

I brushed the question away with my hand as if I was now embarrassed by the subject. "I hate to be a cultural desert, but I've never seen a polo game, though I hear they're exciting and dangerous."

"Then you have never seen poetry in motion," Rubi said. "It is polo, not horseracing, that is the sport of kings. The game originated in Persia as practice for horse soldiers going into battle."

I listened attentively as Rubi enthusiastically described the play of the game. Two teams of four players on horseback used mallets to knock a wooden ball down a greenway, scoring goals by getting the ball between goal posts. I wanted to say it sounded like croquet on horseback, but kept my mouth shut.

Hotel staff removed the banquet table and brought out an entirely new assortment. We ate and drank and talked. After a while, Ramfis played a little poker with some Cubans who Rubi told me were high-ranking members of Batista's foreign service, but he played without enthusiasm. I suspected that having so much access to money without working for it had left him a little bored about money. No one seemed to be into gambling. I was eating caviar on a cracker when Luz appeared at my side.

"I'd like to get some air. Would you take a walk with me?"

I hid my surprise behind a blank look and followed her out of

❖

the inner sanctum. Crossing the gaming floor, she asked, "I notice you don't have much interest in gambling."

"It's rigged for the house. I'd rather try my luck at something with an even playing field."

"You're very fortunate, you come from a society in which you have great personal freedom. From my vantage point, everything is rigged for the house."

I didn't know if she meant having a dictator running the country or the way women were pigeonholed into the traditional home-and-sex roles by Latin men.

"You must forgive me, señor, I realize it is a man's world, but occasionally I ask myself why it isn't also a woman's world. There are a growing number of women in Western Europe and the States who ask the same question. Unfortunately, the world of the Caribbean and Latin America lags far, far behind, eons, not years behind."

"Personally, I'm all for liberated women."

"As my father would say, you are full of *mierda*."

"Nice language. I guess you think that being equal to a man means you have to talk like one, too."

That shut her up. It wasn't easy, not when you were dealing with a woman who was much more intelligent than you were. Of course, there was the kind of book-smarts she had—and the street-smart, smart-mouth, wise-ass intelligence people got when they've been forced to fend for themselves at an early age. I had street-smarts, but I admired someone like Luz who had that more refined, finishing-school, political- and social-awareness upbringing.

We went out of the casino and walked along a wooden boardwalk that ran along the ocean. Like I said before, I wasn't used to looking over my back in Havana, but now that things had gone to hell politically, I used panoramic vision. I'd just as soon have stayed inside where there were lights and action, but my chances of making it with this beautiful woman were better under a romantic moon than casino lights.

"I want you to answer a serious question," I said.

"You're not trustworthy."

Nothing like getting quickly down to the bottom line. She had guessed that I wanted her to define why she didn't like me.

"Okay, give me one reason why you don't trust me."

"I'll give you two. One, Cuban revolutionaries don't throw Molotov cocktails into arenas. By the time the man lit the wick on a bottle of gas and reared back to throw it, he would have been shot at least twenty times. They use hand-grenades, of which they seem to have an almost unlimited supply. A Molotov cocktail is something a Russian would think of. You are a Russian. And you denied knowledge of what a Molotov cocktail is."

"Half-Russian. I'm also British."

She shrugged.

"Have you shared your thoughts with your friends?"

She stopped and leaned against the wood railing. "Should I?"

My turn to shrug. "Do what you like."

She touched my face, cool fingers caressing my cheek. "Latin men like women with blond hair and blue eyes. Latin women like men with blond hair and blue eyes. My brother went to Finland once. He said the women were crazy about his dark skin and hair."

I kissed her hand and held it against my chest.

"If I told them my suspicions," she said, "you would be picked up by Batista's secret police and they would take turns with Trujillo's secret police and beat you. You're not too pretty now, but your face would look even worse when they got through."

I pulled her to me and kissed her. My lips melted into hers. I felt the kiss down to my groin. After the kiss she stared at me intently for a moment and then let me kiss her again. With her breasts pressed against me, my blood surged.

She drew away from me and walked slowly down the promenade.

"I need your assurances that you mean no harm for my friends," she said.

I shrugged. "I'm a businessman. I want to buy into your country. That was my only motive."

"Was?"

❖

"Now that I've met you, my interests in the Dominican Republic have gotten broader."

She paused and leaned against the railing. A cool breeze teased us and made the night magical.

"Why are you interested in, as you put it, 'buying in' to my country?"

"It's obvious that Batista's losing the war. I don't know what's going to happen, whether this communist rebel Castro is going to win, whether the Americans will intervene, or if there'll be a coup and Batista will be kicked out. Whatever happens, Cuba is slowly going down the drain. However the cards fall, it's not good for business. Smart people are already bailing out. I've got an offer to buy into a casino for chump change. I'm not buying in. My holdings are in the outskirts of Havana and in the Pinar del Rio region. I have a distillery that processes thousands of gallons of rum every day. The molasses for the distillery comes from sugarcane fields and a processing plant for the cane. In the last month, three of my trucks have been hijacked by the rebels. Naturally, the bastards took the finished product coming out of the refinery and not the raw stuff coming in.

"It's not just the rebels taking the rum. It's Batista's militia. They're as out of control as the insurgents. And it's getting worse every day. I've started paying 'protection' money to keep the road open, to the rebels and the militia. The barbarians are at the gates and Batista is drinking piña coladas and doing the rumba."

"So your plan is to relocate to my country."

"Relocate and retool. Just like Cuba, your country is one of the world's major sugarcane producers. I need the cane for my rum. And tobacco's a big product in the Dominican Republic. I understand your family owns a tobacco plantation."

"Yes."

"Good, I'll expect it as part of your dowry."

"Excuse me?"

"You don't think I would reveal all of my secrets without marrying you, do you? When Cuba falls, most likely Castro will take over. The Americans are already foaming at the mouth at the idea, but they're doing nothing to stop it. I told you I don't gamble in casinos, but life is a gamble. Right now I'm putting my money on this Fidel guy to win by a nose—no, make that a length or two. When that happens, the Americans are going to get uptight and self-righteous and slam the door on Cuban imports. When the market for Cuban cigars closes, who's going to fill the void?"

"I see. The Dominican Republic has a like climate to Cuba and can produce like tobaccos. In fact, it was there that Columbus first saw the Indios smoking cigars through a tube they called *tobago*—thus tobacco got its start and name in my country. I can see now that it is because of Christopher Columbus you wish to marry me."

"You're a smart woman."

"No, if I were smart I'd say no to your proposal."

"Which one?"

"That I marry you. However, before we marry, I must tell you that Rubi told me to take you outside and use my feminine wiles to get some information for him."

I broke into a smile. "He wants to know about the treasure map."

"*Exactimente*. You knew he would be fascinated by the mention of the archives. There is only one archive that is important to treasure hunters in the Caribbean, and that's the Archives of the Indies in Seville. It has the records of all the treasure ships sunk on the Spanish Main back in the days when the Caribbean was a Spanish lake. Supposedly a man employed for many years as a curator in the archives has tried to sell a map that he claims shows the location of a Spanish treasure fleet galleon."

"That's right."

"And you are in contact with this man?"

"No, I'm in possession of the map. I bought it from him a week ago."

"Does it show the location of a sunken-treasure fleet galleon?"

"That's what it claims to show, but so do a lot of other maps. But what makes this map unique are the qualifications of its seller. He is the former curator, and I had him checked out. He took off from Seville with his children's seventeen-year-old baby-sitter

❖

and a bad case of midlife crisis, and knocked around for a while until he ran out of money in a casino where I know the management. I bought the map after he had a bad run at the roulette table. Havana casinos being what they are, I arranged for the bad run."

She shook her head. "Your schemes know no bounds. You knew Rubi would be fascinated because he was once involved in a treasure hunt. He lost a lot of money but he loved every moment of it. You do your homework, don't you, Señor Cutter? When you set out to ingratiate yourself with the men who run my country, you were professional to the extreme. *Criminally* professional."

"Nick, call me Nick. If we're going to be lovers, it'll look funny if we don't use first names."

We were entering the casino when something occurred to me. "You said there were two reasons you didn't trust me. What's the second?"

"You're too damn attractive. There's something about a good-looking bastardo that attracts a women." She frowned at me. "Even one that should know better."

Dominican

REPUBLIC

36

❖

Ciudad Trujillo, Dominican Republic, 1960

Lua put down the telephone and sat very still. Her mind and body froze. She was seated at her dressing table, staring at herself in the mirror, shocked by the news she received.

"*Las Mariposas son muertas,*" the voice on the phone had said.

The Butterflies are dead.

She was in the apartment she shared with Nick in the capital of the Dominican Republic. They had been together for nearly two years, living together outside matrimony, to the scandalization of her family, because she refused to marry Nick. Havana and the rest of Cuba had fallen to Castro on January 1, 1959, when the dictator Batista fled the country—flying to the Dominican Republic and the arms of Trujillo—with bags of money at the conclusion of his annual New Year's Eve party for his loyal supporters—many of whom soon found themselves in Castro's prisons or before his firing squads.

"Señorita?"

Rosa, the housekeeper, stood at her door.

"Are you and the señor dining home tonight?"

❖

247

Luz stared stupidly at Rosa. It took a moment for the question to filter into her consciousness.

"Señorita, are you all right?"

"I—yes, yes, Rosa, I am fine." The words came out like an automated computerized voice. "No dinner tonight. We're eating out with businesspeople. Call Don Quixote's and reserve a table for six, please."

Luz got up and went into her bathroom. She shut the door behind her and leaned against the door, taking deep breaths to calm her nerves and get her breathing back in control.

She left the apartment fifteen minutes later. Their penthouse occupied the entire tenth floor of a building overlooking the bay. It was a very expensive piece of real estate but Nick had an ability to make money—and spend it. Their life together had been mostly ships not passing in the night but occasionally bumping together—he was busy building a business empire to replace the one he had had in Cuba, and she was busy with her friends at the university and her job teaching Spanish literature. They came together at night, for late dinners and lovemaking. "That's all we seem to do together," she told him one night, "eat and fuck."

He hadn't seen anything wrong with the scenario.

The only quality time they had together were trips they made to her "secret" place. She had inherited a small house, not much more than a beach cottage, in an isolated area on the north coast of the country, near the ruins of La Isabela, one of the first European towns founded in the New World. She had inherited the property from a maiden aunt. It was her secret place because few people knew she owned it and she told no one when she went there. When she lived alone she had gone there to hide out and work on her university projects in complete isolation. She managed to lure Nick there twice, but he went stir-crazy with the isolation.

Her mind swirled with thoughts as she waited for the elevator. She realized that her whole life had changed because of a single phone call, that someone had shifted the sands of time, that the life she had known was no longer possible.

She came out of the building's underground parking lot in a

❖

1960 Ford Thunderbird that Nick had bought for her. A pearl-white convertible with red seats, it was the only one like it in the city, making it both special and noticeable. But being noticed was not something she wanted at the moment. Six blocks from the apartment, she pulled onto a side street in an affluent section and left the car. She walked back to the main street and flagged down a taxi.

"Parque Colon," she told the driver.

The park dedicated to Christopher Columbus—"Colon"—was near Rio Ozama, the river that ran through the city and met the Caribbean, in the heart of the city's historic colonial district.

Santo Domingo, the city's name before General Trujillo renamed it "Ciudad Trujillo" in his honor, was over four hundred years old, making it the oldest European city in the Americas. It was a city of American firsts—the first true city, first cathedral, first palaces of the great, first true seat of government as Columbus, the "Admiral of the Ocean Sea," and then his son, Diego, the "Viceroy of the Indies," ruled as princes. It was where Hernando Cortés came first, before he sailed from Cuba to conquer the vast Aztec Empire with five hundred soldiers and sixteen horses, where Ponce de Leon dreamt of the Fountain of Youth and went on to discover a place he named for its many flowers—Florida.

But it was also a city of contrasts, where the language and culture was supposed to be Spanish but most of the people had an African heritage, where people with old and new money lived in luxury and the streets were crowded with people whose only possessions were the rags on their back and hopes for their next meal, where sidewalk cafés hugged buildings or lined plazas constructed a couple centuries before the American Revolution.

But dominating the city weren't the glories of the colonial past, but the contingencies of the present—and the pivotal contingency was Generalissímo Rafael Trujillo, "El Jefe," the Chief. He was omnipresent, more important than God, almost as visible as the weather. No issue of a daily newspaper was complete without his picture. No hour went by on a radio station without some mention of the Great Benefactor. His picture along with phrases like "Tru-

jillo and God" and "the Benefactor" adorned walls of buildings—
with Trujillo's name usually in first place. Songs were sung about
him. The Twenty-third Psalm was revised for schoolchildren to begin, "Trujillo is my shepherd. . . ."

A less obvious but ever more dramatic evidence of his domination of the city and country were the black Volkswagen vans of the
SIM, the Military Intelligence Service. The secret police, an internal and external spy organization, helped Trujillo maintain a reign
of terror against dissenters, not a few of whom ended up as shark
bait after the SIM paid a midnight visit to their houses.

It was truly the city of Trujillo. What was most strange to Luz
was the basis of the dictator's support—it came from the bottom. It
was the poorest, most underprivileged, most socially, politically
and economically oppressed people where the dictator found the
core of his support. The wealthy gave alliance only because they
wanted to protect their assets and lives. The middle-class kept
quiet because they were in a comfort zone that they wanted left
undisturbed. But it was the lower classes where the shouts for the
dictator were loudest and the most real. Perhaps in having nothing
material, they found something to be proud of in the reflected glory
of El Jefe. And in his vast wealth, most of which was obtained from
corrupt government practices.

*Can people have so little in body and soul that they fill them-
selves with the glory of a tyrant?* Luz wondered. Perhaps that was
why so many people sought God—to fill the voids within themselves.

Luz left the taxi at a corner of the park and slowly walked toward El Conde street. She saw no one she knew. When she was certain she wasn't being followed, she went up El Conde two blocks
and turned onto a narrow side street, little more than an alley. At
the back of the alley she entered a small store that specialized in
clocks and watches.

A man working on a clock spoke without looking up from his
work as she entered. "Señorita."

"Manuel."

She went by him and through a curtained doorway, down a

❖

narrow, dark hallway crowded with shelves jammed with merchandise. Out a back door, she walked quickly across a small cobblestone courtyard with a stone bird bath in the center. On the other side of the courtyard she paused at a wooden door and knocked. A man's voice told her to come in.

She entered the living room of a small apartment. The room was dimly lit from a single lamp next to a stuffed chair. Books were everywhere, books on all subjects, some on political theory that would not find favor with the present administration. A man with gray in his beard got up from the chair as she came in.

She went into his arms and broke into tears.

"Las Mariposas son muertas," she sobbed.

The Butterflies are dead.

37

❖

The Big Man from Chicago, Sam Giancana, was in town and I was baby-sitting him. I met him at the airport and put him in the back of the limo with me and Vincent. This was the same Vincent who tried to get me to buy a Havana casino at better than fire-sale terms—as Castro's guerilla army was entering the city limits. He knew all about casinos. I knew nothing. He had contacts in the States with men willing to invest in casino operations that involved beaucoup payoffs to local officals and risky political situations—and I had the contacts with the crème de la crème of Dominican Republic politics.

It wasn't a marriage made in heaven, but at the bank. I got 10 percent *tax free* of the casino's bottom line and all it cost me was a lot of black-slapping b.s., a few bribes, and another piece of my soul—the latter according to Luz, who saw my talents in a different light than I did. She accused me not only of dealing with American gangsters but said I was beginning to talk and think like one.

Personally, I didn't care what she said about me as long as she put up with me. I still found love as the deepest, most unfathomable mystery of life. God, UFOs and the Sphinx were not as difficult to

❖

fathom as why a person like me loved someone like her. "Opposites attract" may have been the result of our being together, but it didn't explain how we got there. Part of it was just plain sexual chemistry. When we went to bed, our passions melded us and we became one, not just physically, but with our hearts beating together.

SAM G. WAS A mob boss from Chicago. He had "interests" in clubs along the Las Vegas Strip and in "roadhouses" in Arkansas and Mississippi. I also heard that besides his gambling investments, he collected revenues from prostitution and protection rackets.

In other words, he was a gangster, American style.

He was one of the investors in Club Paradise, the casino-hotel project we put together on the beach a few minutes from Ciudad Trujillo.

I don't think that Luz really ever understood or appreciated exactly what it took to walk a line between gangsters who would kill you for cheating—real or imagined—and local police and government officials who would occasionally spit on the slate and wipe it clean, like Castro was doing in Cuba. And spilling a lot of blood along the way. There was book-smart and street-smart, but these mob guys had the intellect of jungle predators.

Vincent offered Sam G. a cigar.

"The best in the world now that Havana's gone Commie," he told Sam. "They ain't hand-rolled, you know, Nick has them rolled between the thighs of virgins."

"You're shitting me."

I assured Sam G. that it was the gospel, wondering to myself how men who made millions of dollars and ran big business enterprises could be so damn stupid. "We're reproducing the same fine cigars here in the Dominican Republic that they have in Cuba." It was a lie, but what the hell did he know about growing tobacco?

Sam bit off the end of the cigar and spit the piece out the window. "The take in the casino looks bigger than the money in my pocket," he said. "All's I got out of it has been pocket change. Why is that?"

❖

There was a not-too-subtle threat underlining the question.

"We're doing classy additions to the casino, big crystal chandeliers, private spas in suites, that sort of thing," Vincent said. "The boys from New York have opened one, too, not far from ours, and we have to make sure that everything is a class act to get the Stateside crowds into ours and not theirs. Then, you have to know, the payoffs here are murderous, worse than Havana. Even with that, we're returning a profit. You see big money when the overruns are finished."

"Just make sure none of the overruns end up in your pockets. If that happens, despite my own tender feelings for you boys, and I think of you as the brothers I never had, there are guys back in the States who would see to it that you come down with a fatal dose of Bugsy disease."

"Bugsy disease?" I asked.

"Bugsy Siegel," Vincent said. "Caught a slug in the eye after the Flamingo in Vegas got too expensive for the investors' tastes."

Talk about being stupid, I thought they were talking about something like malaria.

"What's this shit I heard about some rum you got that gives you a hard-on?" Sam asked.

"Garcia's Widow, good stuff," Vincent said. "Nick has it made from a secret formula created by a voodoo queen. You'll find some in your suite, and we're having a case sent to your house in Chicago."

Sam's eyes narrowed. "You think I slap my own dick up?"

Vincent went pale. "Hell no, Sam, it's just for laughs. Pass 'em around to the boys back home, they'll get a kick out of it."

I leaned back and decided to keep my mouth shut. Sometimes I wondered if Luz wasn't right—it might be easier to make an honest buck than a dishonest one. But playing on the shadowy side of business was in my blood. Not the blood my mother and father gave me—that was full of idealistic dedication to the Cult of the Common Man, the original give-a-sucker-a-break mentality. No, this was the corrupt blood I picked up in my years on the streets of Leningrad.

And throw in some of those years in British Honduras, too. It

❖

was pretty damn difficult to earn an honest living in the colony. Jack had tried it, although toward the end I was sure he was skimming from the till to buy expensive gifts for his lady friends. It was impossible because the deck was rigged—the businesspeople who got the breaks did so with influence in London. The ones who failed typically were strangled with red tape.

Bottom line, and that's what it always came down to, you could not do business in the Dominican Republic honestly. I suspected that was true for most of Latin America. The Spanish had laid a solid foundation of mordida, a system where government offices were literally sold to the highest bidder who then got paid by those wanting to do business in the country, where policeman and regulatory officials were so underpaid, they were expected to be on the take in order to feed their families.

Graft and corruption were the name of the game. If you wanted to play, you had to do it by their rules.

We arrived at the hotel-casino and started the Cook's tour with a drive-by. To save on building costs, the hotel wings were long, narrow, one-story units coming off the casino. The casino itself was cheaply built, but with a lot of fancy trim. Costs were kept down because you didn't need the quality building structures required in cooler climates, and who the hell knew when the next revolution was coming and we'd be out on our butts? If the revolutions didn't get you, the hurricanes did. We closed up shop in the hot, rainy hurricane season, and figured that we'd just rebuild if the place got flattened.

We turned around at the end of a hotel wing and were heading back to the casino when we spotted a man painting something on the low white wooden wall at the entryway to the casino driveway. Vincent yelled out the window and the man, a dark-skinned local, took off running.

Julio, the casino manager, met us out front as we stared at the words painted on the wall.

Las Mariposas se asesinaron.

"What is it?" Sam G. asked. "Some religious nut who's got a hard-on about gambling?"

❖

"It's about butterflies," Julio said.

"C'mon, Sam." Vincent grabbed Sam's arm. "Let's get something cold to drink and I'll show you the best green felt layout in the Caribbean."

Once they left, I said to Julio, "The sign says the butterflies were murdered. What the hell does that mean? What's this butterfly stuff?"

He hesitated and looked around as if he was wondering whether the flowers had microphones in them.

"Have you not heard of the three Butterflies?"

"No, why should I?"

He gave me an odd look, as if he questioned my answer, as if I had admitted not having heard about God.

"The Mirabal sisters. They have spoken at the university where Señorita Luz teaches, and have many friends on the faculty there. I didn't know if they were friends of yours and the señorita."

I shrugged. "Luz tries to keep her university friends away from me. She thinks I'm ignorant and crude. What's this about murder?"

"I don't know anything about murder," he said, defensively.

"The sign says the butterflies have been murdered."

"I have heard rumors—"

"Goddamit, Julio, spit it out. What's going on? This is your boss, not the SIM, asking the questions."

He spoke in a low tone. "It's trouble, Nick. The Mirabal sisters and their husbands opposed El Jefe. They called him a tyrant and enslaver of the people. They were the loudest in their criticism. You have to understand, such criticism is not tolerated. He put them and their husbands in prison. The women had been released, but instead of keeping their mouths shut, they have publicly spoken out against El Jefe."

"He bumped them off?"

"I don't know. First word was that the car with the three sisters and a friend went off a cliff and everyone was killed. But people who saw the bodies say that not only were their bones broken, they were strangled, too."

❖

Julio looked around again. "The three sisters, they had a code name in the underground that worked against El Jefe."

"Butterflies?"

"Yes, Las Mariposas. Now the Butterflies will fly no more." Julio's eyes misted.

I had no inkling about his political feelings. Being a casino manager was a tough job, not one for a sentimentalist.

He caught my thoughts and interpreted them as a weakness on his part.

"Understand, Nick, it is not a political opinion I have. The Generalissimo is said to have done evil things, but the country was in very bad condition when he took over. He did many good things. The Mirabal sisters believe that he is an anachronism, like Batista and the banana republic dictators, that his time has come and gone. You understand, señor, I have no opinion, I am just repeating what they say. But these were three very lovely women. The thought that they might have been—" He broke and walked away.

I got the picture. SIM agents stopped the car at an isolated spot, beat and strangled the women and driver, then put them back into the car and rolled it over a cliff. I didn't know the people, couldn't remember if Luz had ever introduced the sisters called Mirabal, but I had instant empathy for them on several levels. The similarity between SIM thugs and the NKVD, what they were now calling KGB in the Soviet Union, the secret police that murdered my father, wasn't lost on me.

Neither was the fact that if Luz was involved in any underground activities against Trujillo, we could get a midnight visit from the SIM.

The thought of Luz's lovely little neck being twisted by SIM chief Johnny Mena put a shudder through me.

❖

38

❖

"Did you know the Mirabal sisters?" I asked Luz.

We were in bed, our meeting place. I had tried to call her all afternoon, but she wasn't at home or at her university office.

"Yes, but I wasn't close to them."

"Do you know they're dead?"

"Yes, I've heard."

She lay back as she spoke. Her eyes were closed, no expression
on her face. Her breasts were visible through her flimsy, sheer negligee. I always stared at her in wonderment. How many times had I
seen her naked breasts . . . but the see-through sexy lingerie never
failed to arouse my hunger for her. I felt the surge in my loins.

"Is that all you have to say? You've heard? These friends of
yours were murdered!"

She opened her eyes to give me one of her looks.

"I said I knew them, Nick, not that they were friends. Mostly I
knew *of* them. They were openly opposed to El Jefe, neither a very
smart nor very healthy attitude to have in our country. Some say
they were killed in an accident, others say the SIM murdered

❖

them. There are as many different rumors as there are people spreading them."

She rolled over to go to sleep, her signal that she wasn't in the mood tonight. I was always in the mood, but knew better than to push her. I snuggled up to her back and put my arms around her. It wasn't long before my hard-on started growing and pushing its way into the softness between her naked thighs. She wore no panties beneath her short negligee, so there was nothing to impede its journey.

She leaned back harder against me and used her hand to direct my penis inside her. "Make love to me, Nick," she said, "I need you inside me."

I gently stroked her, then moved her into a position where I could massage her breast and her clit. She reared back against me, pushing harder and harder, until she began to shudder and gasp. My own explosion quickly followed.

Afterwards she lay in my arms and breathed softly against my face as she slept.

I lay awake, staring up at the dark ceiling, unable to sleep, because a thought kept nagging me. I didn't think Luz would lie to me—but there had never been anything between us that would cause a need for deception. Yet I wasn't completely satisfied with her explanation about the Mirabal sisters. It was the way she had brushed off their death as not being that significant. I couldn't say Luz was a wild-eyed revolutionary. Hell, I was so busy doing my own thing I hardly knew what she did with her time. For sure, she was very knowledgeable and somewhat opinionated in political matters. Like everyone else in the country, apparently except for the Mirabal sisters and their husbands, she mostly kept her views private. I didn't even know exactly what they were because we just didn't talk politics. She had plenty of opportunity to harangue about the Generalissimo if she thought he was the monster that so many other people thought he was.

One thing that was certain in this "man's world," she was a strong advocate of feminine causes. It was the one subject where I never saw her give quarter, privately or in public.

❖

With the whole town talking about the suspicious deaths of three women, literally feminine heroines who opposed a vicious dictator, why didn't she have more to say about their deaths?

Maybe I am just getting paranoid. I thought of that night they came for my father.

What would I do if they came for the woman I loved?

It wasn't a hard question to answer.

I would kill them.

❖

39

❖

Two months after the incident with Sam G. and the death of the mysterious "Butterflies," I was in the central tobacco growing region of the Dominican Republic checking out a cigar operation that was for sale.

On the auction block were tobacco fields, a drying facility and a small on-site factory for rolling cigars. It was a small but premium-quality operation. The property was owned by a former Deputy Minister for Economic Development. He ran out of patronage with El Jefe when a large public works project in the capital went to hell—a bridge collapsed before the first vehicle went over it. It seems the money that was supposed to go into steel reinforcement went into the pockets of the Deputy Minister and his pals. The fact that Trujillo and his clan got less of a share of the "steel money" added insult to the public-relations fiasco it created for the dictator.

I walked the fields and facilities with Francisco Gomez, the "blender" from my cigar operation. He sniffed at dirt, the growing tobacco, at the stuff hung up to dry, the mounds fermenting, and even the water before we checked out the rolling operation.

"As you know, señor, if you plant tobacco in two fields with

❖

slightly different soil composition, it will affect the flavor of the to-bacco. Tobacco acts like a child in his first year at school—it catches everything around it. The soil, fertilizers, water, air, the amount of sunshine, it all goes into developing the flavor. Even in a country the size of ours, there are only a few places where the filler, binder and wrapper can all be grown. What is interesting is that this area can produce a good quality puro by itself, perhaps not as good as the Vuelta Abajo valley in Cuba, but better than most here in our country."

I did know, but I let him ramble on. A *puro* was a cigar made from a filler, binder and wrapper all grown in the same country. I wasn't sure I was that interested in the operation. I wondered what would happen if I bought the place at fire-sale prices and the Deputy Minister came back into favor next week. For economic reasons he would probably come gunning for me.

Francisco smelled and tasted a piece of bitter green tobacco as we walked toward the drying sheds. He said, "I have heard that the finest wrapper in the world is not Cuban, but one that is grown in the United States. Is that true, señor?"

"There's a Connecticut shade-grown leaf that is the best." I knew that because I occasionally made claim on some of my cigars that the wrapper, the tobacco leaf that is wrapped around the filler and binder, was Connecticut grown. Like the heady world of fine wines, there are a few people who can tell the difference between good and superior, and a lot of people who can be fooled because they believe what they've been told.

We had begun at the farm's nursery where seeds were planted and pampered for six weeks. After they sprouted, they went into the ground, in straight rows the same as sugarcane, although the cane plants were much larger. Some of the plants were selected for shade-cultivation. These were protected under mesh. As the plants were growing, they were primed to remove leaves that would go into cigar making, with the lower leaves having the mildest flavor, and the upper ones the strongest.

Once the leaves were picked, they were sized and graded and hung in curing barns from several weeks to several months, depending on the weather and what the operator wanted to get out of the leaves. After this, bundles of leaves were piled into *burros*, mounds five or six feet high. Tight packing in the mounds kept out air and permitted the tobacco to ferment, a process known in the trade as "sweating" the tobacco over a period of months. The mounds heated up, and the leaves inside released nicotine, ammonia and other elements. It was at this point that the tobacco progressed from plants to what people smoked.

When it came out of the warehouse, the tobacco was brittle. It was graded again for filler, binder and wrapper, and turned over to a blender. Guys like Francisco were not unlike the blenders who selected various whiskeys or rums to blend into a finished product. Blending was an art, and a good blender was worth his weight in gold. I made sure I got the best when I stole Francisco away from another operation.

After the blender selected the tobaccos, in a hand-made operation like this one, the leaves were turned over to a roller who cut and rolled the tobacco until it was in the familiar cylindrical rolls that men suck and puff on.

We were coming out of the rolling room when a car drove up. The man in it was Ramos, someone I employed for "special" assignments. He was a low-life I used to dig into the backgrounds of business people I dealt with. It was good to know the motives of people who were selling—you never knew when a messy divorce or legal problems could drive the price down. And that's what I had Ramos for, to gather the dirt that drove down prices. With a beer belly bulging way over his belt, a shaggy mustache and two-day old beard, and baggy clothes with sweat stains under both arms, he looked like a caricature of a *bandito*. I couldn't stand the man, his methods or his smell.

One of the most painful things I'd ever done in my life was turn him loose on Luz.

Things had changed between us. Over the past few months we'd grown more and more distant, pulling apart even as I frantically tried to keep my hands on her.

Yeah, I was busy buying and selling the world, but we had

❖

lived that way for a couple years, each busy with our own lives. Something had happened, I wasn't sure what, but it was a no-brainer that things were different. We hardly made love anymore. Hardly had dinners together. There was always something, some reason why we couldn't get together. When I tried to talk to her about it, she became evasive and tense, once bursting into anger and storming out. The real killer was when she stayed out one night, telling me she had to stay with a sick friend, a woman who taught at the university.

Finally, I told Ramos to follow her. I felt like a shit for doing it. I knew a real man wouldn't have stooped so low. But I couldn't face her with accusations, couldn't make threats or demands on her. Luz had a hold on me that no one else on earth had—and the fear of losing her was petrifying to me. I had lost my mother and father and had carefully avoided romantic attachments that would make me sweat emotionally.

When I fell for Luz, when we moved in together and in essence became a family, I had made a commitment that wouldn't be easy for me to break. She was a part of me, just as my parents had been. And I couldn't stand the thought of losing her.

"Hola, señor, cóme está?"

"Bien, gracias. What did you find out?"

His shifty eyes darted around a little before they floated back to me. "You asked what she is doing with her time. She goes to the university, spends most of the day there."

"I know that. What else?"

He shrugged. "It is a difficult task you give me. I cannot run around the university looking through keyholes."

"I didn't ask you to look through keyholes. Where does she go, other than the university?"

"I have not seen her with a man, if that is your question. Not, at least, in the way one might call a compromising situation."

I knew the bastard was playing a game with me. He knew something. I saw it in his cocky walk and the little smirk on his face. He had something to tell me but wanted to take his time about it. He was an ankle-biter, a little piss-ant. I was the Big Boss

❖

and this was his time to gloat. Worry and jealousy over what Luz might be doing, who she might be seeing, whose arms she might be in, was building up a rage in me that I was finding hard to keep suppressed.

I spoke quietly, calmly. "Tell me exactly what you know. Don't fuck around with me. Is she seeing someone?"

He took off his hat and examined the brim. "Señor, I can only tell you this. When you wonder where she is at, I believe that you will find she is safely at the estancia."

"The estancia?" It was a type of ranch or farm. "What estancia?"

"La Fundacíon in San Cristóbal, the country estate of El Jefe."

"El Jefe? Trujillo? The generalissimo?"

It suddenly dawned on me. "She's seeing Ramfis, isn't she." I almost grabbed him and shook the truth out of him. She was seeing Trujillo's son. It made sense. Ramfis was good looking, the second most powerful person in the country.

"No, señor, I have spoken to a cousin who works in the kitchen of the estancia. She is not going there to meet with Ramfis."

I shook my head. "Okay, so maybe she's going there on university business. The estancia is probably where El Jefe conducts government business when he's not in town, right?"

"No, señor, she is not going there on university business. I have made certain of that."

I was tired of playing games with the bastard. I grabbed him by his shirt and pushed him back against his car.

"Listen to me, you little dirt bag, spit out what you know or I'm going to kick your ass from here to hell. Why is she going to the estancia?"

"El Jefe."

"El Jefe what?"

"She goes to see El Jefe."

"You told me that already. What else?"

"She doesn't go there on business, señor."

I couldn't comprehend what he was getting at. El Jefe ran the country, ran the people in it. He was about seventy, ugly as a turd, a stone-eyed killer who pretended to be a savior of the people—

❖

yeah, a humanitarian like Stalin and Hitler and Batista. No one said anything about him in public, but he was well-hated. Luz didn't bad mouth him because she would have lost her job.

When Ramos finally told me what he had found out from his cousin who worked in the kitchen, I hit him. My right fist came around and caught him across the side of the head and banged him, and my left fist came around and hit him on the other side of the head before he went down. When he was on the ground I kicked him until he was bloody and toothless.

I staggered away, the words he had spoken earlier chasing me like a dog with sharp teeth yapping at my heels.

"She is fucking El Jefe," he had gloated, "she goes to the estancia to service our chief's cock."

40

❖

Generalissimo Rafael Leónidas Trujillo Molina, known to the people of the Dominican Republic as "El Jefe," the Chief, rode in the backseat of his chauffeur-driven light blue 1957 Chevrolet sedan. The car was well-known in the city, not just for its color but for its twin fender horns.

The vehicle followed the city streets out of Ciudad Trujillo and went along the coastal highway that led west to the dictator's estate in San Cristóbal.

It was evening, just after dark. There was no police escort. But other than his "subjects" waving or shouting their admiration as the car went by, no one would have thought of approaching the vehicle.

There was no police escort because of Trujillo's contempt for his enemies and his refusal to show concern. He was one tough hombre. And he had a street fighter's mentality that if you showed a weakness to the mob, they'd get up the courage to attack you.

As he grew older and developed prostate problems, he made up for his lessening male sexual power by resorting to younger females, and perversions.

He was a man of enormous political and economic power. Un-

❖

like the infamous producer's couch in Hollywood where an actress—and sometimes an actor—could get the opportunity for stardom by taking their turn on the couch, it didn't take any talent to be successful by way of El Jefe's couch. It took a willingness. And as his tastes got more wicked, as did his appetite for younger girls, there was always a mother or father—and a daughter—who were willing to ensure the girl and the family's well-being by taking a turn.

He preferred his assignations at his ranch rather than the palace he occupied in the city. He was an old-fashioned Latino male, very macho, very domineering toward "his women," but respectful toward them as well. Although he was a man who had people tortured and murdered because they disagreed with his autocratic rule, he had enough good old-fashioned breeding not to fuck young girls under the same roof with his elderly wife and grown children.

Some people might consider such sentiment as hypocritical, but perhaps it would be something in his favor when he finally met his maker—wherever tyrants go after they have run out of violence and rage.

41

❖

Anna Maria was nervous. She fidgeted as she sat on a backless couch in a sitting room off the master bedroom in El Jefe's San Cristóbal estate. She was dressed in white—"the color of purity and innocence," her mother told her that morning, as she helped select her clothing for the girl's trip to the ranch. The color went very well with her copper-tone skin color, large, round brown eyes and full red lips. There was both a little of the Latino and the country's African heritage in her shape and looks.

Well-developed for her age, she had a tendency to be a bit fleshy and soft while in her mid-teens, probably looking forward to managing a weight problem after she had children.

She was a very precocious sixteen-year-old, in terms of her ability to deal with everyday situations, but this was not an everyday situation. She was reasonably well-liked at school, but had many more boys as friends than girlfriends. Girls tended to find her too competitive, especially when it came to their boyfriends. She was also well-liked by teachers, who found her ambitious enough to study hard and get good grades.

It had been a dance recital that brought her to the attention of

❖

El Jefe. The dance team at her high school had won a national competition to perform before the country's ruler. They performed modern and classical dances. The high point of the performance was the merengue, a dance that originated in the Dominican Republic and Haiti and spread throughout Latin America. Danced by couples with a limping step in 4/4 time, the weight always on the same foot, it was the dictator's favorite dance. After the merengue, the group did another classic, a bolero, not the lively Spanish step in 3/4 time but the Latin American version, a slow, romantic rumba with simple steps. Her own favorite dancing was swinging to rock-and-roll, especially the music of Elvis Presley, someone that oozed sex appeal to her.

A few days after the dance recital, Anna-Maria's parents had received a call from one of Trujillo's attachés, telling them how impressed the dictator had been with their young daughter. At first the parents thought that it had just been a courtesy call made to all the parents of girls who had performed, but they soon found out that they had been the only ones who had received a call.

The first call was soon followed by another. The attaché invited the parents and Anna-Maria to lunch at Trujillo's palace. Trujillo himself could not attend, there were important matters of state that were demanding his attention, but the attaché was his surrogate in letting Anna-Maria and her parents know that El Jefe had been struck by her model Dominican Republic looks, that she was the epitome of what the chief considered to be the flower of young womanhood.

Anna-Maria was pleased and again surprised. She had not been singled out by Trujillo during the performance, not even when he placed a pink ribbon with a gold-colored medal on the end around each girl's neck. She had merely curtsied and murmured, "Gracias, Excelencia," as she had been told to do.

During the lunch, the conversation had come around to the father's business. He was a former engineer who ran a small business importing machine parts for farm equipment. The downturn in the economy had been particularly bad for the business, increasing competition for fewer markets. Even worse, decreasing govern-

❖

ment revenues had resulted in higher import duties on the equipment he dealt in.

The attaché had listened sympathetically to the father's woes, nodding his head. Nothing more had been said until the attaché was escorting the family to the exit and then, giving the father a warm handshake, the attaché mentioned that there might be something he could do about the financial predicament. He smiled graciously, mentioning again how pleased El Jefe had been with Anna-Maria's classic looks. "Perhaps," he said, "it might be arranged to have El Jefe meet with Anna-Maria again, this time in private so that our chief can have some quiet time to appreciate her great beauty and charm."

Anna-Maria's mother and father were silent as they drove home, but they had exchanged looks as they walked away from the attaché to get into their car. Neither of her parents were dummies, though it was her mother who was the sharpest when it came to life situations. It was she who convinced her husband that he had to be more ambitious than teaching an engineering class in college, and urged him to go into business. And she was the one who was shaping her daughter for a good marriage instead of a career. There was little opportunity for a woman in business or government, but she wanted a good education for Anna-Maria and the sort of social and business connections that would guarantee her a stunning marriage.

"Why does El Jefe want to see me alone?" Anna-Maria asked during the drive home.

It was a question her mother dreaded answering. She brushed aside the question and told her it was not their place to wonder about what was in the mind of the leader of their country.

But Anna-Maria had an inquisitive mind, one that kept processing data even when it was told to shut down. She thought about the day the great man put the winner's ribbon-medal around her neck, about his smile and the look in his dark eyes.

"*Sexo!*" she suddenly screamed.

Her father jerked on the steering wheel and went over the white line, pulling back just in time to avoid a head-on collision.

❖

Her mother twisted in the seat of their car and said, "Be quiet! Don't you ever speak like again."

She was ready to challenge her when her father shouted, "Silence! You can't ever say that. It could cost us our lives."

Anna-Maria was no fool. She understood the fear that the generalissimo generated in the country.

And she was no fool when it came to men. She was a virgin; it was mandatory for young girls of her age and culture. Like her friends, she wasn't a virgin by choice but by necessity—there was no sure birth-control method. There was talk of oral contraceptives that would prevent pregnancy, but in Anna-Maria's country in 1961, as in most of the world, oral contraceptives were rumors, not reality.

Her dating experiences had been restricted to letting boys pet her breasts with her bra still on. Occasionally a boy would try to put his hand up her dress, but she would push it out. Only once did she let a boy cup her vagina with his hand and she remembered the tremendous sexual urge she felt, but her mother's training and warnings kicked in and she had knocked the boy off the couch they were occupying as she shoved him aside.

Following lunch with the attaché, no word passed between Anna-Maria and her parents about the incident for a week. She knew, however, that her parents had been discussing the situation because they became silent when she came into hearing range. And she overheard a comment her father made to her mother about the attaché calling again at his work to discuss business problems.

Anna-Maria never thought about which parent would approach her with the subject, but when it happened, she knew instinctively that it would be her mother. Men were weak when it came to some things—they much preferred to remain in the dark about ugly things.

Her mother had been circumspect about the subject, but Anna-Maria was smart for her age. She got the picture well-enough, had hit the nail on the head when she exclaimed that El Jefe wanted to have sex with her. She also understood without having a picture drawn for her that her family's future and her own was about to be radically affected by what came down between her and the country's leader.

Without specifically stating what needed to be done to get the desired result, her mother told her that if everything went all right, she would go to the finest university in the country, perhaps even to a world-class university in America or Spain, that a brilliant marriage would follow with a leading family of the country. It was a rosy prospect for her, not to mention that her parents would be bailed out of severe financial straits and be rewarded with rich government contracts.

All she had to do was have sexual intercourse with a man four or five times older than herself.

That was how she thought of it when she lay in bed that night after the roundabout, never-get-to-the-point, see-no-evil-speak-no-evil conversation she had with her mother.

She was vain enough to be thrilled that the most powerful man in her country, literally in the whole world, as she knew it, was attracted to her. But the prospect of having sex with the man was scary.

Anna Maria knew what a penis looked like—she had seen enough of them on little boys who ran naked in yards and on the streets. She had not seen a grown man's penis and had an inflated notion of what the size of one might be. She also knew how babies were made. As she lay in bed, she spread her legs and cocked them back, trying to imagine what it would feel like to have El Jefe on top of her, his naked penis slipping into the opening between her legs.

No matter how she imagined it, the paunchy dictator of the Dominican Republic looked slightly ridiculous naked.

❖

42

❖

Luz came up to the guard gate at La Fundacíon Enstancia and slowed enough for the guard to recognize her and see that no one else was in the car. She pulled the convertible Thunderbird up to the front of the main house and got out, leaving her keys and her purse in the car. Both were safe on the guarded property of the country's ruler.

The door was opened for her by an old woman who looked to be approaching the hundred-year mark. She had no idea whether the woman was an old family retainer that Trujillo kept employed out of loyalty or if she was someone he inherited when he took over the ranch. It once occurred to her that the old woman might have been Trujillo's lover when the dictator was young and the woman middle-aged, but she couldn't imagine the hunched, shriveled-up old thing being sexual. She hoped that she wouldn't live to see the day when she was old and hunched herself and people could not imagine a time when she had been sexual.

She permitted the woman to lead her to a suite with a large bathroom done in rose-colored Italian marble. She slipped off her clothes and stepped into the warm bath that was already drawn

❖

for her. She lay back in the luxurious bubbles, letting her body relax. A silver goblet filled with a fine Madeira, something to relax her further, was on a tray next to the sunken tub.

After soaking in the bath for half an hour, she cleansed her vagina with a douche, then took a shower, using a shower cap to keep her hair dry. She dried herself off with thick, soft towels of Egyptian cotton.

She applied a musk scent on her body, not putting any on her neck or shoulders because it would conflict with her perfume, and applied the scent liberally to the inside of her thighs.

During the preparation, she was careful not to look at herself in the bathroom's full length mirror. She used a small mirror to apply a new lipstick that claimed to be smear proof, then combed out her hair. Her hair fell into natural curls, which made it easy to deal with.

On the bed laid out for her were black-lace panties and a black bra. They were gifts of El Jefe and expected to be worn. She slipped into a light black linen shift that would keep her cool during the warm evening.

After applying eye shadow and a touch of color to her cheeks, she slipped on her sandals and once again fiddled with her hair, using a small mirror rather than the full-length one in the room.

She didn't like perfumes, they tended to give her headaches, but El Jefe had given her a gift of L'Aimant from Paris's House of Coty, a scent promoted as the "passionate woman's perfume." It would have been inexcusable not to have used it. She put a dab of it behind each ear.

When she was done, she looked for a third time in a small mirror to make sure her hair and makeup were perfect.

❖

43

❖

Anna-Maria looked up from where she was seated on the couch when Luz walked into the room. Generalissimo Trujillo had arrived a few minutes earlier. He had told Anna-Maria to sit back down as she stood when he entered the room.

"Relax, little one, you are here to enjoy yourself. We are not formal here at my country estate."

She couldn't help being in awe of him, but she found it hard to relax in the presence of the man called the Benefactor. Her entire life had been spent under his rule. From her first day in school, she was taught to sing songs in praise of the great man.

They had engaged in small talk for a few minutes before Luz walked into the room. The generalissimo asked polite questions about her family and school, intimating that he had heard good things about her school activities. The generalissimo oozed so much charm, she found herself relaxing.

She started to get up when Luz walked into the room but Luz waved her back down. Luz kissed the generalissimo on the lips. Anna-Maria had not seen her before, did not know who she was in relation to the generalissimo, but the kiss on the lips told her that the two of them must have a sexual relationship.

For sixteen, Anna-Maria was sexually inexperienced, but she had inherited her mother's sexual competitiveness with other women. She immediately felt jealousy toward what she considered the "older woman." Luz was only about ten years older than Anna-Maria, but any woman out of her teens seemed older to her.

She noticed one thing very quickly—her bosom was fuller than the older woman's. So was her whole figure. Luz was much thinner and even though she had an interesting face, even a sensual one, Anna-Maria had an innocent girl look. The difference was Luz had sexual maturity that made her more exotic than a mere girl.

Trujillo whispered something to Luz and she nodded. The small smile, a saintly smile to Anna-Maria, never left his lips.

Luz went to both doors and locked them while Trujillo kept up a conversation with Anna-Maria about her dancing skills. Anna-Maria's eyes followed Luz as she went to each door.

After locking the doors Luz came up behind the girl. Anna-Maria thought she was going to sit beside her on the backless couch, but instead she stood behind her. She heard something, a swish of clothes from behind her, but kept her attention on El Jefe, who was speaking to her.

Luz leaned down and whispered in her ear. "Our Benefactor suspects you have a very beautiful body. He would like to see your breasts. May we show them to him?"

She felt a sudden surge of nervousness, but she nodded. She was even pleased that he wanted to see her breasts. Her mother had told her that they were her best assets in pleasing a man. She didn't know how she was supposed to show them, the palms of her hands had become sweaty from sudden anxiety, but Luz took care of the matter.

Still standing behind the girl, Luz leaned around with her arms in front of Anna-Maria and unbuttoned the roll of buttons that went all the way down to the waist of the dress. Luz spread the top of the dress open, exposing Anna-Maria's white bra lined with white lace with a thin pink ribbon woven in. She squeezed her breasts. Luz undid the clasp on the front of the bra and pulled it aside, freeing the breasts. She cupped the breasts, holding them up so the Benefactor could see them.

"*Magnifico*," he said, "truly splendid." He saluted her by kissing the tips of his fingers.

Anna-Maria noticed that he was rubbing his crotch with his other hand, but no bulge had appeared. She had overheard her mother and father once talk about El Jefe having prostate problems, but she didn't know what that meant.

With Luz's hands still cupping her breasts, Luz leaned down again and whispered to her. "El Jefe has had many women during his life, hundreds perhaps. Now he enjoys watching two women. Do you understand?"

"Watching two women?"

Luz sat down beside her, facing opposite her on the backless couch. For the first time, Anna-Maria realized that Luz was no longer wearing the linen shift she had had on. She had taken it off and sat beside her wearing black bra and panties.

Luz used her finger to gently caress the girl's nipple. It stiffened and hardened under the touch. "I'll show you what he likes," she said.

She leaned forward, her lips brushing the girl's. She kissed Anna-Maria on the cheek and her lips came back over her mouth, circling the mouth with her tongue, going down the side of the her neck, and crept atop the lush mound of the Anna-Maria's breast, taking the nipple in her mouth and arousing it with her tongue. Anna-Maria felt the sexual stirrings building in her body.

Luz guided her to her feet and pulled the dress off. They sat back down and Luz kissed her lips again, teasing her mouth. Luz undid her own bra, slipped it off and placed Anna-Maria's hands on her own breasts. She responded by squeezing the breasts, kneading them. Luz guided her breasts into Anna-Maria's mouth.

Anna-Maria had resolved herself to whatever El Jefe had planned to do to her. She found herself first startled, even shocked

❖

by the fondling from a woman, but became more and more aroused as Luz touched her.

Luz pulled off her own panties and then Anna-Maria's. Standing up, she hugged the girl, bringing the girl hard against her breasts. Luz kissed her passionately, her lips going down to each of the girl's breasts, wrapping around each nipple. She guided the girl to be seated again and she knelt in front of her and kissed each of her knees. She spread the girl's legs, and slowly, kissing the inside of the thighs, her lips made their way to the pink between the girl's legs.

Still sitting, Anna-Maria spread her legs and cocked back her knees as the older woman found a spot in her pink area that she had not realized could give such an electrified sensation when it was caressed by a warm tongue.

Her mouth slightly agape, breathing uneven, she felt sensations that she only felt once before when she had touched herself in bed. She looked over at the Benefactor.

The front of his pants was wet.

There was no bulge.

❖

44

❖

I came home from the tobacco country in a quiet rage. Beating Ramos until he was unconscious had spent my hot rage to kill. Now I had a cold rage to kill. I didn't doubt Ramos's information or conclusions. He wasn't stupid, nor would he have risked bandying around El Jefe's name. Now I understood Luz's sudden absences and coolness toward me.

I drove back by myself, thoughts and feelings neoned inside of me like fevers, emotions galloping through me—I hit all the high points, shock, murderous anger, mindless jealousy. One moment I was ready to choke the lies from her and the next I had the impulse to cry at her feet and beg her not to leave me. Begging only lasted momentarily—the thought of her in the arms of Trujillo made me want to puke.

There was just one problem, one tiny doubt that existed in my mind—it just didn't seem like Luz. She wasn't a social climber, she wasn't a bootlicker or someone who would be a sycophant for status or career gain. I don't think she would be impressed with God. But she was a woman and he was the most powerful man in the

❖

country. Hell, he *was* God as far as she was concerned. He had already been dictator when she was born, and she had gone to school like everyone else singing praises of the great Benefactor.

I had learned long ago that women liked power in a man, masculine energy, financial clout, inter-personal dominance, raw power that is found in politics, entertainment and sports. Men like Rubi, who had a lot of experience dating Hollywood stars, joked that Hollywood was the only place in the world where a short, pudgy middle-aged man could go to bed with a tall, lush blonde. But he was wrong. Women went for powerful men *everywhere*. Hell, even I was constantly having the make put on me.

The only explanation I could find for Luz's infidelity was that she somehow became awed by the mystique of Trujillo. Unless she was being forced to service the old bastard to protect her family, but her father, mother and brother were living in Madrid where her father was a distinguished visiting professor at a university.

I called her acts infidelity, and that's what they were. We weren't married, but we lived together, professed our love for each other, shared the same bed, understood that we would someday be married when we were both ready.

My gut was raw and boiling as I drove through Ciudad Trujillo and headed for our penthouse. I kept telling myself over and over that I had to hear her out, let her tell me what was going on, and not just launch into brutal recriminations. I felt sick as I approached the building. *Loss, loss, loss,* that had been the story of my life. I should have known better than to permit myself to love, I should have protected myself better.

I parked in the underground garage. Her white Thunderbird was not there. In some ways it was a relief. I needed to go up and get my bearings, have a drink, sit down and think before I confronted her.

When I entered the penthouse, Rosa, the housekeeper, came into the living room. I could tell from the expression on her face that something was wrong.

"Where is she?" I asked.

❖

"Gone. They came and took her belongings. All of them."

I felt dead inside.

"Where has she gone?"

"I don't know."

"Who came?"

"Government men. SIM."

Jesus.

"Was she forced?"

"No, señor. No, she directed them in the packing."

I went into the bedroom. The cosmetics and grooming items on her vanity were gone. I didn't bother checking the closets—I knew they would be empty.

One thing was odd. The full-length mirror near her vanity was broken.

Rosa came in behind me.

"What happened to the mirror?" I asked.

"Broken, señor, she did it. She smashed the one in the bathroom, too. I don't know why, can you tell me why?"

I stared at the mirror and shook my head. I had no clue.

"Señor Cutter."

The voice came from behind me. I turned and faced Johnny Mena.

I hadn't seen Trujillo's chief of the SIM since we had met in Havana nearly two years ago. But I had heard plenty about him. He was his master's dirty tricks thug. I suppose every dictator has a Johnny Mena—Stalin had his Beria, Hitler his Himmler. They needed someone to pull the trigger, spill the blood, spread the terror.

Two SIM agents entered behind him.

"We will wait while you pack," Johnny Mena said.

"Am I going someplace?"

"*Si*, señor, you are being asked to leave the country—in lieu of a prison term."

"What did I do to deserve a prison term?"

Johnny Mena's eyes widened in mock surprise. "For illegal business activities, of course. The Minister of Economic Development is shocked to discover that you have been paying bribes to public employees."

"Funny," I said, "I don't remember him being too shocked last time we had lunch and I slipped him an envelope full of American dollars."

45

❖

San Cristóbal Highway, May 30, 1961

Salvador Garcia was nervous—piss-your-pants, shaky-knees, sweaty-palms anxious. He was riding shotgun in a car with a group of men who intended on waylaying the generalissimo's car as it drove along the coast highway from Ciudad Trujillo to El Jefe's country estate near San Cristóbal.

When he was a teenager and got a ride in other boys' cars, the privileged seat, other than the driver's seat, was the front seat next to the passenger window. They called occupying that seat "riding shotgun," adopting the phrase used during the days of stage-coaches when a man with a shotgun rode next to the driver.

Salvador was an unlikely candidate to be involved in a plot to assassinate El Jefe. Salvador was a product of old Dominican Republic money—his family's ownership of a sugarcane plantation predated the country's declaration of independence from Spain in 1821. His family managed to stay on the good side of the succession of dictators who ruled the country, literally from the time an occupation by Haiti, which came on the heels of independence, was thrown off.

❖

In terms of the color of his blood, it was blue indeed. From the standpoint of his family, the Trujillos, who had ruled the country for three decades, should have been just a speed-bump in the family's history, someone they had to pay off and show their support for as they always did.

But Salvador lacked the discretion of his long line of sugarcane planter ancestors. He made the mistake in a moment when he had had too much to drink and started running off at the mouth, calling two of Trujillo's brother's pimps because they had been on the take from the prostitution rings in the capital. His father always said he had diarrhea of the mouth, and this time he flushed the family fortunes down the toilet. He couldn't get labor to harvest his sugarcane crop, but that didn't really matter—he couldn't have sold the cane to a processor even if he managed to get it cut.

It was the same story for all the dozen and a half other *con spiradors*. Each had an ambition stilted, a wrong unredressed, a humiliation suffered, a reversal of fortunes, all at the hands of the Trujillos.

These men were not the idealistic Cubans who battled Batista for Castro and then fought Castro for liberty, or who had died on the beaches trying to unseat the despotic Trujillo regime. There was no idealism in their ranks, merely ambition. They wanted to kill Trujillo for personal gain.

And they had strange bedfellows on their side—the United States and the Catholic Church.

It was nighttime, shortly after ten o'clock when Salvador and his cohorts got word that Trujillo had left the city to go to his San Cristóbal estate for a rendezvous with his mistress, his driver taking him along a route that ran along the shore of the sea. It was not a well-traveled route at night, which is why the assassins had chosen it as the best place to ambush the dictator.

They knew only two men would be in El Jefe's 1957 Chevrolet—El Jefe and his driver. Both men would be armed with handguns and machine guns. Trujillo was a very capable marksman.

The idea that a small group of military officers, businessmen

❖

and government officials would attempt what larger radical groups had failed at added sweat to Salvador's wet fears.

Salvador knew that some of Trujillo's bravado was based simply on longevity—he had been around so long, he was thought of as invincible—and thought of himself the same way. Like most of the people in the country, Salvador was under the age of forty. That put him in with the majority of the people in the country who either were very young or not yet born when Trujillo started his reign thirty-one years earlier. To them, Trujillo was more omnipresent and omniscient than God.

Much of the time during those several decades of rule, he had provided economic progress and stability to the country. As things started going to hell politically and economically in the 1950s, two special-interest groups still supported him—the Catholic Church and the United States. As it was put to him by President Kennedy, Trujillo was a bastard, but at least he was *our* bastard.

By the end of the 50s decade, at a time when Cuba was falling to the Red Menace, the Dominican Republic's economy took a dive. Radicals started raising their revolutionary heads, and Trujillo began to lose the support of his main allies, the Americans and the Church.

Six months after Cuba fell to Castro on June 14, 1959, with help from Castro, Dominican Republic exiles invaded the country but were stopped on the beaches by Trujillo's forces. Those who survived the murderous machine-gun fire during the beach landing were taken to a military base where they were questioned under torture and then killed.

Frightened that Trujillo's brutal, anachronistic brand of despotism was creating the alchemy for another radical Red revolution, Castro-style, the Americans decided that it was time for a change.

The harbinger of political change, American CIA style, circa 1960s, was assassination.

It was with the CIA's implicit consent that Salvador and his cohorts took three cars out on the San Cristóbal road on a warm May night and waited for a light blue Chevy to come along.

❖

Salvador was deep in thought when a conspirator in the back-seat suddenly yelled, "It's him!"

The blue Chevrolet shot by, picking up speed as it left the city behind.

The car Salvador was riding in pulled onto the road and accelerated. Salvador said a prayer and wiped his wet palms on his pants. The shotgun he held—appropriately, he had insisted upon bringing his own shotgun rather than use a military rifle—felt slippery in his grip.

Once they were behind El Jefe's car on a straightaway, they flashed their brights to signal the two cars waiting ahead.

As their car pulled alongside the Chevy, Salvador pulled the trigger of the shotgun only to realize, to his horror, that in his anxiety he had been popping shells in and out of the chamber and that there was no shell ready to be fired. A burst of gunfire exploded from the man in the back seat. The back window of the Chevy disintegrated as the burst hit. The Chevy went off to the side of the road as Salvador pumped a shell into the shotgun's chamber. More fire came from the rear-seat assassin as Salvador finally let loose with the shotgun.

El Jefe's Chevy had stopped. Trujillo was firing from the back-seat and his driver out the front driver's window by the time Salvador and his companions got out of their car. The fire-fight continued between the two sets of weapons, momentarily a stand-off, then the second vehicle of assassins arrived and four more men joined the fight.

Generalissimo Trujillo, Benefactor of the Republic, a man of iron nerve and grande cohunes, bleeding from a wound received in the first volley that came through the rear window of his Chevy, stepped out from the back of his car and fired from the hip.

He went down, hit again and again, his body jerking as the bullets hit him.

The king was dead.

One of the stories that would be told and retold about the battle, is that after the first volley, Trujillo's driver had yelled that he was turning the car around to go back to the city because they

❖

were outnumbered and that the generalissimo told him not to turn around—that they would stand and fight.

He was mucho hombre.

And one hell of a bastard.

❖

PARADISE LOST

FREEDOM

"*WE* prefer to do things comfortably."

"But I don't want comfort. I want God, I want poetry, I want real danger, I want freedom, I want goodness, I want sin."

"In fact," said Mustapha Mond, "you're claiming the right to be unhappy."

"All right then," said the Savage defiantly, "I'm claiming the right to be unhappy."

"Not to mention the right to grow old and ugly and impotent; the right to have syphilis and cancer; the right to have too little to eat; the right to be lousy; the right to live in constant apprehension of what might happen tomorrow; the right to catch typhoid; the right to be tortured by unspeakable pains of every kind."

There was a long silence.

"I claim them all," said the Savage at last.

ALDOUS HUXLEY,
BRAVE NEW WORLD

46

❖

San Juan, Puerto Rico

I was in my suite at the Day Club Hotel when I got the telephone call.

I still had my feet in the Caribbean. Other than my state of mind and finances, Puerto Rico wasn't a hell of a lot different from the Dominican Republic or Cuba. It was in the same neighborhood, across the Mona Strait, about fifty miles east of the Dominican Republic. The people had the same type of mixed Spanish and African heritage, they spoke Spanish, had an "old town" historic district along the waterfront—hell, the island was even discovered by Christopher Columbus. Added to the list was the fact that the island was cursed by that same unholy trinity of sugar, rum and tobacco.

The place was under American rule, grabbed during a war with Spain about sixty years ago, so it was a bit more peaceful than the Dominican Republic or Cuba, but that observation came with a caveat—Puerto Rican insurgents tried to kill President Truman back in 1950, and in 1954 they opened fire in the U. S. House of Representatives in Washington, D. C., and wounded five congressmen.

❖

Like I said, it wasn't much different than the Dominican Republic or Cuba. I just hoped I got out of town before the next revolution.

It had been almost a month since I'd been taken to the airport in Ciudad Trujillo, carrying my passport, a suit of clothes and the money in my wallet. Since that time, my business interests in the Dominican Republic—my distillery, sugarcane fields, cigar business—had been "sold," although that really wasn't the right word for it. "Stolen" at ten cents on the dollar was a more accurate description. And that 10 percent got eaten up by "taxes."

The one thing they could not take from me was the Garcia's Widow brand of rum. They took the distillery, but the rum was still blended from Sarita's secret formula. The first thing I did when I hit San Juan was license the brand to a major rum distiller. I called Sarita to arrange for the ingredients she had been sending to the Dominican Republic to be shipped here to Puerto Rico instead.

"I saw it in a dream," she told me, alluding to what had come down in Ciudad Trujillo. "Men with black masks came and took you away. I reached for you but your hands were always too far away."

I believed her. And even if Johnny Mena's men didn't wear actual masks, the masks were there, anyway, a metaphysical extension of their black hearts.

I lived in mortal fear that some asshole in the Dominican Republic would counterfeit my rum labels and put an inferior product on the market. I had counterfeited labels myself many times, but that was different. And I never sold an inferior product. At least, not completely inferior.

My one financial regret was that I had not seen the blow coming and had not stashed a big wad outside that rat-hole of a country. I had put all my eggs in one basket. The Trujillo gang made an omelet out of mine—and swallowed it whole.

At least I had enough survival instinct to get the brand licensed right away. That would keep the legitimate stuff on the shelves so there couldn't be room for the phony labels, if that's what was going to come down. But that bit of business savvy stretched the limits of my emotional wire. I did the licensing deal

❖

before I sat down and just gave up, too damn traumatized emotionally to face the fact that the woman I loved had pissed on our life together.

"You worthless wimpy bastard," I told myself.

Any man with red blood in his veins would not have let a woman screw him over and take it sitting *down—he'd take it lying down*, poking his cock into everything that wore a skirt, ramming it in so hard, he'd blow their asses out, make them sorry they were fragile women in a tough world run by men.

That was the kind of man I always thought I was, the macho type who wouldn't give a second thought about some bitch that did him in. I'd just go out and fuck everything in sight . . . only it hadn't turned out that way. Wimpy bastard that I was, I thought of nothing but Luz from the time they put me on the plane in Ciudad Trujillo. I endlessly ran our relationship over and over in my mind, trying to figure out what I did wrong.

Goddamn women—they just have no mercy on men. Us poor guys are sweet, lovable, affectionate dopes and they just grind their spike heels into our hearts.

I called Sarah the moment I hit San Juan to tell her what had happened. She was still my favorite person in the world—next to the woman whose name I wanted to forget. She was back in Merry Ole England, even had a beau, a decent chap who worked for the Underground, the London subway system. But she still couldn't get over that bastard Jack who had treated her like a doormat.

"You have to give up the ghost, Sarah," I told her, full of sage advice. "Jack was a shit, you're better off without him."

"Then I guess you must be better off without Luz," she said without any pretense of innocence.

Bitch.

But I still loved her and knew I deserved her caustic rebuttal. I was the most deserving guy in the world when it came to needed punishment, at least that looked like the reasoning of the gods who were raining bad things down on my head like a plague of frogs.

"What *are* your feelings about Luz?" she asked. "No macho stuff, tell me really what you feel."

❖

"About the same if she had ripped out my heart and threw it in a vat of acid, about the same if she had whacked off my nuts and fed them to her dog. I have a few more feelings, like I want to kill the bitch and fuck her, but I'm not sure in what order."

Poor Sarah. I think she had always thought of me as basically sane, albeit a little criminal, but after our conversation I'm certain she thought I should be committed. My language alone made the poor girl question my mental state. Hell, I could have easily told her what my mental state was—murderous rage fighting with black depression.

One lesson I learned from Luz walking out on me was one I would never forget—I knew how love quickly could turn to hate. Hell, they were just flip sides of the same coin. Heads I love her, tails I hate her. It was that easy. And it switched to tails since I found out she was balling the old bastard who terrorized millions of people.

But even with all the hate and rage, I still loved her.

I had been drowning in an alternating current of loss, self-pity and rage when I got the call.

"Of course you know, amigo, El Jefe is dead."

The voice on the other end of the line was Rubi himself, Porfirio Rubirosa, polo player, international-set playboy, expensive gigolo. Last but not least, compadre, baby-sitter or whatever the hell of Ramfis Trujillo, the new dictator of the Dominican Republic.

"I read the papers."

Calling me "amigo" was not Rubi's style. His voice on the phone revealed a hint of stress. That wouldn't be an unusual reaction to the fact his former father-in-law and chief benefactor had taken a couple dozen rounds in a violent gunfight.

When he called, it took me a moment to orientate myself. I'd had a couple drinks, actually maybe even a couple too many, but hell, it was almost noon—at least it would be in a few hours.

"I am assisting Ramfis," he said.

"Long live the new king. The newspapers say you and Ramfis were in Paris when word came that the old bastard had been as-

❖

sassinated. Spending some of the money you and your pal stole from the poor of your country?"

There was silence on the other end.

I'm sure Rubi wasn't used to being spoken to like that. I didn't care. If he was an "amigo," where were he and Ramfis when I was getting thrown out of the country and my property stolen because an old man they served lusted after my woman?

"You better watch your ass, Rubi. Ramfis isn't like the old man. He doesn't have the balls to run the country. He's good for a few good knocks, killing a few people, stealing more money, but he doesn't have the staying power to be a despot. That takes the sort of murderous lust for power which the old man had. Ramfis has had too many soft landings. You stick around and hold his dick, you'll end up on the chopping block with him."

More silence.

Yeah, I had a few shots of Moskovskaya, not my counterfeit stuff, but the real stuff before the call came in. I wasn't a rum drinker. It was pussy booze compared to a good, clean shot of vodka that would knock you on your ass and burn the hair on your soul. Like any good Russian, I took my vodka neat, straight out of the bottle, not even stopping to pour it into a glass, and none of that olive and shake-but-don't-stir crap, either.

I never really understood how Russian I was until I began to drown the damage to my soul with vodka.

I was on a roll with Rubi, the vodka had oiled my tongue, I'd become a velvet-tongued devil, in my own opinion, so I kept it up.

"If you called to tell me that it's all a big mistake, that the old bastard didn't mean to steal my woman, that Johnny Mena and his shithead thugs didn't mean to steal everything I'd worked so hard for, then hang up and call someone who cares—or buys into the bullshit. You wanna know what I think about your fuckin' little ankle-biting, chickenshit—"

"I called you about Luz."

It was my turn to shut up.

I shook my head to clear some of the alcoholic haze. He had used

❖

the "L" word, had spoken the unmentionable name. The emotions that had been tying my stomach in knots rose up and grabbed me by the throat and choked me. I wanted to call her. The moment I heard Trujillo had been assassinated, I had thought of little else except her. I had picked up the phone a dozen times and slammed it down, swearing to cut off my own hand if I did pick up the phone and try to dial her. The king was dead. My whore was available again.

Yeah, since I heard the news, I'd thought about getting together with her again, thought about telling her I loved her, even about luring her into a position where she would be emotionally and financially dependent on me—and then dumping her. I thought about calling her and simply asking, "Why?" Had it been something I did? Was there some way to heal the past?

Sometimes I fantasized that the phone would ring and I would hear her voice on the other end. What would I say? What would she say? I was certain that I would take her back if she wanted to come back into my life. And I hated myself for my weakness.

It all hurt.

Rubi's voice came back over the line, a little irritation underlining the edge of stress.

"As you know, Nick, I am back in the country. And yes, I was in Paris with Ramfis when the sad news came in of the treachery of those who should have kissed the feet of our Benefactor. We flew back together. Now I must assist him in this hour of our country's need."

I almost puked. Someone had to be listening on the other line, probably Johnny Mena. Rubi was loyal to the Trujillos, hell, he married one once, but he wasn't into kissing feet, not unless the secret police were listening—or the feet belonged to a rich widow.

The gears in my head began to churn. My first instinct was that Rubi had called to sell me back my own property, probably to raise money for Ramfis, to buy guns for his new government. But he had spoken Luz's name, so I shut up and listened because it sounded like there were going to be some twists to the game.

"As you might have read in the newspapers, Ramfis is firmly in the seat of power here in Ciudad Trujillo. And he has been unmer-

❖

ciful to the murderers who shed the blood of El Jefe. They have gotten more justice than they gave our poor Benefactor." He paused for a moment. "The murderers disclosed their dirty secrets under questioning."

Questioning, in Dominican Republic police parlance, meant torture, the kind that makes you pray you die soon.

I was beginning to wonder if he had dropped Luz's name just to get my attention and really was calling to make a buy-back deal. My mind was calculating how much I should pay if a deal was put on the table—and where I'd get the money if he offered me a chance to buy back my businesses.

Was he assuring me that they had the situation under control so I would feel comfortable coming back and doing business in the country?

Maybe I had the guy wrong, too. Everyone liked him, regardless of his connection with the Trujillos. And we had been friends of a sort, not really close but on a comfortable first-name basis during the couple years I spent in the country. But not close enough for a government insider to call me up just to chat up current events, not unless there was an ulterior motive.

One thing I knew—Rubi was an all-right guy in most ways. He wasn't as cruel or as stupid as the Trujillos. He was just loyal to them. Frankly, I always thought the guy had too many brains and too much class for people who were essentially thugs with fancy titles.

"Are you aware of how the murder of El Jefe came down?" he asked.

"You mean assassination. When you run a country, they call it assassination, don't they? 'Murder' makes it sound like he didn't have it coming. All I know is that he got pumped full of lead and went down fighting."

With a strained voice, Rubi said, "It happened at night. El Jefe finished conducting government business in the capital, stopped by his daughter's house, and then headed out for his estancia at San Cristóbal."

Mention of the country estate brought back an old memory, the day I kicked the crap out of that swine Ramos, making him pay for my pain.

"El Jefe was on his way to visit his mistress," he said.

The knot in my stomach twisted tighter, reaching up and choking me. "Why did you call? What do you want?"

Silence. The only sound was the tick of a clock on the fireplace mantel. I had puzzled over the fireplace earlier as I drowned my sorrows in sixty-proof vodka—who the hell needed a fireplace in a place like San Juan? I listened to the silence, unconsciously counting the ticks of the mantel clock.

"Would it interest you to get back the millions you lost when the generalissimo no longer desired your presence in the country?"

"You mean when that old shit fucked me over by stealing my girl and my property? However, I guess that's just how business is done where you come from. Let's get down to the bottom line, what's it gonna cost me to get back what is rightfully mine in the first place?"

More silence. Rubi must have led a sheltered life, or he was used to dealing with guys with a lot more charm and class than I had. I was running a little short on both after being royally fucked over. I tried to control myself, but the bitterness just kept boiling over.

I heard Rubi sigh. I'm sure he wished he was in Paris on a polo field and not taking care of dirty laundry for the new king. During the couple of years I spent in Ciudad Trujillo he hadn't been around much, but he was always an object of conversation. I heard he had spent every cent he got from the rich women he married. I didn't know if his loyalty to Ramfis and the now-dead El Jefe was due to love or money.

"Not everything about the investigation into El Jefe's murder is public knowledge," he said.

Okay. Ask me if I care. He seemed to be having trouble getting down to the bottom line.

"Under . . . questioning . . . certain facts were revealed that have been kept from the public because the matter is still under investigation. Especially certain matters about coconspirators."

"Rubi, you haven't called to give me a lecture on Dominican Republic police methods, most of which were probably learned from the Spanish Inquisition. Why don't you just tell me how much ransoming my property will be so I can see if I can raise the money?"

He went on, smoothly, every bit the gentleman he was. "One of the pieces of evidence that has not been made public is that El Jefe took the road to San Cristóbal late that night he was ambushed because he received an urgent call from his mistress."

Urgent call from his mistress. Out on the road late at night. Ambushed.

I froze. Somewhere in the alcoholic haze bred in my brain by too much Moskovskaya, an alarm bell started going off.

Rubi went on, his words smooth and oily. "You understand, my friend, the assassins were informed of the time El Jefe would be on that road." His voice dropped down to a whisper. "Someone made sure that El Jefe would be on the road so he could be murdered."

I stayed quiet. My mind was processing information. I was beginning to get the big picture. Tense breathing was my listening response.

"Under . . . questioning . . . we found out who arranged with the assassins to put El Jefe on the road that night."

I pulled the phone away from my ear. There were so many thoughts, so many feelings erupting in me, I was ready to burst. If I'd been in the same room with Rubi, I'd have gone after him and beat the truth from him.

"Have you ever heard of the Butterflies?" Rubi asked with a silken voice. The man could grease race cars with his charm.

I could understand why the richest women in the world paid for his company. It had nothing to do with the size of his cock; it was his golden tongue that hypnotized them, that made them open their purses and their cunts for him. I could actually see it coming, see the punch through the alcoholic haze, but I was too mortified to duck.

"Three sisters," I said. "Las Mariposas. Part of the underground to overthrow El Jefe."

"There were four Butterflies."

❖

47

❖

My mind was racing. Fuck your mother! Luz had lured the old bastard out onto the highway so he could be killed. She was part of the underground freedom movement.

My hand shook so bad I supported the phone with both hands. I cleared my throat and spoke calmly, clearly, without emotion, smothering the volcanic eruptions surging from my stomach.

"What do you want?" I asked.

The mantel clock ticked so loud, the noise banged between my ears like the clash of cymbals.

When he finally spoke, I listened carefully to his answer to my question, took down his callback number and hung up. I stood up and took the bottle of vodka and dropped it into the trash can under the room's vanity. From now on, I would need a clear head.

I gathered my thoughts and all the feelings tearing me apart, out onto the balcony. As I leaned against the railing, I looked at San Juan Bay and the rusty-blotched ghost of El Morro, the sixteenth-century castle that once protected the city. Chalk up another Caribbean similarity for Puerto Rico—Havana had an El Morro bay fortress, too.

❖

From the manager of the hotel I found out how the town got its name—Puerto Rico, Spanish for Rich Port, was once the name of the town and San Juan was the name of the island. But over the years the names got switched. The Dominican Republic claimed they had the bones of Columbus and Puerto Rico had its claim to historical discoverers—Ponce de Leon was buried somewhere around here, when he died in Cuba after he took a Seminole arrow in Florida and missed finding the Fountain of Youth.

My volcanic emotions had become a tornado of feelings and thoughts swirling and clashing in my head. A month ago, I had been picked up by the feet and shook upside down until my pockets were empty and my emotions scrambled, staggering ever since then. Now I was on the roller coaster again, hanging on for dear life with both hands, as it barreled down a track that looked more like the side of a cliff than a slope.

Rubi never did get around to expressly stating the reason for his call, but it wasn't hard for me to figure out. There were three possibilities—one, he called to shoot the breeze, letting me know Luz had left me for Trujillo to help rid the country of a tyrant; two, he called in the hopes that I would help Luz; or lastly, in the hopes I would lead them to her.

Anything was possible, but the most likely reason—the one I'd put my money on—was the last one. Rubi wasn't a bad guy, but getting down to that bottom line I always liked to reach, he was in bed with the Trujillo's. Hell, in a lot of ways, he had been more of a favorite son to the old man than Ramfis.

No, this was no altruistic call from Rubi, no matter how he felt personally about Luz and El Jefe. I had no doubt Johnny Mena was listening in on the call, or at the very least had arranged it. The motive was clear—Luz was a loose end for the new administration. They had to find her and punish her or they would invite a million others to join the anti-Trujillo cause. It was good that her family was out of the country. Johnny Mena would handle the punishment of the conspirators about the same way Batista, Stalin and Hitler had let their secret police interrogate suspects—not only torture and kill the actual participants, but arrest and imprison

❖

their families so the next group of anti-Trujillo conspirators would know that they were betting more than their own lives.

I didn't have to analyze my feelings about Luz. I felt pain for her, and fear, mortal fear. If the SIM got ahold of her . . .

I didn't want to think about it, but I couldn't help it. I couldn't chase out of my head an image of the three Mirabal sisters having their bones broken, three young women who were brutalized before being strangled.

Could men do these horrible things? I asked myself. But the answer was obvious—they were all around us. No despot ever had trouble finding thugs to do their dirty work. They don't do it for the money—I'm sure the animals who beat and strangled the sisters didn't get rich from it, any more than their spiritual brothers who murdered babies in Nazi death camps did. Mostly they do it because they enjoy it. Wrapping their fingers around a woman's neck, or breaking bones with clubs or bare hands, must be a blood lust instilled in some human genes from the days when we were savage apes.

I ordered up a pot of coffee and a batch of eggs and spicy sausages. I was suddenly hungry. While I waited for room service, I shaved and showered, something I hadn't been doing on a regular basis since I hit Puerto Rico and wallowed in self-pity and recriminations.

After I hogged down the food, I sat with my feet up on the banister and watched the boats in the harbor. Mena had put me on a plane for San Juan for little more reason than it had been the next flight out, but it had turned out to be advantageous for me in terms of what I knew how to do. Like other areas of the Caribbean, sugar and rum were king in the islands.

For the past several weeks, I had been telling myself to check out business opportunities in the territory, but other than getting my rum brand licensed, I had hardly left the hotel to do anything.

"I know why you called," I spoke aloud, lost in my thoughts about Rubi.

"Are you talking to me?"

The response came from the balcony to my left. Sam Denver, a middle-aged American, and a Puerto Rican woman too young and cheap-looking to be his wife, were having breakfast. I'd bumped into the guy around the hotel. Denver was an ex–U.S. Navy submarine officer who had picked up a decommissioned training sub and brought it to the Caribbean in the hopes of making it a tourist attraction. He had talked my ear off one night in the hotel bar about how people would pay to take a dive in a real sub.

"Sorry, I was thinking out loud."

"By the way, did you give any thought to my proposition?" he asked.

His proposition involved my investing in his tour sub, fronting the money he needed to get the operation going. I couldn't picture why anyone would want to go under the beautiful, exotic Caribbean sea in a steel coffin. I'd take a ride on a glass bottom boat any day over being trapped in a sub.

He had served in World War II in the Pacific and knew the name of the ship, tonnage, captain, and casualty count of every Jap ship his sub sank. His only regret about the Korean War was that the North Koreans had so little navy to sink. He was so enthused and gung-ho, if a war didn't happen soon, he would probably start one.

I shook my head. "Sorry, but investing in a submarine sounds like a hole in the water to throw money in. I'll stick to liquids you drink rather than float in. With all the revolutions going on in this part of the world, maybe you can rent it out to combatants instead of tourists."

He didn't find the idea amusing. He went back to his breakfast and puta without dignifying my comment with a response.

I stared back out at the bay, running the phone call through my mind. Rubi said they were sure Luz had not gotten out of the country, that she had left the San Cristóbal estate soon after getting a call that Trujillo had been gunned down, but from what they learned from the conspirator who was "questioned," her plan and that of the others was to go into hiding rather than risk getting caught at the airport.

They wanted to spook out Luz. They assumed I knew something, maybe even thought I had been in on it with her. But they were still fishing because they didn't know where I stood—or what I knew. It was a good bet that if they questioned me, the man she lived with for a couple years, they might at least get some idea of her thinking, where she might be hiding.

There was nothing wrong with their line of reasoning. I knew of at least one place where she might hide.

Rubi had intimated that I would be rewarded with a return of my assets if I cooperated. In other words, tell them where Luz was hiding, turn her over to their thugs, or at least cooperate in trying to flush her out, and I would get well again financially.

There were two things wrong with that scenario.

The first was that the Trujillo gang were completely untrustworthy. If Johnny Mena got his hands on me, I was sure he'd "question" me the same way Spanish Inquisitors did with people accused of religious heresy. They would take me apart and not put the pieces back together.

The second was that they misjudged my feelings about Luz. I felt Rubi was a sensitive-enough guy when it came to romance to catch the fact I was crazy about her. But to the rest of them, women were merely sex objects to be used and discarded.

Now that I knew the truth behind Luz's relationship with Trujillo, I had one overriding, almost overwhelming desire to save her from Ramfis and his SIM thugs. I loved her. I loved her when we were together. I loved her even when she betrayed me. Her saving grace was that she did it all for a good cause. Yeah, it was a great cause. I lost almost everything I'd worked for.

The strange thing about it, I was lucky Trujillo had his boys give me the bum's rush out of the country. If I'd been allowed to stay around, I'd be in the SIM's hands already.

I glanced over at Denver, the germ of an idea growing in my head. If my hunch was right about where Luz was hiding, he might be able to help me.

Did I know for sure? Had we been that close, so connected emotionally, that I could accurately second-guess her? I hadn't second-guessed her before, but now I was certain that I was the only hope that she had. They were going after the assassination crew with a vengeance. It wasn't a very big country, it wouldn't take long to find her.

Right now, as I looked out at San Juan Bay, I couldn't help but wonder what she was doing, what she was thinking.

❖

48

❖

Luz stayed in the water, keeping all but her head submerged as she hung onto a rock in the surf, hiding from a government helicopter. She had walked down to the beach for a swim to cool off from the oppressive heat when she first heard and then spotted the helicopter. It was a few days short of July and the Dominican Republic was unseasonably hot, even for what was considered the warm season.

She had kept hidden, clutching onto rocks, as the helicopter flew overhead and along the coast. She didn't know if the helicopter was looking for her. Had they found out she was in the area? She'd been there for nearly a month now, ever since the night Generalissimo Trujillo was killed and the plot to assassinate him began to unravel. But it didn't make sense that they would just send out planes and helicopters to look for her at random. If, and when, they found out where she was, they'd descend on her like the hounds of hell fueled by demonic fury and bloodlust. To play it safe, she had to keep out of sight.

She wasn't staying on the beach. The cottage she was hiding out at was on a plateau a mile from the beach. The region was

❖

along the north coast of the country, in the area between Puerto Plata and Monti Cristi. This part of the coast was the country's unspoiled, barely developed region, a place of natural beauty lined by mostly deserted beaches. A dirt road ended two miles from the cottage, making the rest of the way available only by Shank's mare unless you had the wings of an angel.

Not many miles from the cottage was the ruins of La Isabella, the first settlement built by Columbus in the New World. It was the scene of suffering, tragedies and disappointments as the exploring Spaniards fought the indigenous Carib Indios and suffered setbacks in their lust for gold.

Luz had walked the ruins during earlier visits to the area, reflecting on a tale that the ruins were haunted. There were only a few visible stones left of this town that had for a brief time been the capital of the New World, and it was rarely visited except by hunters or fishermen. The legend said that terrible cries were heard by those who came near the deserted ruins on nights of the full moon, and that a headless caballero, with a cloak and sword, rode through the town. She had seen neither when she camped amidst the ruins, but she had spoken to a hunter earlier that day and carefully recorded his description of the headless caballero so she could relate the story to her literature class at the university where she taught.

Rather than the horror story, she preferred a romantic fable about the ruins, a tale that a wandering Spanish picaro-adventurer, Miguel Diaz, fell in love with Cathalina, a queen of the southern coast of Hispaniola, and that because of the lady's love, Columbus and his men were invited to build a new city in her territory. That city became Santo Domingo, which was now known as Ciudad Trujillo.

BETWEEN THE COTTAGE AND the beach were fields of abandoned banana trees. Her aunt had cultivated the bananas, but it was not a profitable enterprise. The area was remote, the transportation costly, the labor too expensive, and although for a time there were huts for workers, she could not keep year-round workers. When Luz inherited the property after her aunt's death, she had been forced to let the trees revert to their natural state. People came from a village several miles away and picked the fruit for nothing and all she asked in return was that they not damage the trees.

There were no close neighbors, and she knew no one at the village well enough to call or be called by name. She had intentionally kept it like that. The house had been her secret place from the time she inherited it when she was eighteen. She often came here to study for final exams during college but never invited anyone else. There was something about having a place that no one else on earth knew about, where no one could bother her. The house was simply furnished in crude wood furniture that would attract no thief, and she kept linens and kitchenware in a secret compartment under the floor for the same reason.

The only person she had shared her secret place with had been Nick.

She cringed when she thought of him—and he was never far from her mind. She knew she had betrayed him. She had destroyed their relationship, destroyed him financially, humiliated him. He deserved none of the abuse she gave him. She had left him and went to the bed—to the perversions—of another man.

That she had done it for what she considered a good cause didn't diminish her crimes. Some would even call her courageous.

But she knew she hadn't been brave. If she truly had courage, she would have killed El Jefe herself, would have plunged a knife between his shoulder blades as he lay asleep on his stomach next to her on the bed, his head turned sideways, snoring like a boar hog.

Instead, she used her body to set him up for assassination, had submitted to his perversions to gain his confidence. Finally, she had made a pleading call for his company, the kind of call no man could refuse. And he had been brought down by a blaze of bullets, like a bull elephant too strong to kill with one volley.

After she had arrived at the cottage, she went down to the isolated beach frequently. She felt dirty and needed to wash away the filth. And the sins.

❖

Her life was over. She knew that. It was only a matter of time before Johnny Mena and his SIM thugs found her. Her only connection to the outside world was a hand-cranked radio—there was no electricity at the cottage. She heard the news that Ramfis had come back to the country, that most of the conspirators had been rounded up. She had no illusions about what happened to them. Or what would happen to her when they found her.

Should I kill myself? It was a question she had asked herself many times. And the answer was always the same. *I don't have the courage.*

She was too hard on herself. Most people would have argued that joining a resistance against a tyrant was a monumental act of courage. Using her body to trick the tyrant into a mistake was nothing less than martyrdom. But she didn't feel that way about herself.

She had joined the resistance against Trujillo the previous year, after the Mirabal sisters were arrested the first time. She had come into the movement to help plan the overthrow of Trujillo. With his domination of the police and army, it had become obvious that the underground's best chance of getting rid of the dictator was to kill him rather than fight his overwhelming army.

After the murder of the Mirabal sisters, she met with ringleaders of the resistance. The discussions revolved around El Jefe's weakness, his Achilles' heel. That vulnerable point was the women in his life. He had a habit of installing his current mistress at the San Cristóbal estate and making his visits unannounced, making it difficult to track his movements in advance so an ambush could be set up. Not even the staff in the household knew when he would come and go.

Finally, the decision was to have a woman establish a relationship with him that would give her the opportunity to request his presence suddenly—but at a time when men with guns would be waiting for him.

El Jefe already had a wife, mother and daughter. The only other female relationship available was a mistress. And to do that, Luz would not only have to hook the dictator, but be prepared to put up with his perversions.

It had cost her the loss of the man she loved.

The loss of her dignity.

And now it was going to cost her life.

Her only regret was that she wouldn't know if what she had done would make a better life for the people of her country—or if Ramfis or another strong-arm personality would simply step into the shoes of the last tyrant.

After the helicopter was out of sight, she made her way back up the hill to the cottage.

She knew she didn't have long to wait. Someone would make the connection to the cottage. A simple check of government records would disclose her ownership. When that happened, men from the SIM would come.

Would they break her bones and strangle her and put her over a cliff as they did the other Butterflies?

No, she was sure they would not. Ramfis had other plans for the conspirators. Plans that would make the devil shudder. She knew death wouldn't be quick or easy. But a sort of peacefulness had come over her. While she would avoid capture as long as she could, in a way she had already accepted death.

Mostly because of Nick.

She found it impossible to redeem herself after betraying him. She had broken the mirrors in their penthouse because she couldn't face herself. Facing Nick would be infinitely more painful. She would never be comfortable living with the knowledge that he must hate her. Worse, she knew how much he truly loved her, how deeply wounded he must be by her treachery.

❖

49

❖

As I sat out on the balcony, I started laying out the deal, point by
point. It was like doing any business transaction—I had to know
everything about the deal, including the seller's motivation and
any hidden points.

Ramfis, his henchman Johnny Mena, the SIM—they all
wanted Luz. But they weren't coming clean with exactly why they
wanted her. They either wanted to give her some old-fashioned justice for her part in the plot to kill El Jefe—torture and kill her
slowly—or they wanted to torture and kill her slowly *and* get her
to roll over on whoever else might be involved.

They had called me because (a) they figured I might know
where she was, or at least would have a good guess since we had
lived together; (b) I was greedy enough to trade her for the millions
they stole, or (c) I wanted revenge for what she did to me.

I could toss in the fact that they knew enough about my business methods to appreciate the fact that I was probably morally
corrupt, thus would not pass up an opportunity to enrich myself at
someone else's expense, especially if it was someone who had
screwed me over. If the someone was a woman, all the better. Rubi

❖

was a gentlemen, but the rest of them and their attitudes toward women could be summed up by a joke Johnny Mena had told me at an Independence Day party I attended with Luz.

"Know what you say to a woman with two black eyes?" he had asked.

I took the bait. "No."

"Nothing. You already told the bitch twice."

Shades of Jack the Wife-Beater.

Sure, I howled with laughter like the rest of the losers and ass-kissers in hearing range. But I only did it because I was making a buck in the country. That set me apart from the ankle-biters.

Okay, maybe it didn't. Maybe these guys had my number. Maybe they were right about me. A guy who always walked a crooked line doesn't change. Yeah, I was a bastard, I could be bought. I was willing to pay my dues to make a buck—millions of them—but I was one of those rare breed of bastards that couldn't screw over the woman I loved. Maybe it was because of what happened to my mother. My mother would have crawled over broken glass for me. She did more than that, she gave her life for me. That started me out with a rather good impression of womankind—except for the times when I got the pointy end of a spiked high heel slammed into my heart.

That brought the whole nine yards down to one answer to the offer: Those bastards could fuck themselves.

I was going to get Luz out alive.

Or go down with her.

IT WAS LATE EVENING, the sun had finally disappeared and a cool breeze was coming in from the bay when I took a shower and slipped into light slacks and a pullover shirt and took a walk. Old San Juan, with its narrow streets and wide history, had little attraction for me. Neither did the whores or hustlers that were waiting in front of bars and at the head of alleys.

I had been running the situation over and over in my mind, nibbling on it, chewing it, ripping it with my teeth. I was pretty sure I knew where Luz would go. There was a special place she loved, a hideaway that was her own secret place. She was a romantic. She'd go there because unconsciously she would believe that the place had some sort of magic, that it could protect her like an enchanted fairyland. Now that I knew her motive for throwing herself at Trujillo, I was once again sure I knew her.

She would be no match for the SIM. The only smart move would be to get out of the country, but that would not have occurred to her—and if it did, it wasn't something that she would do because she would see it as a betrayal of her comrades. No, she'd stick around to tough it out. Even when the SIM thugs put a garrote around her pretty little throat and choked the life from her.

I was walking along the waterfront, getting as close to the water as I could to pick up the cooling breeze, deep in thought, when someone bumped into me.

"Pardon—" I said.

A gun was in my stomach and I looked into the stone eyes of a killer.

"In the car," he told me in Spanish.

The car was parked a dozen feet away. As he shoved me toward it, another man got out.

"In the back," he said.

I got in, with the two for company, one on each side.

I knew who they were, SIM. Johnny Mena's boys. I was sure the man who had gotten out of the car as I approached had been with Mena when I was given the bum's rush to the airport.

I said nothing. I knew it was no use. These guys were errand boys. They were going to kill me, hurt me, scare me—they had already done that—or whatever was on the agenda Mena gave them. Whatever it was, it was a done deal. There was nothing I could say or do. But what the hell, never say die.

"I'll pay you each a thousand dollars to pull over and let me out."

An elbow came around and hit me across the face, smashing my nose, spattering blood across my face. I doubled over on the seat, holding my broken face, wavering on the brink of passing out.

❖

"That was for Ramos," the goon on my left said. "He is my cousin."

"Fuck Ramos. Fuck your mother," I said.

A fist caught my unprotected left ear. Fireworks exploded between my temples. I guess the guy didn't realize that it was just an old Russian expression, no insult was intended toward his mother.

I had no idea where they were taking me. I was in too much pain to wonder or care.

"You're a woman and your mother's a whore," I told the bruiser on the left. I threw a right at him, twisting in the seat. He caught it with his hand. I think he twisted my arm, I'm not sure, because the guy on my right began to pound my head with the butt of a gun.

THE CAR PULLED UP somewhere. I don't know how much time had passed—minutes? Hours? Were we still in San Juan? The suburbs? Countryside? I could have been on Mars.

When we got to wherever we were, Lefty pulled me with him as we got out of the car. I had a gnawing, clawing, irritating, piercing pain that went from my head down to my groin.

As soon as I had solid ground under my feet, I threw a punch at him, bringing it up from down low, putting my shoulder into it.

He brushed it aside and hit me in the stomach.

I collapsed on the ground and puked, the contents of my stomach coming out in a terrible violent eruption. I got the bastard's shoes and he went nuts, kicking me, landing one in the nuts.

Someone, two someones, pulled him off of me.

"Stop, he has to be questioned."

Lying on the ground, my mind in a haze, I realized that my benefactor had interceded only so I could be spared for some more painful maltreatment.

I was pulled, dragged and kicked into a building. I didn't know what it was, a palace, shack, something with a door and walls. Inside, one of the thugs threw a rope over an exposed crossbeam and tied one end to my feet.

❖

Even in my pain and haze, I thought it was curious—why would they tie my feet to a rope dangling from a crossbeam?

Two of them pulled the other end of the rope, hoisting me up so I was upside down, my feet pointed toward the ceiling, my head toward the floor.

I was held still so the man who had been on my right in the car, apparently the group leader, could lean down and talk to me.

"Where is your woman?" he asked.

"Fuck your mother," I whispered.

Someone held me while another person plugged one of my nostrils and put the pointy end of a funnel in another.

The man on the right poured water into the funnel.

My brain exploded. I'm sure I blew gray matter out my ears. My bashed nose, the kick in the nuts, slug in my stomach—child's play. This was the real McCoy, this was the kind of torture Torquemada of the Spanish Inquisition got his rocks off on.

I blacked out, a merciful dark shadow seeping into my brain. I heard a slew of Spanish curses, angry accusations that they had gone too far, as I lost consciousness. I wasn't sure if my face had a grin on it, but I knew I grinned mentally. The bastards had overplayed their hand.

They had probably killed me.

50

❖

And then there was light.

It came at me so hard, I screamed, screeched, and made inhuman noises.

"He's drunk," a disgusted voice said. "Too much booze, too many whores. He fell into the gutter and smashed his face."

"Akabaajabazka," I said. It wasn't Russian. It wasn't even human.

Eventually the unsympathetic hands of a San Juan street cop pulled me out of the gutter and lay me on my back until a couple of unsympathetic ambulance attendants scraped me off the sidewalk and took me to San Juan Central Hospital, where an unsympathetic ER doctor patched me up.

"Your nose will be crooked," he said. "There's nothing I can do here about it. You American?"

I had to think. "British." That was the country on my passport.

"They can probably straighten it out in London." He surveyed my face. "Not that it makes you any uglier than you already are."

No smile. I guess he wasn't kidding.

"They say you got drunk, got rolled by a prostitute and fell into

❖

a gutter, flat on your face. Looks to me like you got your ass kicked, maybe even gang-stomped. You don't get the multiple injuries you have from a single fall. Is there something I should be telling the police?"

"You have the bedside manners of an axe-murderer," I said. "You should be working in a butcher shop, not a hospital. Tell the police to fuck their mother."

He didn't have the faintest idea what I was talking about.

That was okay, neither did I.

I took a taxi back to the hotel, my face bandaged, my body crying. I had the doorman pay the taxi based upon a promise I'd pay him later and I staggered to the elevator.

In my room, I managed to get to the bed before I was down on my knees.

Russians are tough, I told myself, not as convincingly as I had said earlier.

I lay on top of the covers, too hot in the sultry tropical night to sleep, too tired and beat—literally—to take off my clothes.

I started laughing.

It began as soon as I had stretched out on the bed, shoes and all. It started in my stomach and worked its way up, coming up my throat and bursting out my mouth, hurting every inch of the way. I laughed and laughed and choked and cried. Tears streamed from my eyes. I laughed because I had learned something very important that night.

Ramfis, Rubi, Johnny Mena, all of them, were real smart hombres, real tough, too, much smarter and tougher than me.

I was a pussy compared to them.

I laughed some more. It hurt like hell. God, *everything hurt.* And that fuckin' axe-murderer of a doctor had refused to give me pain pills. I saw the look in his eyes when he turned me down. *Fuck you,* his eyes said, you think you're a tough dude, so tough it out, you mouthy bastard.

Take it by the numbers, you smart, mean Russian hombre, I told myself.

Rubi hadn't picked up the phone at a random moment and di-

❖

aled me in Puerto Rico. Hell, no. They had tracked me down and had men in position before the call was made.

And they hadn't been fooled by my vague, noncommittal listening responses during the call. These smart bastards knew what I was thinking every second I'd been on that phone, could tell from my tone of voice that I was in pain from Luz, that I wasn't going to give her up for revenge or money. I thought I was so damn smart, and maybe I was when it came to making a buck, but these people were professional people manipulators, whether it involved one person or a nation of millions.

They knew by the time the call was over that I would not be a help, but a hindrance to them, that I would play the hero, not the betrayer, that I would make a play to save Luz.

That's why they picked me up.

Running it back through my mind, I don't believe they really thought they'd get Luz's location from me. People readers that they were, they realized Luz would not have let the man she was screwing over know her plans.

No, they knew they'd get nothing of value from me. I think the number they did on me was intended to scare me off, teach me a lesson, disabuse me of any heroic notions about jumping in and saving Luz from the SIM. Something short of actual murder, because it was on American soil and the last thing Ramfis wanted with his new regime was to show bad faith to Washington by murdering someone in a U.S. jurisdiction.

"They have my number," I told the ceiling as I lay in pain and agony, my nose ballooned.

They had only made one mistake.

They had overestimated my good sense.

I laughed until tears rolled down my face from the pain it caused.

I'd show them.

Fuck their mothers.

❖

51

❖

"What happened to your nose?"

Sam Denver stared at me like he had never seen an inflamed, crooked nose before. I went looking for him and found him hugging a Bloody Mary in the hotel lounge.

"Bite a shark. He bites back. Tell me, does that submarine of yours really go underwater?"

"Why do you think they call it a *sub*marine?"

"Can it travel somewhere, say a hundred miles, surface, and go back under, that sort of thing?"

Denver stared at me. "Why the sudden interest in my submarine?"

"Is it a toy?"

"Hell no, it's not a toy. It's a decommissioned U.S. Navy submarine. It got sent to Panama after the Big One as war surplus. You know how much Panama needed a submarine?"

I shook my head.

"Like teats on a boar hog. I got it from a Panamanian admiral in exchange for a sixty-foot gunboat that had been converted into a luxury yacht. You know how much use Panama has for a gunboat?"

❖

I gave him another shake.

"They use them to protect the smugglers and gunrunners." He roared with laughter.

My face was too battered to join in. It had tightened as it was healing and a good laugh would have shattered it.

"You've been wanting to buy a pier to dock it by, one that tourists can use to board. How would you like to have enough money to get your submarine raking in tourist money instead of collecting rust and barnacles?"

"Who do I have to kill?"

I thought about it.

"No one. Maybe just start a war."

That got his attention.

"Think you can attack a small country with your sub?" I asked.

Yeah, Ramfis and his SIM had overestimated my good sense. I should have been on my way to New York or London, one of those places where you only have to worry about tax collectors and other muggers. But here I was, planning and scheming. They had probably overestimated my intelligence and sanity, too. No one with brains and a mind in good working order would do the crazy things I had planned.

Like I said, the Russian in me came out when my back was to the wall. When Hitler invaded Russia, Stalin had ordered his troops to institute a scorched earth policy, destroying bridges, burning crops, killing farm animals, making sure the enemy didn't get any benefit from its conquest. You don't get any crazier than having the willingness to destroy your own country in an effort to defeat an invader.

That was my philosophy, too. Scorched earth. I was taking names and giving no quarter.

I told Denver what I wanted from him and his submarine and went back to my room to call an old friend in British Honduras.

❖

52

❖

Ciudad Trujillo

"A what?"

As he asked the question, Rafael Leónidas Trujillo, Jr., known as Ramfis to distinguish him from his now dead father, stared at Johnny Mena, the head of the SIM.

Ramfis had returned to the country on the heels of his father's assassination and took his place as head of the army, which made him de facto dictator of the country. But the crown of kingship sat uneasy on his head. Ramfis was junior in more than name when compared to his father. The generalissimo had ruled the Dominican Republic for nearly thirty years, using a iron fist more often than a velvet glove. He had spilled blood not by the bucket, but filled the gutters and sewers with it.

Had the generalissimo been born on the south side of Chicago or the Fort Apache area of the Bronx, he might have ended up as a mobster kingpin. Had he been born in Russia, El Jefe would have filled the shoes of Khozyain, "the Boss," after Stalin died in 1953.

Trujillo had been smart and totally without conscience. Murdering to stay in power was just part of a day's work. It was the mark of dictators and conquerors from all ages, from Julius Caesar

❖

to Genghis Khan, from Hitler to Stalin and Mao; mass murder to achieve political and military gains was just part of the job description. To paraphrase Stalin, a few deaths were a tragedy, a million was just a statistic.

Junior had none of the brutal "advantages" of his father. El Jefe rose from the lower classes and pulled himself up by the bootstraps until he ran the army. Poor Ramfis. He became a colonel hardly out of diapers. Now he was a goldfish in a pool of sharks. Not a comfortable position for a man who had had a lifetime of soft landings.

Ramfis stared at the head of his secret police. Johnny Mena had interrupted a party Ramfis was throwing for the country's elite in order to discuss an urgent situation with him. Mena himself had had his dinner at a Ciudad Trujillo nightclub interrupted by a Dominican Republic navy admiral and rushed to the Ciudad Trujillo palace that Ramfis was using as his headquarters.

The two of them were in Ramfis's office now, along with the dictator's aide de camp, Colonel Ramírez.

"A submarine," Johnny Mena said.

"A submarine," Ramfis repeated. "Off our south coast, not far from San Cristóbal. Could it be American?" he asked Mena.

"I'm certain it is American, but not part of their active navy, not anymore at least. In the reports I received from San Juan, one of the people Nick Cutter was seen talking to repeatedly was the owner of a salvaged submarine, a smaller boat used for training purposes. They are staying at the same hotel, with adjoining rooms."

"What are you getting at?"

"That submarine was anchored in San Juan Bay. When I got word of the sighting of a sub off our coast, I immediately contacted the agent in charge of our surveillance of Cutter. He has confirmed several things—Cutter is not at his hotel, and has not slept in his bed."

"And?"

Johnny Mena leaned forward. "The submarine has left its mooring. At least, our man believes so. Naturally, it's still dark in

❖

San Juan, but there was enough moonlight for him to get a good view of the bay."

Ramfis asked, "So you believe that Nick Cutter has hired a submarine to rescue Luz?"

"The submarine was seen off San Cristóbal, so it fits," Colonel Ramirez said. "The woman dropped out of sight immediately after El Jefe was murdered. The easiest situation for her would be to hide at a fellow conspirator's house and await rescue."

"But it's been a month," Ramfis said.

Ramirez shrugged. "A month in which there has been an intense hunt for the conspirators. She would have naturally kept her head down until she thought it was safe to make a run for it."

"But why a submarine? A submarine can't come that close to land. Can it?" Ramfis asked.

It was a stupid question. Both men exchanged looks but neither pointed out how naïve the question was.

Johnny Mena's tone of voice was smooth when he answered Ramfis's question. Before his father was killed, Ramfis had not made any attempt to hide the fact he disliked Mena and his brutal methods and reputation. In the weeks since he got back from Paris, Ramfis had fully underwrote Mena's vicious police methods.

"Not underwater, of course, but they don't draw the same sort of water a large ship of war or freighter would, especially a small sub like this one. It could come reasonably close to shore, and of course, they would send an inflatable motorboat ashore to bring the woman back."

"If the rendezvous point has enough water for the submarine to get within a mile or two from shore," Ramirez pointed out, "a rubber speedboat could cover the required distance back and forth, probably in minutes."

"Do we know exactly where the submarine is?" Ramfis asked.

Mena was careful not to commit himself to a reply that could later be used against him. Capturing—and punishing—the killers of El Jefe was Ramfis's most pressing political and personal concern. Mena didn't want to be caught guessing wrong about anything arising from the manhunt. He had many enemies in the

❖

government. If Luz escaped and Ramfis had an excuse to punish him, Mena had no doubt he'd get a taste of his own painful SIM methods.

"It was spotted heading for the San Cristóbal area just before darkness fell," Ramirez answered. "That was several hours ago. We have ships and planes in the area, and they had occasional electronic detection of the sub." He spread his hands on the desk. "But what that means, I'm not completely certain. It was detected again less than an hour ago. We have helicopters with searchlights patrolling miles of coastline in the San Cristóbal area, and police and troops in vehicles searching on the ground. The sub has to surface to launch a rubber speedboat to attempt any rescue."

"Unless the person on the beach has their own boat."

Mena kept a straight face. Colonel Ramirez was right. He had not considered the obvious. "Regardless, there are no reports of a powerboat coming or going from the coast to the submarine. It's dark, but a powerboat makes engine noises that are heard over a great distance. But the fact that the submarine was detected a short time ago and is still in the area is our best insurance that an escape has not been made."

Mena made his excuses and left the meeting. Unlike Ramfis who supped his entire life with the proverbial silver spoon, he had survived hard knocks time after time in his life. Not just the machinations of envious souls who wanted his position of power, but attempts to kill him.

Now the hounds were gathering, snapping their jaws, trying to get up the courage of a pack so they could attack him. The SIM had not detected the plot to kill El Jefe. Blame was being laid at his door. He had to make sure he rounded up and punished each of the conspirators.

If Luz escaped by submarine, there would be recriminations. But he was already preparing damage control. Submarines were not within the power of the secret police. They were strictly a military matter. He would recommend the firing and disgrace of the admiral who was in charge of the country's small navy.

As he rode in the back of his chauffeur driven car, he thought

❖

about the submarine spotted off the coast. He had one observation that he hadn't shared with the other two. He had a logical mind, and something did not fit properly in the logical arrangement of the facts.

Submarines were exceptionally hard to spot. Under ordinary circumstances, one would never have been spotted off the coast of the republic. The country had no enemies among nations of the world that would attack it, not with the Americans waiting in the sidelines to come to its defense. And it had only a very small navy, mostly just patrol boats to fight smuggling and potential bands of rebels. The navy was not well equipped to spot a submarine and track it. Not unless the sub wanted to be spotted.

It was the latter point that bothered him.

The sub had surfaced twice near government patrol boats on the south coast near San Cristóbal.

"Why?" Mena asked himself, aloud. Why would a submarine blow its own inherent ability to remain hidden by surfacing in an area that was the most watched in the country?

"Put out a bulletin to agents at all points, including the north coast," he instructed his aide who sat next to the driver. "Any suspicious activity is to be reported to me immediately."

"What about the submarine?" the aide asked.

"The submarine is the navy's problem. My problem is to make sure that no snakes slither under the threshold while we are waiting for the navy to act."

Something was wrong. The finely honed survival sense that kept Mena one step ahead of his many enemies was buzzing louder and louder. Mena liked no one, but he respected dangerous enemies. And Nick Cutter was a dangerous man to buck.

"When you put out the bulletin," he told his aide, "tell them to be on the lookout for a man with four fingers on his left hand."

❖

53

❖

On a Puerto Rican fishing boat on the north side of the Dominican Republic, I wondered how Sam Denver was doing with his submarine on the south side. And I asked myself for the hundredth time if I was completely crazy.

I was operating off of pure gut reaction. The place Luz had always found most comforting during times of stress had been the cottage and little banana plantation she had inherited from a maiden aunt when Luz was still a teenager. The cottage, about a mile from the shore on the northwest side of the country, was my destination. I hired a commercial fishing vessel in San Juan to make the short jaunt across the Mona Straits and down the Hispaniola coast. Once we were in range, I'd slip into the rubber dinghy equipped with an outboard we were towing and take it to shore.

That was part of the plan.

Another part was Sam Denver and his submarine. I sent him and his submarine to the opposite side of the country to draw attention to the San Cristóbal area. "A red herring," as he put it.

If for some reason Luz was in that area, I'd be putting her into

❖

even more danger. But my bones were telling me that she'd gone to the plantation to hide out. I had to admit that I didn't have a history of batting a thousand when it came to predicting Luz's behavior.

"I am not a happy man," the captain of the fishing boat said.

It was dark, after nine o'clock. I had gone below when the captain spotted a Dominican Republic patrol boat. The fishing boat had headed further out to sea, making sure it was in international waters. I was at the stern, checking to see if the rubber dinghy we were towing was still attached, when the captain approached me about his negative state of mind.

"That is the second patrol boat I have seen."

"Uh huh." I didn't know what else to say.

"I have fished these waters hundreds of times. Do you know how many times I have seen two"—he held up two fingers—"*two* patrol boats?"

I had a pretty good idea just from the way he was shaking his head.

"Never, never have I seen two patrol boats on the same day. I have never seen more than one patrol boat in a single week. And that is what makes me unhappy."

"Hmmm." Another brilliant listening response because I had no answer for his unhappiness.

"I am unhappy also because these patrol boats are out here at night. Do you know why the patrol boat crews are usually home with their families at night instead of patrolling?"

I shook my head.

"Because that is what they are paid to do, paid by the smugglers who come at night. You see why I am so unhappy. Two boats? At night?" He made the sign of the cross across his chest. "Maria mother of God, this is very unusual, don't you think so?"

I cleared my throat. "Captain—"

"Can you tell me, señor, why I would see two patrol boats in these waters, at night, and on the same night?"

Yeah, I could tell him. For the past month, ever since El Jefe's death, the whole country'd been an armed camp, with the army,

❖

navy, air force and police throwing everything they had into the manhunt. I could have told him that, but he probably would have stuck a hook in my ass and trolled me behind the boat as shark bait.

I didn't actually tell him why I had hired him to drop me off along the coast of the country. I had a waterproof duffel bag with some personal effects in it, part of a back up plan in case I needed it. I just let him assume I was smuggling drugs in. It was a perfectly acceptable explanation. Smuggling was considered a respectable occupation in the Caribbean.

"Your silence, señor, tells me you are not going to offer me an explanation as to why I see these two patrol boats. But I have to say that I misspoke earlier. There was a time when I saw these waters infested with police boats. That was in 1959, just two years ago, after rebels supported by Cuba landed and tried to overthrow the government."

He gestured at my duffel bag. "Would you like to show me what is in your bag, señor?"

"I'm not a smuggler. Or an insurgent."

"Then what are you?"

Telling him that I was dropping in to rescue one of Trujillo's killers would definitely get the hook up my ass.

"I'll double our deal," I said.

"A hundred times what you offer would not pay for my boat or the lives of me and my men."

Two of his men flanked me. They each had a big gaffing hook used to haul in sharks.

"You are getting off my boat, señor. Now."

54

❖

The captain of the fishing boat told me that the lights I saw along the coast were the town of Puerto Plata, the "Silver Port." All it meant to me was trouble.

The banana plantation was in a rural, undeveloped area about twenty miles up the coast. I couldn't have gotten more than a quarter of that distance with the gas that was left in the outboard by the time I reached the coastline.

I had to give the fishing captain credit, he was an honorable man. I was the bad guy in the scenario. He had me climb into the outboard, threw my duffel bag in after me, and cut the tow line after I got the outboard going.

If our situations had been reversed, I would have thrown the lying passenger overboard and kept the rubber dinghy and outboard motor as a well-earned bonus.

I made it to the coastline off the silver port without being boarded or run down by a patrol boat. It was a warm night, without a breeze, and the surf running up on the beach was manageable. I beached the boat, set aside my waterproof bag and then let the air out of the dinghy. When it was deflated, I dragged it into the

❖

bushes, did the same with the outboard, and covered them with palm fronds.

From my waterproof duffel bag, I took out my backup plan—a good pair of slacks, shirt, sports coat, shoes and a small overnight bag with a change of clothes.

It wasn't much in terms of equipment for a guy making a one-man invasion of a small, Caribbean country, but there was some logic to it, at least in my own small, twisted mind.

If Luz wasn't at the banana plantation, I would have to go to the next best bet, San Cristóbal on the other side of the country-island, and see if I could nose her out there. I would have to backtrack to Puerto Plata and take public transportation to the capital and then to San Cristóbal. I needed to look respectable to make that trip. And I needed a disguise. My blond hair and eyebrows, a real tipoff to the police in a country of dark complexioned people, were now medium brown.

It was the best I could do short of plastic surgery—some passable clothes and brown hair.

That and a passport in the name of Sam Denver. Sam would report his passport as stolen. It cost me another arm and a leg to go with the limbs I gave for renting his sub for red-herring duty.

And there was no gun in my bag. I had thought about it, that I might get into a situation where I had to shoot my way out, but weighing the pros and cons, the idea of packing heat kept coming up snake eyes. Unless I had my trump card to use on myself, a gun would only help me get to hell faster than the speeding bullet I was already riding.

I was east of the town, the banana plantation was to the west. Between the town and the plantation were miles of jungle and other rugged terrain. It wasn't a trip I would be able to make on foot, especially during the hot months. I needed transportation and a cover story.

I thought about both as I meandered from the beach through a thinly populated area that seemed to have more barking dogs than people and finally made it to a stretch of highway that appeared to be a main road into town.

❖

I wasn't sure how many people lived in the town, probably about forty or fifty thousand I imagined, but it was even less of a town than that in terms of its sophistication. The southern part of the country, which had the capital, was a much more developed region. It was the main area that attracted tourists. That meant I would stand out more on the north coast.

I had that comforting thought as I came into the outskirts of town and spotted a battered taxi parked next to a shanty. I needed wheels under me. A taxi wouldn't fit the bill, but taxi drivers are better sources of information than city hall and the tourist offices combined.

Pounding on the door brought first a little girl with a big smile and ragged dress and then her father, a short, black Dominican with a belly built upon too much rice, beans and cerveza.

"I need information," I told him.

"It's late, my taxi is cold for the night."

"I need to rent a car."

"A car?" He shook his head as if to clear his hearing. "Señor, it's nearly midnight. Perhaps you could steal a car at this time, but you couldn't rent one, not even if you were in Ciudad Trujillo."

"I know it's unusual." I grinned. "I have a small problem."

"A problem, señor?"

"A woman problem. A husband problem. I came here with a woman, in her car, to her beach house. Unfortunately, her husband showed up. Now I don't have the woman or transportation."

"Mañana—"

"I can't wait until tomorrow. I'll be dead by then." I spoke with great sincerity because I believed it. "I need to get to Santiago tonight." Santiago was to the south, a good-sized city in the heart of the agricultural region. I had been through and in it a number of times doing tobacco and sugarcane deals. I didn't want to get to Santiago, but I couldn't tell him my real destination.

He shrugged. "No cars tonight, maybe tomorrow. My taxi, I lost water, a radiator hose. I will replace it mañana."

Mañana could mean tomorrow morning or a week from tomorrow in this culture, usually the latter. Like British Honduras and everywhere else in the Caribbean, it was hot much of the time, and no one was in a hurry to sweat anymore than they had to. Besides, he thought I wanted to hire a taxi. I didn't want a taxi ride to Santiago. I wanted a car under me so I could head west up the coast.

"I have a lot of business to attend to in Santiago, mucho running around, comprende? I need to rent a car, not hire a taxi. You know where I can rent a car?"

"Tomorrow I will help you rent a car. No one can help you tonight."

He was probably right. It was too late to rent a car to an honest man, even if I was one. I was stuck.

"For tonight, you can stay in a hotel. Very good, just half a mile down the road. I drive you."

"I thought you said you blew a radiator hose?"

"I tied it with my handkerchief, it will last that long."

A hotel was a good idea. The next best thing to a taxi driver for getting things done around a town was a hotel clerk.

The hotel turned out to be a small dump. The creature that answered the office door after some pounding by the taxi driver, whose name I found out was Manuel Hidalgo, looked like he could be Manuel's older, long-dead brother.

Before Manuel left, I took a wad of bills out of my front pants pocket and unpeeled a couple. "Mañana," I said, "early. Get me a car."

My room had a dumpy bed that looked like something the office clerk had once been buried in—or got sick on.

It was hot. I threw open the windows and hoped for a hint of breeze, enough to make it worth the blood I would be donating to the mosquitoes.

❖

55

❖

The theory that taxi drivers knew more about what was going on in town than almost anyone else had not been lost on Trujillo and his police. Manuel Hidalgo had something in common with most of the taxi drivers in the country—he was on the payroll of the police.

In addition to the almost daily "want list" that the SIM issued to taxi drivers, hotel clerks and local police agencies, an alert had been issued less than two hours earlier from SIM headquarters in the capital to be on the lookout for a blond foreigner.

Manuel was not a stupid man or a particularly clever one. He was smart enough to realize he could make good money from the stranger who had showed up at his door. Had the man been wanted by the local police, Manuel would not have hesitated to help him for a substantial fee, enough to pay off the police if they found out. But the want lists were being issued by the SIM. And everyone knew they related to the assassination of El Jefe.

El Jefe had been a hero of Manuel's. He had been proud of the dictator's accomplishments. And now that he was dead, Manuel would be proud of the next strong man who ran the country.

No, it was not his loyalty to the memory of the Chief that

❖

caused Manuel to go directly to the local police office immediately after settling the foreigner into the hotel. It was because the situation was political and the SIM was involved.

When the secret police came for you, they took you and your entire family. He had heard stories of children being raped in front of suspects to draw confessions—or just as punishment for a wrong.

Manuel scratched his two-day-old beard as he waited at the police station for the arrival of SIM agents. Perhaps this foreigner would be important and he would get a reward.

He kissed the St. Manuel medallion that never left the chain around his neck. Nothing was impossible for a man who honored the saint he was named after.

"I have met a man," he told the SIM agents, "like the pamphlets said, a man with four fingers on one hand."

56

❖

I must have dozed off for a while as I sat in the bamboo chair when I heard a discreet tapping on my door. I jerked awake, my adrenaline on fire. It was a little past two in the morning. Nothing but trouble would come knocking at that hour.

I could go out of the window, but I knew there was no place to run. I froze in place, contemplating my next move.

"Señor, it is me."

I went to the door and opened it.

"I have a car," Manuel the taxi driver told me. "It is my cousin's car." He shrugged. "Not fancy, señor, but the motor, it is more reliable than a burro."

The car was nosily idling on the street. A man who could pass for Manuel's cousin—same belly—was standing by it.

"Okay."

I didn't know if it was a trap, but I didn't have any options if it was. And having a Caribbean tell you there were no cars and showing up an hour later with one was par for the course for the islands.

I grabbed my bag and followed Manuel to the car. Five minutes later, I pulled away, half of my wad of money gone—I had more

❖

strapped to my leg—and a gas pedal under foot. The car was a 1949 Ford two-door sedan. It sounded like a bucket of bolts being shaken, but I was on my way.

Luz and I had visited the abandoned banana plantation twice, driving from the capital in a jeep I had shipped over from the States. But she liked to drive and I liked to read business reports and deal memos, so I wasn't as familiar with the route as I should have been. Not that there was that much to know. I knew I had to head out of town, going west up the coast, and that civilized roads would soon degenerate into dirt roads that would ultimately deteriorate into two-wheeled dirt tracks—except for the places even the holes and ruts had been wiped away by torrential bursts of rain.

Damn—damn—damn.

I should have bought a fishing boat and taken it to the area myself instead of putting myself in the hands of strangers.

But at least I had wheels under me.

❖

57

❖

Johnny Mena was in his office at SIM headquarters and wide awake. It was still dark outside, would be for a couple hours. Three of his staff were with him. He was excited. Any one seeing him would have thought his jerky movements were signs of being nervous, but when he got excited, he became hyper, bursting with nervous energy.

"Keep the radio transmission open at all times to Puerto Plata," he instructed his aide, who was dozing until Mena snapped at him. "Tell our people there that if we lose contact, they had better wade into the sea and let sharks feed on them."

"Should we notify the military?" his aide asked.

"The military?"

"They would be able to cover the area much more completely than we can," the aide said.

"Don't be a fool," Mena snapped. "That would tip off Nick Cutter that we are tracking him." What he didn't say was that he didn't want the military to steal his thunder. To Johnny Mena, there were two things that motivated men—sex and money. They had already given Cutter a hint that he could get back his money if

❖

he cooperated and he had not taken them up on it. That meant he was only here for one reason—to rescue Luz.

"What if we lose him?" the aide asked. Unlike Mena's hyper condition, his nervousness was exactly that. There was nothing as important to the new dictator right at the moment than capturing the conspirators who killed his father. If the SIM screwed up, someone would be severely punished. And he had been a part of the system long enough to understand that the person taking the blame was rarely the person on top.

"We won't lose him," Mena said.

But the aide had made a good point. He needed a backup plan.

"Why the north coast?" he asked.

His staff looked at him rather stupidly.

"Do you mean, Why is Cutter there?" his second in command asked. "Obviously because the woman is somewhere around."

"I'm not asking why Cutter's there, you fool, I know he's there to rescue the woman. *But why is she there?*"

More stupid looks.

"The woman is hiding out," someone offered.

Mena slammed his fist on the table. "I should have you all chopped up and fed to the sharks. I ask you again, *Why is she there?*"

"She knows someone who would hide her," the aide offered.

"Of course. I want a list of every suspected subversive in the area west from Puerto Plato to the Haiti border. And I want it *now*."

His aide left to start the process and Mena pursed his lips as he looked around the table.

"All right, why else would she be there? None of you can think of a reason?" He banged his fist on the table, sending a jolt through the men in the room. "She either has someone who will hide her . . . *or she has somewhere to hide.*"

He stared around the table for a moment to let his words sink in.

"Check property records in the area, tonight, get people out of beds and into the records office. Find out if the woman or anyone in her family owns property in the area."

❖

58

❖

I was five miles outside the city, traveling at a snail's pace on a road that made dirt tracks in British Honduras seem like autobahns in comparison, when I pulled to a stop, put the transmission in neutral and let the car idle. It was not a black night, but it was dark, and I had to keep the speed down to a crawl because I was driving without lights.

Getting the car was a lifeline thrown to a drowning man. But now that I had my head above water, and was at least treading water with a dog-paddle stroke, the hair on the back of my neck began to fan. It was the same feeling I'd had once when I was a starving kid in Leningrad and I'd entered a dark house in search of food. I'd tripped over a man sitting in a chair. He was dead. And I almost jumped out of my skin.

That's how I felt now, like I should be running like hell. Something was wrong.

I stopped thinking and listened to the night.

All I heard was the sound of the bucket of bolts in the car engine shaking.

I twisted in the seat and squinted out the rear window at the

❖

darkness, wondering if I was being followed. There were no car lights behind me, which was not surprising, there was little traffic on the road. I had passed only a few cars and had gotten passed once by a drunk going too fast.

I turned off the engine and got out of the car to check out sounds. I heard something and strained to listen. I was pretty sure it was the *chop-chop-chop* sound of helicopter blades. I was near the coast and the sound seemed to be coming from far out, over the water, but it must have really been a long ways out because I couldn't see anything.

It struck me that the car might be bugged in some way, that there might be some sort of transmitting device in it that permitted a copter to follow me without being in sight. Had I been in New York or London, maybe even the capital, I would have been sure there was a transmitter, but the more I thought about it, the more I was certain that that sort of sophisticated technology didn't exist in the Dominican Republic. And if it did, if some clever bastard like SIM chief Johnny Mena bought it, it was sitting on a shelf somewhere because no one in the country would know how to use it.

So what was it? I had come to the conclusion I was being set up. Manuel the taxi driver and his middle-of-the-night cousin were too pat. And the cousin was too clean, too nicely dressed. I was sure the swine of a hotel clerk was Manuel's cousin, but not the guy with the car.

I checked the car. It was clean. That wasn't unusual, ownership of a car was a big deal in the country. But this one had an official look to it. What was an official look? I wasn't sure. It looked like it was kept in good repair, except for the taillights. The red glass coverings had both been broken, as if the car had backed into a wall or something.

I started the engine again. When I put the car in reverse I noticed there were no backup lights, but I could see behind me because the tail lights sprayed white light. So did the brake lights.

I put the car into first gear and let out the clutch and started moving forward when it hit me like a bang across the head. I

❖

slammed on the brakes, turned off the engine and jumped out of the car, staring back at the car like it was a red-hot piece of coal.

I knew what the game was.

I listened to the night again, this time intently, not for a car, but anything airborne. I heard it, that *chop-chop-chop* of a helicopter. But where was it?

It was the middle of the night, the moon was low, but there were plenty of stars in the sky. I leaned up against a tree with my back and started looking at the east side of the night horizon and slowly made my way across the sky toward the west. I was halfway across when I saw it. Actually, it wasn't so much what I saw but what I didn't see. A tiny area of the sky was blanked out, with no stars, just a black void. But it wasn't a void. It was a smudge in the night sky. Studying it, I could see the faint outline of a helicopter.

There was a chopper out there, idling in the sky, watching and waiting, its running lights off.

It knew what it was following. Yeah, I was a smart guy, all right. I'd turned off the lights and drove without taillights or headlights. But I had to ride the brakes throughout as I went from one rut and hole to another, and each time I hit the brake lights, instead of glowing red, the lights shined white, alerting the copter hanging out there over the water that they were still on my tail. It wouldn't be hard for someone in a helicopter to keep track of me with a pair of binoculars—hell, I had two white lights flashing every time I hit the brakes.

Jesus H. Christ.

I was leading them to Luz.

I busted out the taillights and brake lights. The red glass housings were already broken; what I broke were the lights themselves. Then I broke out the headlights to avoid the temptation of turning them on.

I wondered how much time I had.

One thing I knew, Johnny Mena was no fool. I was a pro at making money, even making it a little off center. But Johnny Mena was a bloodhound. He was a professional at finding people—and exterminating them.

My adrenaline was in high gear. Mena didn't know where she was; if he did, he already would have her by now. And I would be in SIM custody, suffering the same torture that opponents of the regime were put through.

But that was before I headed out of Puerto Plata, heading due west up the coast, pointing an arrow directly at Luz's heart.

Now it was a race.

Johnny Mena knew where she was by now, or had a pretty good idea.

I had to get there before he did.

59

❖

It was nine o'clock in the morning by the time I was on the plateau overlooking the sea and had the cottage in sight. I had abandoned the car three hours earlier when I made a wrong turn and ended up high-centering it trying to get out of a gully. I couldn't have driven all the way to the cottage, anyway; whatever road had existed had long since gone back to nature.

It was going to be another one of those hot-wet Carib days when the air was so thick with humidity that you could swim in it. It was still early, but I was already drenched in sweat. My clothes looked like I'd swam up the plateau. Except for a snake, I'd been bitten by everything that jumped, flew or crawled.

I pushed myself, breaking into a run the last hundred yards. I called her name as I ran to the house. I hit the front door so hard it flew open and broke off a hinge.

"Luz!" I cried out.

The living room was empty. And gave no hint that anyone had been there. The kitchen was empty. I checked dishes, cups, shelves. A coat of dust was on everything. The sink had a hand pump to a well. There was no moisture in the sink or the end of the faucet. It was completely dry. No one had used it in a long time.

❖

I slammed open the door to the bedroom. The bed was not made, dust was everywhere. No one had been here in months, probably not since Luz and I were here the year before.

I spun around, almost in a circle. I was ready to cry.

Wrong—I had fucked up, I was completely wrong. She had not come to the cottage.

Now what the hell was I going to do? It was one thing to fantasize that I'd search the whole country for her, but the SIM knew I was in the country. If they didn't drop out of the sky at any moment, I'd be picked up before I made it back to Puerto Plata. I was probably as close to the Haiti border as I was to Puerto Plata, but they would be watching border crossings.

I went outside, cursing my stupidity. I thought I knew her. But hell, I thought I knew her after living with her for two years only to find out that she had one layer of secrets stacked atop another.

I couldn't stick around here long. I had to get away from the cottage and plantation, pronto. They couldn't have kept track of my car during the night after I got rid of all the lights, but once I pointed the way, I had no doubt Johnny Mena would figure out where Luz was hiding. He had all the resources of the country at hand. And I had tired feet and a million mosquito bites.

"Nick."

I felt like I had fallen off the edge of the world.

Luz stood at the bottom of the clearing that separated the cottage yard from banana trees. She was thin and haggard and looked like she had been through the ringer, which she had.

But she was the most beautiful woman in the world to me.

"What—" She stopped. "How did you get here?"

"Mosquitoes flew me." I slapped one on my neck.

"What happened to your face?"

"Mena's boys gave me an attitude adjustment."

"Why did you come?" she asked.

"There's no one else in the world for me, Luz."

"No, no, you have to go. You don't understand, they're going to find me, it's just a matter of time."

I heard the familiar *chop-chop-chop* sound in the near distance.

❖

60

I ran to her and grabbed her arm. "Let's go. We gotta get out of here."

She stumbled along with me as I led her into the thick plantation growth. "It's no use, they'll find us. Go hide, I'll distract them. They're after me, not you."

I stopped and stared at her.

"Who the hell do you think you are? You're not the only hero in this world. I came here to get you and I'm not leaving without you. C'mon."

I led her into the thick terrain. We passed a campsite. It was Luz's. She hadn't been staying in the house, but camped out nearby. It was a smart move. Searchers might have shown up and left figuring the house looked empty and not recently occupied.

A couple hundred yards from the house, the terrain started climbing until it peaked several hundred feet above the flat level where the cottage stood. After that, there were more peaks and valleys as the elevation rose higher.

We stopped for a breath at the top of a ridge. We crouched in the bushes to stay out of sight. Beneath us a helicopter had found the cottage. It was hovering near it.

"I'm sorry I got you into this," she said.

"Yeah, me too. You should have just shot me."

Her eyes misted. She touched the raw scratches and raised insect bites on my face. "I don't know how you can forgive me."

"I haven't forgiven you, you're a bitch. I came because I love you. Forgiveness is something else."

She shook her head. "There's no place to go. I can already hear another helicopter. They'll beat these bushes until they find us."

"We're going over there." I pointed to a point southwest from our position. "There used to be a lake there, if I remember right."

"What good will that do us?"

"I need a bath. C'mon."

I led her through the dense growth. From the sounds coming from the other side of the ridge, another chopper or two had arrived. I didn't need a crystal ball to get the picture—they would be unloading men to make a search. And they would know I had been there. Luz had been careful not to disturb the dust in the house. I hadn't been.

I heard the yelp of dogs and exchanged looks with her.

"Bastards," I said. "They've got bloodhounds. You really know how to piss off people, don't you? Let's go."

We kept pushing toward the lake. When we reached the top of the ridge overlooking the lake, we could see the helicopter on the ground near the cottage and another one making sweeps over the plantation.

The lake was below us, a narrow dark green, murky puddle of warm water, a couple hundred yards long and only forty or fifty feet wide.

Luz had been quiet up to now mainly because she was too busy breathing as we made our way up the hills and vales.

"Nick, I don't understand. What are we doing here? How are we going to get away?"

"Shhhh. Listen."

❖

We listened. There was the sound of helicopter chopper blades, and the bay of hounds.

"All I hear is—"

"Shhhh. I think I hear it."

She shook her head. She thought I was mad. Maybe I was.

"Hear what?" she whispered.

"The wings of an angel."

The sound became more obvious. It was a buzz, not unlike the buzz of an electric saw.

The plane came over the top of the ridge, flying low—a seaplane, not something off the production line, but the kind of plane that Lindbergh would have flown if he had wanted a puddle-jumper with pontoons.

"Who is it?"

"Suez."

WE DIDN'T GET MUCH chance to talk until we were in Corozal. I figured it was a safer bet to have Suez fly us back to the colony than Puerto Rico. San Juan was too close to the Dominican Republic, too infested with SIM.

Suez left us off at his house while he went to stay with friends. I guess he figured Luz and I needed some time alone. I walked around his backyard, getting reacquainted with the Suez Canal, while Luz sat in the shade. I had been the one who did what little talking there was along the way, mostly just explaining how I got involved, how I had sent Sam Denver and his submarine out as a decoy and arranged with Suez to pick us up and fly us out.

Now that it was all over, I don't think either of us knew how to start an intimate conversation. I wasn't interested in hearing it and she wasn't eager to provide details about what happened between her and Trujillo.

This wasn't about another man, a country, or a revolution. I didn't give a damn if millions had a better life because of her sacrifice—I wasn't into sacrifice to save anyone. And I really didn't believe anyone would give a damn about her sacrifice, or that the poor bastards in that country were going to be any better off just because one strongman got his comeuppance. There was always another waiting in line to take the place of the recently departed.

This was between the two of us, no one else, and nothing else. It was about love and love lost, about betrayal, redemption, giving up or starting over. It was about whether it was possible to forgive and forget without getting answers to questions that were sure to doom the relationship.

I didn't know what to say, what to do, how to approach her, what to ask, whether there was forgiveness in me.

"You're never going to forgive me, are you?"

I was kneeling by the canal and stood up as she came up beside me.

"You always said you feared the loss of someone you loved more than anything in the world. Now you'll never forgive or forget."

I shrugged. "Forgiving and forgetting is bullshit. Those are words people use. No one really forgives and forgets, they just stop talking about it, stick it under covers and pretend it went away."

"I don't want to lose you again, Nick," she said.

"Yeah, it was tough throwing me to the dogs while you went out saving the world." I shook my head. "I was hurt. I don't like what you did to me, I don't even like what you did to yourself."

"I don't like what I did either." Her eyes were serious. "Love means trust, and I broke that trust. I wanted to save my country but I lost something even more precious to me. I hope you can find it in your heart to forgive me, because I love you, Nick. I never stopped loving you." Tears welled in her eyes.

She meant everything in the world to me. No matter how hurt I was that she betrayed me, I never lost my longing for her. I knew she spoke the truth.

"I promise I will never hurt you again," she said, as tears streamed down her face.

I knew her promise would be kept. My voice was lost in my throat. I pulled her to me and felt the warmth of her body. She buried her head against my chest.

❖

"Never let me go, Nick." Her arms tightened around me. "Promise me."

"I promise," I told her, as my own tears spilled down my face.

What she didn't know was I had already forgiven her. When you love someone with all your heart and soul, you find a way to forgive. You may never forget, but love means forgiving.

True love never dies.

❖

Historical Note

Nick's evaluation of Ramfis as having too many soft landings to fill his father's shoes was correct. Ramfis and Rubi did, in fact, come back from Europe after El Jefe was assassinated on his way to visit his mistress. But they didn't stay long.

Ramfis lasted only about six months as dictator of the Dominican Republic. During that time, he wreaked revenge on the group that ambushed his father. After questioning and repeated torture, the captured conspirators were chopped up and fed to sharks. When the United States withdrew its support of Ramfis because it believed he was brewing a Castro-type revolt, he fled in his yacht, taking the untold millions that his father had robbed from the people during his thirty-year dictatorship.

Rubirosa also left the country, returning to Paris and his life as the most fabulous of the jetsetters. He was truly the ultimate man's man, a sports star on the playing field and in bed, a person of great charm and intelligence.

Both Ramfis and Rubi died in auto accidents in the 1960s. No one knows whether it was coincidence, the fickle finger of fate, or darker forces at work.

❖

Sam Giancana, the Chicago mobster, was gunned down in 1975 by "unknown assailants" after he was scheduled to appear before the U.S. Senate Intelligence Committee to discuss his involvement in a CIA plot to assassinate Fidel Castro in the early 60s.

Las Mariposas, the Butterflies, died young and tragically, but they left behind them a rare heritage of national feminine heroism that ranks with Joan of Arc taking up sword and riding at the head of the French army.

The Mirabal sisters, Patria, Minerva and Maria Teresa, age thirty-seven, thirty-four and twenty-six respectively when they were viciously murdered by Trujillo's secret police, are not just national heroines of the Dominican Republic, but to the world at large. They became a symbol of the crisis of violence against women.

In 1999, the fifty-fourth session of the United Nations General Assembly adopted a Resolution designating November twenty-five as the International Day for the Elimination of Violence Against Women. November 25 was the date in 1960 that the three Butterflies were killed.